Bao Ruo-wang (Jean Pasquali...) son of a Corsican father and a Chinese mother. He was brought up as a Chinese boy at home and educated as a Westerner at a Catholic school in Tientsin and at a technical college in Shanghai, where he specialized in machine tool operation. In 1945, at the age of nineteen, he worked for the American Marines. He remained a French citizen, although he never left China, where he married a Chinese wife; hence his Chinese name Bao Ruo-wang and his French name, Jean Pasqualini. After the proclamation of the People's Republic, his parentage and career made his arrest in December 1957 inevitable.

In 1964, the year France and the People's Republic of China officially recognized each other, he was released as 'a special gesture of extraordinary magnanimity', and crossed the border into Hong Kong with a dollar in his pocket. Since then he has lived in Paris, where he now teaches Chinese at the Institut National des Langues et Civilisations Orientales.

Rudolph Chelminski was born in Wilton, Connecticut, in America, and went to Taft School and Harvard College. He worked for *Life* Magazine from 1962 until its demise. He first worked in Paris and then in Moscow as bureau chief from 1968 to 1969. In 1969 he met Jean Pasqualini and their collaboration on this book began at his instigation.

PRISONER OF MAO

Bao Ruo-wang (Jean Pasqualini)
and Rudolph Chelminski

Penguin Books

Penguin Books Ltd,
Harmondsworth, Middlesex, England
Penguin Books, 625 Madison Avenue, New York,
New York 10022
Penguin Books Australia Ltd,
Ringwood, Victoria, Australia
Penguin Books Canada Ltd,
41 Steelcase Road West, Markham, Ontario, Canada
Penguin Books (N.Z.) Ltd,
182–190 Wairau Road, Auckland 10, New Zealand

First published in the United States by
Coward, McCann & Geoghegan, Inc., New York, 1973
Published in Great Britain by André Deutsch 1975
Published in Penguin Books 1976
Copyright © Jean Pasqualini and Rudolph Chelminski, 1973

Printed in the United States of America
Set in Linotype Times

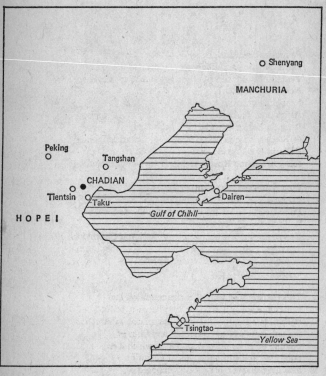

Sketch giving an approximate location of Chadian site of the
Clear Stream (Ching-ho) Labour Camp

Author's Note

I first met Jean Pasqualini towards the end of 1969 in Paris, where I had arrived as a *Life* Magazine (remember?) correspondent after a two-year stint in the Moscow bureau. When I learned that he had a second, Chinese, name – Bao Ruo-wang – I was hardly surprised: His physical appearance, after all, was far more like a younger Mao Tse-tung than the Corsican syllables of his Western name suggested. We became good friends and I quickly found myself addicted to his apparently endless reminiscences about the Chinese labour camps. As astonishing as his experiences had been, I was doubly impressed by the fact that he is one of those rare and curious persons who possess a virtually perfect memory – names, dates, even conversations sprang effortlessly from his mental archives, even if the events he was describing were ten or more years old.

And then there was the fact, the simple, extraordinary fact, that he had spent seven years in Chinese prisons and labour camps. There aren't many people like that around. Probably hundreds of Westerners have been interned in one way or another by the Chinese Communists but none of them – none – went through the forced-labour camps. He is unique in this.

And there he was, telling those amazing stories.

'Why in hell don't you write a book about it?' I suggested one day. 'You could be the Chinese Solzhenitsyn.'

'I'm not a writer,' he said. 'I've tried, but it doesn't come out too well.'

And that was how our collaboration began. I still don't understand how he was able to spend five years in Paris after his release from the mainland without some writer or journalist leaping at the chance to do his story with him.* Writers and journalists aren't very smart.

Jean and I spent something over three years on the project because we wanted the picture of the camps to be as complete and accurate as possible (everything we write of is precisely as he lived it, except for the fact that Jean changed most of the names involved, for evident reasons), but also because we were both working full-time at our other jobs and could get together only on weekends and vacation. As we got deeper into the writing I realized (to my surprise, I admit) that neither Jean nor the book we were developing was anti-Chinese or even anti-communist. In the camps he had been frankly employed as slave labour, and yet he couldn't fail to admire the strength of spirit of the Chinese people and the honesty and dedication of most of the Communist cadres he met. Even though nine years have passed since he was released, his story is every bit as pertinent now because it is in large part the story of the building of the new China. And the camps still exist today.

Those seven years taught Jean as much about himself as it did about the Chinese among whom he was born and raised, and not the least of the lessons was that the best way to affront hardship is with humour. That is why he thought it might be fitting to dedicate the book to the man who put him in prison and the man who got him out: 'To Chairman Mao Tse-tung and General Charles de Gaulle, both of whom did so much for me without ever being aware of it.'

* *Reader's Digest* ran Jean's account of the prison camp mass of Father Hsia in a 1970 issue. But they stopped there.

All the names and proper names of the prisoners mentioned in this book, with the exception of that of Louis Fourcampre and that of the author, have been changed to protect their identities.

Chapter One

On the afternoon of Friday, 13 November 1964, a political prisoner was released at the Chinese border checkpoint of Shumchun, the principal land entrance to Hong Kong. He was hardly important enough for any consideration: There were no delegations to meet him, no press, no relatives. Only the usual English colonial policeman was there at his post on the other end of the Lo Wu Bridge. Across the way he could see the uniformed Chinese busying themselves around the grey brick buildings of the frontier station and beyond that the Shumchun freight yards, where steam locomotives ferried back and forth, drawing boxcars covered with slogans in huge Chinese characters. 'Long Live the General Line', the slogans read, 'Long Live the People's Communes' and 'Long Live the Great Leap Forward'.

At precisely 1.30 p.m. the policeman saw at the far end of the bridge the man he had been notified to meet. He had a typically Chinese face set off by black-rimmed glasses, walked with a busy, hunching gait and appeared to be in his mid-thirties. The grey woollen suit he wore was obviously government-issue, and the collar of his white shirt was absurdly too large for him. He crossed the bridge with a face void of expression, never looking back. All the policeman knew of him was that he was a French citizen and that his name was Pasqualini. All that must have appeared rather odd, considering his thoroughly Asiatic appearance.

That prisoner was myself. I was about to start my new life in the West with six Hong Kong dollars in my pocket – U.S. $1. I was on my way to France, my homeland even though I had never set foot there. Nineteen sixty-four was the year that France and the People's Republic of China officially recognized each other, and it was as a special 'gesture of extraordinary magnanimity' that I, a passport-holding French citizen, benefited from remittance of the remainder of my twelve-year sentence and deportation. By then I had spent seven years in Chinese prisons and forced-labour camps. As I crossed that bridge I was leaving behind an entire culture into which I was born, every friend in the world, a wife who had had to divorce me for her own sake and two sons whom I shall probably never see again.

But I had learned about *Lao Gai*.

Lao Gai – short for *Lao Dong Gai Zao** – is a twentieth-century invention, an institution presented to humanity by the Chinese Communist theoreticians. It means Reform Through Labour.

In our fair and pleasant world there is no shortage of countries that have built their modern civilizations on a foundation of deportation areas, concentration camps and prison farms. The Soviets have been especially notable achievers in this line. Their complex of forced-labour camps was impressively vast in its prime, but it was brutally cruel, unsophisticated – and inefficient – compared to what the Chinese developed after the victory of the revolution in 1949. What the Russians never understood, and what the Chinese Communists knew all along, is that convict labour can never be productive or profitable if it is extracted only by coercion or torture. The Chinese were the first to grasp the art of motivating prisoners. That's what *Lao Gai* is all about.

Those seven prison years I lived – often in abject, despairing misery, sometimes literally starving and always haunted by hunger, in perpetual submission to the authority not only of guards and warders but even more so to the 'mutual surveillance' of my fellow prisoners and even to my own zealous self-denunciations and confessions – constitute my own story, of course, but far more important, they are the story of the millions upon millions† of Chinese who endured the camps

Lao Dong: manual labour; *Gai Zao:* to change, reform.

† How many prisoners are there? The estimates of the Chinese forced-labour-camp population vary wildly, depending mostly on the political

10

with me and are still in them today. I am their only spokesman. The story of *Lao Gai* has never been told before.

Let us avoid polemic here; the purpose of this book is neither to slander the People's Republic of China nor to invent fantasies for the CIA. What follows on these pages is only what I personally lived and saw and heard about from others. I don't pretend to be a scholar, but I was born and raised and spent thirty-seven years of my life on Chinese soil. And what I learned about the prison system came firsthand.

There is a simple, basic truth about the labour camps that seems to be unknown in the West: For all but a handful of exceptional cases (such as myself) the prison experience is total and permanent. The men and women sentenced to Reform Through Labour spend the remainder of their lives in the camps, as prisoners first and then as 'free workers' after their terms have expired.

Labour camps in China are a lifetime contract. They are far too important to the national economy to be run with transient personnel. It was convicts who reclaimed and made flourish the vast Manchurian wastelands which had defeated all past efforts and which today still offer the only convincing proof that a Sovkhoze-style state farm can operate profitably; con-

---

convictions of the person making the estimate. There are even some distinguished authors, intellectuals and academics in the West who appear to believe that there never was a labour camp or political prisoner in mainland China. At the other extreme are certain Sinologists who affirm that upwards of twenty million are being held in servitude for ideological reasons. Obviously, the Chinese Government furnishes no statistics, but I can assure the reader from personal experience that the camps exist and that their population is colossal. An interesting hint of the possible scale is contained in a phrase dear to Chinese rhetoricians: 'Only a small minority, perhaps five per cent, is against us; these are being forced to build socialism.' No one who takes a stand against the government can remain out of jail, but if we take only two per cent as a reasonable possibility, this still gives us a figure of sixteen million prime candidates for Reform Through Labour. This figure does not include those individuals undergoing the standard three-year terms of *Lao Jiao* – Education Through Labour. These are persons who have committed 'mistakes' rather than 'crimes'. In theory, they maintain their civic rights while in the camps. There are at least as many undergoing *Lao Jiao* as *Lao Gai*; in fact, probably many more.

victs who began China's plastics industry and run some of her biggest factories and agricultural stations; convicts who grow the very rice Mao eats.* To achieve these successes one thing was indispensable: a stable supply of manpower, willing to work hard. With this assured, the Chinese reached a goal that had eluded even Stalin – making forced labour a paying proposition. China surely must be the only country in the world whose prisons turn a profit. It is an exploit of which they can be rightfully proud.

'A living hell' is the popular image inevitably conjured up by the idea of Communist labour camps. There is truth in the image, of course, but it is distorted because it is incomplete. The reality, the most exquisite irony that I discovered as the years slipped by, was the same that had already been testified to by the survivors of Stalinist camps: Not only is the society within the camps in many ways purer than the larger one outside, but it is also freer. It is in the prisons and camps that the notions of friendship and personal freedom are the most highly developed in China.

There is an impressive fund of partial knowledge and downright misinformation in the West concerning China, in spite of the many doors that have recently been opened; when it is a question of her prison system, that fund absolutely overflows. There has been no shortage of Westerners – journalists, priests, businessmen, soldiers – who have spent some time in confinement on the mainland and written books about the experience. Almost all of them were hampered from the start by the basic fact of speaking little or no Chinese. But even more important, being round-eyed foreigners, they invariably received special treatment – their own private cells or rooms, different rations and isolation from Chinese prisoners. No Westerner has ever been allowed to visit the camps, not even Mao's friend Edgar Snow. And certainly none has ever won the doubtful honour of being selected for Reform Through Labour.

I did because the police authorities for all intents and purposes considered me as just another Chinese. I was a very rare

* At Branch Farm #3 of the Ching Ho State Farm, northeast of Tientsin. I worked to grow that rice with my own hands.

animal – a foreigner born in China, speaking the language like a native, with the face of a Chinese. A snake in the grass, the interrogators called me, and they had a point.

I'm a strange mixture. I have confused people for years. My name, Pasqualini, comes straight from my Corsican father, an adventurous character who left his native island at the turn of the century (in something of a hurry, as I understand it; I have often wondered if he had been involved in some sort of vendetta), joined the French Army and eventually found himself on garrison duty in Peking – those were the days when just about every Western power had a piece of poor, humiliated China. With the end of the war and demobilization my father elected to stay on in China. He went into business for himself and took a Chinese wife. As their only child, I grew up first as a Chinese boy with my playmates and then as a Westerner when I attended Peking's French Public School and three different mission schools, run by the Marist brothers and the Salesian fathers. It was, as my jailers often pointed out to me later, a most thoroughly rotten and reactionary, bourgeois education.

English, the tongue I now prefer, came to me by a funny boyhood accident. At an age when I already spoke Mandarin Chinese and French, my father sent me away to a Catholic boarding school in Tientsin. On opening day I stood in the wrong line and found myself in a section where they were speaking English instead of French. That was all right with me – I preferred the kids in that group. When I returned to Peking for vacation my father met me at the station.

'*Comment vas-tu, petit?*' he asked affectionately.

'Oh, fine, Dad, how are you?' I answered. When he had recovered from the culture shock, he decided to let me stay on where they spoke that strange, unknown language.

To the Salesian fathers I was known as Jean Pasqualini; to the Chinese as Bao Ruo-wang, a name roughly derived from the 'P' sound in Pasqualini and the Chinese appellation for St John. Very young, I recognized that I had been born into the classic dilemma of the *métis*, the half-breed who participates in both societies but feels truly at home in neither. The great exception was the clan of other *métis* who attended the mission schools

13

with me. All my closest friends were half Chinese like me and a multiracial cocktail on the other half: Irish, Russian, Polish, Czech, Jewish, Italian, German and God knows what else. We were a special society, a subculture closed to the rest of the world. Of them all, I was the one who looked most completely Chinese.

Throughout my adolescence China was swept by great waves of afflictions, some natural like the recurrent floods, droughts and famines and some man-made, like the several foreign incursions, the Second World War, the Japanese invasion and occupation, the Civil War and finally the purges and retributions after the total victory of the Communists. It was a confused time in which to be growing to manhood – protean and unpredictable, often dangerous but undeniably exciting. The situation changed from week to week and it was a rash man who thought he might know the future. My own was formed for me young, because of my education and because of personal tragedy – both my parents died before I reached my majority. I became a ward of the church and the French embassy, living in a tiny cubicle in the isolation ward of the French hospital and being watched over by nuns. There was no money allotted, or no will, to send me on to the university, even though I had passed the tests at the top of my class. On graduation from an industrial school, just after V-J Day, I began looking for work. By personal preference and instinct, I gravitated to the Western diplomatic and military missions, where my biracial background and four languages (I had added Italian) could be useful. That was already a giant step in the direction of trouble.

The first two jobs I held did more for my spiritual education than all the years of the mission schools. I was nineteen in September of 1945 when I started working for the Fifth U.S. Marines. I began as a jeep driver but quickly rose to interpreter and civilian specialist for local affairs with the divisional military police. My experience with these easygoing Americans was overwhelming – they treated me not only as a human being, but as an adult! It was the first time that had ever happened to me. (Could they have been the same Americans as those who committed atrocities in Vietnam? I cannot conceive it.) In my youthful enthusiasm I regarded the Marines' life as ideal – I even asked once if I could go to Parris Island for training. When I was only twenty I was a big wheel – a uniformed civilian with the privileges of an officer, earning good money and shopping in the PX. Life would have seemed rosy, if it hadn't been for my second job.

My mentors of the French embassy put me onto that one. It taught me something about the French, the Chinese and myself. At the time the French had vested interests in the Peking Tramway Company, which owned the trolleys the ordinary people rode. They were looking for foremen. I could do that during the day, I thought, since most of my work with the Marines was in the evening and night. As a Frenchman by birth I was fit for this middle-level technical work, but since I was a *métis*, the responsibility they entrusted ended there. The higher, executive posts went to the Frenchmen of pure blood.

The French representative introduced me to the Chinese director, who immediately made me an Inspector First Class, a position a Chinese might reach after twenty years. My education began the first morning I reported for work at the depot and I saw the kind of people who were soon to bring Mao to power. They were huddling around little coal stoves, coughing, dressed in rags and eating meagre bits of cornbread, such as I got later in the camps. In the mission schools and in the foreign concession with my family, I had been thoroughly sheltered. They were the drivers, ticket-takers and maintenance men. They were earning four American dollars a month. After a few weeks I fell into the habit of bringing them antiseptics, sulfa pills and APCs I had wheedled from the medical corpsmen. They began calling me *Ban Mei Shi* – 'the one who does things the American way'. I wonder if Americans realize how much good will there is towards them in China, at least among the older people, built during the days before they became conquerors or lesson-givers.

One cold December afternoon of 1945 I was taking a tram home. It was already nearly dark, but in the chilly, swaying car I clearly saw the ticket-taker dip into his till. It was incredible,

15

one of those rare moments when you can watch someone who thinks himself unobserved. I was shocked. Without a second thought I strode over and denounced him. The tram stopped. I looked down the nearly empty car and saw the driver advancing at me with his big brass steering key in his hand. He stopped dead in his tracks when he recognized me in the dim light.

'It's you!' he said.

'I've got to do my job,' I told him righteously. In the missions I had always been taught that stealing was a terrible sin. But I hadn't learned much about compassion. The driver looked at the poor wretch, weeping in his corner.

'You got no luck,' he said.

There was someone else behind us. A Chinese inspector had boarded the tram. He was an older man, and still in uniform. Within a few seconds he had surmised what was going on.

'If you're going to write a report,' he said, 'you'll have to do it right. Here.'

He handed me a printed Report Sheet. Then, as if he were suddenly changing his mind, he told the driver to take the car back to the depot and motioned for me to step outside with him.

'Come with me,' he said. 'I want to show you something.' I didn't know the man, but his manner commanded respect. I plodded along with him in the dark, wondering where we were going. We penetrated deeper and deeper into the poorer quarter, where the streets were like mazes and the people like shadows who slipped silently by us.

'Don't worry,' he said, sensing my nervousness. 'We're almost there.'

We crossed over a muddy little *hutung* (lane) into an unlit courtyard where a wooden shed hardly higher than my shoulders stood precariously in the far corner. Without knocking he thrust open the door. Nine faces, softly outlined by a kerosene lamp, turned in surprise to regard us. There was a woman, an old man and seven children. No one said a word. After what seemed like minutes – though I suppose it could have been only ten seconds or so – the inspector closed the door again.

'He feeds them all on four dollars a month,' he said. 'That's that ticket-taker's family. Do you still want to write that report?'

'I was off duty,' I said. We walked back out of the slum together.

I quit the tramway job after a few months and went to work full time for the Americans. There is one last footnote, though: Several years later, after the Liberation but before my arrest, I caught sight of that same inspector in a busy Peking street. This time he was in the uniform of the People's Police. Obviously, he had been a Communist all along. Instinctively, as much to spare him embarrassment as to avoid an encounter with authority, I turned away, assuming he would do the same. To my surprise he hurried through the crowd to greet me and shake my hand.

'Don't be worried,' he said. 'As far as I'm concerned you'll always be in our good graces. You did something for us once and we haven't forgotten.'

A year after I began working with the Marines I got married. It was a typical Chinese union – part affection but mostly a carefully thought-out bargain for mutual benefit of the parties concerned. The story of the bargain started in 1937, when the Japanese were openly looking for pretexts to take control of China. My father had become friendly with a large and powerful family of Mandarins who owned a sprawling, 270-room palace in the north of the city near the Drum Tower. Foreigners, especially Westerners, were a commodity in terrific demand by wealthy Chinese every time warfare seemed imminent, since the colonialist concessions and diplomatic areas were almost automatically safe from attack. At the time of the Marco Polo Bridge incident* (7 July 1937) the affluent merchants of Peking paid huge sums of money to hole up in the basements of legations. Another system, somewhat riskier but more satisfying when it worked, was to place their residences under foreign flags.

Old man Yang, the patriarch of the clan with the huge

---

*Japanese garrison troops manoeuvring near Peking deliberately provoked a battle with the Chinese army to use as a pretext for full-scale war, much in the manner of their later ally, Hitler.

palace, made my father a very lush proposition: If he would come and live on Yang's grounds, he would be given large and elegant quarters rent-free, plus a salary of 200 Chinese dollars a month. Never one to turn down a good proposition, my father packed us up to go live with the Mandarins. The French flag flew at the peak of the highest roof.

What a fantastic person Old Yang was! His life was like a melodramatic Chinese film – there was adventure, intrigue, elegance, violence, sex and even murder. A Manchu by birth, he had been a close confidant of the last emperor and held the high ceremonial function of Master of the Clocks. Every day, wearing the proper gown and followed by a suitable retinue, he would go from clock to clock in the palace, winding them with a gold key on a chain at his waist. With the treasure he acquired from his years of royal service he built himself one of Peking's most splendid private residences. I remember clearly playing by a little pond in one of his numerous courtyards with his granddaughter, Yang Hui-min, the girl who later was to become my wife.

After my parents had died and I was on my own, Old Yang called me to him for another proposition. He hadn't changed his ways a bit. Would I marry his granddaughter, he asked. There would be a dowry, of course, and I would be given a nice house for us to build our family. My part of the bargain would be to help the family through my connections with the Americans. Working for the Americans, the Chinese used to say in those days, was like having a tiger skin – no one dared touch you.

I accepted. I must admit that it was more because of the advantages I received and respect for the old man than for love or even passion. If this appears strange to a Westerner, it is normal for an Oriental. Unions in China are much less emotional and the rapport much more distant than in the West. My wife and I got on correctly, no more. When I was jailed, she suffered because of me and starved almost as badly as I did; I felt no sense of betrayal when eventually she decided to divorce me. It was the best for her.

After our marriage we moved into Number 17, *Chien Ma*

Chang Hutung – Back of the Horse Shed Lane – a little one-storey, three-room Chinese house, facing auspiciously south as all houses should, with grey brick walls and a pointed roof. My eldest son, Mow, was born the next year and followed two years later by a daughter, Mi, the one I preferred. Poor little Mi died of typhoid when she was only three. Our second son, Yung, was born in 1953.

When the Fifth Marines withdrew from Peking I moved over to the U.S. Army, first as a technician with the Signal Corps and later as civilian liaison with the CID, the Criminal Investigation Division. That job counted heavily against me during interrogation and judgement. If the Chinese Communists (and Communists everywhere for that matter) tend to view diplomats and journalists as spies, then my employ with the CID absolutely cemented their conclusion that I was a full-time agent of imperialist aggression. In reality, my duties were far more mundane: keeping track of the Chinese whom the Army hired and fired. I stayed on with different U.S. military establishments in Peking until their hasty departure in November 1948, less than a month before the city was invested by the omnipresent Communists.

The siege of Peking began in the middle of December, and it was carried out in a manner that probably no one but the Chinese could accomplish. Above all, the Communists wanted no bloodshed or destruction of what was to be, after all, their own capital. They had already taken the countryside; now they were waiting for the city to fall into their hands 'like a ripe fruit'. Which is exactly what happened. We inside the city lived, worked and ate normally; the only signs of conflict we saw were distant reflections. The Nationalist Army was evident everywhere inside Peking and around the walls, but they were surrounded. The invisible Communists waited patiently, allowing food and normal civilian supplies to pass through their lines toward the city as if nothing had changed. They held the powerhouse twenty-five miles outside of town but continued supplying electricity. Only now and then – to remind the people who was running things – did they cut off power for an hour or two.

As the vice tightened the Nationalists showed increasing signs

19

of desperation. They even became almost virtuous. For once their soldiers were no longer looting or trying to extort money – they all knew the Communists would hold them implacably to account for every witnessed misdeed. The commander of the Kuomintang (KMT) forces, Fu Tso-Yi, even instituted roving courts, military tribunals mounted on the back of Dodge trucks, which were dispatched to the scenes of alleged crimes. The court would hear witnesses, judge and sentence the offenders on the spot. Sentence was carried out by firing squad. Martial law was total.

When the outlying airfields fell into Communist hands, the Nationalists were at their last gasp and knew it. By then it had become a question of simply getting out with as much as they could. They began building airstrips inside the city. Their first attempt was foiled, ironically enough, by the Japanese. The logical spot for a strip, it seemed, was the *glacis*, the broad, grassy promenade in the eastern section near the legation quarter, where the foreigners used to play polo, bounded on the south by the inner wall and on the north by a big marketplace. The *glacis* was shaped like an 'L' and the longest part, about a kilometre of grass, ran east to west. Unhappily for the KMT, the Japanese had built a mighty series of reinforced concrete bunkers right in the middle of the long run, and every effort to blast them out proved futile. There was no choice but to build the strip on the short length of the L, north to south. To allow extra space for the C-47s to get airborne, a pickup crew of engineers levelled the roofs of buildings in the flight paths to the north.

The emergency strip was more or less satisfactory but there were bound to be accidents. The most memorable – the one that all Peking was discussing for days afterward – was the time late in December when a too-heavily-loaded C-47 stalled shortly after it became airborne and crashed into a populated area, spraying gold ingots over a path of several hundred yards. A lot of poor folk got rich that day and some general was without his treasure trove. As they had always done before in times of trouble, the diplomats began flying their countries' flags over their residences.

Liberation day was 30 January 1949. The top KMT brass had long since fled and the officers left behind to keep house negotiated their skins with the Communist emissaries. Their vanguard was already there, moving expressionlessly and methodically around the city in their padded winter uniforms, arranging for the arrival in their style. In the afternoon the full complement of the besieging army marched in through the Yong Ding Men and Hsi Chih Men gates, the infantry in big fur hats and the armoured units driving old Japanese tanks and towing American 105-mm howitzers behind Studebaker trucks. It was the equipment they had captured in battle from the KMT, or bought from the KMT's corrupt commanders. The soldiers carried portraits of Mao and Chu Teh, head of all the armed forces. It was a cold, windy day. The citizens lined the streets waving little red flags they had made at home.

'Welcome to the People's Liberation Army,' they cried over and over.

The new China was being born, but I was out of work. After a short stint as interpreter and leg man for the Associated Press correspondent, which ended in June, I began what turned out to be more than three years of unemployment. We foreigners were left pretty much alone, but our activities were circumscribed. The new regime was getting itself established.

On 1 October 1949 the People's Republic of China was officially proclaimed and gained immediate recognition from the Soviets. At the time, it seemed the dawn of a bright new era for Communism. The most populous country in the world had joined with the biggest one in a holy alliance that would inevitably bring a new way of life to mankind. Wave upon wave of technical and military advisors arrived from Moscow. The people were encouraged to refer to the Soviet Union as 'Elder Brother'.

Strangely enough, though, the Soviets botched the job as the years went by. The country that fancied itself the leading force against imperialism began treating China with an arrogance that bordered on scorn. Naturally government circles were circumspect, but it wasn't long before the people formed their own disabused opinions about the Elder Brothers from the north.

The Russians mishandled it badly. In spite of all the new revolutionary teachings, the Chinese remain a profoundly prestige- and face-conscious people. Everyone knew that the Soviets had just been ravaged and bled by a murderous war, but their experts on foreign relations should have been more clever about appearances. The advisors became objects of disdain.

'Poor bald eggs', the Pekinese used to call them – a Chinese image signifying the abject, third-rate style they uniformly projected. They were boorish and overbearing even while making laughing-stocks of themselves. The Russians, it was said, always arrived at night to be whisked by bus directly to the Grand Hotel des Wagons-Lits, so that the natives would not be able to catch sight of them. In the hotel were tailors who quickly stitched them up dark, boxy two-pair-of-pants suits with those extraordinarily wide cuffs that became a Russian trademark in those days. When they were suited up, they would make for the nearest retail stores to snatch up enormous lots of any consumer goods in sight – luggage, bolts of cloth, food, utensils . . .

The Chinese referred to the Soviet women as 'walking barrels'. The Russians had lost face. What a contrast to the American 'tiger skin'! One of the most popular moves Mao ever made – and a good part of the reason why the Chinese follow him as lovingly as they do – was kicking the Soviets out of the country.

There was some rapid house-cleaning when the Communists took over. The first victims were the obvious criminal elements and exploiters of the people. Yang, my rich old grandfather-in-law, was arrested as a degenerate, money-hoarding rascal and died in a Peking prison camp where he had been put to digging ditches. The city's numerous corps of prostitutes was rounded up and witnessed the execution of their pimps and madams, by firing squad at the outer walls.

Within three years of the Liberation, the campaigns started. In 1951 was the First Campaign for the Suppression of Counterrevolutionaries. Every day brought dozens of public trials, and the people were encouraged to watch. Trials of People's Courts were broadcast over loudspeakers in public places, as the crowds shouted for death. The most to be shot in one day was 199, but in the countryside many, many more were put to knife, bullet and garotte. The fury of vengeance continued throughout March and April and then abated, as if out of breath. The camps were beginning to flesh out. Already in that first movement some of my foreign and *métis* friends were arrested for their ties to foreigners. I passed the time making myself inconspicuous, visiting with a few trusted friends and reading voluminously in the public library.

When the pitch of retribution rose to what was beginning to look dangerously like hysteria, I applied for an exit visa, the first time I had ever done so. It was refused. Or rather, it was ignored. Every time I queried the foreign ministry about what was happening, I was curtly informed that my application was 'still pending'. It continued to pend right through to 1955, when the Second Campaign for the Suppression of Counterrevolutionaries began. More of my friends were taken away. Still no answer from the foreign ministry. I was stuck. Apprehensively, I carried on.

I had finally found work in 1953, as personal assistant to an officer of a Western embassy – which one I cannot say, because of people I worked with who are still in Peking. The work I did there was no different from the normal duties of any cultural, political or economic attaché; but for the New Order it represented espionage. If I reported to my boss on the latest rationing measures or passed an afternoon in a popular teahouse listening to rumour and gossip from the workers, I was helping him assess his country's relations with the young republic. That my work wasn't entirely appreciated I learned in 1954, during the Census of Foreigners.

It occurred in November. Because we were about to be issued identity cards and resident permits we were summoned to the headquarters of the Peking Bureau of Public Security to fill out two large biographical forms, giving a detailed report on everything we had ever done in China and enumerating our personal resources and property. One by one, the personal interviews followed. My turn came late in November. I was led to a comfortable sitting room in the foreigners' section. There were sofas and easy chairs and tea and fruit. Three men in grey uniforms met me but only one of them, the oldest, did the talking.

23

'How are things going with you?' he asked pleasantly. 'How's your work? How's the family? We apologize for some of the shortages that still continue, but that situation will improve. However, if you need anything special, or have any requests, don't hesitate to ask us.'

'Thank you,' I said, 'but everything's fine.' I was wary about this excessive good humour.

'You're doing all right, then, aren't you?' he continued.

'Oh, yes.'

'Well, if I were you I'd keep it that way,' he said. Now there was the slightest hint of an edge in his voice. 'You see, we know all about you. We're ready to draw a curtain over your past, when the KMT was in power. As for the period after the Liberation, it might be a case of ignorance – after all, you haven't been warned, have you? But you should know that we don't tolerate for long people doing things against us. We're ready to wipe out the past, but you mustn't think you're too smart, Bao Ruo-wang. You mustn't think we're ignorant. You mustn't look on us with contempt. We know more about you than you imagine – as much as you know yourself. We're not threatening you or bragging. We're simply stating a fact. The eyes of the masses are as bright as snow. They report to us everything that is suspicious. So don't think we don't know what you're doing right now. We know. Be law-abiding. Observe regulations and don't indulge in any activities that could be harmful to us. If you act in a law-abiding way, you will be allowed to stay on in China with your family. If not, you will stay on in China away from your family. We are generous, Bao Ruo-wang, so be generous with us.'

'Thank you for your kind advice,' I answered, 'but I'd like to assure you that I'm not doing anything against you . . .'

He didn't let me finish. His face revealed exasperated impatience.

'Look, don't make statements like that. Don't make yourself guilty of another sin. We've warned you. That's all.'

I left the building even more worried than before, but my self-confidence hadn't left me entirely. After all, I reasoned, they can't really know everything about me. How wrong I was.

Now that I look back I can see my arrest like a film of events that began there in the offices of the Peking Bureau of Public Security, gained momentum during the Second Campaign for the Suppression of Counterrevolutionaries and climaxed because of Nikita Khrushchev.

The Soviets were already actively disliked because of their advisors, but the figure of Stalin himself had remained sacrosanct. Khrushchev chucked a formidable stone into the duck pond in February 1956, with his now-famous anti-Stalin speech before the Twentieth Party Congress. The Chinese leadership at first reacted cautiously, with an article published on the front pages of newspapers and magazines throughout the country: 'On the Historical Experience of the Dictatorship of the Proletariat'. The authors were presumably Mao and Teng Hsiaoping, and they weren't clients for the Khrushchev line. The article admitted that Stalin had committed some serious mistakes, but reiterated the good he had done the socialist cause and concluded that his merits far outstripped his faults. The homegrown de-Stalinization campaign that ensued was so mild as to be practically nonexistent; and even that came to an abrupt halt with the Polish student riots in Poznan.

For the international Communist movement, 1956 was like a string of firecrackers going off, and the Chinese Party orthodox were happy to blame the explosions on the slackening of central authority and leadership by the Soviet Union. The Hungarian revolution only proved the thesis that de-Stalinization had been ill-conceived. At the end of the year Mao published another article, 'More on the Historical Dispute of the Dictatorship of the Proletariat'. Directed primarily against the Soviets, the article scorned Hungary as neither a dictatorship nor a democracy, maintained that the uprising could and should have been prevented, and cautioned the Communist world to take a lesson from the lamentable bungling that surrounded it. It was Mao's bid for ideological leadership.

But his forwardness made problems at home. Mao stirred the pot of dispute so energetically that an atmosphere of controversy and contradiction grew around him. Students and intellectuals grew restive and started asking questions themselves.

Before long the party hierarchy began feeling the first stings of criticism. And for once Mao made a mistake.

Let us go to the masses, he decided. If we indeed have done nothing wrong, we have nothing to fear; if the criticism is constructive, we can learn from it. Let us welcome criticism. Let a hundred flowers bloom together. Let diverse schools of thought contend. The campaign got under way in March of 1957 and immediately yielded spectacular results. In public debate, articles, posters and even song, the critical response was overwhelming. Ordinary citizens found the courage to demand lower prices and an end to rationing. Scholars and teachers heaped odium on the party hacks who controlled education. Students brazenly circulated the Khrushchev speech and pointedly invited Communists out of their unions. It was a dangerous and explosive period. Many were even calling for an outright dismantling of the government structure and saw the future of China as a sort of Oriental Yugoslavia.

There is still debate as to whether the Hundred Flowers was an error on Mao's part or a coldly calculated ruse to make the regime's enemies speak up and thereby entrap themselves, but whatever the original planning, Mao reacted swiftly. As of June, criticisms were no longer received as commentary, but rightist provocations. The Hundred Flowers was finished. Its place was taken by the Rectification Campaign. As the party counterattack gained force, this in turn became the Struggle Against the Rightist Bourgeois Elements.

The campaign rolled furiously over the country and did not end until December 1957 – the month of my arrest.

Chapter Two

It finally happened on a freezing Friday night two days after Christmas. Six weeks earlier the police had told me I must remain in or around the house until further notice; ever since, I had been waiting for the other shoe to drop. When it came down, the only sound it made was a soft, very polite knocking at the door. I was reading in bed and my wife was already in a deep sleep. I jammed on my old slippers and shuffled over to the door.

'Yes, who is it?'

'Lao* Chia, from the police precinct.'

Well, that was certainly friendly enough. For a brief, hopeful instant, I felt a surge of optimism: Maybe it meant things were going to be okay. I was, as the Chinese say, having illusions. As I swung the door open, a harsh rush of cold air hit me and I was literally propelled backward into the room by five grim and very determined visitors – three large cops in padded blue winter uniforms, each one bearing a pistol, Chia, and a dour, expressionless woman from the Street Security Committee. No one was being polite now. Their theatrical entrance and the stamp of their booted feet woke my wife, who looked up, squinted and asked what was the matter. Stupid and panicked, all I could mumble was the usual ritualistic 'nothing'. It was the understatement of my life. The tallest of the policemen planted himself ceremoniously in front of me and another stood by my side. The third sat gingerly on the edge of the bed. Chia and the security woman, obviously enjoying her work, barred the door.

*Lao is Chinese for 'old' and it is commonly used, coupled to a person's family name, as an amicable form of greeting between friends or people with whom one is well acquainted. It is used in much the same way as the English saying 'old chap' or the American 'ol' buddy'.

'What is your name?'

'Pasqualini.'

He didn't like that. 'What is your Chinese name?'

'Bao Ruo-wang.'

'Your nationality?'

'French.'

That was all he needed for the moment. Slowly and carefully he opened his briefcase, extracted a printed card and unfolded it to show a photograph of myself stapled to one corner. Enunciating with studied clarity, he spoke the magic formula:

'Bao Ruo-wang, known also under the original name of Pasqualini, you have been discovered to have been engaged for a lengthy period of time in various counterrevolutionary activities and to have violated the laws of the People's Republic of China. I hereby announce your arrest in the name of the law. This is the warrant for your arrest.'

The word 'arrest' was a cue. The cop at my side seized my wrists with surprising force and the third bounded forward from the bed and snapped a pair of steel cuffs over them. The tall one, very much the leader, thrust the warrant at me to sign, which I did, awkwardly.

'And put down the time, too.' He consulted his watch. 'Forty-seven minutes past nine.'

They frisked me and made a cursory check of my papers until they came upon my passport. It went into the briefcase.

'Take him away,' the tall one ordered.

As they hustled me out, I caught one last glimpse of my wife. She was terrified. 'Go, and learn your lessons well!' she cried.

God, she had certainly learned *her* first lesson in a hurry. But what else could she say under the circumstances? In China one is expected to react in a certain correct manner to every given situation. Prison is not prison, but a school for learning about one's mistakes. What counts is not what a thing is, but what you call it. By being refractory, or failing to show the proper spirit, my wife could have been imprisoned herself, for having knowingly lived with and harboured a counterrevolutionary. The two kids were still sleeping as the door closed.

It was in a black Russian Pobeda that I rode to my first rendezvous with prison, jammed in the back seat between two Sepos – Security Police. There was no traffic whatever, and we sped easily past the Drum Tower, the back of the Winter Palace and finally into a small, twisting back road. It was the entrance to the famous Tsao Lan Tse Hutung – Grass Mist Lane Prison. The Chinese have the most poetically named jails in the world. Through a side door we swept into a wooden-floored reception office, where I was left with a surly young guard for my first taste of arbitrary authority and my first lesson in humility.

'Squat!' he ordered. 'Head down!'

To help me along he shoved my head roughly down until my chin touched my chest. Five minutes of tomblike silence, and then he whistled and made a gesture for me to stand. Meticulously he searched me again, taking papers, my ball pen and identity card. He put it all in a little heap, drew up the list, which I signed – with his pen. Once again, he invited me to squat. I contemplated the floor until another guard appeared to trot me across the compound to an empty office where there was a chair for him and a ridiculously tiny stool in the corner, as if meant for an evil child. For twenty minutes we sat in silence, the guard reading a book – not Mao, I noticed. The phone rang, he grunted a few unintelligible answers, and we were off again, with me leading the way (the prisoner, I was learning, always goes first, for obvious reasons). What we came to was finally the real thing – a true prison block. A fat little warder with bulging black eyes was already waiting for us. In trio we padded down a corridor lined with thick, look-alike wooden doors. Halfway down the row he stopped at one of them, pulled back the latch and looked over at me. We went in together.

The place was lit by a single twenty-five-watt bulb high in the ceiling, and I could make out a long row of men sleeping on a communal shelf-bed that ran along the entire back wall. The warder shook a prisoner awake and told him to make room for me; somehow, heaving and pushing around him, he managed to make a little clearing not more than a foot and a half wide. The warder turned and went out. I took a brief look at my surroundings. The cell was no more than eight feet deep and about twenty feet wide, and the shelf-bed took up all the space except for a narrow walkway in the front. Set in the whitewashed brick walls were two small, barred windows with panes thickly frosted over; on the ledges underneath were two neat stacks of books, pamphlets and newspapers. A pair of tar-lined iron buckets sat in the far corner, one on top of the other. The men sleeping in front of me appeared dishevelled but clean. Each one lay on a palletlike mattress with a thin cotton quilt over him; a few had even placed coquettish little pieces of cloth under their heads to keep the pillow clean.

The prisoner who had been awakened for me put a finger to his lips and motioned me to lie down. In my state of mind, I would have obeyed anyone. I took off my shoes and clambered up onto the shelf. As I was arranging myself, the warder suddenly appeared again with a quilt. He tossed it over me and went back out. I lay staring at the ceiling, too confused and depressed to sleep.

My wife, I knew, would be in for a rough time, but maybe she would be able to find a job. What worried me most was the kids, who from now on would have to face their schoolmates with the stigma of a counterrevolutionary father. My wife wouldn't be able to shield them from it indefinitely. It wouldn't be easy . . .

I huddled miserably under the quilt as the north wind swept past outside the window and the cell grew chillier. The only heat was from a warm stovepipe, which poked into the cell over the door, crossed the room above our heads and then ran out the back wall through a hole by the window. Sleepless as I was, I sat up and crept across to the tar buckets to take a leak. Just as I started thundering nicely a chorus of angry shushings arose behind me. So apparently pissing at night was against the rules. I shuffled guiltily back and drew the quilt around me. What a hell of a way to start my new life.

I must have finally dozed off, because it seemed only a minute before a whistle was blowing furiously out in the corridor and everyone, before I could even collect my senses, was on his feet. Utterly astonished, I watched for the first time the incredible precision of reveille in a Chinese prison. Two men stood at either end of the bed and began folding pallets and quilts into neat, triangular stacks not unlike the napkins in a Chinese restaurant. Another one crouched down, dragged a glazed terracotta basin from under the bed and began ladling cold water into six enamel wash basins. While six prisoners were occupied washing their faces at the basins, four more brushed their teeth over the slops bucket in the far corner. At precisely the right moment four of them changed places with four of the face washers and received a fresh scoop of water. The silence was total, except for the spittings and splashings. No one said a word. Not knowing what part I was to take in this mechanism, I simply held my place by the bed and watched.

After everyone had finished, the basins were emptied into the slops bucket and the piss bucket, which two others in turn toted over to the door. My cellmates fell into a precise line behind the buckets. Automatically, I joined them, not sure what the line was for. We were eighteen in all. I should have guessed: We were making our morning trip to the latrine. We marched silently out, down the corridor and out a side door, across a courtyard, into another building facing ours, out again and onto a little pathway that ran along the side of the prison's high outside wall. At the end of the path were two long cement trenches, very clean. Above the other end of the ditch rose a watchtower from which a Sepo stared blankly down at us, Kalashnikov hitched up his shoulder. Poor bastard, if a bunch of prisoners shitting was the most interesting thing he had to look at, his life couldn't be a very rich one. Even out here the organization continued, and the two men with the slops buckets set briskly to cleaning them with little pieces of broken brick. We marched back to the cell, climbed up on the bed, sat cross-legged and began the meditation period in which we were to ponder our sins. We were exactly like a flock of Buddhist monks.

'What's your name?'

I was startled from my thoughts by the voice of the man next to me. When I looked up, I noticed it was the same person whom the guard had awakened the night before. He asked me if I knew what I had been arrested for. I wasn't sure how to answer – I hadn't learned the drill yet.

'I'm not sure,' I said.

He regarded me with immense calm, and in an avuncular voice said, 'You are a counterrevolutionary. All of us are. Otherwise we wouldn't be here. Do you know where you are?'

Curious to see how much he could tell me, I pretended complete ignorance. There followed a perfect example of what was to become as familiar to me as the morning prayers when I was a student with the missionaries: the admonitory discourse. As always in China, where the prisoners reform the prisoners, his speech was heavily laced with religious imagery. He must have known it by heart.

'This is the Detention Centre of the Peking Bureau of Public Security. It is at number 13 Tsao Lan Tse Hutung, West City. Only counterrevolutionaries and political offenders come here. Some of us are here because of things we did before the Liberation. These individuals are called Persons with a Counterrevolutionary Past. Those who have been arrested for things they did since the Liberation are called active counterrevolutionaries. Some of us are both . . . But whatever category we fit into, all of us have committed our crimes because we had very bad thoughts.'

He gave a sweeping glance around the cell to emphasize the totality of his indictment. His voice was loud enough for the others to hear, but none of them showed any signs of participation. They probably knew the speech as well as he did.

'We must reform these thoughts and become new men again. Twenty-four hours after your arrest you will be interrogated. Step lively when they come for you. Be quick and eager – you must not make the wardens wait for you. When you go outside, walk briskly, with your head bowed down. Keep your eyes on the ground and don't try to look forward or to the side; the guard will give you directions and tell you when to turn. At the interrogation you have to confess your crimes without giving the government any trouble. Be frank and sincere. Your salvation lies in the attitude you adopt during the interrogation. Your interrogation hall will always be the same for as long as you are here, so make sure you remember the number. You will have to send all your written reports and confessions to that number.'

As he continued I felt an old familiar emotion welling up in me, compounded of confusion and anxiety, but also of a certain expectant excitement. It was exactly the same feeling as when I first went away to the mission schools – there were so many routines to learn, so many pitfalls to avoid, such a great effort to be made in so many directions. Already I was beginning to slip into the role of the well-intentioned pupil, eager to reassure the masters of his good behaviour.

'Soon we'll be having breakfast, or rather our morning meal. There are two meals a day, one at eight o'clock and the other at four in the afternoon. Each one of us gets one *wo'tou* [a rough cornbread], a piece of salted vegetable and a bowl of corn gruel. My name is Loo Teh-ling, and I am monitor of this cell. Here we call each other either by our full names or *tung-hao* [cellmate]. We are all here for the same purpose: Facing the government we must reform ourselves together and learn from one another.' I could almost hear him mentally capitalizing the slogan. 'If we are frank with the government, behave ourselves properly and observe the prison regulations faithfully, if we help the government in its work and correct our ideology by ridding ourselves of the bad thoughts in our heads, we shall be shown leniency.'

Carefully, he unfolded a little slip of paper and handed it to me. It was the keystone of his discourse. I looked dutifully (and ignorantly, since at the time I could speak, but not read Chinese) at the ideograms as he spoke them: 'This is the policy of the government. Leniency to those who confess, severity to those who resist; expiation of crimes through gaining merits; reward to those who have gained great merits.'

Loo took the paper back, slowly folded it and put it away in his shirt. His visage was serious, calm, relaxed, the very image of a man who was pleased to have done his duty well. Was that a product of brainwashing? I wondered. It was difficult to sort out. As a Chinese I recognized the desire to perform well and display good faith and willingness. It is a typical national characteristic. But this man, and the others, too, apparently, seemed to feel a need to display a permanent zeal of fealty. And this, of course, is the simple and powerful gist of what is known as brainwashing: submission of your will to that of another. Once the act of submission has been obtained, it is not difficult to increase it from begrudging to enthusiastic – or even to fanatic. It is only a question of how powerful the authority is. I hadn't yet had any contact with the total pervasiveness of that authority, but I would very soon. It didn't take me long to submit, either.

Breakfast time came around. Two of the prisoners climbed down, brought two big earthen basins from under the bed, and stood by the door waiting for the warder to open up. Someone else passed out bowls and wooden chopsticks; a few of the men pulled out little private bags of salt. When the breakfast detail returned I saw that jail was going to be a hungry place. The wo'tou bread was a meagre thing, not half as big as those I had been used to eating at home; it weighed no more than five ounces. Each of us received only one slice of boiled turnip maybe half an inch thick. It looked like a hydrox cookie. And the corn gruel was as watery as clear soup. Christ, I thought, if that's how it's going to be ... It was.

After the meal Loo took me aside. He wasn't finished yet. 'Some of the cellmates have a criticism to make against you,' he informed me. 'Last night you woke everyone up when you got up to urinate. You must learn to do things slowly and silently at night. Take the cover off the bucket gently; urinate against the side of the bucket and not down the middle. And pay attention to the floor.'

I nodded. Loo turned to the others. 'The newcomer didn't know the way we do things. I have explained it to him and criticized him. He has accepted your criticism with humility. I suggest that we excuse him.'

I was beginning to like this odd man more and more. Beneath his portentous manner he was human and generous. He just happened to take his job as cell monitor very seriously.

At nine o'clock a whistle blew in the corridor and everyone assembled on the bed once again, Buddha position. It was study time. Loo began reading aloud from the *People's Daily*. In the middle, though, he was interrupted by the latch clunking back. When the door drew open, the tall cop was there, the one who had arrested me.

'Bao Ruo-wang!' he called. I jumped down, slipped on my shoes and dashed outside. I hadn't expected to be called so soon. It made me nervous.

The big cop took me only as far as the warder's desk, where he handed me over to a Sepo in a yellow-green padded uniform. As I approached he slowly drew a monstrous Browning .45 from his hip holster and with a flourish pulled back the slide to snap a round into the chamber. I figured he was putting on a little show just for my benefit, but the assumption didn't help any. I was still scared as hell.

He told me to get moving and I rocketed out the double doors. Only I had forgotten about what Loo had told me about the posture.

'Keep your head down!' he screamed. 'Further!'

What a situation. I couldn't see a damn thing except my feet and the floor. I hadn't been locked up even twenty-four hours yet, and already this unknown man could make me walk into a wall if he wanted.

'Left! Get a move on! Right!' I trotted along, panting more from terror than exertion, blindly doing as he said. We moved out into a courtyard, and soon I was shivering from the cold as well. We passed a long row of doors and I could hear shouts and threats from other interrogations. Welcome to the club. Left-right, left-right, out through another courtyard, and finally my man brought me up in front of a dark green door with a frosted pane set in the middle. A wooden plaque above read '41st Room'.

'Report your arrival!' I made a modest try, but it wasn't to the Sepo's liking. 'Again, and louder!' This time I shouted, but my voice was strangely squeaky.

A quiet voice invited me to come in and I found myself in a large, high-ceilinged room that could have been in a hospital: tile floor, whitewashed walls and fluorescent lights. Two desks at the back wall faced me; between them was a wooden locker and above, a large red star. I didn't see it until I left, but directly above me, peering down at my back, was a colour poster of Mao. Behind the desks sat two young men, both in the dark-blue flannel uniforms standard for all party functionaries.

Neither looked more than thirty. One wore black leather army boots and fiddled with a gold Parker 51, that great status symbol of the Communist world, and it indicated that he was the more important of the two. This, it turned out, was my interrogator. His companion was the recorder. His boots were only padded cotton.

The interrogator made a gesture toward a short stool in the centre of the room. As I sat I noticed a piece of chalk placed carefully on the floor between the two front legs of the stool. The interrogator gazed contemplatively down at me and started from the beginning.

'Your name?'

'Bao Ruo-wang.'

'Your original name?'

'Pasqualini.'

'Take that piece of chalk and write it on the floor in big letters.'

So that's what it was for. The routine continued – address before arrest, employment, nationality . . . He went through the detail mechanically and with obvious boredom. He showed no signs of animation until he reached the point where he could begin making speeches. Interrogators are born speech-makers.

'Now then. Before we start, there are some things I have to tell you. The people in your cell have probably told you the government's policy toward those who are arrested for counter-revolutionary and political activities. Can you read Chinese?'

'No,' I admitted. Despite the fact that I spoke Mandarin like a native, I had never been taught to read or write it. That came later – in the camps. The interrogator pointed to the characters on a banner pinned to the wall. This was the official version, which he read off for me:

Leniency to those who confess; severity to those who resist; redemption to those who obtain merits; rewards to those who gain big merits.

I noticed the slight differences between this and the version Loo told me in the cell. Evidently he had done some embroidering.

'This is the government's policy,' the interrogator continued.

'It is the way to salvation for you. In front of you are two paths: the one of confessing everything and obeying the government, which will lead you to a new life, the other of resisting the orders of the government and stubbornly remaining the people's enemy right to the very end. This path will lead to the worst possible consequences. It is up to you to make the choice. The sooner you confess your crimes, the sooner you will go home. The better your confession, the quicker you will rejoin your wife and children.

'You need not worry about your family. The government will look after them. You are the guilty one, not they. The families of counterrevolutionaries are not discriminated against in any manner. If they are in difficulties, the government is there to help them. So set your heart at ease and confess your crimes thoroughly. If you behave properly, we might recommend you for leniency when the time comes for that. But if you show yourself to be stubborn and a die-hard imperialist without an ounce of regret, then the outcome is too frightful to contemplate. Do you understand me?'

I nodded. I was, in fact, very relieved by what he said about the government taking care of my family. It was good news at the time. Only later I learned that it was a lie – when I was in the camps, my wife and children were hungrier than I was.

'There are two types of confessions. We call them Toothpaste and Water Tap. The Toothpaste prisoner needs to be squeezed every now and then, or else he forgets to keep confessing. The Water Tap man needs one good, hard twist before he starts, but then everything comes out. You are a reasonable person, an intelligent person. I don't think we need to resort to persuasion. Do you understand me?'

Silence. I nodded again and waited for him to go on.

'Good. So we'll begin. Do you know why you were brought here?'

I made my first mistake. 'When I was arrested they told me that I was a counterrevolutionary.'

My interrogator leaned forward in his chair angrily.

'*Told* that you are a counterrevolutionary? You *are* a counterrevolutionary! You are a spy of the imperialists! No one tells you – it is a fact! You will have to be frank with us or things will go badly for you. Speak!'

I suppose it must have been the arrogance of his manner that briefly raised what was left of my hackles. I hadn't been inside long enough to realize that a prisoner has no defences, no justification whatever. I committed the presumption of answering back. For the last time in China, I was a wise guy.

'How can I be a counterrevolutionary,' I asked, 'if I am not Chinese?'

He stared at me, dumbfounded for a tiny moment, then exploded in unfeigned rage.

'How dare you ask us questions? Your activities have brought damage to the revolution and have caused great losses to the government. You are a counterrevolutionary through and through. All your life you have engaged in activities against the Communist Party and against the people. We have proof of it – plenty of proof.'

He calmed himself quickly. 'Now we are going to start again from the beginning. You will tell us your history properly.'

'Where shall I begin?'

'Before the Liberation, when you started working for the American imperialists.'

I began the long list, from the Marines, the Signal Corps, the Associated Press, but the interrogator was showing increasing signs of impatient discomfort. He broke in.

'We are not asking for your biography. We know where you have been working. We have records for that. What we want is a confession of your crimes. You are giving us all these details but nothing about your crimes against the people. Do you realize what you are? You are an agent of the imperialists and a loyal running-dog of the Americans. Tell us all the dirty work you did for them. We have complete records in our files and we have formal accusations from people you victimized in the past. Tell us about your duties as interpreter for the Marine Military Police. Was interpretation the only work you did?'

It was easy to see what he was getting at. It was also easy to see I was in trouble. No matter how much I might try to minimize my role as interpreter, I couldn't avoid piling incriminations on my head. The Communists had always regarded the military police as an organization of repression against the Chinese people and as an intelligence-gathering agency. I had not only accepted their pay and their orders, but had quite willingly worked in the middle of all their activities – some of which were painful. I had been along on raids against black-market rings, confiscations, all sorts of vice-squad dealings, interrogations of civilians. I was well known. There were plenty of black marketeers, night club operators, pimps, whores and God knows what other characters who could have poured out their meretricious tales of suffering under the Americans, once the Communists were in power and puritanism became the call of the day. I began talking about the Marines and went on until half past noon, when he ordered me to stop and called for a guard to return me to the cell.

'How did it go?' Loo asked me.

'Well, I don't know. They told me I'd be called again.'

'Of course you'll be called again.' Loo spoke with the amused indulgence of a schoolmaster. 'Perhaps dozens of times. That is what we are here for – to be interrogated. Interrogation is a good thing. It is the solution of our problems and the settlement of our cases. The sooner we end the interrogations by being open and frank, the sooner we will leave here. You must make efforts to leave as soon as possible.'

That was something he didn't have to tell me twice. Loo was a very unsettling person, though. I was really liking him a lot by now, but it mystified me why in hell he talked like a Communist functionary. That was something that would be cleared up for me in time, step by step. My interrogation, it turned out, was to last a full fifteen months, at the end of which I, too, was speaking like Loo. And I was begging to be sent away to a labour camp. Life is strange, but the human mind stranger.

It doesn't take a prisoner long to lose his self-confidence. Over the years Mao's police have perfected their interrogation methods to such a fine point that I would defy any man, Chinese or not, to hold out against them. Their aim is not so much to make you invent nonexistent crimes, but to make you accept your ordinary life, as you led it, as rotten and sinful and worthy of punishment, since it did not concord with their own, the police's, conception of how a life should be led. The basis of their success is despair, the prisoner's perception that he is utterly and hopelessly and forever at the mercy of his jailers. He has no defence, since his arrest is absolute and unquestionable proof of his guilt. (During my years in prison I knew of a man who was in fact arrested by mistake – right name but wrong man. After a few months he had confessed all the crimes of the other. When the mistake was discovered, the prison authorities had a terrible time persuading him to go back home. He felt too guilty for that.) The prisoner has no trial, only a well-rehearsed ceremony that lasts perhaps half an hour; no consultation with lawyers; no appeal in the Western sense. I say in the Western sense because there actually is a possible appeal, but it is such a splendidly twisted, ironic caricature that it is worthy of the best talents of Kafka, Orwell or Joseph Heller. We shall see that later.

Very soon I realized that I could expect no help from any quarter. My wife was petrified with fear, poor and in danger of being locked up herself. At the time France had no diplomatic relations with People's China and the Quai d'Orsay certainly wasn't prepared to make any trouble over me. I was nothing more than a half-breed who happened to be holding a French passport by luck of birth. I was no Jenkins, and no one was going to war over my ear ...

My brain was flailing away trying to get all this business straightened out when, unexpectedly, I was called for a second interrogation. Again, I was taken aback and unnerved. Why another session at 8 p.m.? Everyone had indicated that they always took a few extra days to digest the material from the first session. The only explanation I could find was that my output that morning had been completely unsatisfactory, and that they were planning to try again, from another angle. And how right I was. It was pitch dark when a cop – a new one this time, but with the same fat pistol – led me away through the maze of passageways and corridors. My apprehension mounted as we crossed the big courtyard in silence, and it was an almost friendly sight when we came upon the green door marked '41st',

I barked out my name and trotted in, head down, aiming crab-like for the stool in the corner.

'Don't sit down.' It was the interrogator who spoke. 'We're going somewhere else this time.'

I stood studying the floor for another five minutes before another Sepo came in. We trooped out en masse. This time I had the privilege of four guards and four big pistols. We pushed bravely off into the night, me blindly leading the way as always, left-right, left-right. We came up before a huge, three-storey structure that I took to be some kind of administration building, then inside and across a big, sparsely furnished meeting hall. I found myself at the head of a flight of red brick steps, lit dimly and twisting steeply downward. Down I went, boots creaking behind me. An iron gate stopped us, but one of the guards came forward with a key. I could make out another set of steps, even darker, plunging into the penumbra. The walls were closer, too, barely the width of my shoulders. With each step the air seemed to grow damper, warmer and more sickly. I felt as if I were walking into a plague. My mouth was dry. I was scared as hell. At the end of it all was a wooden door sheathed in iron.

'*Baogao!*' someone ordered behind me. 'Report!'

I shouted out my name and the door flew open. Two men in blue padded uniforms were there to jerk me inside and at the same time lock my arms behind me. There were ten more little steps down, then an opening and then – I found myself in a torture chamber.

I don't think a person screams when he is terrified. The first instinct is to freeze up. It's not possible, I thought, it's not possible, but there was a tiger bench before me, just as bright as life. I contemplated it numbly and felt cold. A tiger bench is a simple device, really, just a sort of articulated board. The client is tied firmly in several places, and then the bench can be raised in many different and interesting ways. Eventually it is the hip bones that crack first, I have been told. Next to the bench were water and towels, indispensable accessories for that great classic, the water torture. The towel goes over the prisoner's face and the water is poured gently on it. The man suffocates or drowns.

It is a handy little torture, because it is light and portable. It is a technique that was much in vogue during the war in Vietnam. I looked around and saw bamboo splinters and hammers, and even a set of chains heating over a coal fire. I think I would have sunk to the floor if the two cops weren't supporting me by my arms. His face a stone mask, the interrogator stepped up before me. The faithful scribe followed, notebook in hand. And finally, after a long theatrical pause, I discovered the truth of this routine.

'This is a museum,' he said. 'Don't be afraid. We wanted you to have a look at this place so you could see how the Nationalist reactionaries used to question their prisoners. Now we are living in a different era. We are in a socialist society, under the humane regime of Chairman Mao and the Chinese Communist Party. We do not use such crude and inhumane methods. People who resort to torture do so only because they are weaker than their victims. We, on the other hand, are stronger than you. We are certain of our superiority. And the methods we use are a hundred times more efficient than this.'

He looked over the room with disdain, looked back at me for a long moment, then ordered the guard: 'Take him away.'

Long Live Chairman Mao, I thought as I shuffled out. From that moment on, my interrogations started going smoothly.

The next time I saw the interrogator he had a bit of psycho-political explaining for me.

'You see, Bao, the reason you became frightened when you saw our museum the other night was that your mind has been poisoned by imperialist propaganda. What we showed you was just our way of letting you know that it is only the criminal Chiang Kai-shek regime that ever used torture. Now that you have learned the lesson you will see that the only way for you is to confess. It saves so much time for you and me. And there are so many advantages.'

'What do you want me to confess?'

He looked pained. 'We don't tell people what to confess. If we did, it would be an accusation and not a confession. Don't you see that we are giving you a chance? We already know everything about you, Bao. We want you to confess only to give you the opportunity to obtain some leniency. If what you tell us tallies with what we already know, then I can give you my word that you will be leniently treated. But if you tell us only five or ten per cent, then you'll never go home.'

'Where do I begin?'

'There are many ways. Some people prefer to start with the most important things and then work their way down to the details. But most are the opposite – they start with the trifles and little by little work their way up to what is really important. You might say they try to save the best part for the last. That's all right with us. We know we will get it eventually. And then there are some people who suffer from loss of memory and can only talk about the most recent things; they don't seem to like to talk about their past. It's all up to you, Bao. We have lots of time. Only one thing: Don't try to make fools of us. I can promise you it won't work.'

I began the story of my life, from age eight onward. The interrogator hardly interrupted again and listened with complete attention. The scribe took it down in Chinese characters with admirable speed and precision. That session lasted six hours in all. As the sessions continued the gaps between them gradually grew larger and larger. I had plenty of time to think, to observe my new home and to slip into its routine.

Our little world of Grass Mist Lane was so poetically named, I learned, because there had once been a Buddhist monastery on the spot, razed by the Nationalists to make way for the prison. The great, square compound was itself divided into four smaller squares or subcompounds, each with its own courtyard. They were called, naturally enough, the South, East, West and New compounds. The whole thing was surrounded by a brick-and-plaster wall about twenty feet high, topped by the inevitable electrified barbed wire. Each compound was divided into blocks and each block into cells and offices, storerooms and so on. The cells varied in size. In Block A of the West Compound, where I spent my entire interrogation, the cells were designed for twenty men. The floors were concrete, the bars on the windows, stout wood, and the windowpanes were covered on the outside, to block the view and make the feeling of isolation complete.

From the first time I saw it I was amazed by the organization of life in Grass Mist Lane. Every one of us had a certain housekeeping job to carry out, and a time for it. Our existence was governed by a routine as fixed and unvarying as the seasons. Confessions and interrogations occupied five days of the week, with Sunday free for political study and meditation and Tuesday for cleanup. Two cellmates would scrub the floor then, while the rest of us remained on the communal bed and cleaned windows, curtains and walls, or else mended clothing. Another detail would take the cotton quilts to the courtyard to be sunned. If some of us had ripped or worn through quilt, pallet or jacket, the cell leader could request needle and thread.

Tuesday was also the day for shaving and nail trimming, both jobs performed with the same little pair of nail clippers. It took me an hour to take off my beard with the clipper, whisker by whisker, but when I was done it was as close a shave as if I had done it with anything as potentially dangerous and forbidden as a razor. Each cell kept a little box for toenail parings, passed around from man to man as he snipped himself. At the end of every month the warder collected the boxes and turned them over to the central prison authority for sale to the outside. Mixed with other equally exotic ingredients, the toenails were used in traditional Chinese medicine. I never did know what they were supposed to cure, but it was enough that they paid us a movie every four months – a dreary propaganda movie, to be sure (there are no others in China), but it was still a break from the routine.

Like everything else, there was a certain accepted form for requesting the instruments we needed. Loo would stand by the door at a certain time of the morning and wait for the warder to pass. When the spy window flew open he would chant out the formula:

'Cell Number 14 reporting. We would be grateful to have four clippers, two big needles for quilts, six small needles, twenty white threads and forty black ones.'

When the slot opened again, the requested gear would be

shoved through, each clipper with a tag dangling from it, followed by the needles and the bits of thread, each one about a yard long. Every clipper and needle had to be returned by nightfall. If anything was missing, no one could sleep until it had been located. If a needle had been broken, both pieces had to be returned. Prisoners had been known to commit suicide by swallowing needles. This care to keep any potential weapons from us was reflected everywhere. The big bed of course contained no nails or screws but was constructed like a set of blocks; it could be dismantled in a moment. A cloth toothbrush holder, like an ammunition bandolier, hung on the back wall with a homemade calendar next to it. For free time, such as there was of it, each cell also had one deck of Chinese cards, a box of checkers, two penholders and a bottle of ink. Paper, of course, had to be requested, as did the nib to be attached to the pen holder.

Every second Tuesday was bath day. The bathing area was a walk-in swimming pool of rough cement in the next building, and it serviced about a thousand men each time it was filled. For the bath, everything depended on the luck of the draw. If our cell happened to be called early, it could be a healthy and even pleasant experience, But if we went toward the end it was nothing short of revolting to wade through the grey, greasy water up to our chests. We left dirtier than when we went in.

After a man had been in prison for ten days his family had the right to send him one quilt, one cotton mattress, a basin, a toothbrush, toothpaste, some soap, a towel and one change of clothes. If the man had no family, or if it were too poor, the government would issue him one white coat, one mattress, a blue enamel basin (theoretically to be returned at the end of his sentence), a piece of Sunlight brand soap, a wooden-handled, pink-bristled toothbrush (Lion brand), a coarse towel two feet long by one foot wide, and one greyish sheet of toilet paper about the size of a newspaper folded out. In winter he would get an old army uniform of padded cotton.

About once a month the barber, a freed worker, would make the rounds of the cells. For each one of us he would pass the hand clippers first around the head and then a couple of times over the face in the guise of a shave.

And then there was food – the single greatest joy, chagrin and motivating force in the entire prison system. I had the bad luck to go to Grass Mist Lane only one month after rationing had been introduced as a formal part of the interrogation process. No greater weapon exists for inducing cooperation. The distressing thin, watery corn gruel, the hard little loaves of wo'tou and the sliver of vegetable became the centre of our lives and the focus of our deepest attentions. As rationing continued and we grew thinner, we learned to eat each morsel with infinite attention, making it last as long as possible. Rumours and desperate fantasies circulated about how well the prisoners ate in the camps. These, I learned later, were often plants sent in by the interrogators to encourage confessions. After a year of this diet I was prepared to admit virtually anything to get more food.

The starvation was admirably studied – enough to keep us alive but never enough to let us forget our hunger. During my fifteen months in the interrogation centre, I ate rice only once and meat never. Six months after my arrest my stomach was entirely caved in and I began to have the characteristic bruised joints that came from simple body contact with the communal bed. The skin on my ass hung loose like the dugs of an old woman. Vision became unclear and I lost my power of concentration. I reached a sort of record point of vitamin deficiency when I was finally able to snap off my toenails without even using the clipper. My skin rubbed off in a dusty film. My hair began falling out. It was miserable.

'Life here didn't use to be so bad,' Loo told me. 'We used to have a meal of rice every fifteen days, steamed white bread at the end of every month and some meat on the big holidays like the New Year, May first and October first. It was all right.'

What changed it all was that some people's delegation came to inspect the place during the Hundred Flowers period. They were horrified to see prisoners eating enough. It was intolerable, they concluded, that these counterrevolutionaries – the scum of society and the enemies of the people – should have a standard of living higher than many peasants. From November 1957 on there was no more rice or meat or wheat flour for prisoners on festive occasions.

Food obsessed us so completely that we were insane, in a way. We were ready for anything. It was the perfect climate for interrogations. Every one of us began begging to be sent to the camps. No one left Grass Mist Lane without specifically requesting it in writing. There was even a form for it: 'Please give me the authorization to show repentance for my sins by working in the camps.'

Later, no matter how unbearable conditions became in the camps, every warder could truthfully tell us we were there only because we had asked for it.

Chapter Three

1. The instructions of the government must be obeyed in all things.
2. All conversations within the cell must be conducted in a normal voice and within the hearing of at least two or three other persons. Conversations in a foreign or secret language are strictly forbidden.
3. The exchange or lending of objects between prisoners is strictly forbidden. Exceptions, however, can be made upon the approval and permission of the warder.
4. Prisoners are not permitted to seek sympathy among themselves, nor are they allowed to shelter criminal activities. Mutual surveillance must be practised at all times and reliance upon the government should be cultivated.
5. Prisoners may make requests of the government either by writing or orally; in the latter case the prisoner must stand three metres away from the warder he is addressing.
6. It must be remembered that good behaviour during the period of interrogation will be taken into account when one's case comes to be dealt with.

The rules governing my new existence were printed on a little card pinned to the wall, and as the weeks slipped past I gradually grew accustomed to the environment and Cell 14 became my world and my home. In the very beginning, not more than five days after my arrival, Loo and the others introduced me to my first Weekly Examination of Conscience, in which every one of us promised to be good-natured with fellow-prisoners, co-operative with the interrogators and reliant on the government. Loo ended it with another lecture and then opened the conversation about the work assignments. There were jobs for everyone in the cell, but before any one of them was taken it had to be discussed, analysed, volunteered for. At the end of our consultation I found myself a floor sweeper. I was startled to see that the prisoner who had been cleaning the urine buckets – manifestly the most unexalted and repulsive job there was – volunteered enthusiastically to continue. My surprise proved that I knew nothing yet of prison psychology: He was only trying to be 'progressive' and give evidence that he was on the road to self-reform.

Shang was his name, and he had been a Communist cadre, but he had made the common mistake of talking too much during the Hundred Flowers. The former Communists were a special breed wherever I met them in the prisons. Disciplined by their years with the party, they were model prisoners, always ready to give the example and explain the latest convolutions of the official line. But in spite of their ready submission to the government, they always bore the realization that since they were locked up with us they were Enemies of the People. It imposed on them a strange, sad dualism that must have been hard to live with. Withal, they were good friends to their fellow prisoners. Never did I know a former Communist to turn informer or denounce a cellmate.

Shang was always trying harder. One day he devised a cardboard cover for the urine bucket and later, when he managed to scrounge a bit of old cloth, he covered the cardboard with a tapestry-like effect. Loo was pleased, and gave him a written citation for his concern for the communal welfare.

Loo's vigilance ran even to supervising our subjects of conversation; at all times, even in casual small talk, he was there to ensure our ideological soundness, and when talk lagged he indefatigably launched us into group discussions or stories with guiding moral principles. Everything else that might make the mind wander – home, food, sports, hobbies or, of course, sex – was absolutely prohibited. 'Facing the government we must study together and watch each other', was the slogan, and it was written everywhere around the prison. The admonition was hardly necessary, though; we were all too tired and enfeebled by hunger to even think about sex. Any one of us would have preferred an extra wo'tou to a woman.

For half an hour every day we were herded outside for

exercise, and we ran in tight little circles in the narrow opening between the cell buildings and the main wall, behind which we could often hear the squeals and laughter from the children's school, which lay just on the other side. The order in which we lined up and ran rigorously followed our sleeping arrangement on the bed; it was imperative for the guards to be able to identify any prisoner by simply looking down at the cell chart he carried with him.

It was during these exercises that I first noticed a squat Japanese with a shaven head who perpetually busied himself in the prison yard, mumbling to himself. He was a war criminal, Shang told me, an ex-sergeant in the imperial military police who had been arrested by the Nationalists and thrown into Grass Mist Lane. When the Communists arrived they simply confirmed his life sentence. Over the years he had become a sort of general-purpose orderly, notably in charge of cleaning out the trench latrines, which were remarkably neat. Like the warders, he had his own cell and complete freedom of movement – but of course he never left the prison.

Another of the permanent fixtures was the prison doctor, a tall white-haired scholarly type, who apparently had been around Grass Mist Lane for at least twenty years. Even though he was a civilian he wore the blue uniform and cap of the cadres and everyone called him Officer Wang. Like the Japanese orderly, he was directly inherited from the Kuomintang and he had managed the transition to the new ideology so effortlessly that he became one of the best agitprops I ever met.

Wang had a good heart, but when a prisoner came to him with a physical complaint, he almost always responded with a speech, parable or object lesson. What the Chinese create by talking alone is truly wondrous. Study, he told us. Study what the government tells you or you will slip back and never learn. Study because in the camps you won't have the time for it anymore.

That was an exaggeration. In the camps we studied, too, but it was here in the interrogation centre that we learned its importance. The studies brought home to the prisoner the government point of view, explained to him why he had been arrested and why it was just to have been arrested and why he must at all times continue striving to please the government. Every cell had its daily session, and every man had to participate.

The most ordinary session would be an extract from the *People's Daily*, read by the cell leader and then commented on by all the cellmates. One of the prisoners, appointed cell clerk, would note each man's words and then make up the résumés that would be placed in the individual dossiers. If a prisoner says something unusual or criminal, his words enter the dossier in full and later he pays: a stretch of solitary, years added to his sentence or perhaps a Struggle. The Struggle is a great Chinese invention. We shall come to that presently. Realizing the consequences his words can bring, the prisoner quickly learns to talk in noncommittal slogans. The danger to this, of course, is that he might end by thinking in slogans. Most do. Generally it takes the realities of camp life to pull him out of it.

Whenever an event of special importance occurred, the ordinary study sessions were replaced by *ad hoc* meetings designed to present the government's interpretation of that event. In 1958, for example, the American landing in Lebanon was considered of such great importance that all interrogations were stopped in favour of prison-wide study sessions. It was the same with the Formosa Straits crisis and the time the Nationalists shot down a Chinese plane with one of their newly acquired Sidewinder missiles. The sessions concluded the Americans were exporting inhuman weapons. We had other meetings to learn about the People's Communes Movement, the General Line and the Great Leap Forward: The Three Red Banners, they were called.

The first such special session I experienced concerned Mao's pamphlet 'On the Correct Handling of the Contradictions Among the People'. I will try to re-create it at some length – verbosity, sloganizing and all – for it is absolutely typical of China (study sessions happen everywhere, on the outside as well as in prisons) and a certain knowledge of this process is essential for anyone who would like to understand the post-revolutionary Chinese mentality.

The study sessions always began in the afternoon; when the interrogations had finished and a calm had settled over the prison. We congregated in the cell and sat cross-legged on the big bed around Loo.

'Now listen carefully,' he warned, 'because afterwards everyone will have to speak. There will be no exceptions.'

Loo read a passage about a page long. Like the famous Red Book of selected quotations, this pamphlet is divided into small, readily digestible portions. Loo slowly read the passage, then put the book down and looked around.

'Now is everything clear? Have I read it too fast?' There were no comments or complaints. 'Good. Now let's meditate for a few minutes.' After a long silence he cleared his throat (even *that* he managed to do ceremoniously) and continued with one final consideration. 'Before we start our discussion I will explain a few things for those who are on a lower cultural level.'

This sort of plain talk is not considered an insult in China. Some of the prisoners were barely educated peasants and no one took with ill grace Loo's statement of fact. And he had a second purpose: In the past some prisoners had tried to use their cultural backwardness as an excuse not to study. Loo had clear instructions to let no one off the hook. He slipped easily into his practised presentation style.

'First of all, what we read today was a famous work by Chairman Mao. It is a report he made during the Hundred Flowers. This work is now being used to settle all the differences and misunderstandings among the people. It is the basis of the rectification of the party and for the struggle against the bourgeois and rightist elements.

'There are two kinds of contradictions – those within the people and those between the people and the enemy. The contradictions among the people consist of errors which are not usually so serious. The second kind is more dangerous. These are not just errors or mistakes, but crimes. Sins. Disagreement over policy. Counterrevolutionary activities. Wilful acts against the state. The first kind can be corrected among the people themselves, by discussions and patient explanation, but the second cannot be solved that way.

'As far as we prisoners are concerned, we have been given the time to acknowledge our crimes and to show our remorse;

we will make a clean breast of everything. Each one of us has been given a tremendous opportunity. If we reject that opportunity, it only means that we still want to rebel. That we remain at odds with the people. If we persist in our erroneous ways, we become targets for the dictatorship of the proletariat. We were given the chance to talk but we didn't. So our errors, which could have been solved easily and quickly, become only more grave. If we distrust the government, the government can only distrust us. And that is why we are here.'

Loo's calm rhetoric was tremendously persuasive for a cellful of dejected and hopeless men who knew they were utterly dependent on a bureaucratic judgement to decide their fates. Every day the prisoner was taught to believe that it was not judicial process, evidence and courtroom contradiction that would mitigate his future sentence, but rather his manner – *the way he behaved*. Our relationship with the state was that of child-parent, rather than adult-adult as traditional in Western jurisprudence. The child must put his entire trust in the parent because he has no other choice.

'All right, now,' he continued, 'let's get started with the discussion. It is very important for us to understand how this discussion can help us. In spite of our dishonesty and insincerity, the government is giving us a chance to redeem ourselves and realize the errors of our ways.'

Loo motioned to a thick-set, fiftyish man at the far end of the bed, a peasant named Wu who was in for agricultural counter-revolutionary activities. He was part of the second wave of farmers to be attacked by the new order. First, of course, were the landlords, who were dealt with immediately – and harshly – after the revolution. Wu had owned land, but farmed it entirely with his own family, exploited no workers, minded his own business, bothered no one and, so far as he knew, committed no crimes. Slowly, though, he had turned into the classic case of the obstacle to progress: He had refused to join the Cooperative Movement.

'I was arrested,' Wu said, 'because some guy accused me of obstructing the Cooperative Movement. They say I was a hurdle. But before that, when the Communists came, they told us that the farmers were free to do as they liked. No one would be forced to join the Cooperative Movement, they said. So what am I supposed to think when they accuse me of not joining? It was supposed to be all right to work for myself.'

Wu still hadn't learned to be repentant, but this very session was to set him on the road. As unruffled as ever, Loo asked him if he had anything more to say. Wu shook his head and Loo asked the rest of us to comment. The litany began.

'Wu is looking down on the workers,' someone piped up.

'Wu has bad ideas,' barked out another cellmate with all the rectitude of a girls' school monitor. 'We have to help him realize this so he can make a good confession. We don't want to see him shot or given a life sentence. We've got to try to help Wu out of the goodness of our hearts.'

As each man raised his hand Loo nodded and the accusations flew out, one after the other. Each prisoner's participation was meant both to help the guilty cellmate and to gain a personal expiatory enthusiasm. And what the hell – these sorts of comments looked good in the dossier, of which each one of us was painfully aware. We went on.

'Wu wanted to be something special.'

'He was throwing a monkey wrench into the Cooperative Movement.'

'Anyone who doesn't join the Cooperative Movement is against it, and if you are against the Cooperative Movement, you are against the government.'

'The government gives us good advice, like a parent telling a child not to steal. But Wu doesn't care about the rest. He just wanted to make a fortune for himself.'

'Wu doesn't have a place in our society. Certain landlords must be eliminated and he is one of them. Lenin taught us that.'

It was probably the half-knowledgeable reference to Lenin that persuaded Shu Li to break into the talk. 'Let's not be so drastic there,' he said. 'Let's look at it from another angle.'

Like Shang, Shu had been in the government, as an economist in Shansi, and he also came to his downfall during the Hundred Flowers. An innovator, he had conceived a scheme to reward individual higher production with bonuses, but this got him into trouble during the Rectification Campaign. He was arrested and charged with materialist molestation. He was in his mid-forties now, thin and ascetic but speaking with all the authority of a professor who had spent years studying Party-Think.

'Let's look at it from another side of Wu's story. He says he was not obstructing the Cooperative Movement because he wasn't in anyone's way. All right. He is under the impression that a man who works hard deserves more in return. We must keep in mind Wu's background when we consider these views. He is a rich peasant; and being a peasant, he loves to exploit the land for himself. It is in his blood. It is passed on to him right from his ancestors. He doesn't want to share his crops with others, but if the others were to put in even more work than he does, then he'd be willing to share their goods, wouldn't he? What we have to do is convince Wu that what the government charges him with is just.

'The Cooperative Movement is a mass movement. Millions of pieces of land are being joined together. Instead of 30- or 40-acre plots, we have hundreds and thousands of acres now. So what happens if right in the middle of that you have ten acres owned by a private farmer? If the rest decide to plant rice and he wants to plant corn, he disrupts the entire system. They can't plough through his fields, so they have to detour around them. And then maybe he will give the others second thoughts about having joined the movement and sharing their crops with others. He is a bad example. But the most important is that the Cooperative Movement was decreed by Chairman Mao himself, so Wu was disobeying the directives of Mao.'

Shu was getting hot now, ready to make his point. 'If that is really the case, then I am afraid I have to agree with our cell-mates that he has no place in our society.'

As far as pure demagoguery went, he could hardly find an argument stronger than that one, but as a good Communist, even fallen, he really did want to convince Wu, and he knew there was a way.

'Classmate Wu,' he asked, solicitous now, 'how much food did you have in the days before Liberation? What was your yearly yield?'

'About 250 kilos a head,' Wu answered respectfully. 'Not counting the husks.'

'And what is it now? I mean, what was it when you were arrested?'

'About 320.'

'How is it that you get 70 kilos more?'

'There are less losses now. Irrigation was bad then, and we used to be robbed by the soldiers.'

Everything was falling into place, as Shu knew it would. 'Don't the soldiers come and ask for food now?'

'Why, no, of course not.' Wu seemed almost indignant that there could be such a suggestion. 'The people from the Provisional Army don't do that sort of thing.'

'And how is the irrigation now?'

'You know we had the Irrigation Movement in 1953. That improved things.'

'So instead of being grateful to the Communist Party for improving things you try to throw a monkey wrench into their system. Do you see what a bastard you've been?'

Loo cut in, and his voice was tinged with anger. He had to remind Shu of the rules of the game. 'Don't call him a bastard,' he said firmly. 'You know there's no swearing in study time. We can't use that sort of language for cellmates.'

Shu descended one notch in the lexicon of officialese pejoration. 'All right. Rotten egg, then.'

'No,' retorted Loo, shaking his head, 'not even that. You can call him a bad element if you like, or a reactionary or a stinking landlord. A landlord who doesn't even rate that name. We can call him a small-time rich landowner.' Now he turned to Wu with all the dignity of a superior-court judge. 'Do you see all the trouble you have caused?'

Grateful, intellectually overpowered and a bit frightened, Wu nodded, but that wasn't enough of a signification. What Loo was waiting for was the testimonial, the formalistic declaration.

'Yes, I am beginning to see my error,' Wu said cautiously. 'I didn't realize how much damage I was doing by not joining the Cooperative Movement.'

But even now Wu's case was not completely framed and packaged. To make it final, Loo had to decorate it with homilies.

'Mao issued the directive out of the goodness of his heart,' he said. 'It's not up to you to judge it or not. You thought you would be smart to stay out of the Cooperative Movement. You thought you'd have it easy. You were wrong, Wu. You were very foolish. All you got out of your attitude was to be sent here, and now there's nothing you can do about it. Now, does anybody else have anything to say?'

He looked around for further comment. No one spoke a word. Wu was finally off the hook. Loo signalled to a skinny little balding man with a grey beard. Wei-I-sha was his name, the Chinese transliteration of Isaac. Wei was a Methodist pastor, and he spoke with the ease of a man used to addressing crowds.

'For the benefit of those of you who have never heard me talk before, I am a Protestant pastor, that is to say a missionary. I joined the church in my early twenties and I have been with it now for over forty years. I make no secret of the fact that I worked for the Americans.'

'Imperialists!' shouted a couple of the most zealous cellmates.

'There's something I still don't understand. When Peking was liberated by the People's Government, they said they would grant freedom of religion, but that the running dogs of imperialism and everyone who had worked against the security of the state would be punished. All right. Then they said that to liberate the church from the influence of foreigners they had decided on reformations that would keep the church Chinese. Well, I was all for that. I didn't want to see the interests of the Chinese sacrificed to foreigners. As a matter of fact, I was on the first reform committee. I began to worry when they appointed a layman to the committee. He was supposed to be in charge of future projects, but he just wasn't qualified for the job. What the job needed was an ordained minister, but I assumed they had their reasons. The church had been ruled by clerics for centuries. Maybe it was time for the laity to have a voice. Maybe we could learn from his outlook. Well, time went by and we worked with this man, but then in 1955 they did

57

something I'll never forget – they appointed a Communist Party member to supervise our activities. Our chief! That was when I really began to realize that the purpose of their reform was to do away with the church. Pretty soon we weren't allowed to teach children religion anymore. Then the committee began warning us to pay less attention to religious affairs and more to our means of livelihood. What they had in mind was a church without preaching. What is the use of a church when you can't preach in it?'

Hostile faces studied him, but no one tried to answer his question.

'So at the next meeting of the committee I voiced my views. I told them that while the Communists said they tolerated the principle of religious freedom all their actions aimed at doing away with it. The committee told me my views were harmful to the government. The next day they arrested me. Here I am.'

As a matter of course Wei was labelled a running dog of the resisters and charged with working for foreign powers. Like so many of the Chinese men of religion, his faith made him difficult to break down. He had a stubborn sort of tenaciousness that was close to naïveté.

'Up to now, I don't understand my interrogators,' he continued. 'They say I was a spy. But I never spied.'

Wei's simple affirmation may sound mild to the Western reader, but in the context of our cell, the prison and China in general, he was being strongly defiant.

'Shut him up!' one of the prisoners cried. 'He's defying the government.'

Loo intervened. 'This is a special case,' he said. 'So far Wei hasn't made his confession. In other words, he doesn't acknowledge his mistakes. That is why he has behaved so badly so far. It is up to us to help him as best we can. Today I am going to break custom and start asking him questions myself.'

This time Loo didn't feel so bound by his usual restrictions of proper behaviour. Instead of interrogating the pastor, he rolled into a long and surprisingly passionate denunciation.

'The trouble with you, Minister, is that you're no longer Chinese.' It was a low blow, but when Wei tried to protest, Loo silenced him and continued implacably. 'You don't even think like a Chinese anymore. You have accused the Chinese government of being a gang of liars!'

It was a perfect bit of demagoguery, and it brought forth a predictable chorus of indignant cries. Wei sat silently.

'If you don't trust the People's Government, then you can't believe the assurances they gave you. No wonder you haven't confessed yet. All you are doing is getting deeper and deeper into the mess you've made. You refuse salvation. One of these days they're going to take you out and shoot you, Wei. You say you're not a running dog of imperialism or an agent of foreign powers, but for forty years you have been carrying out the orders of a foreign religion without even questioning them. Are you foreign or Chinese, Wei? If the People's Government wants to make changes in religion, it has every right to. But you won't see this, will you? You've had it too good for too long. You're rich. You're fat.'

Wei took it all without a word. What else could he do? Loo had thought of an ingenious syllogism to tie it all up.

'Don't think you'll end up a martyr, Wei. You're only a traitor. Your own people are turning against you. Tell me – do you think like a Communist?'

'No.'

'Do you act like one?'

'No.'

'Then you shouldn't be surprised to be here.'

As if he were snapping a book closed he ended the questioning of Wei and moved on to the next man. The session ended at 4 p.m.

The natural complement to the study meeting is the Struggle. It is a peculiarly Chinese invention, combining intimidation, humiliation and sheer exhaustion. Briefly described, it is an intellectual gang-beating of one man by many, sometimes even thousands, in which the victim has no defence, even the truth. The first Struggle I ever met with indirectly took place in the cell adjoining ours a few months after I arrived at Grass Mist Lane. The entire cell was working over a newly arrived prisoner, and the din of their shouts was so passionate that our peaceable study session was hopelessly derailed. The technique, as I heard it, was a thing of utter simplicity: a fierce and pitiless crescendo of screams demanding that the victim confess, followed by raucous hoots of dissatisfaction with any answer he gave them. The horrible, ear-splitting din continued for a couple of hours, and it ended only when the man was led away in chains to solitary.

A guard slammed open the slot in our door, and Loo beckoned us over one by one to get a glimpse of the spectacle. There was plenty of time; he could barely move. His feet were in fetters, an iron bar a foot long, ringed at both ends to pass around the ankles. Bolts held the rings fast; two chains rose from the middle of the bar to the wrists, which themselves were joined by another chain. In all, the outfit weighed thirty-two pounds. The prisoner was obliged to carry the vertical chain from his feet looped several times, since it was long enough to drag on the floor and that was forbidden.

The Struggle was born in the thirties, when the Communists first began making headway in the great rural stretches of China. Developed over the years by trial and error, it became the standard technique for interrogating the landlords and other enemies who fell into the hands of the rebellious peasants. There is a system and a very real rationale behind it all. The Communists were and remain extremely formalistic: A man must be made to confess before he is punished, even if his punishment has been decided beforehand. The captured landlord was pushed, shoved or carried to a handy open area and forced to kneel and bow his head as dozens or hundreds or thousands of peasants began surrounding him. Screamed at, insulted, slapped, spat upon, sometimes beaten, hopelessly confused and terrorized, no victim could hold out for long.

The Speak Bitterness meetings were in the same psychological vein. As they were liberated from serfdom, the peasants were invited to testify to the horrors they and their families had undergone at the hands of their class enemies. Like mad mirror images of revivals, Speak Bitterness campaigns drove the participants to vociferous frenzies of hatred, which was precisely the intention. Orwell had perhaps heard of them when he wrote of the daily 'Five Minutes' Hate' in *1984*. The reasoning is simple: To kill an enemy you must hate him. Without hatred it is only murder.

Of course Struggles continue to be used in prisons today, both as punishment for improper attitudes and as a tool for extracting confessions. But they are also prevalent in ordinary civilian life. In a half-dozen or so campaigns of political zeal that had swept over China since 1949, Struggling became a fact of life for everyone. As in prison, a man might be Struggled for something he had said weeks or even months earlier; for in civilian life, too, scribes are present to note down what is said. Or he might be trapped by one of the omnipresent denunciation boxes which proliferate in every city. A foreigner might mistake them for mail boxes, since they are painted bright, optimistic red, slotted at the top and padlocked closed. Underneath is a shelf space for standard forms and above it a little notice in Chinese characters: 'Denunciation Box'. The forms are neatly categorized:

> Name and address of denunciator
> Address of employment
> Name and address of person being denounced
> Age
> Sex
> Date of birth
> Native of what province and town?
> Physical traits: hair, eyes, height
> What are his hobbies and pastimes?
> What special knowledge does he possess?
> How did you come to know him?
> What are your relations with him?

Separate pages are provided for the actual denunciation. One denunciation per page, please. The police collect from the boxes daily. Denunciation boxes also exist in prisons and camps, and there are also the so-called Constructive Criticism Boxes.

If a denunciation leads to a Struggle, the victim is well advised to submit immediately, because there is never any time limit to a Struggle: It can go on indefinitely if the leaders of the game feel that not enough contrition has developed. Like all the other non-physical interrogation techniques, the purpose is to bring the victim to accept anything that may be judged for him. Thus a Struggle is rarely resolved quickly; that would be too easy. At the beginning, even if the victim tells the truth or grovellingly admits to any accusation hurled at him, his every word will be greeted with insults and shrieks of contradiction. He is ringed by jeering, hating faces, screaming in his ear, spitting; fists swipe menacingly close to him and everything he says is branded a lie. At the end of the day he is led to a room, locked up, given some food and left with the promise that the next day will be even worse.

Often there will be a day off, on Sundays for instance, but this, too, is an exercise in sadism. Locked in his room, he will be perpetually surveyed by at least one of the Struggle team. If he happens to look out the window, the guard will rebuke him for allowing his mind to wander from his problems, which must totally occupy his thoughts. If he nods off to sleep, the guard will grab him by the hair and jerk him awake. After three or four days the victim begins inventing sins he has never committed, hoping that an admission monstrous enough might win him a reprieve. After a week of Struggling he is prepared to go to any lengths.

In China the thought counts as much as the deed, and the Struggle is one of the most effective weapons for weaseling into a man's mind to control his thoughts. I was given a vivid reminder of this some years later in the camps, when our cell was assigned to Struggle a prisoner who had stolen two extra pieces of bread. We worked him over for three days during the evening rest period following our work in the fields. For three days, from 5.30 p.m. to lights out at 9 p.m., we shouted and screamed while the prisoners in the other cells took it easy or played cards. It was exhausting. Finally, I went to beg indulgence from the warder.

'Look, Warder,' I said, 'we've been at him for a total of ten hours now, over the last three days. He *admits* he stole the bread. He was hungry. Isn't that enough? Do we have to make him say he is a dirty bourgeois because he was hungry?'

I should have anticipated it: I was in for another classic object lesson. 'How can a man absolve himself,' he asked me, 'if he doesn't know how and where and why he went wrong?'

The warder reached over to a bottle into which he had stuck some ragged flowers. Pulling out the flowers, he emptied the bottle of its mucky water and handed it over to me.

'Fill it from the teapot,' he said. 'Just fill it. Don't rinse it out.' Already I could feel the waves of didacticism washing over me as I replaced the bottle, murky once more because of the thick sediment that had swirled up into the fresh water.

'The water won't be clear as long as there are dirty things in the bottle, will it, Bao? That's how it is with your cellmate. There are dirty things in his head that he doesn't even know about. As long as they remain, none of our friendly criticisms will be able to sink in.'

So we went on Struggling our cellmate until he realized the ideological implications of two pieces of bread.

Loo, our impeccable spiritual leader, began his trip to Grass Mist Lane after being Struggled. A government functionary and party member in good standing, he had had the bad judgement to open his mouth during the Hundred Flowers. After several months his words returned to haunt him, and he was invited to speak to the government. Locked in his office at night, Struggled during the day, he gradually made a full confession, admitting his evil thoughts and actions piece by piece, even to the fact that he had previously served in the Nationalist army. The climax of his case came when he gave a one-man show of his complete confession to a full assembly of his fellow office workers. When it was finished, he was allowed to return to work. He assumed his case was finished, but three weeks afterward his local party secretary called him in for some heavy news: 'You must be prepared to go and undertake some very serious study. We think your ideological situation needs clarifying. Ideologically speaking, you are in a bad state. The party is concerned about your political welfare.' Three days later he was arrested.

By the time I met him, Loo had outgrown my feeling of bitterness. He agreed that it was a perfectly good thing for him to have been locked up. 'After all,' he told me, 'if everyone who confesses his sins were to get away scot free, then China would be a country riddled with criminals.'

Loo was the model prisoner – humble, energetic in carrying out orders and positive in his thoughts. The poor man was under the impression that his behaviour would earn him a better sentence. He was wrong.

After Loo the man I remember best from the interrogation centre was Wong Ai-Kuo. What an incredible life he had led! And how incredible that he should end it ignominiously in a prison. It was the first day of Chinese New Year when our cell met him, just as we were finishing our afternoon-evening meal. The door swung open to admit a sturdily built, distinguished individual in black leather shoes and a Western suit. He appeared to be in his sixties, was tall for a Chinese, broad shouldered and white haired. He carried his belongings wrapped in an American army blanket. Routinely we made room for him and Loo called him over to ask him his name and the other usual information.

'Wong Ai-Kuo,' he said. 'I'm from Peking.'

'You're a native of where?' Loo continued.

'No place. That is, I don't know.'

Loo left it at that for the moment. It was evident he didn't feel like talking. Later, at bedtime he had a grand surprise for us – he pulled a pair of striped pyjamas from his kit! It was an unheard-of elegance in a proletarian prison, where we all slept in our underwear. One of the cellmates couldn't resist the temptation to come up with a class criticism.

'Stinking bourgeois!' he barked out.

Holding the bundle of orange and blue stripes in his hands, Wong gazed over with regal contempt. 'And what are you, then? If you're better than I am, what are you doing here?'

He slipped into the pyjamas and Loo told them both to shut up. I picked up Wong's story as the weeks passed. Born of unknown parents, he had been an orphan begging in the streets of Tien Tsin when an American Protestant missionary couple took pity on him and brought him home, fed and clothed him and enrolled him in the mission school. The childless couple ended

64

by adopting him and sending him through international law studies in the States. He married an American girl and just after World War II was sent briefly back to China with the OSS to help build cases against Japanese war criminals. His short stay was ample, though, for him to develop a deep and well-founded scorn for the corruption and viciousness of the Nationalists. Shipped back to the States, he followed with growing fascination and pride the developments of the civil war leading to the Communists' triumph. Like so many overseas Chinese, he determined to go back and offer his knowledge to the young republic. After numerous travails and difficulties – Communist sympathizers didn't have an easy time of it in the States in those McCarthyite days – he finally managed to board a freighter for Japan and from there a small passenger ship for Hong Kong, where he arrived at the end of 1950.

It was months before he could contact the Chinese and persuade them of his sincerity, but in March 1951, he crossed the border to a prodigious welcome. When the congratulations were over, he took a job as a legal adviser to the minister of foreign affairs. With the job he received his own house, a chauffeur and a top-level salary. As the years slipped by, however, his special privileges began melting away. What he was discovering was that the regime harboured an ardent distrust of persons from overseas.

In 1953 he was asked to contribute a month's salary for the soldiers in Korea. Reproachful party types commented heavily on the ostentation of his house and his elevated salary. Wong's class consciousness, after its long bourgeois dormancy, was being shaken awake. Surprised and pinned in a corner, he could only agree that he had been a selfish profiteer and request that his salary be reduced by fifty per cent. Even after this, though, he was far better off – strikingly so – than other Chinese of his level of employment. The next deprivation was crueller – his book-ordering privileges were sharply curtailed. 'We have no objection to your reading English or American magazines,' they told him, 'but we feel that you should start learning more about your own country's literature.'

Apparently Wong had outlived his usefulness, but he was not

yet in any deep trouble. But then he raised a contrary voice: He accused his hosts of having wilfully deceived him and others he knew among the overseas Chinese who had voluntarily returned after the revolution. *You* gave me the house and chauffeur, he told them; I never asked for them. And now you accuse me of not having the proper class spirit. And as for the magazines, I need them to keep abreast of international developments.

It all may have seemed logical enough at the time, but each word was just another brick in the prison Wong was building for himself. He refused to make the retraction demanded and maintained that he had told no lies. He was arrested two months after me.

In the camps I met another one like Wong – James Ch'in. Jimmy was a Western literature scholar who had gone through Cambridge and had taught in England for twenty years when he heard that the motherland was in need of teachers. He, too, found himself in a mad, surreal academic world, where advanced courses in the English language were to be taught from translations of Soviet propaganda documents. His basic text was the English translation of *Pravda*. Try as he might, Jimmy couldn't help being intellectually and academically offended. After a few meek remonstrations he found himself in the greased chute to the camps. Independent thought is not appreciated.

Chapter Four

I spent the entire year of 1958 in Grass Mist Lane. It was a strange and memorable period for China – the year of the Great Leap Forward. An enormously unrealistic enthusiasm gripped the country during those harebrained months. Production and construction were to rise dramatically, as if by an act of will, to demonstrate once and for all the greatness of the Chinese people and the thought that was guiding them. Newspapers wrote of new techniques for fantastically increasing the yield per acre of the rice crop and printed pictures of stalks growing so closely together that a man could stand on them. (Months afterward, the same papers neglected to report that the miraculous rice suffocated before it was harvestable.) Vast new amounts of cabbages and other vegetables would be grown. Every little village had one of those jerry-built furnaces with which they hoped to make steel. The furnaces even invaded the prisons, though we undergoing interrogation at Grass Mist Lane, being as yet unworthy of productive labour, missed that privilege. Personally, my finest symbol of the whole campaign was when my wife wrote to tell me she had donated our iron bed for the steel drive.

Simultaneous with the Great Leap Forward was the People's Commune Movement, Mao's Bailey bridge to Communism. The coexistence of these two campaigns made for some astonishing situations. They were, in fact, mutually defeating, but no one could realize it until it was all over and the poor Chinese, wheezing but game as ever, had to start from scratch again.

In contrast to their brethren in the Soviet Union, the Chinese peasants generally supported the commune idea with enthusiasm. To hell with individual life, they reasoned, since the party tells us everything will be better if we act and live in common.

With energy and good cheer they built their community mess halls and, by extension of the same logic, ate their fill of the free meals. Home kitchens were out of style; many peasants broke their clay vessels and donated their metal pots and pans to the all-consuming furnaces, which roared and glowed and produced trickles of what they all took to be steel. Marvelling at their ingenuity – hadn't Mao said that all wisdom lies in the peasantry? – they concluded joyfully that engineers were mere parasites, since demonstrably anyone could make steel.

As this naïve, bucolic hubris grew, the production, both in foodstuffs and the utterly useless steel, began to fall. The peasants spent more and more time in the mess halls and around their homes. Individual profiteering followed naturally enough and soon the mess-hall crews were selling food on the side, or at least reserving the best for themselves. And worse yet, if a peasant became bored with the country life, or was unwilling to invest the harsh muscle power to work the land, he had no problem, for the Great Leap had created an insatiable demand for labour.

Everywhere construction projects abounded. The peasants flocked to the cities where they found instant employment at prime rates. Hiring gangs even took to stalking them at the city gates, importuning them with half-witted patriotic slogans to come and work on their particular jobs. On fourteen dollars a month the peasant found city life to be a thing of beauty – and there was electricity and running water to boot.

In short order the farms began suffering from lack of hands. It became a governmental problem of highest importance: The nation's crops were in jeopardy. But nothing would induce the peasants to return to the land. Party secretaries pleaded fruitlessly with rural families to bring their prodigals home. Finally the government reacted by suppressing the ration cards of the families involved. The threat was clear and simple: Either get your men back or you won't eat. This was known as the 'Cease Food Policy'. If there were any protests they threatened to call in the army.

Slowly, reluctantly, the young peasants began trooping back to the farms. But they couldn't quite forgive the party for what it had done. They took up their work again, but with only half a heart. Their sulky lassitude paved the way for the disastrous agricultural years of 1960, 1961 and 1962.

We in Grass Mist Lane were treated to double doses of study sessions on the Great Leap. Guards, warders and interrogators never missed an opportunity to inform us of what useless scum we prisoners were, lying about while on the outside everyone was giving his all for the building of Communism. The only way we could demonstrate our revolutionary ardour was to confess well. Our sessions with Loo became more and more charged with verbal signs of devotions. We chatted away our platitudes like Stakhanovite parrots.

After my fifth interrogation I was accorded the privilege of being allowed to write my confession. Since I was a foreigner, I could do it in English. In all, it took me somewhat more than three months, from 20 February to the end of April, and 700 typewritten pages to tell the story of my life. Three days a week I was led, head down, through the corridors to a tiny interrogation room where there was a typewriter, paper and a guard to watch me. Since his sentry duties were not taxing, he spent the time working on a fabulously detailed map of Hong Kong. Every traffic light and police box was marked. God knows why he was preparing that map, or who had ordered it, but someday the residents of that pretty city might discover the reason.

The two of us worked in silence as a kettle of hot water simmered on the stove. I was permitted to drink as much hot water as I wanted – an indulgence, but one I had to be careful with. Water-drinking is the standard prisoner's answer to the perpetual pangs of hunger, but it can be dangerous. I had already heard stories of starving prisoners who died from œdema. Disciplining myself away from excessive water consumption was easily as tough for me as when I finally quit smoking.

Like everyone else, I wanted to have my confession accepted as quickly as possible, take my sentence and get away from the slow starvation of Grass Mist Lane – to the camps. God, how I longed for the camps! Every day we heard and repeated the yearning tales of how much food there was in the camps.

69

One night late in March I discovered how closely my literary output was being studied. It was 10 p.m. and the cell was asleep when I was summoned before a panel of three interrogators. I recognized one of them from my arrest. He was very pleasant, almost solicitous. Apparently, it was his idea of a joke.

'How are you doing, Bao?' he wanted to know. 'You've been here quite a while already, haven't you?' They were the kinds of questions which answered themselves. I wasn't supposed to answer and didn't. His concern for me was touching. 'You've grown thinner, Bao. Maybe your problems are doing that to you. That's what I'd like to talk to you about. I've been reading your confession. So far there's not much to it. Maybe you're acting like a serial writer, just trying to keep up our interest enough to make us want to buy the next instalment. Is that it, Bao? There are lots of names you don't mention. Do you remember Linda Lee?'

So that was it. Linda was a Chinese girl who taught painting and, I knew, had had affairs with a number of diplomats. She was a good friend.

'It might make you happy to know that she's not far, Bao. In fact you are both in the same compound. I thought that might help you with your confession.'

It did, indeed. Linda knew all about my connections with the Western embassies, and obviously had told them everything she knew about me. The interrogators were merely making it clear that there was no use in my trying to hide anything.

Still, I made my modest little efforts at dissimulation. I omitted mention of my work with the CID. I was certain that no one but the Americans knew about that job, so I left it out and finished up my confession and awaited word from the interrogators. It came on the night of 4 June, and they had another surprise in store for me.

The interrogation room was quite dark this time, with only a single weak lamp illuminating my questioner's face. The arrangement was deliberately theatrical. The interrogator flipped indolently through my 700 pages and asked me over and over if I had nothing more to add. For an hour we went over the insignificant details of my life, still the insinuating questions continued and still I told him there was nothing more to add. Then, dramatically, a third voice rang out from the penumbra behind me. This one spoke English, and it sounded familiar.

'Turn around, Pasqualini.'

The interrogator flipped on the overhead light and there before me I saw Robert Chen, the man who had sat at the desk facing mine in the CID office. My good friend Robert. He was wearing the uniform of the Political Police. So he had been their agent all along. Jesus.

I broke down. I told them absolutely everything. In the end they indeed got their 'full and frank admission of sins'.

For the next three months I met no more with the interrogators and spent the mostly idle but hungry time dreaming of the camps, chanting my liturgical responses during Loo's study session masses, shouting out my portion of insult and menace whenever a Struggle was called, and generally keeping myself occupied with housekeeping chores. The only significant change occurred late in June, when a new decree came down stipulating that we all would take a two-hour nap in the afternoon. As usual, there were no exceptions to the rule: Even if he were not tired, the prisoner was expected to lie in his place and keep his eyes closed. Guards periodically peered in through the peephole to check us out; anyone with his eyes open would receive a written reprimand. Enough reprimands and he would be ripe for Struggling. We were very well behaved. Model children.

In mid-September the warder called me in to tell me I was nearing the end of my problem. It was time for me to write my self-accusation, officially called 'statement by one's own hand'. The self-accusation is one of the masterpieces of the Chinese penal system. Not only does a prisoner undergo months and even years of infinitely patient questioning, but he must bring it all to a climax with a handwritten and signed précis detailing his crimes. The prisoner takes care to build the case against himself as skilfully as he can, for an unsatisfactory statement will always be bounced back, and he will continue to wait in the Interrogation Centre. When a prisoner has finally produced a satisfactory statement the government holds a document with which, depending on emphasis of interpretation, it can sentence him to virtually any desired number of years. It is a prosecutor's dream.

It took me four hours to write my statement of sixteen pages, and I didn't have long to wait for the response: Favourable. The very next day I was called in for a final session with the scribe who had been present at all my questionings.

'Have you got anything more to add?'

He insisted heavily on the question, and he was right to do so. One of the greatest horrors of prison life is that a prisoner can always be brought back from the camps for further interrogation if any new crimes come to light. The whole painful career in Grass Mist Lane can start over again. A sentence of ten years can mushroom to alarming proportions for insincerity with the government.

'I can't say for sure that I have confessed everything,' I admitted, 'because I might have forgotten some minor details. But everything important is there.'

'Are you quite sure?'

'Yes,' I said. 'Quite sure.'

'Good. Stand up.' He took on the important manner proper for such situations. 'We hereby announce that your period of interrogation is over,' he declared. 'Have you got anything to say?'

I certainly did. I was ready with the standard phrase which every prisoner learns and waits for this very moment to bring out. It has been passed from mouth to mouth for years, and everyone knows that it is the required response:

'I hope I will be leniently dealt with by the People's Government.'

Now it was the scribe's move; he had *his* ritualistic words: 'You will be leniently treated if you behave well, and then we will see. But if you do not behave well, no amount of requests will ever earn you an ounce of leniency.'

I was expecting a somewhat longer speech, but he surprised me by changing tack. 'Tell me, Bao,' he asked, 'did you ever have the feeling that perhaps we tricked you into confessing some things you didn't need to tell us? Or that we had made a case against you where there had been none? Do you ever think that maybe you talked too much?'

'No, not at all,' I answered quickly. Of course I said no. What else could I say? Still, he insisted.

'Don't say that so easily. What we're saying now is very important for you. It will affect your behaviour later on, when you are undergoing Reform Through Labour. You see, I am here to dispel any doubts from your mind. This is the last thing I can do for you to prepare you for what's in store for you. So tell me truthfully: Did you ever have those sorts of thoughts?'

'All right,' I admitted. 'Sometimes during the past year I did wonder whether I went further than I really had to.'

That seemed to please him. 'Good. Very good. Now come over here and look at this.'

He pulled from the drawer a thick folder about the size of a Sears and Roebuck catalogue.

'We want you to read this, Bao. What you are going to see is a number of accusations and denunciations concerning only one person – you. You will see that your confession tallies with them almost perfectly. The reason we are showing you this is not to give you vengeful feelings about these people who did their duty to the state, but rather to prove to you that we have had a case against you for years. Now you can sit down and read it.'

I was at a loss. I didn't know the drill for this situation. Playing it safe, I decided to try the modest and contrite approach, generally a good bet. 'It's not necessary for me to read it,' I offered. 'I believe you.'

'You may believe me now, but later on you might have doubts. Take this and read it thoroughly. Read every accusation.'

I took the massive document and as I couldn't read Chinese then, the scribe did it for me, sitting next to me and reading aloud. It took several hours, and it was a frightening revelation. On those hundreds of pages were handwritten denunciation forms from colleagues, friends and various people I had encountered only once or twice. When I returned to the cell I was relieved to have reached this important moment in my prison career, but my head was spinning – how many persons whom I had trusted without a second thought had betrayed me! My resentment was all the deeper in that I personally had never filled out a denunciation form.

The following morning I was summoned for one final ceremony. My interrogator himself was there. His voice was almost friendly.

'Congratulations.'

'I beg the government to show me leniency.'

But it wasn't quite over yet. I was having more illusions.

'Leniency?' he asked ironically. 'You may earn leniency through your acts. Confessing your own sins doesn't make you perfect, Bao. There are also the sins of other people to be denounced. Do you understand?'

Of course. Now it was time for me to do in my friends and colleagues.

'We're not asking you to be a stool pigeon,' he assured me, 'only you weren't alone in your crimes and errors. You had associates. We want you to reform, but how can we consider you to be truly on the good road unless you tell us about your associates? Denunciation of others is a very good method of penance. You still have a few weeks here before you will be transferred to the transit centre. As you leave this room you will be given some denunciation forms. I hope you will show your appreciation by helping the government to ferret out its enemies.'

I took the forms and dragged myself back to the cell. For the next two weeks I filled them out as innocently as I could, trying to be certain that the people I mentioned were only the ones who would already have far worse accusations against them. It was an exhausting effort of concentration. Throughout, I was obsessed with leaving Grass Mist Lane and being able to eat once again. My hair was falling out and what had been my stomach was a concave triangle. A new rumour had it that the camps in Manchuria were especially wonderful – teeming with fish and game and vegetables that sprang from the soil like magic. I lost myself in reveries of food and slowly filled in the forms.

The transfer from West Compound finally happened in the first week of November, when the last member of our cell had finished his full confession, delivered an approved self-accusation and had requested that the government dispose of him. We were to move en masse into the Eastern Compound. At nine o'clock of a chilly, sleety morning a warder bustled in and ordered us to get our things together. We bundled up our personal belongings, clothes, bedding and notebooks, leaving behind all the tubs and pans and other housekeeping gear, and waited for the guard in the prescribed marching order. Heads down, the eighteen of us tramped the 500 yards across to the Eastern Compound, stopped, squatted by the entry way and awaited orders. I was disappointed to realize that our group was to be completely broken up when a guard arrived to read off the names on his lists. I was sent to a small cell with only five others. The leader was a Manchurian not more than thirty. He indicated my spot on the communal bed and gave a routine little speech. 'I'm glad to see you've solved your problems. Now that we've come this far, let's continue studying and try not to make the government disappointed in us.'

One of the prisoners, I learned, had already been sentenced, and the rest of us were burning to know how many years he had gotten – it might have been an indicator for the rest of us. At the same time we knew very well that such information was forbidden. Our cellmate never said a word. In theory a prisoner never has the right, during the entire period of incarceration, to reveal his sentence; but it is only the beginners who worry about the rule. All we could tell from our friend was that he appeared deeply depressed. Two days later I was transferred again. My new assignment turned out to be something of a family reunion.

When I trotted into my new cell, the first man I laid eyes on was Anthony Liu, a good friend who had worked as liaison in another Western embassy. And then, four days after that, Johnson Wong was led in among us. I had known Johnson for years. An overseas Chinese, like me, he had worked in a Western embassy but later turned informer to the Political Police. When he was no more use to them, they put him away. Poor Johnson. He was weak and characterless, but in time I felt sympathy for him. I buried him, years later in the camps.

The cellmate I liked best, though, was Bartek, the first non-Oriental I had seen in prison. He was in his early fifties then, with brown hair and beard and a fine, long face, whose deep blue eyes were set in a mass of smile-wrinkles. He had plenty of reading material with him, and in short order the books were to get us both in trouble.

'Welcome to our cell,' he called out jovially in perfect Mandarin the first time I saw him. He was lying against his bedroll, wearing a padded jacket, blue cotton pants and Chinese slippers. Thick glasses perched on his nose; he was glancing over a copy of the *Peking Review* in English translation. As a foreigner, he was allowed to have approved non-Chinese reading matter. For me it was like discovering an oasis. After only the briefest of introductory conversations I fell upon Bartek's books and magazines like a starving man.

The euphoria lasted three days only – I was called into the warder's office, harshly rebuked for having spoken English and reminded that the reading matter was for the foreigner only. I had to get my things together once more and move to a new cell. I was beginning to feel like a commuter.

Anthony Liu, who had also committed the sin of speaking English, preceded me as we were marched out of the new compound and into a large, three-man cell in another building. It was comfortable enough, and spacious, but frightfully cold since they had neglected to provide us with a stove. It was a sort of solitary *à trois*, only there was a big window and an exceptionally bright light hung from the ceiling. The three of us huddled miserably under the lamp, as if it could give us any warmth. Late in the day – but what time was it? No possible way to tell – a guard barged in and demanded to know why in hell we weren't in bed.

'We didn't hear the whistle,' I tried to explain.

'No whistles,' he said. 'Everything is silent here.'

Special discipline. We were allowed to talk only in whispers. On the second day I discovered that there were American prisoners among us.

By an egregious professional mistake, the guards failed to check the latrine before I went in. On the floor I found an empty American cigarette pack! I knew from years before that two American airmen were being held in Peking; this proved at least that they were receiving their Red Cross parcels. Another time, returning from the latrines, I heard an American voice ask if he could have a match. On the warder's desk I saw their food – two big bowls of soup and two bowls of rice apiece. They had three meals a day – soup, Chinese dumplings, rice, meat, vegetables. Compared to us they were fantastically well off, but they had to endure the crippling isolation and solitude of the Western foreigner. That, at least, was spared us. Anthony Liu and I didn't speak together in the cell about the Americans. After all, we knew nothing about the third man. He, too, remained silent, probably because he knew nothing about us. Mutual surveillance works even by assumption.

The days dragged by. No exercise, no games, no reading. We sat staring witlessly at the walls, waiting for the vegetable soup and cornbread that came twice a day. In the course of that week we discovered to our horror that the soup was becoming thinner and the bread loaves smaller! That was too much. Already subjugated by hunger, I was ready for desperate measures in order to get more food inside me. The next day, when I went into the mess hall to pick up our ration, I snatched two extra pieces of bread when the guard wasn't looking. Liu gave me a long stare when I handed him his unexpected bonus. But he held his tongue.

Twenty-four hours later I tried the stunt again; but this time the warder stopped me as I was walking back to the cell and made me show my basin. Seeing the extra loaves he gave a little hiss of surprise and immediately denounced me for stealing from the government. I didn't care. By then I was shamelessly given over to the need for food. When the warder threatened me, I glowered at him sullenly and shrugged.

Still, I hadn't taken leave of my senses entirely. When he ordered me to write a confession and an apology, I complied. Stealing is one thing, but refusing to confess is an attack at the very foundations of the state. I wrote out two little documents:

'Today I stole two extra pieces of bread at mealtime. That is, I stole government property. I promise not to do it again. I hope the authorities will help me to avoid a repetition of this behaviour.'

'Today I acted in a disrespectful manner to the guard. I forgot who I was. I was not feeling normal at the time. I hereby promise that I will do my best not to repeat this kind of action.'

That night I was called in for a predictable scolding. 'It's hard to be good on an empty stomach,' I told the warder. 'When you've been hungry as long as I have, it's almost impossible.'

'Don't be impatient, Bao. You won't be here long.'

It was strange. He sounded positively reassuring. The next morning when I went to fetch breakfast for the three of us, the guard told me to take nine loaves – three apiece. I wondered if it was a trap, but took them anyway.

'Orders from the ideological warder,' the guard said. Even to this day I feel warmth and gratitude to that man for those pieces of bread. Less than a week afterward Liu and I were transferred back in with Bartek. The guard told me I would be allowed to read all his magazines and books provided we conversed together only in Chinese. That began for me a short interlude in which for once, in spite of the ever-present hunger, I was able to remove myself from the cant of the study sessions and examinations of conscience and allow my spirit a certain measure of flight. Bartek's collection included, beyond the inevitable *Peking Review*, *Soviet Literature Magazine* and Russian editions in English of *A Tale of Two Cities*, *Nicholas Nickleby* and *Oliver Twist*. In a copy of the *Moscow New Times* I read that Boris Pasternak had slandered the Soviet people with his new book *Doctor Zhivago*. When I took breaks from reading, I joined Bartek and Liu in working the minor miracle that consisted of maintaining the fire in our stove. The prison-issue coal balls were meagre things compounded of compressed coal dust, bits of wood and dry dirt. To keep them from expiring in the old iron stove one of us had to watch over them with all the caressing attention we might lavish on a sickly newborn child. We sat around the stove drinking hot water, occasionally toasting our pitiful little cornbread and talking. It was on one of those interminable, bone-chilling and eventless winter days that Bartek told us of how he happened to land in jail.

Bartek* was a Pole, a good Catholic who grew up in a wealthy merchant family in Harbin. He worked up a stamp business for himself (quite lucrative in those days) and dabbled in real estate speculation. Everything considered, he was well off and happy to be living in China. He eventually married a White Russian girl who was now keeping him in relative luxury by sending regular Red Cross packages from Australia. Like so many others, Bartek had begun heading for trouble when the Civil War came to Shanghai. As the situation became more dangerous, the American forces hastily decided to clear out and contracted with Bartek for the use of one of his empty warehouses. It wasn't until 1953 that the police decided to have a look around his storage depots. Fearing nothing, he showed them the invoices declaring the contents of the dozens of heavy wooden crates: curios, clothing and machine parts. The only problem was that when the Communists pried the lids off, they fell upon stacks of well-oiled, high-quality Yankee rifles. Searching further, they discovered five thousand American dollars in small bills, forty bars of gold, bolts of rich cloth and several crates of grenades.

Bartek was in deep trouble. The matter was important enough for the personal attention of the central authorities in Peking. They hustled him off to the capital – not Grass Mist Lane at first, but the exclusive little prison of the ministry of public security, the very top rung of them all. Bartek stayed on there a month, and the living was easy. Among other VIPs sharing space with him, he heard, were Fecteau and Downey, the two American CIA agents shot down over Manchuria during an abortive spy-drop in the Korean War, as well as the crew of the CB-29 reconnaissance plane, who were later released thanks to the intervention of Dag Hammarskjöld. The food was good, he recalled, three meals a day. Breakfast was the traditional English spread, supplemented with fried peanuts, rice and salted vegetables. At noon there was Chinese steamed bread with meat

*As late as December 1975, I received reliable information that Bartek is still being confined in a Chinese prison in the Peking area.

or fish and for supper the same. Bartek landed on the cold concrete floor of reality when he was transferred down with us in Grass Mist Lane. The interrogators had never accepted his plea that he knew nothing of the contents of the crates. They accused him of preparing to command a guerrilla action.

Bartek went through fifteen interrogations and was tried in late 1957, long before I met him. Unfortunately, he was stubborn. He rebelled when he learned that his sentence was to be five years in prison and confiscation of all his goods and property. He was prepared to take the five years, but balked at losing everything he had spent his life working for. Bartek appealed. Evidently, he could not accept the elementary truth that any wise prisoner learns as second nature: In China an appeal against a sentence means the prisoner is not repentent for his crimes and has not accepted the government's leniency. *Ipso facto*, it is proof that he has not learned his lesson. An appeal, therefore, is a demand for further punishment.

At the appeal trial the government pressed a single charge and exhibited a single piece of evidence: an old photograph. It showed Bartek in Harbin in 1934, posing with a Samurai sword. The area where he was posing was controlled by the Japanese at the time and he and some friends had been invited by a Japanese officer to come to the scene of a recent skirmish with the Chinese rebels. Not thinking of any consequences, Bartek posed with the sword. He was charged with having participated in a massacre of Chinese patriots. His sentence was changed to life.

Johnson Wong was with us in the cell because he, too, had appealed. Arrested long before me, he had been sentenced to twenty years. He had not gone beyond the first year when he decided he had been unjustly treated. Foolish man. As an appellant he had to go through the entire Grass Mist Lane routine all over again and prepare himself once more for the second trial that was his right by law. Johnson had a special usefulness for us because he had already been through the Transit Centre, our next stop along the road to the camps. The work was hard, he warned us, but at least the food problem would finally be solved – in the Transit Centre everyone could eat his fill. It was

80

a joyous prospect, but illusionary: Johnson had passed through the Transit Centre in the old days before rationing. What he didn't realize was that conditions there would be exactly the same as in Grass Mist Lane. After about one week with us Johnson left to face his new interrogation and trial. I saw him again two years later, in the camps. His sentence, too, had been changed to life.

I took another important step along the road to the camps late in December, when I was urgently summoned back to the interrogation centre for my version of what is known in China as a trial. Being the period of the Great Leap, the order of the day was still to do everything 'quickly, well and with economy'. Consequently, the court came to me, in a free room back where I had started everything in Grass Mist Lane. I was only one of many to be tried, and the atmosphere around the huge, dossier-covered table was one of bustling efficiency.

'This is not an interrogation,' the prosecutor announced. 'You are here for your trial. You are not obliged to say anything. You will answer only when you are told to. We have chosen someone for your defence.'

The usual clerical preliminaries of name, former address, etc., took only a moment, following which the prosecutor read aloud my Statement By My Own Hand and his own official inculpation:

You have been charged with the following crimes –
1. Collecting information for imperialist powers.
2. Engaging in illegal activities and transactions prejudicial to the economy of the state.
3. Spreading rumours with the intention of creating confusion among the masses.
4. Slandering, calumnizing and insulting the Chinese Communist Party, the Chinese People's Republic and the leadership thereof.
5. Distributing imperialist propaganda with the intention of discrediting the Chinese People's Republic and the people's democracies of the socialist camp; and in a vain attempt to corrupt Chinese youth.
6. Undermining the good relations which exist between China and various friendly nations.

I admitted that I had nothing to retract from my statement and that the accusations were true and just. The prosecutor called on my defence lawyer, a young fellow of about thirty in a Mao suit. His plea was concise and to the point:

'The accused has admitted these crimes of his own free will. Therefore, no defence is necessary.'

The prosecutor sent me back to my cell and urged me to devote my time to furthering my studies before sentencing.

About a month passed before anything more happened. During that dreary time the only thing I remember with any clarity was a Struggle session in which I was a direct participant. The cells were emptied and about a thousand of us were herded out into a big courtyard next to the main building. The cadres instructed us to go to the latrines quickly, since the meeting was to start at 1.30 sharp and there would be no departures allowed. Off we trooped, heads bowed, in silent pairs. The guards had prepared things for us by laying straw mats on the frozen earth as an elementary protection against the dampness. Everyone was bundled up as warmly as he could, but we had no proper winter clothing; right from the start we were shivering as we huddled together. A ring of soldiers surrounded us. Up on the roofs the guards were silhouetted against the pearl-grey February sky.

Our victim was a middle-aged prisoner charged with having made a false confession. He was an obstinate counterrevolutionary, a cadre shouted out to us through a cardboard megaphone. For his actions he was to serve as an example for all the rest of us. Perhaps, he said, our enthusiastic participation could help him along to a full and frank admission of his sins. I never did learn the man's name. He sat in the little open space without a mat, head bowed. We surged around him and began.

'Down with the obstinate prisoner,' we screamed. 'Confess or face the consequences.' These sorts of imprecations may sound slightly comical in English, but in Chinese they are terrifyingly real and fraught with menace – especially in the framework of a prison where a man has no counsel or friend. And when a thousand men are shouting at once.

Every time he raised his head to say anything – truth or falsehood, that wasn't our concern – we drowned him with roaring cries of 'Liar!' 'Scum!' Or even 'Son of a bitch!' This time there was no one to reproach us for this breach of the rules, as Loo had done in the study sessions.

'Is he telling the truth?' howled out the cadre, hopping energetically from foot to foot.

'No!' We all hooted in derisive unison. The Struggle continued for three more hours like this, and with every minute that passed we grew colder, hungrier and meaner. A strange, animal frenzy built within us. I almost think we would have been capable of tearing him to pieces to get what we wanted. Later, when I had the time to reflect, I realized that of course we had been Struggling ourselves at the same time, mentally preparing to accept the government's position with passionate assent, whatever the merits of the man we were facing. Our victim finally reached a point where he couldn't bear it any longer. He raised his head and cried out directly at the guards:

'Don't waste their time any longer. Punish me according to the regulations.'

It was a request that was defiance at the same time. The guards came forward with the chains he had earned by his obdurate attitude. In front of us they hammered home the rivets to his fetters and irons.

A week afterward the warder called me to his office to show me a document, written in Chinese, in which I formally requested the honour of going to a labour unit and waived my right to stay on in the Interrogation Centre. I signed instantly. Within a few days I was transferred to the Transit Centre. Anthony Liu came with me. We had joy in our hearts.

Chapter Five

It was in a convoy of closed flatbed trucks led by police jeeps that the batch of jailbirds including Wang and me arrived at the Transit Centre, commonly known to prisoners as the South Compound, to guards as the Peking Detention Centre and to the outside world as Peking Experimental Scientific Instruments Factory. Nicely situated next to the lovely Tao Ran Ting Park, it is the standard next stop for prisoners who have completed their interrogation and are awaiting their court appearance, sentencing or assignment to another prison or camp. Depending on whether we had been sentenced, we were all portentously categorized as 'prisoners whose fate has already been decided' or 'prisoners whose fate has not yet been decided'. Wang and I were in the second group. As we climbed down from the trucks and assembled in the yard, we had a chance to inspect the place.

In front of us angled out the two great grey brick arms of the four-storey main building, designed in the form of a K. Behind us, past the administration buildings and over the twenty-foot fence that runs along the public road called Ban Bu Chiao, we could see the looming form of what I learned later was the Boys' Reformatory, for delinquents under seventeen. Behind and to one side of the K Building was the red brick, three-storey Technical Building, home for the prisoners who were engineers, architects, physicists, translators, etc. – the intellectuals who did the paper work for the various enterprises of the South Compound. In addition to the other various shops, storerooms and staff quarters, one particular building magnetically drew the attention of every one of us standing out there in the cold : the central kitchen. Great clouds of steam – the live steam always used in Chinese prisons to cook the hard, moist, cornmeal wo'tou – billowed up from the vent holes. It was the biggest kitchen I had ever seen. It looked like a factory in itself. We regarded it with hungry fascination.

Next to the kitchen was a much smaller, L-shaped building, hunched up against the angle of the wall. That was death row, we later learned. Adjoining that were rows of solitary cells, which I was to try before too long. The whole ugly group was known to the prisoners as the Northwest Corner. The name rang with a menace that quickly became a stock part of everyone's personal vocabulary: Look out, or you could end up in the Northwest Corner.

It was eleven in the morning when Wang and I set foot inside K Building. If any place ever deserved to be called infernal, this was it. It was like walking into a Hieronymous Bosch fantasy. We found ourselves in a vast, draughty central hall that rose four storeys to a glass ceiling. There was a pervasive odour of creosote. Around the hall ran the open faces of the four floors and fixed on one of them was a monstrous colour poster of a worker, gazing down sternly with a sheaf of paper in his hand and pointing with his right hand like the famous Uncle Sam recruiting poster. Underneath was an admonition in large black ideograms:

To damage a book leaf is to ruin an entire book.
To ruin an entire book is to deprive one person of the chance for education.

There was no doubt that we had arrived in a deadly serious place. Everywhere there was an intense, frenzied, antlike activity. Men rushed back and forth before us, toting stacks of book leaves three to four feet high, disappearing into doorways and then popping out into view again on the steps leading up to the different floors. The din of hammering and footfalls on the cement stairways echoed off the shiny grey concrete floor to create a background for the piercing tenor voice of the agitprop, who moved from floor to floor setting his stool up in a corner and standing with notes in one hand and a tin megaphone in the other. His job was to encourage production. He never stopped.

'Cell Number 17 has issued a challenge to cell Number 1,' I heard him shout.

A guard led us up to the third floor, where a prisoner opened an iron gate to let us pass into the corridor. Wang and I were assigned to B Section of the Third Brigade, and a trusty led us down the corridor lined on both sides with the wooden doors of communal cells. Along both walls were prisoners sitting on their haunches folding book leaves while others bound them into packets. All this activity left very little room and we were obliged to pick our way carefully through them as if we were on a mountain path. No one spoke. It was quieter here than in the central hall – nothing but grunts and the slapping of bamboo against paper. The cell doors were all open. Inside, the communal plank beds had been dismantled to form two large work tables per cell. Each table had eight men to a side and everyone was feverishly folding bookleaves. They didn't have many machines in China then, but there was plenty of prison labour.

It didn't look to be very hard work. Each leaf, about three feet by two, had to be folded four times onto itself and then stacked on the side. On the wall of each cell a printed notice spelled out what was expected of us:

The target set by the government is 6,000 leaves. The average output is 4,500. The beginner's norm is 3,000. All must strive to surpass their targets.

Mealtime was called as we stood in the hallway. Our trusty told us to wait; we would take ours right there. When the food detail came through, we each got a coarse porcelain bowl and a pair of chopsticks. A second prisoner followed with a wide basin full of warm cornbread loaves and gave us three apiece. They were smaller than the wo'tou in the interrogation centre but also heavier, since they had been compressed so that more of them could fit on the steaming trays. Shaped into cones perhaps four inches high, they resembled tall bullets. Was this what Johnson Wong meant about better food, we both wondered. The soup the third man ladled out was richer than usual, though, and in with the potato peels there were little chunks of potato and even a little fat! What a joy that was. Sitting on our bedrolls, Wang and I gobbled it down.

A warder appeared with long foolscap forms that we were to

fill out for our personal files. Once again, for almost two hours, I wrote a synopsis of my life history, the motive for my arrest, my interrogation and sentence. When we had finished the forms another warder assigned us to our cells. Mine was Number 14. The cell leader gave me a cursory greeting, motioned me to a spot on the bed-bench and told my neighbour to show me how it was done. Bamboo stick in hand, I laboriously started folding.

We worked until 6 p.m., broke for the evening meal (exactly the same as lunch) and then continued again until 7.30, when a warder in the corridor gave the signal to quit, wash up and get ready for the study session. We stacked the finished reams, labelled them with our numbers and piled them out in the corridor for picking up. I had managed only 300.

With practised precision my cellmates hefted the table planks and replaced them to form the two communal beds with the narrow aisle between them. When we were all seated cross-legged on the beds a trusty came in with a shoebox containing each man's cigarette packs. Fresh from the interrogation centre, I had neither tobacco nor money to buy it, so I went without. The study session was to be on the Great Leap Forward.

One of my cellmates explained the ration system, which was a model of simplicity: A prisoner's food depended on his production. My portions as a beginner would be low, and I had two weeks to reach a level of output that would either maintain it at that level, raise it to first class – or drop it down to a punishment level. But beyond production, he warned me (and I could have guessed anyway), a prisoner's attitude was equally important for determining rations. Even a good folder could fall down to subsistence rations if he worked without evident enthusiasm, or if he sloughed off in study sessions.

Rations were divided into four categories: beginner, light labour, heavy and punishment. The rate for beginners – those who could not fold a minimum of 3,000 leaves – was calculated at 14 kilos, 250 grammes of cereal per month – about 31 pounds in all. This might not seem too bad, were it not for the fact that our diet contained almost no fat, therefore obliging our bodies to seek their force from starch alone. Meat was almost unknown except on festive occasions – and it was only rarely that the cooks found a little grease to add to the corn mush or vegetable soup. As a beginner I would spend my first two weeks having two bowls of corn mush kasha in the morning, vegetable soup with three wo'tous at lunch and the same for supper. The cooks had so perfected the system for making wo'tous that any one of the sixteen loaves that came from a kilo of cornmeal would always weigh exactly the same as another. This was important for morale: The prisoners always watched each other's rations like hawks, wary lest someone else receive a few grammes more.

The light labour ration, which arrived at 3,000 leaves, was considerably more – just over 41 pounds a month, and it translated into three extra wo'tous a day. The heavy labour ration – 6,000 or more leaves, rose to something over 43 pounds, or five more wo'tous per day than the beginner. In addition, the expert folders got one meal of wheat-flour bread the fifteenth of every month and one of rice on the twentieth. The punishment ration could be anything the warders decided.

What created harsh animosities was the mixing of different levels of rations in the same cell – a common occurrence, and one that a good cell leader tried by all means to eliminate. The vegetable soup was thicker than in the interrogation centre, and it was said that a prisoner in solitary could tell the seasons by noticing the different vegetables that composed his soup. I figured that it cost the Chinese People's Government $3.00 to feed one prisoner for one month. This included the meat we were given on Chinese New Year.

When the study session was finished and it was time for lights out, a warder came to our door for roll call. The forty of us were too many for the cell to hold, even in the tight conditions normal for Chinese jails. Twelve of us slept on each big bed, four more on the floor space of the aisle between and then four more on a set of planks laid over them, making the aisle a double berth. The remaining eight moved out and slept in the corridor. We were so tightly shoehorned into our spots that no one dared move, let alone get up to go scrambling over the supine bodies to the latrine. When we were awakened the next morning, I was surprised to learn that it was only 5 a.m.

'I didn't think we got up until six,' I remarked to one of my cellmates.

'Shao shuo hua' – 'Shut up' was his only answer, tossed over his shoulder as he began disassembling the bed. Within a few minutes the work benches were formed up again; without a word everyone had tossed his bedroll into a little heap in the corner, seized a bamboo stick, took his place on the bench and began folding leaves. I watched it all stupidly until one of them shouted at me to get going. Groggy and confused, I started folding. By the time I had finished my first leaf the man next to me had done a dozen or more.

It wasn't until 6.30 that the trusty came by with breakfast. Still naïve, I put down my stick and made ready to eat. My neighbour gave me a dirty look.

'Here we eat while working.'

The trusty placed a saucer of salted vegetables and a small bowl of corn mush on the table before each one of us. To a man my cellmates slopped down the vegetables and plunked their portions of mush down on the floor to let it cool. Right now the only thing that mattered was to fold and fold.

The experienced prisoners knew it was 10 a.m. when the music from the loudspeakers in the yard meant the guards were doing their calisthenics. Ten was an important hour. The rule of thumb was that if a prisoner hadn't finished a quarter of his daily quota by then he wouldn't make it at all. At lunchtime we all drank down our soup with hardly a hitch in the rhythm. By the end of the day I had done only 1,500; even 3,000 seemed like an impossible dream. My arms were so stiff it hurt me to move them, and my back felt as if it had been sledgehammered.

Three days afterward I was called in for a routine medical exam. It was nothing special, only the most cursory of check-ups, except that for the first time since my arrest I saw myself in a full-length mirror. I was appalled. My weight had dropped to 110 pounds, and the skin hung loosely on my frame, blue and calloused where it had been in contact with the benches, ashen elsewhere. I couldn't sleep that night.

Directly after the medical exam I had the good luck to be transferred to Section A of the Third Brigade, where I joined a much less crowded cell – only twenty-two in all. The cell leader was a handsome young boy of only twenty-one named Howe, a native of the northeast who was in for twenty years because of an intemperate speech during that great flytrap of the Hundred Flowers. He came from a good bourgeois family and even, he told me, had a girlfriend in Canada. I was surprised and pleased to see that he knew as many American traditional tunes as I did, and we used to break the monotony of folding by humming along together as we folded. I suppose the irony of the strains of 'My Old Kentucky Home', 'Swanee River', and even 'Long Long Ago' sweeping out of a cell populated exclusively by Oriental jailbirds was lost on the occasional guard who passed by.

In spite of his educated and even privileged background, Howe was a prodigiously energetic worker, and he constantly encouraged me to get my output up. He paid only the basically required lipservice to the didacticism that old Loo took so much to heart in the Interrogation Centre and aimed only at getting us all first-class rations. With all his good will, though, the only route to those rations was increased production.

By the end of March I was up to 3,500 leaves and the light-labour ration. The important thing was to start each day with a personal goal to aim for, Howe told us, and thereafter we announced our plans every morning, deliberately committing ourselves to a target. Of course we never had the time to read our work, but we folded quite a variegated selection of material over the months: *The Farmer's Dictionary*, a simplified manual of words and phrases with explanations of historical events and ideological terminology; technical textbooks on electricity; politically oriented mysteries published by the Popular Press (which worked under the direction of the Ministry of Public Security), relating the usual tales of catching spies; a de luxe edition of *Don Quixote*; magazines such as *Harvest* and *Problems of Peace and Socialism*; and, lastly, Mao's works and poems, the folding of which we took as a political task demanding special attention. After our output was bound it was sent to the New China Bookstore, the big state-run outlet downtown, for sale to the general public. Howe told us that hand labour was preferable to the mechanical devices available then because the machines weren't reliable. Prisoners made fewer mistakes.

It was during this period of apprenticeship that I saw my first show in prison. The ostensible occasion was International Women's Day, but there was an ulterior purpose. Little matter. Live entertainment would be a welcome break from the study session routine. At 6.30 in the evening, just after supper, we bundled up in our warmest clothes and filed out two by two into the courtyard, each one of us carrying a bit of cloth to pad his poor, shrivelled ass. It was getting dark as we took our places.

'How come you're not smoking?'

Like everyone else, the man sitting next to me had lit up as soon as he sat down. I had seen him in the corridor, but didn't know him personally.

'I don't have any cigarettes.'

Without a word he handed me one of his own – Big Fortune brand, one of the cheapest produced in China. But it tasted fine. It was the first I had smoked since my arrest more than fifteen months before.

'I don't have anything I can give you in exchange,' I said.

'That's all right. Good things should be shared.' He handed me four or five more. 'Maybe I'll see you in the camps some day. It's a small world. You can pay me then.'

I never did run into him again, but his gesture was the first example I had of the spontaneous generosity that was usually the rule in the camps.

The evening's spectacle told the story of the Hsing Kai-Hu labour camp in Manchuria, and it was entitled 'The Dam'. It was the opening salvo and central masterpiece of the Mobilization Campaign for attracting volunteers to the camps on the Sino-Soviet border.

We all knew something about these camps, of course. The Barren Lands, they were called, and they were a rich source of folklore. Heroic tales of exemplary Communist enterprise flowed from them as naturally as they did from the war years, for the Barren Lands were one of the greatest challenges the party had ever tackled. For centuries it had been known that the Manchurian steppe had the potential to become fabulously productive for agriculture, but no one had ever been able to overcome the obstacles of climate. Even the gifted and industrious Japanese gave up after spending fourteen years (and thousands of Chinese lives) labouring to reclaim the land. The Nationalists hardly even bothered to try. The first batch of Lao Gai prisoners – 4,000 of them – arrived there from Peking in 1954 and was producing food within two years. By the time of the Great Leap, 1958, there was enough food coming from the Barren Lands to feed a million people for a year. There were nine camps up there, spread out through sixty-four villages.

Hsing Kai-Hu inspired strangely mixed emotions in us beginners. On the one hand, life in Manchuria was commonly rumoured to be far more healthy than what we were now undergoing. The eating was good, we heard, consisting mainly of soybeans, some wild boar meat every now and then, plenty of fish, poultry and eggs, and even milk, since the government had installed processing and canning factories up there. What was more, the earlier batches of prisoners to be sent up were accorded the indulgence of bringing their families with them as nuclei for future settlements, rather in the same way as in the founding of modern Australia. Those were appetizing details, but the harsh sides of life in the north were even more notorious. The winter temperatures dropped to as much as forty below often enough for some newly arrived prisoners to have died from simply inhaling the air without a mask, their lungs and throats frozen. Since the whole area was marshland, summer brought not only heat but the plague of mosquitoes as well – huge, tough mosquitoes that could sting through two layers of shirts.

So we didn't know. Somewhere along the line, in God knows what central planning office, some intelligent bureaucrat with agitprop experience apparently had figured that a good way to generate enthusiasm was to produce a full-scale recruitment show. The result was the hundred-strong cast of the New Life Theatrical Troupe – prisoners themselves – and by the time we saw them they had honed their spectacle to such a level of technical perfection that I am convinced the very same show could run and make money on Broadway. And who knows? Probably even produce more volunteers.

The stage darkened and the narrator came forward under a little spotlight. He looked like a true Chinese hero in his splendidly tailored Mao suit. The man who had slipped me the cigarettes was unimpressed by his glamour.

'If he's one of us,' he whispered, 'he must be pretty special.'

In a way he was right. Chances were that he had been a successful theatre or film actor who had been done in by his personal life. Almost all theatrical troupe prisoners had been arrested for fornication, adultery, household-breaking or suspected homosexuality.

'Schoolmates,' he shouted in the dramatic, stentorian tones common to spectacles in people's democracies everywhere, 'we come here from the great barren northeast. The show tonight tells of the beginnings, struggles and future of the Hsing Kai-Hu camps. We come before you tonight because we need your collaboration. These camps are testimony to the greatness of the programme of Reform Through Labour. Please watch and listen closely and try to understand our pride. This is a success story!'

From the wings two others in Mao suits strode out bearing the mockup of a large book. Across the front the title was written in huge letters: THE DAM. As the two actors opened the book to the first page, the lights came up and the stage sets displayed a rough, overgrown, marshy swampland. From stage right an old couple in traditional peasant work clothes trudged wearily on their way, passing directly over the marsh. Towards stage centre they both began to sink; the more the old man struggled to free his wife the deeper they descended. Presently the lights dimmed and only two gnarled, grasping hands showed above the surface.

The second tableau brought dozens of optimistic settlers bustling around the area during the years of the Great Famine. The climate and the fickleness of the soil doomed their efforts, though, and the tableau ended with a field of bones bleaching in the sun. The third tableau illustrated the war year of 1931, when the Japanese occupied Manchuria and drove something like

150,000 Chinese slave labourers to the task. The actors playing the fiendish Japanese wielded bayonets and whips over human teams ploughing the soil by brute force. From time to time a team would sink into the quicksand and even, occasionally, the Japanese overseers with them.

And so it remained until 1945, when the Nationalists took over. They were the fourth tableau, made up mostly of property owners and generals, none of whom felt any interest either in the fate of the Chinese people or the barren lands. Such was their scorn that they left the lands untouched, sometimes exchanging chunks of land as bribes or presents. The place was as wild as a moor, and covered by a semiperpetual fog. And then, through the fog and murk, there came the tiny hint of a point of redness, growing slowly into the unmistakable ray of a rising sun. The red glow grew larger and stronger, and it slowly lifted from the horizon, to become – Mao, rising in the east! The Liberation was upon us.

'But what sort of Liberation is this?' asked one of the actors. 'When a land that is reputed to be so rich is left untilled and barren? The land must be liberated, as well as the people. But who can do it?'

Who, indeed? That was what Americans call a loaded question. Who else but prisoners?

The Chinese people had been undergoing the hardships of the Korean War, the narrator continued, and the national economy was still struggling to free itself from the misdeeds of imperialism. It was then that the government gave us the chance to make good! Accordingly in 1954 the first 4,000 prisoners arrived to affront the place that had thwarted every previous effort. The tableaux succeeded each other majestically, showing how the prisoners first lived in holes dug into the wintry ground and covered at night with branches. Surveying teams spread out; agronomists took samples of the soil; and the engineers concluded that there was a satisfactory emplacement for The Dam – the dam that would tame the waters of the marshy steppe, form an artificial lake and drain the fields for planting with soybean, maize and sorghum. The 4,000 dauntless prisoners began work on The Dam on the first day of 1955, even though the temperature was forty below and they still had no barracks to live in. It was eight months before The Dam was finished, and three dozen workers had perished. These exemplary deaths had occurred when the earthworks gave way and the waters came flooding through. Most of the men drowned while trying to block the water flow, and they were all given the exceptional honour of posthumous rehabilitation, from Enemies of the People to Model Workers. Their families in the villages were no longer required 'to wear the black hats of relatives of enemies of the people' and could thenceforth refer to themselves as 'families of heroes who contributed to the building of socialism'.

Once The Dam was properly completed, the following tableaux demonstrated, other teams set to maintaining the soil's fertility by spreading dried wheat stalks and setting them afire for the rich ash that would remain behind. Here, too, ten men died when they were caught by a sudden change of wind and engulfed in the flames. Like the others, they were upgraded to heroes.

Further tableaux showed the arrival, late in 1955, of the Construction Battalion. The Construction Battalion! It is the most perfect Orwellian triumph of Chinese scientific socialist thought. It shall always remain my personal symbol for the masterpieces of absurd irony of which the human spirit is capable. The 400–500 architects, supervisors, surveyors, transportation specialists, engineers, carpenters, masons, etc. who constitute its squads are entirely prisoners, in for life like the rest of my 'fellow students'. Their speciality, in fact their unique *raison d'être* was – is – to travel around China building prisons. Once they finish an assignment, they move on to another, packing up their baggage, field kitchen and tools like some sort of Oriental circus, always perfecting their craft and winning red banners for their zeal and ingenuity. Prisoners make the best prison-builders.

Touched by the trials the Barren Lands settlers had undergone growing food for the people, the Construction Battalion set new records, working day and night, and in little more than four months had built some 1,000 units or cells, comparatively luxurious prison houses of red brick with hollow walls where heating fires could be lit. The solidarity between the settlers and the builders was exemplary.

The last scene brought us to the sixty-four villages that have now infused life into Hsing Kai-Hu, each one of them peopled by smiling, enthusiastic and well-fed prisoners, happy to be building a New Life for themselves and their families. We poor paper-folders shuffled silently back to our overcrowded cells, wishing we could be out of Peking and up with the heroes in Manchuria: The show had succeeded as planned.

The following day was declared a period for rest and reflection; we were herded from one lecture to another, all of them extolling the joy and virtue of life in the northeast. New villages and farms were being planned and the state urgently needed fresh hands to work them, at least 2,000 from our Transit Centre alone. But now the night's sleep and the blatantly exaggerated optimism of the recruiting talks had dampened our enthusiasm. We began getting cold feet. The northeast camps did, indeed, sound splendid, but every prisoner knew he would never return from them, and never is a long time to be up on the frontier. If we could at least bring our families . . . ? The recruiters cut these illusions short quickly: Only a selected few would be permitted to bring their families. Families created more problems for the administration than they solved. The government would decide who could bring his family – after everyone had volunteered.

Volunteered? Even that, it turned out, was superfluous. We soon found that the show and the pep talks had been only gestures. Once again we had a demonstration of the party's passion for the form of things. Early the next morning we were called out into the humid courtyard and formed up into long lines. A tough, businesslike character in a padded black Mao suit – no hortatory blandishments from him! – strode rapidly down the rows, looking and choosing.

'I'll take this one, and this one, and you, and you . . .' we heard as he went along. An assistant jotted down the numerical position of each volunteer. Since we were standing in cell sleeping order, it would be easy to fish up the names later. Occasionally the selector would stop to ask a prospect if he had ever done any farm work. And then he went on.

'Okay, he's quite fit, take him, yeh and that one, too . . .'

The Germans, I couldn't help thinking, chose their press-gangs of wartime factory workers in about the same way. Oh, my God – he passed me over. I was too thin for his taste.

Later that evening when we were back in our cells the warders called out the names of those who had been selected, and they were promptly marched out to another part of the compound to sleep. It was like a quarantine. Then they locked us in our cells. Every damn door in the building was bolted. No one was allowed to sleep in the corridors. At three or four in the morning we were all still awake and we heard the buses and trucks that had come to pick them up. Twelve went from our cell. The next morning life resumed as usual.

Paper folding was in such demand in those days that private citizens were encouraged to take bunches of leaves home with them to fold at job rates – the going price was the equivalent of thirty American cents per thousand. We prisoners were credited (purely in theory) at the rate of thirty cents per thousand. Thus, an excellent folder could pay for his month's food in a single day. Little wonder we were constantly pushed to produce more. By the time I moved away from the Transit Centre seven months later, I had almost no fingernails left and the little finger of my right hand looked like a blackened twig. But I was folding 10,000 leaves a day. I learned to respect books.

On April first the warder called me into his office to announce that my wife had come with a small packet for me – three packs of cigarettes and the equivalent of $1.50 in Chinese money. I was bitterly disappointed at the penury of the gift – for that much she shouldn't even have bothered. I returned to the cell full of self-pity. It wasn't until May, after I had been sentenced, that I learned how much that packet had represented to her.

And then I saw Loo again. Poor Loo. I had left the cell for a minute to go to the latrine and there he was, shuffling quietly down the corridor. I was delighted to meet him again.

'Well, well, Loo,' I said, 'what a pleasure to see you. How are you?'

'Not good, Bao,' he answered, and I could believe him. He looked terrible.

'Have you been sentenced?'

'Very heavy, Bao.' He shook his head like a man in a daze. 'Everything's finished. My wife's divorcing me. They gave me life.'

'Even after all your good behaviour?' It really was amazing.

'I don't believe it myself. I don't know what to do. Let's not talk about it anymore. It makes me too depressed.'

After that meeting I felt myself pursued by the nagging fear that I would never get out of prison, for if they were so harsh with Loo for his Nationalist past, how could they judge my own association with the Americans and British? Psychologically, I was already prepared to accept with gratitude anything less than life.

It was around this time that I made the foolish mistake of publicly opening my mouth in opposition to the government line. The Chinese army had just taken over Tibet; naturally enough, every cell was instructed to devote special study sessions to the 'liberation'. Howe dutifully read us the documents and newspaper accounts provided by the ideological warder and continued in the classical pattern by inviting us one by one to speak his thoughts and analyse the situation. Most of the cellmates trotted out the atrociously racist old wives' tales, which the Chinese have repeated for centuries, concerning the savagery of the Tibetan aristocracy, their penchant for killing Chinese by the hundreds, and even the story that they tanned their victims' hides and made drinking goblets from their skulls. These banal stupidities bored me. I tried to present things more honestly.

'Since the party expects us to speak our minds,' I began, 'I think that all these stories are just pretexts to justify our annexation of the territory of Tibet. What's the use of inventing other reasons? We in China have always been taught that Tibet is part of our national domain. We were simply annexing our own land.'

Howe even congratulated me. 'Bao,' he said, 'it was good that you got rid of the thoughts in your head.'

I felt momentarily proud, but I got the bill for my words later.

Once a week we had a bath. It was a welcome break from the folding (fairly enough, the bathing time was deducted from our quotas) and meant a nice walk, but most of all it was a chance to savour the atmosphere of Prison Number One, where the bathhouse was located. Lying just beyond the wall to the east of our K Building, Prison Number One was like a dream for all of us. It was a model jail, a humane and decent place where the prisoners were truly happy. There was no rationing whatsoever – a man could eat his fill – the work was real and dignified and the prisoners were even paid for it. Obviously, Prison Number One is still one of the best attractions of the standard Peking tour for foreign visitors, and they react predictably. How many pages of emotional praise have I read since my release concerning the wisdom and humanity of the Chinese prison system, all of them due to the good offices of Prison Number One. I finally was to have a brief stay there myself and I remember it with nostalgia, almost pleasure.

The contrast between that paradise and our own beehive was appalling and depressing. Not long after my first bathing trip across the wall I was visited with another little object lesson in humility. I had developed a painfully virulent boil on the back of my neck, and Howe sent me to see the prison doctor, a character named Ma. I was flabbergasted when, instead of giving me any treatment, he gave me hell for coming!

'*Hun-dan*,' he shouted – good-for-nothing son of a bitch! – 'Don't you know where you are? This is a jail, and you're here to work. Get out of here! And the next time you'd better make sure you're really sick before you come to see me.'

He threw a couple of compresses at me and sent me packing. The worst of it was that he, too, was a prisoner. Howe shrugged and told me not to worry. Some men just couldn't handle authority.

On 13 April, my big day finally arrived – the sentence. I was folding 4,500 leaves by then and already dreaming of making it to 6,000 so I would be eligible for heavy rations. In the afternoon a guard called out my name and told me to go to the warder's office. I dropped my bamboo stick and jumped up without even bothering to consider my appearance. I was a pretty unappetizing sight. Since it was hot and close in the cell, I was wearing only a pair of grey shorts, a dirty white undershirt and slippers. By now the best I could do for my boil was to cover it with my old handkerchief. It wasn't a very sanitary solution, but at least it might keep the lice out of the wound. I hopped over the piles of book leaves and hurried down the corridor. In the warder's office I met a handsome young man in an olive drab jacket and blue pants.

'This is a representative of the People's Court,' the warder said. 'He wants to see you.'

After the usual formalities – name, former occupation, address – he opened his briefcase and brought out a sheet of paper covered with Chinese characters.

'You have been called here to hear your sentence,' he said. He began reading from the paper. 'The accused is charged with having participated in the repression of the Chinese people by having been a faithful running dog of the imperialist powers, with engaging in illegal activities and black marketing, with spreading rumours with the intent of creating confusion among the masses, with slandering the Chinese Communist Party and calumnizing its leadership and with distributing imperialist propaganda with the intent of corrupting the Chinese people.

'The accused, having admitted all these crimes by himself under his own free will and under no pressure whatsoever, the People's Government hereby sentences you, Bao Ruo-wang, to twelve years' imprisonment, counting from the date of your arrest on 27 December 1957. You will carry out this sentence in units of Reform Through Labour.'

Long Live Mao, I thought. It could have been life or twenty years, and I was getting only twelve. What a relief! I think that at that moment I truly loved Mao, his police and the People's Courts.

My particular sentencing process was unusually straightforward and free of ruse, probably because I was a foreigner. The party decided I had earned twelve years and that exactly is what they gave me. This was quite different from the usual sentencing procedure, as a fellow prisoner, a former judge, explained to me in the camps several years later.

First, he said, there is nothing in China to limit the sentencing power of the government. The common analogy is the rubber band – a sentence can be stretched or abbreviated, depending on dozens of nonobjective factors. A man sentenced to life might well become a free worker before his cellmate who was sentenced to ten years. A committee of three or four persons who know the prisoner makes the judgement of sentence. One of them might be a policeman who had been watching him on the outside, another the interrogator and another his scribe. Together they decide on a fitting sentence and then, depending on their attitude toward the accused, begin embroidering on it. If, as in my case, the actual sentence was twelve years, they might announce twenty to him, or even life. As always, the prisoner is told that he can lighten his sentence by making the necessary efforts and showing himself to be a model for the others. So perhaps after one year of furious effort he will be rewarded by a gift from the state: a sentence reduction from life to twenty years. Radiant and grateful, he becomes even more so the perfect prisoner, and after three more years he is reduced to only fifteen years. Two years later the sentence is reduced to ten years – ten more years only! Since he has already served five and continues to behave with zeal and gratitude, they wait until he has served seven more (to make his original twelve years). It is at this moment that the government, in its generosity, decides on an amnesty. Twelve years instead of life! The man becomes a free worker with a song in his heart, thinking only of helping to build socialism.

Another interesting invention of the Chinese Communists is the suspended death sentence – the execution to be carried out only if the prisoner misbehaves himself in some manner determined by his warders. It tends to make model prisoners. Lo Rui-Qing, formerly China's number-one policeman (he was stripped of his powers during the Cultural Revolution, and I wonder where he is now), took it upon himself one day in 1959 to explain and justify the system:

Among the punishments to be meted out to the criminal elements of our country there is one sanction called 'capital punishment with two years' suspension of execution and forced labour with observation of the effect.' Imperialists have denounced this as a most cruel punishment. We say that it is the greatest possible clemency. The criminals themselves understand this. Capital punishment with suspension of execution gives a last chance for reform to these persons living under the sword of the government. In fact, most of the criminals who receive this punishment are saved. Where was there ever, in ancient or modern times, in China or abroad, so great an innovation? Where in the capitalist world can such a humanitarian law be found? (*People's Daily*, 28 September 1959.)

'Do you have any objections to this?' the court representative wanted to know. Of course I did not.

'Do you wish to appeal?'

God, no. Bartek and all the other horror stories I had heard had cured me of that. 'No,' I said with emphasis. 'I realize I have the right to appeal, but I am satisfied with my sentence. I do not wish to appeal. I only wish to sign my name.'

'Raise your right hand,' he ordered me. 'Do you hereby accept that you were given a fair and just trial and a just sentence?'

'I do.'

'Sign.'

When I got back to the cell I was bursting with joy. I told Howe that I was the happiest man in the world. He agreed that the sentence seemed an unexpectedly good one. The soup tasted good that night. Only after the lights went out did I begin thinking of what lay before me. Ten more years. It began to seem longer and longer.

Chapter Six

I launched my very first satellite right after the Anti-Lice Campaign. I'm not likely to forget either one of them. The Anti-Lice Campaign opened one evening with a cell-by-cell sweep through our living quarters, during which the guards gathered together all our clothes and bedding and handed out thin little blankets in return. The nights were still chilly then, and we huddled unhappily on the wooden benches, naked under our wraps, waiting for the crews to return with our garments, which were being steamed somewhere downstairs. By the time we got them back nearly an hour had passed. The bundles were still smoking and warm when we undid them and as we spread them out we discovered that everything had assumed the same tone of uniform grey. Not exactly the finest Chinese laundering, that, but the worst part was that the delicious, steamy warmth quickly drained away, and we found ourselves in wet clothes lying under clammy blankets. It was terrible. We were colder than before. Hardly anyone slept and that was a pity because the very next evening, just before roll call, the warder hauled us out into the corridor to announce that we were given the honour of launching a satellite.

A satellite signifies the highest production possible. The Chinese Communists adore industrial imagery and every style of labour, every manner of output, has a corresponding title or analogy. Factory hands both inside and outside of prison have their achievements and status totted up at least every month; often their machines or vehicles are marked with appropriate symbols. Thus the very best workers in those days found themselves classified as rockets and the slower ones, progressively, aeroplanes, locomotives, automobiles, bicycles and finally ox carts. I knew one character in the South Compound who failed in his work so miserably that he rated not even an ox cart, but only a turtle! That was a double humiliation, for a turtle is not only slow, but is also the traditional Chinese image of the cuckold. Just to make things clear, they also gave him a week of solitary.

As I discovered on my first morning of folding, even our normal work days surpassed the official standards, since we 'voluntarily' arose an hour earlier than the standard prison reveille time in order to get folding as soon after five a.m. as possible. On High Production Days ('working furiously and bitterly for ...') reveille was at 4.00 a.m. and on both rocket and satellite-launching days at 3.30 a.m. In all, we worked about sixteen hours on satellite days.

The production warder had a speech for us, as warders always do in China. As anyone of any authority always does in China. I can't reproduce precisely the words he used that first time I heard him, but it is the easiest thing in the world to summon back the rhetoric of exhortation I was to hear so often. Picture a narrow prison corridor with 400 or 500 shabby men sitting Buddha-style on the concrete floor. From the cells set into the walls around us the overflow of those who couldn't find room in the hallway leaned over each other, craning their heads out of the doorways. Before us, down by the iron-barred door, wearing a blue Mao suit with a padded overcoat, the warder stood on a stool haranguing us through a tin megaphone. In his right hand he had a tightly rolled magazine which he swung around, slashed and jabbed with, whenever his words required extra force. This was how he spoke:

'Tonight I have something very important to announce,' he announced. 'Even though all of you are in this place undergoing Reform Through Labour, you know perfectly well what is happening on the outside in society. You listen to the radio and you read the papers. The government, in its concern for your cultural welfare and your ideological reform, sees to it that you do not lose touch with the great movements in our society. Now you all know that the labouring masses are taking part in the Great Leap Forward. Filled with revolutionary enthusiasm, they have given themselves over to selfless labour so that they can carry out the directives of the party and the government.

They are determined to realize the glorious goals that have been set for them. They are determined to reach the industrial capacity of England within fifteen years. They have accomplished brilliant results that are almost miracles. Immersed in their activities, they have forgotten what it is to eat or sleep. There have been cases where workers stood twenty or even thirty hours by their machines. Sixteen- or eighteen-hour work days are now common. Machines don't need to rest. All they need is to be manned.

'You who are undergoing reform for your sins are expected to do no less than people on the outside. Because you sought to undermine and destroy socialism, you are now being compelled to take part in the construction of socialism. With this in mind, and with the first of May fast approaching, the government has decided to make tomorrow a Satellite-Launching Day. By emulating the workers on the outside you will show that you, too, are willing to take part in the Great Leap Forward instead of lagging behind with your pitiful production figures. The labouring masses are working sometimes under very trying conditions for the realization of socialism, even though they have committed no crimes. Do you think you should do any less than them? You, who are traitors to the new society, must work harder to redeem yourselves.

'Tomorrow you will increase your targets by 100 per cent. No one, I repeat no one, will be allowed to fold less than 6,000 leaves. Laggards will be treated as saboteurs and will have a taste of gruel in solitary. All cells which fail to attain the targets set for them will go on a diet of corn mush for one week. Before you go to bed tonight each one of you will declare his norms for tomorrow, and the cells will set their targets on that basis. I want these figures before eleven tonight. And in case some of you have some incorrect ideas, let me just tell you this: It is an honour for you to be permitted to participate in the Great Leap Forward, because as far as society is concerned, you have already been written off.'

Before we turned in that night Howe pledged us to something like 200,000 sheets.

After that the only thing that counted was to get to sleep as rapidly and as thoroughly as possible. Sleep meant strength.

At precisely 3.30 a.m. a trusty awoke us without dramatics. He stood down at the bottom of the hallway by the door with the iron bars and shouted out a businesslike command:

'All right, everybody up!'

That was all there ever was to it – no whistles, bells or sirens. (Even if he had wanted to stroll down the hallway he would have been blocked by the sleeping bodies.) Within seconds of the sound of his voice the building was echoing around me with the clattering din of hundreds of men taking apart their plank beds and restacking the wood into the shape of the regulation work benches. The prisoners who had slept in the hallway rolled their bedding into balls and stashed them behind their backs and we in the cells chucked ours willy-nilly into the small, cupboard-like stowholes at the head of the beds. There was no time to fold them or properly roll up the blankets. Every second counted in the Transit Centre since even on normal days we worked doubletime. Within minutes we were all seated at the benches, ready to fold. Blinking, fuzzy and half-asleep but ready.

This seething urgency to get going as rapidly as possible resulted in some amazing behaviour patterns that toward the end of my stay hardly even surprised me anymore. I still clearly remember one prisoner – a stranger I never noticed before or after – whom I met on the eve of another Satellite day. We had gone to bed early, but around 2 a.m. I crawled out of bed for a quick trip to the latrine. This character was down near the entrance to the latrines, and he was sitting bolt upright in his dirty undershirt while all around him in the hallway his comrades slept. He was folding book leaves. I don't know whether he was slow, and afraid not to make his norm, or zealous and trying to impress the government, but there he was, already folding an hour and a half before reveille. I wondered if I'd ever come to that.

While we had been dismantling the bed, our orderly (a cell-mate appointed by Howe) had gotten the book leaves together and now flopped individual stacks of them down beside each of us. We prepared our toilet kits – the square of towelling, the all-

106

purpose enamel mug, the toothbrush and a sliver of soap. Everything in its place, ready. Each of us squeezed a little toothpaste onto the brush, laid it down next to the towelling, put the tube away – and started folding. Once, twice, thrice, four times. Back and forth with the bamboo sticks, into the endless, mindless ritual of folding each sheet four times onto itself. The more regular and machinelike we made our gestures, the quicker it went and the neater the creases. Everything out of the mind. Concentrate on folding. Bury yourself in it.

Outside, we could hear latrine call. 'Cell four,' the trusty called out, or cell five or cell six, 'get ready for toilet!' We went on folding. When our number came around, we jumped up in unison, scrambled to the door and trotted doubletime to the washroom: eight taps with cold water running into a concrete trough set into one wall and a urinal and lines of concrete latrine holes at the other. It never took a cell long to get its synchronization together: Half of us rapidly brushed our teeth on the left while the others relieved themselves on the right. Then switch. Have a quick brush, suck up a mouthful of water, and then hurry over to the hole in the floor, crossing the other cellmates midway. Out with the little square of newspaper, then trot back to the cell, passing the next cell en route. In the cell we hung our mugs up on pegs, strung the towelling on the overhead line to dry – and started folding again.

No. Not right away. First we went through a little ritual that was part of the unique folklore of the Transit Centre – the gluing of three cigarettes, end to end. The point was to make one long cigarette that would last, because we were allowed to light up only one a day. We knocked a little tobacco from the end of the first one (the cigarettes we had were always loose and filled with the lowest quality tobacco shards, so it was easy to empty them partially), stuck another into the opening and sealed the joint with a bit of paper and a touch of paste from the big pot every cell had as part of its inventory, used for sticking labels onto the finished book-leaf stacks. A third one finished up our Chinese version of a super-kingsize, and we were ready to go again. The paste gave a weird taste, but what the hell. A smoke was a smoke.

'Here comes the light,' Howe warned us presently. That was the best time of the day, when the light arrived. The lightup worked in a chain that began down at the iron-barred door, when a warder strolled over and handed the trusty a single match and watched carefully as he lit his cigarette and put the match out. Working slowly and calmly to keep from damaging the coal or mashing the end, the trusty worked his way down the corridor, passing his cigarette one time only to each cell leader, who lit his own and handed it back. The chain of lit cigarettes grew until the entire brigade was smoking from that single match, all of us with the same ludicrously long, drooping creation. It was good to smoke, and since this was a Satellite day there was even the chance that we might get another light after lunch. They did that sometimes to stimulate production.

By the time breakfast came at 7 a.m., I had folded just over 800 leaves, but most of the others had gone well beyond a thousand. I was still clumsy compared to them, but it was coming, it was coming. By the time I left the Transit Centre I could do more than 10,000 on Satellite days. Without moving from our places we gobbled down the food feverishly, begrudging the few seconds it took away from us. The day passed in a weird, dream-like haze of the endlessly repeated motions of folding, never really broken by anything, neither rest break, studies nor meals. We even tried to drink as little as possible, to avoid having to squander a few minutes on pissing. Somehow, we made the quota, even though I contributed less than my appointed share. The others, the more experienced hands, had made up the difference for me. So everything was all right. We would hold onto our rations. We went to bed at 11.15, absolutely dizzy from exhaustion but, I suppose, happy.

Our folding operation was, of course, only one of the several steps along the entire book-production line. The basic material was delivered to the Transit Centre already printed on massive sheets up to six feet wide and four or five feet long. After being cut in half by mechanical knives they became the reams or strips we folded into the various sections that constituted the books. Each man's daily output was then stacked, tied tightly into symmetrical bundles, labelled with his name and cell number and finally carried up to the fourth floor, where a machine punched three holes in the margins.

On the fifth floor they were sewn. There, shifts of prisoners marked and sorted the sections into proper order and heaved them into yard-high wooden boxes placed on a reclining, V-shaped table under which they slept at night. Over by the window was another long table, with clamps and a stapling machine powerful enough to pierce the entire thickness of a book. One prisoner clamped the pages firmly into place and rammed a temporary staple through to hold them together in the form of the final book. This man's mate was the sewer, who ran his line through the three holes and then, when he had finished, removed the staple.

The sewing sometimes wrought terrible damage to their hands, but the worst job of all in the Transit Centre belonged to the runners who carried the folded leaves upstairs. I mean runners quite literally. Each one of these coolies – there isn't any better word to describe their work – serviced two binders, each of whom had a daily quota of 700 books. Fourteen hundred books a day they toted on their backs up the four flights, thirty or forty at a time, stacked on wooden planks attached to their shoulders with a rough cord. They had to run to make their quotas, and if they ever stopped or fell, the man behind would run over them. Most of them were former students from Peking University who had made anti-government statements during the Hundred Flowers. Resisters they were called. They were only up for three-year stretches of Education Through Labour, but they knew if they consistently missed their quotas their Lao Jiao could be transformed into Lao Gai. They worked like hell.

The trick to folding book leaves is the old, universal system of black dots. We had to be careful not only to match up the dots along the borders of each sheet but also, obviously, to keep the order straight as well. Woe to the man who damaged a page. Every one of us bore permanently and vividly in mind the huge image hanging in the central hall of K Building, the poster of the accusing worker. At the end of each day, just before evening study, a warder appeared for the damage check. By then we had had a quick wash and were sitting cross-legged on the bed, ready for his visit. It would have been the perfect time for a cigarette, but smoking was allowed only in the morning. Howe took a sheet of paper and called off our names one by one; successively, we reported our personal damage counts. Three or four were considered natural and inevitable and were generally passed over without comment, but anything beyond that could bring serious trouble. Occasionally some of the more naïve newcomers would try to feign low damage counts by hiding some of their sheets under the bed, but this sort of ruse was always discovered. Nothing can be hidden in a Chinese jail. At the end of the month we received marks on the basis of our output and damage record. All of it went into our dossiers, and all of it counted for our future.

One of the worst incidents our cell experienced happened in May, and ironically enough the victim was one of the most skilful folders, a man named Hu. Even on normal days Hu would turn out seven or eight thousand leaves. He went so fast that his folding would be sloppy sometimes, but little matter – the binders could finish it up for him, he figured. Hu's problem was that he was stubborn and couldn't take criticism. And he was illiterate. It was toward the end of the evening that Howe was called urgently from the cell. When he returned, he was looking grim and mean. I had never seen him with that countenance before. In his hand he bore a folded sheet, ready for the binders.

'Hu, you're going to get it,' he said bleakly. 'You're good for a week.'

Hu, understandably, was startled and angered. 'What do you mean by that? What did I do?'

'What you did is terrible, Hu. I hate to speak of it, even.' I was shocked to hear friendly old Howe speaking that way. He sounded like Loo. Hu sensed the same thing and reacted by lashing out.

'Be careful what you're saying, Howe. You know I didn't damage more than five leaves all last week. And in case what you're thinking about is the window, remember that I was the one who wanted to close it. The wind wasn't my fault.'

Howe shook his head. 'I wish it was only that, Hu, but you have caused grave losses to the state. You have caused terrific damage.'

'Don't you go putting hats on me, Howe.' Hu was quite angry now. By speaking of hats he was charging the cell leader with a frameup.

'I'm just telling you what they told me and what I saw with my own eyes, Hu. It's not a question of five or six leaves. It's 300.'

He blanched. That was a terrible accusation.

'That's not possible.'

'No?' Howe held out the sheet he had brought with him. 'Is this your work?'

Hu leaned over and inspected it carefully, then nodded solemnly. 'There's nothing wrong with it.'

'Look at the bottom, Hu. The numbers don't follow. They start at 25 instead of 16.' Long silence. 'Now do you still say you didn't make any mistakes?'

Hu went into solitary for that. Jailers in China will give a man free time – release from study sessions, for example – to learn to read and write, so ignorance can never be used as an excuse. Hu had no one to blame but himself. It was after his unhappy run-in with a badly stacked pile of reams that I began seriously studying written Chinese with my cellmates. By the time of my release I could read and write the language as well as I had always spoken it. When Hu rejoined us after solitary his face was grey. He'd lost eight pounds.

'If it's any consolation,' Howe told him, 'the guy who cut your paper and lined up the numbers got two weeks.'

At intervals throughout the year – it depended on how production was going – the cells were directed to organize their individual ration-voting sessions. Ration voting was one of the worst aspects of the penal system, for it tended to isolate one prisoner from another and create a tension that dovetailed perfectly with the officially sanctioned Mutual Surveillance. It got us in the belly, the one place where we were all vulnerable. Each cellmate was bidden to assess the other, and when he voted, he was told that he should consider attitude toward work as well as output. The form for the meetings was universal. One by one, going by our lineup and sleeping positions rather than alphabetical order, we made little individual speeches describing our past work, plans for the future and finished with a request for food. The others then commented and voted. One of the early sessions I experienced will give a good idea of how the system works.

'My name is Bao Ruo-wang,' I began in the proper form. 'I am here for counterrevolutionary activities. The government has assigned me to folding book leaves and at present I am on the light-duty ration. Since I am now up to 4,500 or 5,000 leaves a day and since I don't think I'll be able to reach the target set by the government in the near future, I guess I should stay on my light ration.'

Two cellmates briefly commended me for my positive attitude in continuing work while I was in pain from my boils, but it was too much to expect that I would get off without negative comment. Citizens are supposed to criticize each other; prisoners even more.

'Bao Ruo-wang has been commendable in his attitude,' someone piped up, 'but we must remember that rations are not awarded on the basis of attitude alone. His production figures are low. Two weeks from now, if he doesn't make it to the target, the warder will probably punish him. So wouldn't we look bad if we voted him such high rations now?'

Even worse was to come. It was a guy named Liu, a real sour bastard. Liu loved to talk for the record; and he had a high voice to boot – the classical shithead.

'I think Bao should be demoted,' he squeaked. 'He's always making funny remarks. Does he think he's in a hotel? He's here to be punished, not to enjoy himself. He came here in the middle of February, and we're now almost into May. Should he still be eating light rations? That's a waste of government food. It's shameful. He probably thinks he can just coast along and still get well fed. There are other prisoners who just arrived a month ago and are already up to six or seven thousand leaves a day.'

Silence. Howe looked around but no one had anything more to say.

'I have nothing more to add to this myself,' he finally said, 'except to ask that any time one of you feels compelled to throw out accusations, let him keep in mind what his own production figures are. We don't want any polemics or personal arguments. All we are trying to judge here is what rations Bao should eat until the next meeting. One of you suggested heavy rations and another suggested that he be put back on punishment level. Let's take a vote. Who votes for heavy?'

One hand went up. I appreciated the gesture, but I never had figured to stand a chance for that.

'Light?'

Everyone but Liu and myself (the prisoner whose case is being considered never votes) raised his hand. So I was all set: light rations until the next session. Providing the warders agreed with our assessments. While in the Transit Centre I went through three sessions in all, and I can recall with pleasure a few incidents when we managed to get away from bureaucratic form. And Liu, that bastard, figures in two of them.

Chen was a nice little guy who had been arrested as a common thief. For some reason I never discovered, the authorities chose to give him his Reform Through Labour in the Transit Centre itself rather than in a camp. So he was a permanent fixture, an old timer. He had it all down pat by then.

'My production is around 7,500 to 8,000 leaves a day,' he said. 'The government has been generous enough to let me have the heavy-duty ration.'

'Chen is exceptional,' a cellmate commented. 'His production is high and he is very efficient. Since the government can't raise his ration any higher, I suggest we recommend him for a prize.'

'All right,' said Howe, 'we'll put it on the record if there are no objections.' Sure as hell, Liu piped up.

'Schoolmate Chen boasts about his production with self-assurance. He doesn't have the proper attitude. He takes everything lightly. He is always making jokes. I am sure that if he took a more serious view of things and stopped making jokes and went to the latrine less, he could raise his production higher.

I think we should warn him right here that if he persists in his self-satisfied attitude, we will demote him. Let this serve as a warning.'

'All right, Liu,' Howe answered with a sigh. 'I'll put down your remarks. Let the warder make the decision.'

The saddest case I ever came across was a ruddy-faced prisoner whose name I forget. Amid all the sloganizing that governed our existence, he was the one who came the closest to speaking the plain, blunt truth. He even permitted himself undisguised irony in his voice. He had lost hope. He spoke in a weary monotone.

'I am here for counterrevolutionary activities. I used to be a running dog of the landlords and of course I caused grave losses to the revolution. Putting me in prison was only right. By giving me a long sentence the government put me out of harm's way. Now I'm no longer in a position to obstruct the progress of the revolution. My production figure is around 4,500 leaves, but because the government thinks I can do better, I am still eating the beginner's ration. My attitude is not correct. It has been this way for the past five months. We prisoners have no rights so I don't really see why the government asks us to vote the food rations. We eat what the government gives us. All of us have to struggle to put out an extra book. That is how we expiate our crimes, right? How we regain the confidence of the government. But what are we really struggling for here? We're struggling for an extra piece of bread, aren't we? The government may think I can fold more than 4,500, but I can't do it on the beginner's ration. So if you ask me if I want the light-work ration, I will say yes not because I think I can fold more, but because I am hungry. That's all I've got to say.'

We all looked down at the bed in embarrassment, waiting for someone else to speak. Finally Howe broke the silence.

'What ration do you want to request?'

He shrugged. 'You heard what I said. You know what I want to eat and what all of us want to eat. But no matter what I want, I'll eat what the government gives me. We have no right to ask for anything else.'

By now Liu couldn't resist putting in his two bits. He delivered a little sermon about counterrevolutionary talk. Or started to, before Howe told him to shut up.

'What you have said,' Howe continued, 'the warder will learn about. You know there's no question about that. And as for your ration, no matter how badly you feel, you know we can't increase it.'

That ended his case. There was nothing more Howe could do, in spite of the obvious sympathy he felt. The other man nodded without the least expression on his face. He would pay for his words later. We all knew that.

And then there was Lo. Lo was great. He was the closest thing we had to a Marx brother in the South Compound. He was an absolute champion folder, one of the best of all – up to 9,000 leaves in a normal day's work.

'Cell Leader, can I reveal my thoughts? Or shall I ask for an interview with the warder?'

Howe told him to go ahead.

'It's about my rations, Cell Leader. I'm an embezzler, you know that, don't you? I won't say how much I embezzled, but anyway I won't be bothering society for the next twenty years. I am undergoing Reform Through Labour here in the book-leaf division while awaiting transfer to another camp. I have been here for six months. My production figure, and I'm not boasting, is around 9,000 a day – sometimes more, sometimes less.'

He cast a glance over at Liu, but he held his tongue this time. Lo went on cheerfully. He had some arithmetic for us.

'It all depends on the type of sheet, and how I'm feeling. I've been on the heavy ration for the past four months. That's a long time. By next week I might be up to 10,000 leaves – I've discovered a new gimmick to make it go faster. I'll fill you in on that later. But, anyway, I think this heavy ration is unfair. The guy who folds 6,000 a day gets as much food as I do and I fold 60 per cent more than he does. Now then, if the guy who folds 6,000 only got as much food as the guy folding 3,000, he'd scream bloody murder, wouldn't he? If I make 9,000, doesn't it stand to reason that I should get 60 per cent more food than the man at 6,000?'

He spread his palms out in the gesture of the reasonable man asking for an obvious answer. Full of goodwill, he went on. I was intrigued to see what conclusion he was leading up to.

'Of course, I realize that I'm asking for the impossible. There's a limit, isn't there? And the government knows how to reward us. Therefore, I'd like the classmates to vote me the light ration. I feel like taking it easy for the next couple of weeks.'

It was a bombshell, the one request that took us all utterly by surprise. Howe sat speechless. The best he could do was to lightly admonish him not to make jokes.

'I'm not joking,' Lo protested. 'I don't think the light ration will hurt me for another month or so. I feel quite fit now. If I went down to folding, say 5,000 a day, it would be a nice break for me.'

'Do you know what the consequences of your action might be, Lo?'

'Sure I do. But what am I asking for? Special treatment? All I want is a little rest. That's all I want, schoolmates.'

We debated the request and quickly decided to let him have his way. He stayed on the light ration until the next session. And he had scored a small personal victory. Good for him.

During my stays in the Interrogation Centre, the Eastern Compound and in the Transit Centre before sentencing, I had not been allowed to see my wife. The law permitted her only to come to the place of my imprisonment once a month, where she could deposit small parcels, no more than one letter and perhaps photographs of the kids. Naturally enough, her letters were optimistic; that was expected. If they had been otherwise, they never would have been delivered, and she herself would have run the risk of prosecution for dissemination of anti-government propaganda. Even though I knew the drill on this, I had gradually let myself be lulled into an unreal sense of security about the family. They would be doing all right, I figured. Right from the beginning all my jailers had assured me about that. A sinner will be punished, but the state takes care of his family.

I finally saw her for the first time early in May of 1959 – a year and a half after my arrest. I had been allowed to write her one of the official postcards inviting her to come for visitors' day. On the two lines left blank for personal messages I asked her to bring cigarettes and a change of clothes. On the evening before her visit I trotted over to the barber, where according to the custom I had the right to ask for a shave and a quick run-over with the shears for the regulation crew cut. I doubted it would help my appearance much, though. The boils on my back and neck still hadn't healed, and I wore the same old grey shorts, leather sandals and dirty grey shirt that was my standard folding uniform.

At 5.30 in the evening those of us receiving visits were marched downstairs into the main hallway. I carried with me a quilt that I planned to give her to take home and wash. It was filthy, and now that the weather had warmed up I could get by without it. Roll call. A warder barked out an order to line up for examination. The personal body search was only the beginning. The warders looked through every page of any books we were carrying and then slit open the linings of our jackets with a razor blade. Inspected and passed, standing at attention face to the wall, we heard the final directives:

'All right. In a few minutes you will have your visits. Make them as brief as possible. Those prisoners seeing their families for the first time must refrain from dramatics. Speak in a loud voice so the guards can hear you. No dialects allowed – only official Mandarin. Don't try to pass anything to your families. You will be observed. No codes. No contacts. If there are any infringements, the warders will end your visits on the spot.'

About face. We tramped out into the courtyard, where a series of barrier-style arrangements had been set up: wooden planks five feet wide, reposing on stacks of bricks. The planks came up to about waist level. Between each barrier a guard was posted. We jailbirds gazed up and down the line to try to spot our families. Yang was standing on the other side of a plank with our youngest son Yung in her arms. Yung was my favourite. He reminded me of poor little Mi who had died of typhoid. He was six now, and he barely knew who I was. I wondered what he was thinking now that he was inside the prison. My wife had never had the heart to tell the kids exactly what had happened to me. The best she could manage was to say I was away working somewhere. She had promised them that I'd bring them candies when I got back. Yang looked much too thin, even though she had made the effort of putting on her best floral Chinese-style dress. Yung was wearing a white shirt and a pair of khaki pants. He looked at me with big eyes, then turned his face away and all that he went through welled up in him – he started crying. I guess I really looked like hell, too. Yang was shocked.

'How come you're like this?'

I didn't answer.

'No dramatics,' the guard said. He didn't miss a thing.

'How are you, Yung?'

The poor kid was too scared to say anything. He thrust out a little parcel toward me, still looking away. There was a hand-kerchief, a couple of packs of cigarettes, a newspaper and some toilet articles.

It was all so strangely constrained. I told Yang not to worry about me. She said the same for herself and the kids. The oldest boy was in school. Everything was all right . . .

'I heard about the sentence,' she finally said. 'How can I take care of the kids alone for twelve years?'

'You are not allowed to talk about that subject!' shouted the guard.

I gave her the quilt and asked her to wash it. The visit was over. It had lasted six minutes. Yung waved back at me as they left.

A few days later I received a letter from Yang apologizing that she had no money to send me. As she explained, very briefly, what her situation was, I realized what she had gone through to make that visit. When I was in the Interrogation Centre, she had been able to come fairly regularly to deposit parcels for me, because we lived in the north of Peking near the Drum Tower – less than a mile's walk from Tsao Lan Tse Hu-tung. But the Transit Centre was entirely on the other side of town to the south. Yang was so strapped for money that she hadn't had even enough for the bus – which is ridiculously cheap in China. She had walked all the way to the South Compound, with Yung in her arms whenever he was too tired to walk himself, and then had had to make the same trek home – with the quilt I had passed her as extra baggage. It was about eight miles each way.

Withal, something happened that at least restored my faith in humanity. For reasons of speed the bus stops in Peking are quite far apart. As Yang Hui-min was trudging along with the kid, a driver stopped his bus on his own responsibility and asked if she wanted to come aboard between stops. My wife had to admit that she had no money. The ticket-taker, a young girl, waved her aboard anyway.

'That's all right, comrade,' she said. 'I'll pay your fare. You can take my number and reimburse me if you ever get up the cash.'

The bus dropped her fifty yards from our front door.

Yang visited me one other time while I was in the Transit Centre. It was what you might call a command performance. In prison terminology it was a 'dishonourable visit' – something reserved for badly behaved or recalcitrant prisoners. The occasion was my release from solitary confinement. It came on the fifteenth of July, just four days after I was back up from the hole. It was hot then, and I was dozing on the floor during an afternoon break. My snooze was broken up by a businesslike warder.

'Get up, Bao,' he told me. 'You have a dishonourable visit. It is necessary for your family to know what you have been up to and to speak to you about your situation.'

He led me out into the empty courtyard. There, next to the door from the main building, were my wife and both of our sons, Yung and Mow. Mow had been given a day off from school. Little Yung was crying again. The warder allowed me to touch them both. Yang began reciting her speech.

'I have been told that lately your behaviour has been bad.'

The bastards, I thought. Couldn't they have spared her this comedy? Wasn't it enough for me to be locked up and working like a coolie, without involving her and the kids in their goddamn object lessons? No. Of course not.

119

'Your behaviour has not made things easy for me,' she went on in that weirdly loud voice. 'The children in school . . . All their classmates know that their father is a counterrevolutionary prisoner. But there is a difference between a counterrevolutionary who is genuinely trying to reform himself and one who is not. One who is resisting reform. All this is deeply affecting our lives, Bao Ruo-wang. I beg you to listen to the government's instructions. I beg you to work and study hard. Then maybe the government will be lenient and forgive you for your sins.'

The visit lasted maybe ten minutes in all, and I heard nothing but that speechifying. When she had finished Yang Hui-min left me a political pamphlet and two packs of cigarettes. Yung and Mow were too intimidated and mortified to say anything. Neither of them waved as they left.

Chapter Seven

As nightmarish as the paper-folding operation could be, I experienced a little interlude that showed me even worse ways to pass time in the Transit Centre. For one week in April I had been transferred to the Fourth Brigade – the 'technical brigade' – because in my life history I had described the shop training I had received with the Salesian Fathers as a boy. A sudden shortage of personnel, probably brought on by transfers to the camps, had made a dent in the machine-tool production section. I was one of those sent in to fill the gap.

When I left the cell, Howe and the others were happy for me. What, after all, could be worse than the infernal round of folding? Now I would be able to hold my head up as a skilled worker. The rations were rumoured to be better over there, too. I shook hands all around and joined the guard for the walk two flights up to another wing of K Building. When we arrived, I was surprised to see how dirty and unkempt the cells were, but on reflection I could see that logic of it – the inmates stayed away all day at work and returned only to sleep and study. The Technical Brigade was so obsessed with their output that their study sessions eschewed politics entirely and dealt only with ways to increase production.

Early the next morning I picked up my set of tools from the supply room and reported to the lathe that had been assigned to me, a tired, rusted old thing dating from around the time of the First World War. Everywhere around me prisoners were turning, filing and cutting in a confusion of metal chips, smoke and dust. Ting, the shop super, gave me a six-foot length of old steel pipe three inches in diameter. I was to make rings from it, of very precise measurements. Discouragingly precise, considering the state of the machines we were working with. My first step was to trim a fraction of an inch from the outside of the pipe and then lop off an equal amount from the inside. Once it was perfectly prepared, I was to cut away the pipe into rings. The section I had in my machine should give me 110 rings, Ting warned. No less. My quota for the day was to be 600 rings. By the end of the shift I had managed only 450. Ting gave me hell.

The next day I made it up to 600, but I was even more sharply rebuked. Though I had attained the norm I had wasted pipe, averaging only 85 rings per pipe instead of 110. I was caught on the horns of output and economy, those two mutually contradictory goals. Within a few days I was holding the norm, but still averaging only 95 rings per pipe. I lived in an atmosphere of perpetual scolding. At the end of the week my cutting tool snapped. Ting blew up and sent me back to folding leaves.

'You worthless bastard,' he growled, 'you're lucky to get off this easy. The government has shown you nothing but consideration. Prisoners have gone to solitary for breaking tools.'

I knew Ting was breaking the rules by using abusive language with me, but I didn't protest. I was happy to be away from him and his goddamn shop. I left it at that.

Obviously I had no choice in my assignment, so the cell I went to back in the book-leaf division was a new one. The leader was a thick-set Northeasterner named Yen, who had been a doctor before his arrest. Our paths crossed again later on, toward the end of my career in the camps.

'There is a proverb,' he told me as if he were letting me in on a secret. 'A man doesn't know his happiness when he has it.'

Yeah, I thought. A lot of people have proverbs like that. I fell back into the mindless, repetitive rhythm of folding book leaves, struggling furiously and bitterly to increase production.

On 28 April we were marched by cells over to Prison Number One to have haircuts. The occasion was the approach of May First – May Day – one of the great national holidays in China as in the Soviet Union and the entire Communist bloc. We eagerly looked forward to these holidays because they meant extra food, some rest and entertainment. On the afternoon of the twenty-ninth after half a day's work, we stowed our gear and trooped downstairs to the courtyard. Divided into blocks of brigades – sixteen cells to a brigade – we stood under the bene-volent sun guarded by soldiers with automatics. It was time for a new ritual.

'Attention!' shouted out the officer in charge. 'Any of you who have objects that are forbidden by prison regulations may throw them on the ground in front of you and you will not be punished. But if they are found on you during the search that follows this, you will be punished as the government sees fit.'

A book flew out. Some bits of paper, probably notes that had gone back and forth between prisoners. A pencil. The soldiers stepped forward and frisked us, clothes and body. They confis-cated a cheap fountain pen from someone near me. They took his name down. We felt like dirt. Humiliated and picked over like a herd of brutes. In half an hour it was over and we marched back to the cells. What a spectacle *they* were. Every-thing was upside down and strewn around the floor. All our bundles and personal effects had been ripped open, even to the stitching of the cotton quilts. We started scrambling for our gear, but Yen sensibly ordered us to stop.

'We'll all sit on the bed and each schoolmate will go look for his stuff alone,' he said. 'That way we can see what he takes and there will be no confusion.'

And so we whiled away the rest of the afternoon restoring order. If that was what they meant by a May Day celebration, they could keep it.

30 April was a holiday – two meals during the day, one at 10 and one at 4 p.m. That was fine. In the afternoon we were allowed down into the courtyard to do our laundry. And in the cell we could play games and talk of subjects unrelated to poli-tics or production. After dinner, at about 5 p.m., we went down to the courtyard for the show. But first, naturally, there was a speech from the head warder:

'We are here to celebrate May First. In spite of the fact that you prisoners have no right to such a celebration, it is the government's opinion that the constructive work you are doing should be rewarded. As for production, I may say that we are doing quite well. We have brought a certain amount of profit to the state. You have more reasons than anyone else to bring profit to the state, because you owe it your whole lives. Therefore, in recognition of the presents you have made to the state, the government hereby declares that tomorrow you will receive a bonus of two (Chinese) dollars.'

As he clambered down from the platform our only reaction was silence. It wouldn't do to applaud. The show that followed was called 'On the Tracks of the Snowy Mountains' and it was presented by one of the companies of the New Life Theatre Troupe. Comfortably seated on our makeshift rolls or bundles, we lit up and waited. It was underneath a huge banner whose red letters proclaimed 'The Resolutions of the Government Shall Be Carried Out' that the actors gave us the story of how a special commando unit of the People's Liberation Army went into Manchuria and defeated the resident bandits by infiltrating their headquarters. It was a fine show. New Life always did a first-rate job.

For May Day the morning meal included steamed white bread made from wheat flour, a stew of pork, vermicelli and potatoes and two ounces of candy; to digest it we were called to assembly in the great central hall to listen to the radio broadcast of the big parade in Peking. We knew it by heart already and it was a bore to be assailed once again by the same stock phrases and heroic resolutions, but what could we do. We were prisoners and that was our duty. Here were the workers, marching with firm step. Then the women workers. Then the peasants. Then the schoolchildren. Then the athletes. Et cetera, et cetera. On they came in seemingly endless, repetitive bands, everyone chanting long life to Mao. A prisoner near me had a mental lapse and lit up a cigarette.

'Put that out,' snapped a guard. 'You're here to listen, not to smoke.'

If anyone talked, he was told to shut up. If anyone read, he had his book taken away. If anyone slept, he was kicked in the ass. Two and a half hours that parade lasted. They were getting some serious exercise back there in Peking. For us at least it passed the time of day until the 4 p.m. meal – rice, vermicelli, bean curd and soup. Good food by any standards. We were a contented lot to watch that evening's movie, 'Fire on the Frontier', a rambling tale about how the Nationalists persecuted the ethnic minorities and how the new order treated them like brothers. The star, I recall, was a girl named Wang Hsiao-tang, who was later arrested for immoral living. The official charge was 'having sexual relations in a most disorderly manner and breaking up households'. I suppose she ended up with New Life.

At the end of the week that followed May Day we swung into the Ideological Reform Campaign, our own sort of mini-Hundred Flowers. That one didn't work out too well for me. It began in the courtyard at 8 p.m. of a Friday evening with an announcement from the prison director, a tall, bearded native of Shensi Province.

'Most of you,' he began, 'have the mistaken idea that you are here only to work. Well, that's not all there is to it. To reform yourselves you have to not only work, but get rid of your bad thoughts as well. Bad thoughts – about the government, about the leaders, about the government's policy, about the government's allies and about the Communist Party. In order to get rid of these bad thoughts you have to speak up and let them out, so the government can educate you. You mustn't be afraid to speak your bad thoughts, because we know you have them – or else you wouldn't be here in the first place. Therefore, beginning next week, the book-folding division will stop work for one week. The mechanical shops will stop work in the afternoon for the day shift and the night shift will not begin work until 11 p.m. During the spare time allotted you by the government, each one of you must write down all his bad thoughts, beginning with what you think of your own sentence and what you think of your crimes. Those of you who haven't yet been sentenced must state what you think it should be. Your comments must be frank and thorough – remember that this is a campaign to help you, to educate and reform yourselves for your own salvation. Keeping bad thoughts in your heads turns you rotten. They will impair your ideological reform. For these reasons the section chiefs and cell leaders must make sure that each prisoner gives a true document of what is really in his head. No one can interfere in this. Those who don't know how to write will be helped by those who have a higher cultural level.'

So it began. And I, like a literal-minded fool, followed orders. I opened my big mouth. I was still naïve. I took a piece of paper – I still shudder at the memory of that moment of idiocy – and I wrote that my experiences in the Transit Centre led me to conclude that the government's alleged concern for our spiritual well-being was a sham. All it really wanted from us was cheap slave labour, working for highest production. Carried away by my stupidity, I even felt a perverse sort of pride when my cellmates praised me for having such truly bad thoughts. I was the cock of the walk – no one else had thoughts as bad as mine. About a month later I got the bill for them. It came with the Denunciation Campaign. Of course. I should have guessed. Once more, it was the director who told us about it, on the evening of 15 June:

'In order to ensure that you all receive the proper instruction, we are now going to open a Denunciation Campaign. Every one of you is expected to denounce others for what they have said or done against the government. No considerations of sentimentality shall intervene. It is your duty to denounce persons in your cell or in other cells. Do not be afraid to say anything. No one can take revenge. It is better to offend a cellmate than the government.'

We trooped back to our cells and sat meditating a moment, the better to clear our minds for efficient denouncing. Little by little, we found things to say. The scribe took it down. As usual with these things, it started on a low key, with the cell leader moderating.

'I saw so-and-so stealing extra bread from the food trough.'

'When?'

'Two months ago.'

'Why didn't you report him?'

'Because he gave me half.'

That was a nice, light start, but things quickly worsened. One guy was accused not only of stealing from the kitchen, but of trading the food for cigarettes. That was commerce – black marketing.

Someone said he saw me using code in my letters home – and writing in a foreign language.

The atmosphere in the cell grew tense. In case any of us had ever doubted it, it was becoming clear then that we were slipping into a jungle situation of every man for himself. Mutual Surveillance put into action. Precisely what the warders wanted. I was shaken. It was weird and unhealthy.

A week later I learned that the government, too, had been working up its own set of denunciations. I was called into the warder's office.

'I've got something to tell you, Bao Ruo-wang,' he said sombrely. 'You have been singled out for reeducation. You have particularly bad thoughts. The government has decided to take special measures with you. We expect you to accept them with the proper spirit. Just remember that. Be thankful to the government for showing you so much concern.'

He dismissed me and I returned to the cell filled with foreboding. At 7 p.m. that evening we were called downstairs to the courtyard. It was time for the climax of the campaign. We sat in the warm evening sun and looked up to the stage, where the director sat at the inevitable bureaucrat's green baize table with his assistants around him, perhaps fifteen in all. Behind them was a large poster of Mao and a fresh banner with a slogan:

PUNISHMENT TO ALL THOSE WHO REFUSE
THE GOVERNMENT'S REEDUCATION

The director rose to make his speech. I held my breath. I hadn't said anything to my cellmates about our earlier meeting.

'The Denunciation Campaign has been a great success. The results are encouraging. They show that the majority of you are truly concerned with ideological reform.'

He paused. Pregnantly, as they say,

'But there are some of you – very few – who have launched attacks against the party and the government. These people will be severely punished.'

Another pause. Shift of gears to the dramatic, stentorian voice.

'Bao Ruo-wang, counterrevolutionary, thirty-three years old, sentenced to twelve years' imprisonment – on your feet!'

I couldn't have remained seated if I tried. Within what seemed like a microsecond of his signal, my dear cellmates heaved and shoved me upward with remarkable revolutionary fervour. There I stood in the middle of them all. The director and me. He spoke.

'This individual has attacked the state's glorious programme of Reform Through Labour. What is worse, he has dared to insult the Chinese People's Liberation Army by saying that the Pacification Campaign in Tibet was nothing less than imperialist aggression.'

He had rather twisted my words on that one, but what shocked me at that moment was how effortlessly he reached back to that early study session in the cell with Howe. Nothing, I realized, is ever forgotten. The audience took in the director's words in deathly silence. He wasn't through yet.

'For these and other insults too numerous to point out here, the government has decided to put him in chains and place him in solitary confinement until he has shown signs of repentance.'

The director sat down, and as if it were a signal the courtyard erupted in a tumult of clapping and slogan-chanting.

'Long live the Chinese People's Government!'

'Down with the stubborn element!'

'Punish severely the agent of imperialism!'

'We heartily support the decisions of the government!'

It was a hell of an impressive din. My fellow prisoners not only shouted and chanted, but shook their fists in the air for emphasis. All around me I saw faces of hatred turned towards me. I suddenly had the very pertinent certainty that my schoolmates would tear me to bits had the director suggested it. Without being bidden four of them grabbed me and propelled me forward through the crowd to the front of the platform, where two guards took over. One on either arm, they pushed my head down and dragged me over towards the dreaded Northwest Corner, where a warder awaited us. He watched impassively as the guards searched me and removed my belt and shoes.

'Put him in chains,' said the guard, but the warder suddenly looked embarrassed. He had to admit to a situation that I probably would have found comical had I not been so frightened.

'I don't have any chains left,' he said disconsolately. 'We've got them all in use.'

'Put him in cuffs, then,' said the guard.

Arms bound behind my back, head down, I careened into the Northwest Corner. It was dark. Presently I found myself in a long, dank corridor with high barred windows on one side and a series of small doors on the other, as if made for midgets. The place smelled like a lion's cage. A guard swung open one of the doors and another pushed me forward. I stumbled and nearly fell over the thick sill beam. Bent double, I squeezed into my hole. The opening between the sill and the top of the doorway was hardly more than three feet and the cell itself was about four feet long. The cement walls were about three feet apart and the ceiling four and a half feet high. There was just enough to fit one man, sitting or squatting, but it was impossible to stand or lie down. My escorts threw in a dirty blanket and slammed the steel door shut. Hunching along, my arms useless behind me, I managed to get seated back against the wall and look around. The door had two openings, a small peephole for the guard near the top and another, even smaller, circular hole near the base – just big enough for the food spout to fit through. There was a wooden bucket for my latrine and an electric bulb sealed into the ceiling. It stayed lit permanently.

I felt despairing and bitter. They had ordered us to speak our minds and evidently I had been the only one to take them at their word. Some people never learn. My arms hurt like hell. I wondered how I would be able to sleep. At least it wasn't cold; that was some small comfort. I dozed and nodded through the first night. The next morning a guard drew open my door and leaned in.

'The government has decided to be lenient with you,' he announced. For a fleeting instant my hopes soared. Was I about to be freed? No. I was having illusions. The guard told me to lean over so he could reach my cuffs. He unlocked them.

'Put your arms out in front of you.'

He snapped the cuffs back on. So that was the leniency. At least now I could sit in relative comfort. Half an hour later another guard opened the door and thrust at me a rusty can about the size of a Campbell's soup tin. The edges weren't bevelled or filed smooth. At what must have been around 9 a.m. a voice on the outside gave me an order.

'Get ready to take your meal.'

I held the can under the bottom hole. A spout like the end of a watering can pushed through the opening and slopped in a full measure of scalding hot corn mush, some of which spilled over onto my hands. Surprised and in pain, I instinctively dropped the hot tin. That was just what the bastard had been waiting for. It must have been part of the normal hazing for new prisoners in solitary.

'You fool!' he bellowed. 'That's wasting food: blood and sweat of the people. You can be severely punished for that. I shall make a note of your attitude.'

You s.o.b., I thought. I'll bet you will, too. Furious, humiliated and brimming with self-pity, I licked off what was left in the tin. I wasn't quite ready to lick the floor yet. Five minutes later the guard returned for the tin. He was rapidly followed by the turnkey, who handcuffed my arms behind me again. So I was to be allowed to have them in front only for eating ... Even that was something, though. Some prisoners had their arms behind them all the time, even for meals, which they had to lap up like dogs.

I hunched over into the corner and tried to make myself comfortable. From somewhere in another cell I heard moaning. I stayed there daydreaming until I could avoid reality no longer: I had to piss. Even that, I saw, was part of the punishment. I lurched over, turned around and took the cover off the bucket with my joined hands, then turned around again to face the bucket. But – how? The only way to get it into the bucket (pissing on the floor was surely a crime) was to stick my foot in it and piss down my leg. There was no question of pulling my shorts down. And even if I managed that, how would I get them up again? I pissed down my leg.

There was no food at the normal lunch period, though I could hear mush being poured in some of the other cells. The moaning started again. Damp and stinking of piss, I set to day-

130

dreaming again. Some time in the late afternoon a guard came to change my cuffs around to the front again.

'I'm sorry,' I said. 'I wet my pants.'

He looked at me as if I were a caterpillar or a toad.

'So what?'

'Can't I change them?'

'Change them! Do you know where you are?'

He handed me another tin can and closed the door. This time when the food came I was ready for it. I didn't lose a drop, even though it was boiling hot and scalded my hands. It was vegetable soup this time, with some green tomatoes.

'You'd better drink it quick if you want any mush,' warned the voice on the outside.

I gobbled it down, cutting off the pain, forcing my throat to accept the unnaturally hot liquid. I was ready when he came back with the mush. To my surprise, the turnkey didn't put my arms behind me after supper. I had been promoted. From that moment on my hands were cuffed behind me during the day only, from nine to five. I was following office hours. At 9 p.m. or so a doctor came in to look at my wrists.

'Nothing,' he said to the guard. And he had some expert professional advice for me:

'Go to sleep.'

That night and for the next several days I could hear someone singing a demented song to himself. Why in the hell couldn't the guards do something to shut him up? I brooded about it until I came up with the solution: Those were the death cells down at that end. As far as the guards were concerned, he was already finished. Since he didn't exist, why bother to stop him singing?

On the third day a strange thing happened. I was jerked from my reverie by the sound of the guards heaving buckets of water into the cell next to mine. It wasn't until then that I noticed that the cells were sloped slightly downward, like an easy ramp, so they could be flushed of their filth and cleaned the way Hercules did with the Augean stables. The occupant of the cell began shouting abuse at the guards. I was stunned at his daring.

'I don't need a shower, you bastards. I just hope I get my

hands on you someday – I'll make you suffer, too. You call yourselves Communists? You're no better than the Nationalists!'

'If you don't shut up we'll gag you,' warned a guard.

'Kill me, you son of a whore.'

Afterward, there was nothing more. I suppose they did gag him. I have often wondered since what sort of history he had, and how he could be so courageous. I imagine he was an ex-Communist. I met a lot of them in the camps, and they were the bravest and most human of all the prisoners.

The next novelty to come to me in solitary was the lice. It was a revolting experience. I watched them grow fat. My skin teemed with them, and with my hands bound I could hardly reach them, especially during the day when my arms were cuffed behind me. At least my boils had healed in time, though. I don't think I would have been able to keep my sanity with lice and open wounds.

On the fifth day I was taken out and presented to the warder in charge of the solitary block.

'What have you got to say for yourself?'

'I want to see a representative of Public Security.'

'Why him?'

'It's his department that sent me here.'

'So you don't want to talk?'

'Yes, I want to talk, but I want to talk with a representative of the Ministry of Public Security.'

They threw me back in the cage, but three days later I got what I wanted. They'll do anything to make a prisoner reform himself. They led me to a meeting room where I was presented with a uniformed officer of the Peking Bureau of Public Security. I respected them for that. The form on which Chinese Communists insist can often be used to a prisoner's advantage if he knows the rules of the game. I was beginning to learn how.

'What is it?' the officer asked. 'I have come here especially to hear you out, so go on.'

I figured I had to hit hard. But above all things I had to protect myself by staying within the ironclad logic of the dialectic.

'I have been told a bunch of lies.'

'Your cellmates are all criminals,' he answered with a shrug. 'What do you expect from them – the truth?'

I plunged on: 'No. I have been told lies by the People's Government.'

He raised an eyebrow and waited for me to continue. He didn't have to tell me that from that moment on I would have to pick my words cautiously. I was in a fine position to add some more years to my sentence.

Slowly and carefully, I outlined my point of view. I quoted the director's speech, his exhortations for us to put our very worst thoughts on paper, and his assurances that honesty would be rewarded. Having obeyed because of my profound confidence in the government and the party, I was now being rewarded with solitary. Where was my sin? The officer and I had a good talk. He left me with assurances that he would look into the matter.

I am certain today that my accusations of official hypocrisy had an effect on the bureaucrats back in Peking. The Maoist order is inordinately proud of its own special sort of integrity. But since the movement has its own limited literature and a clear set of catechismic rules, it lacks suppleness. It can be used by an intelligent echoing of the catechism. They decided to release me from solitary. But since the Chinese are also face conscious, it would be inconceivable for me to simply stroll back to the cell absolved and victorious. They found a compromise: I would get Struggled.

On a Sunday evening, ten days after my arrival in solitary, I was dragged up, handcuffed, filthy and stinking, to my wing of the K Building and dumped on the floor before 500 of my chosen classmates. The first order they shrieked at me was to hold my head even further down. I complied, but not before noticing that most of my very own cellmates were out there in the bunch. That was interesting. I wondered how they would act. I should have known.

'Bao Ruo-wang has come back to make a public confession,' announced the warder. 'It is up to you to see whether or not he makes it properly. You will judge whether he has recognized his sins.'

133

I spoke.

'I am taking this opportunity to tell the government that in the past I have used various study sessions and campaigns to spread unfavourable ideas.'

That didn't work very well.

'You're not being sincere!'

The catcalling part began.

'You are not telling the truth! *Wan goo bu hua* – stubborn and unmelting.'

I took the initiative again and tried to explain myself, but the warder stopped me.

'Stop talking!' he ordered. Nuance: He had not said 'shut up'. It was fairly polite. It was beginning to look more and more like a *pro forma* Struggle.

'All right, you people,' he went on. 'Start criticizing him.'

One character, whom I didn't know, more or less set the tone for the others. He had it all down pat, especially a nice little set of analogies. He piped them out like a school lesson.

'Bao Ruo-wang is a fox who could no longer hide his tail. He was condemned and sentenced as an imperialist spy. For spreading imperialist propaganda. Now he dares to carry out his imperialist duties right here in prison! We demand that the government punish him as severely as the law allows. Down with the imperialist!'

The others joined in on the theme, sometimes getting together and chanting in unison their favourite slogans and invective. She hui bai lei (bad element of society) was one that recurred quite consistently. Often I could clearly identify the voices of certain of my cellmates, just as harsh and pitiless as the others. So much for solidarity. After about forty-five minutes – only the beginning for a first-rate Struggle – the warder intervened.

'It's getting late,' he said simply. 'You people have to get back to your cells. Thank you for the help you have given Bao Ruo-wang.'

I went back down to solitary, but things were now noticeably better. The next morning the guards unlocked my cuffs and allowed me to wash. When I had finished, they didn't put the cuffs back on. There was no doubt about it: I was on the way out.

When mealtime came, it was the same old corn mush, but it seemed to me that I was getting it earlier than usual. Another good sign. I set to killing my lice, feeling all over my body and grabbing them one by one. They made a satisfactory 'pop' each time I broke one in half with my nail. I must have looked exactly like some scrofulous monkey.

At noon the guards gave me two wo'tous. The next day I was put back on the light-labour ration. We were into the first week of July when I was led up to the doctor's office for an examination. He prescribed a shower and a change of clothes. Solitary was finished. When I returned to the cell, I was warmly greeted by all the friends who had Struggled me and cheered when I was led away to solitary.

'Good to have you back, Bao,' they said. 'Have a cigarette.'

I tried to refuse, but one of them slipped me a pack of Big Fortunes. You'll need it later, he told me, and of course he was right. What puzzled me was how they could act as if nothing had happened. Finally, after a few days, I came to understand. What was the point of harbouring a grudge against them? They had been coerced into Struggling me. They didn't have any other choice. It was simply a fact of Chinese life. Their failure to join in would have meant a bad mark on their dossiers and, probably, an eventual Struggle for them. There was no way out but to roll with the punches, go along with the act and get it over with as quickly as possible – then forget it ever happened. What else is there to do against such an all-encompassing authority?

Chapter Eight

In September 1959, I was transferred to Prison Number One – Peking's model jail. It was the beginning of the happiest nine months of my entire period of incarceration. None of the rumours, none of the quick glimpses from our trips over there to the bath house, had prepared me for the dramatic changes in my living standard.

For a month the Transit Centre had been in a state of flux; new prisoners arrived like waves of immigrants and large batches of veterans shipped out to the various camps under the jurisdiction of the Fifth Department of the Peking Bureau of Public Security. Soon there wasn't enough room for the newcomers, even with the hallways fully occupied. I and about thirty others finally benefited from the situation on 5 September, when a warder strode into the book-folding corridor with a slip of paper in his hands.

'All right,' he called out, 'the following prisoners will assemble in the hall.'

My name was on the list. For the moment none of us knew where we would be going, but it mattered little – how could anything be worse than the Transit Centre? Without even being bidden, we laid our bundles out for the search. When the warders had passed them, we tied them up again and marched down to the courtyard, heads bowed and silent, but secretly exulting. When we arrived out in the sun and saw that no trucks or buses were awaiting us, our spirits soared: It was a sure sign that we were going across the wall to Prison Number One. It was an exciting moment.

The twenty-five-foot red brick wall that faced us, like the rest of the structures of Prison Number One, had been built around the turn of the century, during the reign of the Dowager Empress. Even then it was meant to be a model for the world of

136

Chinese progressiveness in penal theory. Known officially as the Ching Ho (Clear Stream) Combined Factories (the Chinese have always hated to use the naked word 'prison'), Prison Number One lies in one of Peking's loveliest traditional areas near the Altar of Heaven but its street address has been updated and revolutionarily re-baptized – number 125 Ts'e Hsin Lu Road, the Street of Self-Renewal.

The architecture is neobaroque, consisting of five three-storey octagonal hubs (the factories) interconnected by eighteen high-ceilinged spokes containing the numerous cells, offices and store-rooms. The cement floors of the cells now carry Chinese-type raised wooden beds, installed after the Liberation. Previously, under the empress and later the Nationalists, prisoners slept on the beaten earth floor; proud to display the contrast, the Communists have left one of the old cells intact, as a museum. The windows of the cells are unbarred, the wooden doors have no locks and are left permanently open in any case. The danger of a prisoner escaping is virtually nil: Only a mad-man would wish to exchange this paradise against any other place of detention. It is the best jail assignment in China. And even if some strange impulse drove a prisoner to bolt, he would still have to confront the brick wall and the electrified barbed wire on top.

We marched single file through the door in the wall. In the courtyard on the other side a squad of Sepos eyed us while a new set of warders went through our belongings. The search was quick and perfunctory, as if to satisfy form alone.

'Are those all the clothes you have?' one of them asked me with a hint of surprise.

'Yes, sir.'

'What are you in for?'

'I am a counterrevolutionary.'

'What's your sentence?'

'Twelve years.'

'Then you must make efforts to improve yourself.'

'Yes, sir.'

'I see you have some very good cigarettes.'

That was true. Only a few days before I had received a carton

137

of Chien Men Grandes from the consular agent who was representing France in Peking at that time. I had known him for years, and that carton of cigarettes was about all he ever did for me. I have never quite been able to forget the way France wiped its hands of me while I was in prison. For the French government I was just another *métèque*, a half-breed who happened to hold one of their passports.

'You may smoke if you want,' the warder said. He leafed idly through the dictionary and the few other books in my bundle.

'Are these the only books you have?'

'Yes, sir.'

'We have a library here.' He made a little gesture of approval with his hand. 'Everything's all right here. You can put your gear back in order.'

I wasn't used to such consideration. It was almost shocking to be treated like a human being. Just as we began to walk in toward the dormitories another one of the warders ambled casually over and picked up my bundle – not for a search, but to carry it for me! My goodness gracious, I thought. Well, well, well . . .

The corridors in my new home were both wider and more pleasant than in the Transit Centre. Prisoners neither worked nor slept in them. On one side were the lines of cells and on the other, the offices of the warders (the same cells, but occupied by one man), the pharmacy, production office, storerooms, etc. The cell I was led to was about ten feet long and twelve feet wide with the usual raised wooden bed, luxuriously topped with a Japanese-style tatami mattress. A stranger who later became one of my friends – Tang Yung-ming was his name – was propped up on the bed with his bedroll behind him, reading and smoking a cigarette. He was wearing an undershirt and black shorts.

'Hi, schoolmate,' he called out cheerily. 'So you're the one they've been telling me about. Good to see you. This is your spot over here, but if you want to be over by the wall, I'll change with you.'

'No,' I answered automatically, taken aback by his bonhomie. 'That's all right the way it is.'

138

'How come your mattress is so narrow?' There was a point of humour in his eyes. I wondered if he already knew.

'There's not much space over in the Transit Centre.'

'Well, don't worry about that, there's plenty here.'

As he explained the sleeping layout, I realized I would have more than three feet to myself. Unbelievable! I asked him where we could smoke.

'There's a lighted incense stick down at the end of the hall. It's always lit. Just go down there any time you want a smoke. You look tired.'

'I am. When's the next meal?'

'At four. Today's not a working day so we get only two meals.'

'What sort of rationing do you have here?'

'Rationing?' Tang had a nice laugh. 'No rationing, man. You can eat as much as you like. But you'd better watch it. Sometimes you newcomers overdo it and end up getting sick.'

I was tired and hungry and dirty, but it was in a cloud of euphoria that I began stowing away my gear. I took my enamel basin and went down to the washroom to get cleaned up. Tang appeared as I was drying my face.

'Hey, schoolmate,' he said, 'the warder wants to see all you new guys down at the end of the hall.'

I grabbed everything and ran back to the cell. By the time Tang got there I was already dressed and ready to go. I turned to trot out the door and bumped right into him. He was smiling indulgently.

'Take it easy, man. Someone'll think you're trying to run away. What's the hurry? They can wait another minute . . .'

I walked. I actually walked to the assembly point. It was my first gesture of adjustment to the rhythm of my new life. In a few minutes I met Warder Chao – the finest jailer I ever knew.

Chao was a great man. If I could see him today, I would embrace him like a big brother. Coming from the Transit Centre, I expected to meet nothing but gang bosses and slave drivers; instead, what I discovered in Chao was a man who above all respected honesty and morality. If all Communists were like him, the movement would sweep the world effortlessly. As I would soon learn, he was one of the rare warders around who refused to remain distant and aloof from the prisoners. What I saw before me now was a tall man – almost six feet – of about forty, with high cheekbones, a dark complexion, small eyes and a bulbous nose *à la* W. C. Fields. He was wearing a light blue Mao jacket, blue pants and Chinese slippers. He looked pleasantly unmilitary.

'I don't need to tell you where you are,' he began. By his accent I figured him to be a native of Honan Province. 'Here in Prison Number One we are engaged in production in the proper sense of the word. All of you here are assigned to work in the Clear Stream Plastics Factory. We are very proud of this factory, because it was the first one of its kind in China – it is the one that gave China a plastics industry. I know where you've been and what you've been through. Right away you are all going to get a medical checkup. You're not fit to work. You need a rest and we'll let you have it. You'll take it easy for two or three days – maybe even a week if you need it. You'll be eating in two hours. For today, anyway, we're keeping you on a diet of corn mush. Sorry – just corn mush, but you can have as much of it as you want. This is for your own good. Maybe tomorrow you'll be able to try something solid. That's all for now. Dismissed.'

Later in the afternoon as I was having a smoke, a trusty came to the cell with word that Warder Chao wanted to see me personally in his office. The little interview that ensued was a watermark for me. I suppose that Chao saw the other newcomers, too, and gave them about the same reception. And cynics will probably say that the kindness and consideration he displayed were only part of the ancient penal game of carrot and stick. Maybe. Maybe it was a well-orchestrated plan. Maybe it was the classical Pavlovian approach. Call it what you like – but I assure you that it works. His decency after two years of pain and humiliation was absolutely inspirational. I was led to an admiration that bordered on love for that man and for the prison he represented. If that was brainwashing, then I am for it.

Chao's cell was almost opposite ours, and exactly the same

size. He had a little desk and a bed made of three rough planks supported by wooden stools at either end. Everything had its place and everything was immaculate. On the wall next to his bed was a photo of Mao engraved on tasselled silk and on the small night table was another of his own wife and children. The wall calendar of course bore Mao's effigy, and his plaster bust was respectfully placed in the centre of the desk. Behind him, higher up on the wall, was a colour photo of Chu Teh, then commander-in-chief of the Red Army. Warder Chao invited me to sit and we went through the standard biographical questions. When we had finished he gave me a low-key speech.

'Don't be discouraged. The government has assigned you to this place so you can use your skills and talents properly toward redeeming yourself. You will be given every opportunity to gain merits, but you have to have confidence in us. We can't force you to have confidence; but unless you do, we can't make any progress toward your redemption. I am here to help you undergo reform, but all I can do is reason with you. The fact that you had bad ideas and committed crimes means that we have to see to it that you start getting good ideas and never sin again. If you ever have any problems – ideological, political or whatever – come and see me and we'll talk them over. My door's open twenty-four hours a day. Come even at midnight if you have to. No problem. That's my job.'

He flipped open my dossier and came to a part he had already read.

'I see by this report that you don't have much in the way of clothes. If your family is in a bad financial situation, the government can give you some clothes. Talk it over with the trusty. He'll work something out for you. Meantime, keep making efforts to reform yourself, and maybe you'll get out of prison sooner than you think. You may go.'

I was overwhelmed with gratitude and ready to prove it at work. After three days of rest I was assigned to the maintenance section of the plastics factory, responsible for keeping the machines in good running order and well-supplied with spare parts. Compared to paper-folding, it was pleasant and civilized work. Everything about the work and living conditions reflected the immense change from the other side of the wall. Away from work I was a member of Di Erh Tzu – team 2 – and the twelve of us, all specialists for whom no work norm could be set, lived in the relative luxury of three cells, congregating in one of them only for meals and study sessions. There was no cell leader, but, surprisingly, the one who more or less performed that function when some ceremonial need for it arose was the youngest of us all, a squat, little, pale-faced character named Hu Ting-wen. Hu was smiling all the time. He was only twenty-seven when I met him, but he had already been in jail eight years. He had been a street urchin, independent and used to fending for himself, but made the mistake of carrying his notions of liberty of opinion to the point of jeering and making dirty signs at soldiers of the Liberation Army. The sentence was ten years, and it certainly seemed to have reformed him. He was as conscientious and cheerful a worker as I ever came across.

The other members of the team who became my friends, or who at least stick in my memory today, were Ma Hung-fang, a Moslem from Peking who was in charge of setting the norms for the entire plastics factory; Li Ming, a handsome, athletic type who had worked himself up to brigade agitprop; Chen, an accountant in the head office; Liu Kao-sheng, the team orderly; and especially Dai You-ling, a prison veteran whose wise advice pulled me out of trouble more than once. Square-Jaw Dai we used to call him. He knew the ropes, all right.

I was astonished at my classmates' utter unconcern about food. At the first meal I shared with them that evening, their fare was cabbage soup thickly laced with oil. When the orderly began ladling it out some of them actually held him back from putting too much into their bowls! My mind raced. How was it possible? Following Warder Chao's orders, I stuck to mush, a big tub of which was standing out in the hall. After four bowls I couldn't fit any more inside me. I wonder how many people know how good it feels to have a stomach full of corn mush.

At 7 p.m. a guard shouted 'Hsueh-Hsi' – study time. We congregated into the central cell, took off our shoes and placed ourselves cross-legged on the bed.

'Tonight we'll read something from the paper,' Hu said.

'Okay,' someone answered, 'but let's get something interesting this time. Let's not read about production again.'

That sounded to me like heretical self-indulgence, but it was without the least sign of bother that Hu went through the paper to come up with a tale about a general whose peasant father came from his native village to pay him a visit. The general had become decadent and bourgeois during his years of power and had married an elegant lady outside of the working class. He refused to see his father. We were discussing the just punishment he eventually received when we were interrupted by roll call. That meant it was 9.30, somebody told me. That certainly was early for roll call.

Warder Chao called us together for what was the mental equivalent of tucking us in – a little evening speech. He told the others about the thirty new prisoners, gave us new people a bit of the history behind the pioneering Clear Stream Plastics Factory and again reminded us that we should consider ourselves to be not prisoners but workers building the new socialist state. If we were the workers, he was the worker-priest. There was no avoiding that analogy. Chao and the millions of unknown apostles like him are the backbone of the present Chinese regime.

The next morning I jerked awake automatically at 5 a.m., while the others were still fast asleep. I was out of bed and on the way to the washroom before I remembered that there was no hurry anymore. Feeling sheepish and gauche, I crept back to bed and waited for breakfast. When it came, I was delighted to see salted vegetables in with the mush. My cellmates took only a bowl apiece, but I still hadn't got over the novelty: I devoured three.

The weeks passed agreeably. My maintenance work with the machines was challenging and useful and the hours altogether human. More than anything else, Prison Number One resembled an industrial boarding school for men. The day began at six when a trusty awoke us with a shout from the end of the hallway. Between six and seven we had time for latrine, washup (an orderly had filled our basins during the night) and breakfast of mush or kasha with vegetables. I discovered that if I

143

squirted soy sauce over the kasha and vegetables, it became a passable imitation of the canned Campbell's soups I used to eat in Peking with my American friends.

At 7.30 we went off to our jobs, and lunch break was on the dot of noon – thick vegetable soup and corn bread, served from tubs on the spot. Compounding the luxury was the fact that we were allowed fully forty-five minutes to eat, have a smoke and rest. No hurry. At 6 p.m. the next shift took over and we headed back to our cells for a wash and supper. At 7.30 all the Tzus gathered for 'Putting the Heads Together', a group discussion of how to solve production problems. From 8.00 until 9.30 was the traditional study period, at the end of which the flags were issued, for each worker's productive output. Our day ended, naturally, with a talk from Warder Chao, a final cigarette and a sip of tea before lights out. It was a civilized existence.

'I want you to fulfil your norms in an ordinary working day,' Chao was fond of telling us, 'and not by launching you-know-what.'

He was too correct to speak critically of rockets and satellites.

Although Prison Number One was the absolute model for Chinese penal institutions, it was not without its own bittersweet folklore. There was the Translation Brigade, for example. It could have sprung directly from the pages of Solzhenitsyn's *First Circle*. The brigade was made up of 140 specialists, and I learned later that I originally had been picked to join them. I went to plastics instead because they were temporarily over-staffed.

The individual norm in the Translation Brigade was 4,000 words a day. The men worked in teams, one translating and the other checking. Every other day they switched duties. They were a smart and versatile group, translating both ways and into every conceivable contemporary language of any useful-ness at all.

Their great day came as the nation prepared to celebrate the tenth anniversary of the founding of the People's Republic. With the deadline inexorably approaching, some government subdepartment realized too late that it had several untranslated speeches on its hands and no one to work them over. Obviously any party member of any responsibility whatever had to utter some words for the tenth anniversary; equally obviously, their speeches had to be prepared in perhaps two dozen languages for the benefit of visiting dignitaries and for release to the press. When they sent the speeches to the official state translators, they politely refused. Not nearly enough time, they said. We can't possibly get them into all those languages by October first. Besides, we have our own anniversary preparations to worry about.

Disorder and desperation. Then someone thought of the boys over in Clear Stream, who had time on their hands and no celebrations of their own. There was, the story goes, a certain hesitation about handing over what amounted to state documents to a band of counterrevolutionaries, but they had no real choice. It was the Translation Brigade or nothing. The Chinese copies of the speeches were delivered to the Street of Self-Renewal on the morning of 29 September. The anniversary of the Republic falls on 1 October.

The chief warder himself broke the news.

'I've got good news for you,' he began and the translators shuddered. That sort of phrase is fraught with as much menace as when a warder speaks of 'the government's concern for your ideological well-being'. The warder ploughed on: 'For months I've been worried because we couldn't figure out what gift this brigade could give the government for the anniversary of the founding of our state. I was ashamed. I thought we weren't going to be able to participate, as the factories have been doing by increasing their output. Our glorious task will be to translate six speeches by high government officials into twenty foreign languages. Let us approach this task with the spirit of the Great Leap Forward.'

They did it. Everything was ready by 1 October. On 3 October, the Translation Brigade was awarded a red flag.

During the giddy days of the Great Leap Forward, there were slogans everywhere, even more than normal for slogan-hungry China. The official line for the Great Leap was that socialism must be constructed by 'achieving greater, faster, better and more economical results'. To the ordinary citizen, whether he was manning a drill press, planting rice or slopping bogs, it boiled down to a little three-part maxim: 'Do it fast, do it cheap, do it well.'

In Prison Number One every factory, shop and courtyard was decorated with the same set of gold plywood letters tacked on a red background and often floodlit at night:

> KNOW WHAT THE SITUATION IS
> HASTEN YOUR REFORMATION
> STUDY WITH DILIGENCE
> WORK WITH ENTHUSIASM
> REFORM YOURSELF FROM THE INSIDE OUT
> YOUR FUTURE WILL INDEED BE BRIGHT

In our maintenance workshop we had our own personalized slogan framed on the wall:

> BE GRATEFUL TO THE STATE
> HOW?
> BY WORKING WITH ENTHUSIASM
> WITHOUT THINKING ABOUT YOURSELF

In Warder Chao's office the slogan was a paraphrase of Mao's teachings: 'If you have something to say, speak up; once you have started, say it right to the end.'

While I was there, one of the cooks in the big central kitchen earned himself a red flag by applying the maxims to the production of food. One of the great staples of Chinese prison fare has always been steamed bread (usually cornbread, with white bread on special occasions). The moulded lumps of dough were placed on a perforated tray above a large water-filled wok – that ancient oriental cooking pan – and steamed until ready. Since the operation was slow and had to be repeated over and over again, our cook came up with a bright idea: Why not put to use the live steam from the factories and knitting mills? He went to the warder with his idea. Treading cautiously, he said he feared it wouldn't work, bread would be wasted and the prison would get a bad mark. He preferred to leave things as they were. But the cook trumped him with a Mao quote:

'Dare to think, dare to speak and dare to do.'

The cook went down to the boiler room and talked it over with the machinists. To his surprise, it was perfectly simple to rig up what he wanted. He dismantled the section of the stove where the wok had been seated and in its place built a tall rack of six iron pipes. From one of the shops he ordered a set of square steaming trays and stacked them one on top of another over the steam jets. For the first try he put four dough-laden trays on the rack. When he opened the valve the steam blast sent them flying. So it was too light. He added two more trays and installed a more modern valve that allowed him to control the flow of steam. The result was one of the total, if minor, triumphs of the Great Leap Forward – six trays of piping hot bread cooked in fifteen minutes, instead of one in half an hour. The kitchen was immediately presented with a red flag.

Gradually the cook added trays. He soon had the system working so efficiently that fourteen were cooking at a time. He added two more iron cages – forty-two trays in all! He was officially proclaimed Activist of Labour, named chief cook and given a scroll for his wall. When I met him, I asked him why he didn't round it off to fifteen trays per rack. It was a nice number to try for, he admitted, but trial and error proved it to be no good. Fourteen was the limit. On the fifteenth tray the bread was only half-cooked. His system spread throughout the entire camp network. He followed up his triumph by inventing an automatic wo'tou stamping machine that turned out the little loaves in perfect form and order, twice as fast as hands could do it.

In addition to the various corps of specialists and the female section, Ching Ho housed a 200-strong brigade of juvenile delinquents, who would be eligible for the adult camps only after they passed age eighteen. Until then they were kept carefully separate from the rest of us and worked exclusively at grinding lenses for cameras and assorted optical instruments. Their raw material was Coca-Cola bottles. The profligate Americans had left millions of them behind, and the Chinese knew they were made of high quality, nearly flawless glass – thick and clear. Ten hours a day, these boys ground lenses compounded from melted-down Coke bottles. The eyeglasses I still wear today have one of the lenses ground directly from the bottom of the Coke bottle. Since the glass is tinted, my right lens is a shade darker than my left.

My prison paradise unexpectedly turned sour one afternoon toward the end of September 1959, when the Mid-Autumn Festival was drawing near. The festival falls on the fifteenth day of the eighth moon, the brightest night of the brightest moon of all. Traditionally it is the time for settling debts. The Ministry of Public Security had one for me.

I got word of it when a trusty called me from the maintenance shop to the office of the warder in charge of education and discipline. He had a long paper form for me.

'Bao Ruo-wang, the government needs some information from you. Write your name, brigade and section on this and then fill out the rest. That's all.'

I unfolded it as I walked back to the shop, and my heart sank when I read it. At the top of the form was a terse little paragraph: 'The government desires detailed information on the following person or persons: Dr A.P., Mrs A.P. [I am withholding their names]. Relate personal history and dealings, their friends, their activities both legal and illegal, their connections with foreign embassies and the time spent in these activities.'

All afternoon I tried to figure what to do. Back in the cell at study time that evening I went off in a corner by myself and filled out the form:

'Dr P. is an Indian physician. His father was a Parsee and his mother Chinese. He was educated in England and took additional training in France. He returned to Tientsin in 1939 as a doctor on the Chinese railways. He married a Chinese girl and they have four children. They live in Peking. He is one of the physicians for the Western diplomatic corps.'

I signed my name, folded it and returned it to the warder, who slipped it into his drawer without a glance. Clearly, the contents of that paper were not his domain. Less than twenty-four hours later I was called back to his office. He wasn't alone this time. Standing by the desk was an officer from the Ministry of Public Security – olive green uniform, epaulettes, decorations, the works. He spoke in dry, clipped tones.

'For your information, I am the one who sent you the questionnaire. The responses you gave amaze me. What do you take us for, Bao Ruo-wang? We know all this information. We don't need you to tell us that Dr P. is an Indian physician. You have known the Ps very well since 1955. You are good friends. You used to visit their house nearly every day. You know very well the sort of information we want from you.'

Of course I did. Only they weren't going to get it.

'I don't deny anything of what you say. But I have already made my confession.'

Intransigence is not appreciated in these situations. His eyes narrowed.

'Be careful, Bao Ruo-wang. Are you refusing to cooperate with the government? Things could go very badly for you.'

I certainly didn't want a showdown with the cops, but I was damned if I was going to denounce my friends. I decided to face up to him. I knew that I had a certain logic on my side.

'All right,' I said as politely as possible, 'let's speak seriously. If I were a Chinese citizen you wouldn't have needed to pedal your bike all the way over here. I would already have denounced Dr P. and all my other friends. I can understand that Dr P. may be your enemy, but he is not mine. Since I am not a Chinese citizen I have no obligations toward the People's Republic of China.'

The cop eyed me with calm. He wasn't a man given to theatrics, but he had a few weapons left.

'Withholding information from the government is a punishable offence. I wouldn't like to add five years to your sentence . . .'

He had given me a beautiful opening. I hit him with the catechism.

'Five years for what?' I asked innocently. 'If you had told me that in the Interrogation Centre, I might have fainted. But now I have confessed and I have been sentenced. And I also know by heart the eighty-seven articles concerning the punishment and handling of counterrevolutionaries. There are some things you can do and some you can't. There is also the clause of four articles concerning foreigners, which I believe you have read. Since I am not a Chinese citizen, I am not obliged to divulge everything I know for the good of the state. You cannot force me to do that against my will. I have committed sins against the Chinese people, and I am paying for them, but I have no responsibility beyond that.'

The conversation was turning my way. My reasoning was correct and the cop knew it. He didn't dare bully me in the presence of the warder.

'Very well,' he said. 'Perhaps I spoke too hastily. I forgot you were a foreign national. Let me put it this way: If you help the Chinese People's Government, it won't be ungrateful. You may be able to gain merits. I could recommend you for leniency. Wouldn't you like to shorten your sentence?'

'As Mao says, "Fifty years are short when compared with world history." Just a little while ago I thanked the government for its leniency. My crimes are so heinous that I consider my sentence of twelve years more than just. I can only defer to the government's decision and accept my sentence as it is.'

'Is that your final answer?'

'Yes.'

'As you wish. But remember – I made you an offer.'

'I know about offers. I heard about them in the Interrogation Centre. Loo got plenty of offers and he ended up with a life sentence. I don't need offers.'

'I'd watch what I was saying if I were you.' The hint of a threat was creeping back into his voice. I gave him the big trump card.

'Isn't it written here, "If you have something to say, speak up. Once you start to speak, say it right to the end. The man who speaks his mind makes no mistake." '

The cop zipped up his briefcase and went out.

'I hope you won't regret all that,' the warder said.

'Have I said anything wrong? If so, please point it out to me, and I shall be grateful.'

He must have thought he was looking at a monster.

'We'll get to that another day,' he said with a sigh. 'It's getting late now. Go get yourself some supper.'

I never saw the cop again. As I thought about the encounter afterward in the cell, I was horrified by the insolence I had shown him. It really wasn't very smart. But he had backed me to the wall.

The cop was quite right. Dr P. certainly was a good friend of mine. He left China in 1961 or 1962, and is safe in Hongkong now. I knew enough to cause him quite a bit of trouble.

A few days after the Mid-Autumn Festival my family paid their first visit to me in Prison Number One. It was still sunny and warm; the rows of plank tables in the courtyard looked almost cheerful, as if making ready for some picnic. This time I finally had something to give the kids. With the pocket money I had earned in the maintenance shop, I had bought a small portion of candies and two moon cakes, the little round delicacies associated with the festival. The ones I had bought were stuffed with mashed sweet beans. As I approached the visit table one of the guards made a move as if to take the bundle of sweets from me. I gave him a ferocious look and passed by. Probably too surprised to react otherwise, he let me go. My kids got their moon cakes.

That evening I went to see Warder Chao.

'Warder,' I announced, 'I hereby confess that I committed a grave mistake today. I gave one of the guards a very dirty look at visiting time. I forgot the fact that I was a convicted prisoner and that he was a representative of the People's Government. I would like to apologize for my actions.'

He heard me out without expression or comment. He carefully composed his answer, and it was a pleasant surprise.

'I know what you did today. I already have the report. But you seem to think we're not human. We treat each case individually here, on its merits. Most of the other prisoners ate their moon cakes themselves, but you gave yours to your children, even though they can buy them on the outside. Most prisoners ask their families to make sacrifices for them. You did the opposite. I am glad you came to see me, Bao Ruo-wang. You

151

are making your first steps toward reform. But it's still a long march ahead of you.'

If I hadn't been a prisoner, I would have presumed to shake his hand.

As the tenth anniversary ceremonies drew near, we in plastics, like the translators, knitters, electronic technicians and all the other branches of Clear Stream Combined Industries drove ourselves to exceed our norms or to make some other sort of special gesture or 'present' to the government. Our division nearly doubled its production of plastic belts until we were turning out a total value of 40,000 Chinese dollars a day. Naturally this heavy output of one item meant that production of other goods lagged, but the belts made the prison look good. The demand for them was high and they commanded a good price. Over in the stocking factory they invented a machine to turn out stretch nylons in colours. But the one that did the most for the honour of Clear Stream, and became the subject of a special speech by Warder Chao, was the Electrical Division, who put together the two-hundred-watt amplifier, which Mao himself was to use for his tenth-anniversary speech in Red Square. The Electrical Division won a red flag.

At the end of that month I experienced my first full-scale Ideological Review, also known as the monthly lineup. In the Transit Centre, where every spare moment was devoted to brute work, we had undergone nothing more than the Weekly Examination of Conscience – much milder and shorter, amounting to verbal declarations, confessions and *autocritiques*, taken down and registered by the scribe. These, too, were part of life in Prison Number One, but they were insignificant when compared to the major effort in composition that the Ideological Review represented. The reviews were so time-consuming, in fact, that as of the early sixties they were demanded of prisoners only every three months.

Two consecutive study sessions were set aside for writing the personal reports and a third – extra long, this one – for their presentation to the other classmates. Illiterates were helped by the political instructor or the cell's study monitor. The full body of cellmates had to pass each report unanimously, without exception, even for the cell leader. A disapproved paper had to be rewritten until acceptable. The criticism sessions after the reading of each report quickly taught neophytes the limits of tolerance. When a report had been read and accepted, the cell leader wrote his own remarks on the margin before sending it along to the warder.

The principles of criticism and self-criticism applying to the Ideological Review are the same that compose the life of citizens everywhere in China. They boil down to four rules, categorized according to degree:

1. Ideally, confession should be spontaneous and willed; it should occur as automatically as a chemical reaction the minute a citizen commits an error or infringes a regulation.
2. If this does not happen, others should be quick to give the sinner 'patient assistance' to enable him to recognize his mistakes or crimes.
3. If patient assistance is without result, then 'criticism delivered with goodwill by well-intentioned people' should come into play. This criticism should be unaffected by personal grudges and faithfully follow the basic principle that, 'It is the mistake we are after, not the man' (*Dui ren, bu dui shi*).
4. As a last resort, when everything else fails: 'Fix' the sinner with all the severity deserved – Struggles, solitary, etc.

What I reproduce here is exactly the sort of Ideological Review I submitted during my time in Prison Number One, in the form that was expected. If the reader finds it preposterous or exaggerated, he has never been inside a Chinese prison, and he is lucky. It is utterly typical of that country, even today.

ESTIMATION, COMPARISON AND EXAMINATION OF THE PROCESS OF IDEOLOGICAL REFORM FOR THE MONTH OF
19

Name: BAO Ruo-wang
Unit: 4th Brigade, 2d Team

1. RECOGNITION AND UNDERSTANDING OF ONE'S CRIMES AND SUBMISSION TO LAW AND REGULATIONS

After due reflection, assisted by the teachings of the People's Government, I have come to realize how serious and heinous my crimes were. They have caused incalculable losses to the Government, thus impeding and sabotaging the construction of Socialism. They have also caused serious harm to the People. Lastly, they have brought sufferings upon my own family. In spite of the fact that my crimes are so grievous as to merit the supreme punishment, the Party and the People's Government in their generosity have shown me mercy. I am convinced that my sentence of 12 years at Reform Through Labour is a most lenient and just one, and I should like to take this occasion to express my gratitude to the Party and the People's Government. I know very well, however, that thanks should not be expressed by words alone; concrete actions must support the sentiments. Therefore, I am placing my activities and achievements of the past month before the People's Government so that it may judge whether I have done what was expected of me. Since we are all living and working together here I am also asking my schoolmates to judge the sincerity of my statements.

2. PRISON REGULATIONS AND DISCIPLINE

Generally speaking, I have observed all the regulations and matters pertaining to discipline. To my knowledge, I have not committed any serious mistakes over the past month. However, I did commit a number of minor errors. This is nearly as bad as serious breaches of discipline, for several small errors can develop into a major one – without even mentioning the fact that the sum of these errors could seriously compromise my reform. Among others which are too numerous to mention here, and which I hereby request my fellow schoolmates to point out to me, I have disregarded the regulations of mutual surveillance which tell us to always move about in groups of two or more. Several times I have left the cell unaccompanied, notably to go to the latrine. Further, during study sessions I have not always sat in the regulation manner, but leaned back against my bedroll. This is not only a violation of prison regulations, but also a sign that I was seeking to be more comfortable. How can one learn his lessons well if he allows thoughts of comfort to invade him? In the future I shall keep a vigilant guard against such dangers to my ideological reform. Also, I occasionally talk excessively during working hours. We have been taught by the Government that talk should be held to a minimum while working, lest it affect production. That is why we have been advised to set aside shop talk for the daily work conferences before the study sessions. What is worse, my words often have no bearing whatever on reform. This flies in the face of the principle that guides us: 'What helps our reform we should talk about abundantly and often; what has no bearing on reform should be reduced to the minimum; what is bad for reform we should not talk about at all.' Although the subjects I spoke of were not reactionary, the fact that they distracted the attention of others and thus impeded production made them harmful to reform. I have therefore decided not to talk again during working hours. Apart from this manner of talk, I have made remarks about food on several occasions. I have made reflections on the cabbage soup and the quality of the corn meal used in our wo'tous. Complaining about food is a concrete act of discontent about the treatment given us by the Government. I must remember that I will eat what is given to me and that compared to the workers and peasants of the old regime I am immensely better off. The vegetables and cereal that I eat were produced by the labour and sweat of the peasants. Complaining about my food is to treat these peasants with contempt. Being a convicted prisoner undergoing Reform Through Labour, I have no right to do this. I hereby promise to mend my ways and to be more careful in the future.

3. WORK

Being a member of the Maintenance Team, I have no work norms. I should regard this as a consideration on the part of the Government. Although I have generally done what was expected of me during the past month, there are still a few ideological problems that need smoothing out. It seems to me that I have not maintained the correct attitude toward my work, and I would like my schoolmates to help me overcome this error before it becomes more serious. Firstly, I have come to regard the maintenance shop as a kind of elite department, since we are the only ones with no norms to fulfil, but still receive the same pocket money as the more efficient workers in the factories. Pride has blinded me to the fact that we are only there to serve the machines and to make certain that the operators have on hand everything they need to fulfil or over-fulfil their norms. I must remember never to treat an operator with condescension. Secondly, I have a tendency to treat people according to my personal relations with them. I should remember that personal relationships are forbidden, and be guided by the principle: 'It is the work that counts, not the person.' Whether or not I like a person is immaterial; I should look upon him as a schoolmate working for the Government. Partiality hampers production. It has no place in reform. Thirdly, I have at times failed to place all my knowledge at the disposition of the Government. Why bother? has been my attitude. I forget that the Government, in assigning me to the maintenance shop, was displaying a high regard for my talents. The least I can do is to make full use of them.

4. RELIANCE UPON THE GOVERNMENT

I am forced to admit that when it comes to reliance upon the Government and carrying out mutual surveillance, my accomplishments are sad, indeed. It demonstrates that I am still deeply infected with bourgeois ideology. I have not been sufficiently energetic in informing superiors of what goes on around me, in the cell and at work. Being possessed by bourgeois sentimentalism, I have been reluctant to report persons who have been good to me. Further, an evil thought tells me: 'Don't report others and others won't report you.' These thoughts are wrong! We are here to reform ourselves, and there is no place for sentimentality in reformation. While the Government trusts us to the extent of allowing us to carry out this reform ourselves, how do I respond to this trust? Badly. Reporting others is a two-way help: it helps the Government to know what is going on and it helps the person involved by making it possible for him to recognize his mistakes. On the positive side of things, I may say that on several occasions I have exposed my evil and reactionary thoughts to the Government without any prodding.

5. ATTITUDE TOWARDS STUDY

This is the only category in which I have made progress. Of all the schoolmates present I am the one who received the most backward and reactionary form of education. The poison that has been fed me by the agents of imperialism and their running dogs was particularly virulent. I became an anticommunist not only for gain but through actual conviction. However, with study and the education patiently offered to me by the People's Government, plus the kind help of my schoolmates, I have come to realize how wrong I had been about the Chinese Communist Party and the People's Government. It was the rotten education I received at the hands of the imperialists that embarked me upon a career of counterrevolutionary and criminal activities against the Chinese People. It is for this reason that I am particularly attentive at study sessions. As the records will show, I have always been enthusiastic during discussions and always willing to speak out my thoughts and views on a given subject. I hope my schoolmates will continue to give me their valuable help in hastening my ideological reform.

6. OBSERVANCE OF SANITARY REGULATIONS

I have little to say in this matter, since I have done everything required by the regulations. I have volunteered for latrine duty and assumed the responsibility for keeping the workshop neat. Both latrine and shop have received red flags for tidiness during the past month.

7. PLEDGE

I solemnly pledge to overcome all my shortcomings, to consolidate all my accomplishments, to persist where I have been successful, to listen to the Government in all things and to continue my road of Reform Through Labour with all the appropriate conscientiousness. This is the only way I can expiate my crimes and win leniency from the People's Government.

The first times I encountered prisoners actually thanking the government and their jailers for the sentences they had been given, I regarded them with a mixture of astonishment and scorn. Later, as with my Ideological Reviews in Prison Number One, I went through the same sort of motions, but maintained the small mental reserve that I was only protecting my skin: That was the form expected and the way to go through a sentence without trouble. Before I left the Chinese jails, though, I was writing those phrases and believing them.

Chapter Nine

By the time I arrived there, Prison Number One had become something of a repository for the failed espionage efforts of the Taiwan Nationalists and their American friends. One of the best examples of them all was right in my cell – Li Ming, the brigade agitprop.

Agitprop is an institution of key importance in China today, both within and outside of prisons, and the person holding the job is carefully chosen for his qualifications. A good agitprop cannot function without a certain educational and intellectual level, for he must be able to quickly compose elaborate texts, even poetry at times, be familiar not only with Marxist dialectics but with all the *argot* of technique and production as well – and above all he must have the missionary ability to instill fervour and enthusiasm. Li had all these qualities and more. Born, raised and schooled in Shanghai, he had the unmistakable manner of a man of culture. He was also the most enthusiastic supporter of the government line I had met yet – and that was saying something. He was a true activist of labour, the model prisoner.

'A most productive element,' was the official description.

Even though he was my cellmate, I didn't quite trust Li. He was too exultantly inspirational, too sure he was the one the warders depended on. His outlandish efforts to stay on the side of the government, while objectively meritorious, were a pain in the ass for us jailbirds. Here in civilized Prison Number One he had loudspeakers rather than the traditional tin megaphone at his disposition, so he could always reach us with his endless chatter about production figures.

My resentment of his self-righteousness finally had to come to the surface. It happened one day when Li bustled into the maintenance shop, confident and dapper.

'Come on, Bao,' he snapped. 'The warder wants to see you.'

My hackles rose at his abrupt manner.

'Who the hell are you to tell me like that?' I snapped back. 'You're just a con like me, Li. If the warder wants me, he can send a guard.'

That was dumb. Li reported me to Warder Chao, who summoned me in for an explanation. I had been guilty of a sort of second-degree insubordination.

'It wasn't your orders I was disobeying,' I insisted. 'What I didn't like was the way he put it. He tries to place himself above the rest of the prisoners.'

'If you have any complaints,' Chao answered imperturbably, 'you come to see me about them. That's all.'

That was reasonable enough. The subject was finished, but that did nothing to exonerate Li for me. Later I told the story to my friend, old Square-Jaw Dai.

'The trouble with him,' said Dai, 'is that he's been named Activist of Reform Through Labour too often. He gets to acting as if he'd forgotten his origins. He's worse than a bourgeois. He's a Nationalist.'

Though he was technically not supposed to do it, Dai told me Li's story.

'Li was first arrested in 1955,' he said, 'and he's going to be a prisoner for a long time. A lot longer than you or I.'

At the time of his arrest Li had been working as a proofreader in a state publishing house and was caught with his hand in the till. In an effort to impress a girl he made a clumsy attempt to embezzle some money. Since the sum wasn't steep, his crime was considered relatively minor. He was sentenced to six years, to be spent in Prison Number One. All in all, a good deal.

In those days, before the existence of the plastics factory, he was assigned to the stocking-knitting division. His capacity for self-improvement was so remarkable that he was soon promoted to Activist. After three or four years of this idyllic situation, a fresh batch of prisoners arrived. Among them was a man who had been aboard a certain transport plane . . .

The story went back to 1952. An American-made B-25 from

Taiwan was shot down not far from Shanghai, after it had dropped five Nationalist agents by parachute. In line with standard espionage procedure, the men were strangers to each other before the plane ride. Each one knew the others only as a number. One by one, they were picked up in the days that followed – all but the fifth. Carefully and unobtrusively, he made his way into civilian life and eventually landed a job in a publishing house. It was Li.

His charade ended when the new prisoners arrived; one of them remembered him as a fellow passenger aboard the B-25. He asked a guard to take him to the Department of Education and Discipline. His information was so startling that he was rushed off to the Sheng Yang camp in Manchuria to talk it over with the other three ex-agents. The police saw that there was no doubt. Everything about their stories jibed perfectly. All four were hustled back to Peking where Li, unconcerned and blissful, continued his exemplary work in the stocking factory.

The police bided their time and observed their man. Cat and mouse. Except that the mouse, in this case, was blind. After a couple of months they brought Li before the warder in charge of education and discipline. It was time for the test. They gave him the chance to come out with it voluntarily.

'Your behaviour has been very good for the past few years,' the warder said. 'If you are truly reformed, if you are really as progressive as you seem, we will all be very pleased. Now, tell us, Li – is your mind completely at ease about your past crimes? Do you have anything else you'd like to confess?'

He wasn't smart enough to grab at the suggestion immediately. He had become overconfident. No, he had nothing more to confess.

'You'd better go and think it over,' the warder said.

It was grimmer the next day. Now the warder had an old newspaper lying open on his desk. There was a big headline:

FOUR PARACHUTE SPIES CAUGHT IN CHEKIANG

Li stood there, waiting.

'There's a movie playing in town based on this incident,' the warder said. 'I saw it the other day, and I just wanted to compare it with what the newspapers said. You recall the case, don't you, Li?'

'Well, I remember vaguely,' he tried, 'but not much.'

'It seems that one of them escaped.'

'Well, it's a big country, and Chiang's spies are cunning.'

Disgusted, the warder stopped the game. He held up a photograph of Li's four companions in the B-25.

'Maybe you'll recognize this, then.'

Li knew it was finished. The warder came out with a harsh little object lesson.

'You know, Li, you should have told us months ago. The government has been trying for years now to help you. If you had told us even five minutes ago, we would have taken your confession into consideration and recommended leniency. Why do you think I was giving you all those hints? You don't have that chance anymore, Li.'

He summoned two large policemen, who burst into the office in the standard dramatic style, handcuffed him and brought him away to Grass Mist Lane. Three months later he was back in Prison Number One with a life sentence. And a speech from the warder.

'We have taken into consideration your past behaviour. Because of your good work record, we have granted leniency. Usually spies like you go immediately to death, Li. So you see how fair we have been with you. Don't betray this trust. Be thankful to the government.'

In Li I knew I had met one prisoner who truly was grateful for his life sentence. Now it was clear how he could sound so genuine during the Examination of Conscience sessions.

And then there were the tattooed men from the Korean War. They were a strange sight. I came across them shortly after my arrival in Prison Number One, on one of my visits to the bath house over by the machine-tool factory. There were four heated pools in the bathing area, each good for forty people, and the water was uniformly five feet deep. We used to bathe there once a week, by brigades. Although there were 240 of us in each shift, we were allowed to spend half an hour there, compared to the ten minutes allotted us while in the Transit Centre.

In the shift that was climbing out of the pools as we arrived I caught sight of several men in their thirties heavily tattooed on their arms and chests. It was surprising – that sort of thing was supposed to have disappeared with the corrupt old regime. Even in old China tattoos were reserved almost exclusively for hooligans and roughnecks. As I came closer, I noticed that all the tattoos echoed the same motif – thick forests of heavily leafed apple trees and pine.

'What's that all about?' I whispered to little Hu.

'Shh,' he answered. 'I'll tell you about it back in the cell.'

It was quite a tale. These men were among the Chinese 'volunteers' captured by the Americans during the Korean War. While they were in the POW camps, American and Nationalist intelligence had tattooed incendiary slogans on their bodies. Underneath those trees – which had been added later as camouflage – there were inscriptions in bold Chinese characters. 'Down With Communism' and 'Against Russia' were two of the most common.

That was clear enough – a typically devilish trick of the imperialists. But then why were they here in prison? After all, they were doubly heroic – not only had they fought the war, but they had undergone this cruel treatment as well. Hu dispelled my illusions: They were in for treason, and they all had life sentences. Lucky at that, too.

They were a part of the small number of Chinese soldiers who had been 'turned around' by American and Nationalist intelligence officers at Koje, the South Korean prisoner-of-war island. To make the ruse more effective, the agents instructed them to act as 'progressively' as possible in their cells. Many of them became first-rank leaders among the Chinese POWs. In a fictitious act of revenge, Nationalist guards stripped them in front of their comrades and tattooed the stigmatizing slogans on their arms and chests. This, of course, only caused them to act more progressively than ever, chanting patriotic songs, shaking their fists and even spitting on guards and prison personnel. For their intransigence they were rounded up one by one and marched off to solitary.

Naturally, the solitary never existed. The tatooed soldiers

were hustled off at night and flown to Japan for specialized espionage training, notably for transmitting information back to Taiwan. The Americans didn't forget to keep them undernourished, dirty and out of the sun during the training period. It was a hard way for them to undergo their VIP treatment, but at all costs they had to maintain the illusion that they had been roughing it in solitary.

'That's all right,' one of them told me later. 'The Americans were paying us well for it.'

As the war drew to a close they continued their model behaviour in the POW camp. When the armistice was signed, an international control commission of the UN screened all the prisoners to ensure that no one would be forced against his will to return to China or, on the contrary, to defect. At these sessions it was always the tattooed men who screamed the loudest about the debasing humiliation they had undergone at the hands of their captors. The Indians who presided over the commission were shocked and chagrined. They arranged for new artists to come in and tattoo lush forests over the compromising declarations. The prisoners were received like heroes back in their army units.

But the Chinese weren't quite as naïve as the intelligence types had assumed. The poor Americans never seem to realize the extent to which the Chinese are careful and suspicious. They have, without question, the finest counterespionage system in the world: No one gets away with anything for long in China. (Ironically enough, these very qualities made their external espionage system rather mediocre. Too mistrustful to put much faith in foreign agents and too conspicuous in other lands because of their Oriental features, they have to rely largely on the resident Chinese minorities—a generally unsatisfactory solution.)

The political police and military intelligence began a systematic questioning of the newly returned heroes, keeping them rigorously separated to prevent comparison of stories. Gradually the tiny discrepancies began to create a pattern. The entire ring was rounded up within less than a month. Without the doubtful benefit of a sojourn in Grass Mist Lane they were summarily court-martialled, kicked out of the army and sent over to the civilian side of the law to fulfil their life-long debts in Clear Stream. Considering everything, they were lucky not to have been shot. The propaganda material that developed from their stories made them known throughout China. They were our very own celebrities. In the camps I was to meet a few others.

In the beginning of November our team lived through a painful experience – the announcement of the amnesties. It was on the occasion of the tenth anniversary that Prison Director Hsing announced to us that a special amnesty would be declared to commemorate the founding of the republic.* Only those prisoners who had served two-thirds of their sentences and who had earned exceptional merits would be considered. Every cell was directed to discuss the campaign that evening, but none of us could talk with much enthusiasm since most of us were only beginning our terms and had no hope whatsoever

*To celebrate the tenth anniversary of the founding of the People's Republic of China, Mao Tse-tung wrote a letter to the Standing Committee of the National People's Congress to suggest on behalf of the Central Committee that a *special amnesty* be declared, applying to the following categories of convicted criminals under detention:

(a) War criminals of the Chiang Kai-shek clique and the puppet Manchukuo regime, after ten years of imprisonment.

(b) Counterrevolutionaries condemned to less than five years if half of their prison term has been fulfilled, and those condemned to more than five years if two-thirds of their prison term has been fulfilled.

(c) Common law criminals who have fulfilled one-third or half of their sentences as in the conditions above.

(d) Criminals condemned to capital punishment with two years' suspension (si huan), whose sentences may be changed to life or more than fifteen years' imprisonment.

(e) Criminals condemned to life; after seven years' imprisonment their terms may be changed to imprisonment for not less than ten years.

A mandatory condition for applying these remissions was that the prisoner must have truly reformed himself from an evil past to a virtuous present.

The amnesty was passed by the Chinese National People's Congress on 17 September 1959.

By the end of 1959 a total of 12,082 persons were amnestied. Of these, 2,424 were counterrevolutionaries and 9,269 ordinary criminals. The remaining 389 were lifers and those under suspended death sentences.

of benefiting from the government's generosity. We passed the word listlessly around the cell, mouthing the usual phrases a warder expects to see in a dossier. The only exception was little Hu. Poor Hu had great expectations. He got it into his young head that he was going to make it.

'I was thrilled when I heard the news,' he said when his turn came. 'I'm going to make the grade. I know I will. I've been here for ten years now. I was sentenced to fifteen and got three off for good behaviour, so I have only two more to go. In the past ten years I've been named Activist of Reform Through Labour three times. I've won dozens of special prizes. I've never committed any serious sins – you can ask Warder Chao. Now I'm on the selection committee of Activists. I think the government will show me leniency. I'm sure they'll let me become a free worker.'

'That's not for you to say,' growled Square-Jaw Dai, who was almost old enough to be his father. 'Don't be too proud.'

In the first week of November the Peking Bureau of Public Security announced that fifty-four prisoners from Ching Ho were eligible for the amnesty. On a windy morning the next day we marched out into the courtyard to go through the ceremony. Hu was glowing with excitement. Director Hsing and his staff gathered before us on the plank stage.

'Today is a day for great celebration,' he cried out. 'You are going to know which of you have made the grade. A member of the Peking Bureau of Public Security will now read the names.'

The visiting official began with the stocking factory, then the mechanical groups, the Translation Brigade and finally came to us in Plastics. Hu's name never came up.

We had to stay around a few extra minutes to hear another set of names – the lifers who had been reduced to shorter terms and the suspended death sentences that had been reduced to life. As we returned to the cell Hu was in tears – a rare enough occurrence for prisoners anywhere, but especially for the normally stoic Chinese. He was deeply disappointed and couldn't hide it. Warder Chao, who had known about his expectations, came into the cell with a lesson already prepared.

'What's the matter, little Hu?' he asked with fatherly humour.

165

'Feeling bitter? Having tantrums again? Acting like a child? Hmm?'

'I've always been good, Warder Chao,' Hu protested through his tears. 'Why didn't I get chosen?'

That sort of question was made to order for Chao. He was, as they say, like a fish in water.

'You seem to be forgetting, little Hu, that you have no right to question the decisions of the state. The government and the party know much better than you do. If I were you, I'd consider this a test the state has offered you. I think you're failing that test, Hu. The moment the government refuses you anything you start complaining. And you call yourself reformed! Stop your bawling and be realistic. Who knows? Maybe next March when the Activist elections come around the state might make you a present. But what you have to think about right now is making a present to the state!'

Hu blew his nose, shut up and went back to work. As a sad irony would have it, his mother died three months later and Warder Chao made an extraordinary gesture – he wangled a three-day pass for Hu to attend the funeral. As far as any of my fellow prisoners could remember, it was the first time ever that such a special *ad hoc* leniency had been granted.

Around that time I discovered to my surprise that I was sick. I couldn't know it then, but my illness was going to separate me from the comfort of Prison Number One and set me on the harsh road to the camps. My illness came and went in waves, and the most uncharacteristic symptom for me was that it often cut my appetite. The first signs that something was wrong came after a minor incident in the machine shop. I was working on a piece of metal and my drill broke. One of my comrades felt impelled to show revolutionary zeal.

'You must be more careful, Bao,' he admonished me.

As luck would have it Li the agitprop was there. He lost no time in scolding me.

'Hell, Li,' I said impatiently, 'accidents happen.'

'Yes, but you must remember that was the people's property.'

166

'That damn drill wasn't going to last long anyway, Li. You know that.'

Li reported my attitude to Warder Chao, and the two of them returned to the machine shop. Chao wanted to know why I stubbornly refused to acknowledge my mistake. It was getting ridiculous.

'It's not an ideological mistake to break a drill,' I protested. But Chao was having none of that.

'Bao, if you only concentrated a little more on your work the drill wouldn't have snapped. It snapped because it wasn't sharpened properly. Let that be a lesson to you.'

He left without further word. That night I couldn't eat my supper, and since everything abnormal has to be reported to the warder, Chao heard about it. At half past nine he called me to his cell.

'Sit down. What's wrong with you?'

'Nothing.'

'Why didn't you eat your supper?'

'I wasn't hungry. I don't feel well.'

'Was it because I scolded you today?'

'No.'

'Don't let criticism spoil your appetite, Bao. Without criticism there can be no progress. I want you to improve yourself. If you have no appetite, you'd better go see the doctor, because if you can't eat, you can't work. I suggest two things. If you didn't eat because I scolded you, then you have the wrong attitude and you must change it. If it is because you are sick then you have to go see the doctor. Now go to bed.'

The next morning I reported to the infirmary and told them I had no appetite. The doctor gave me some bran pills to ease my digestion. I returned to work, but I never felt quite right again. A recurring fever nagged at me and I became a regular visitor to the infirmary for their regular panacea of aspirin.

One day in the last week of February 1960, I caused a stupid workshop incident that brought me dangerously close to real trouble. I was tempering a piece of steel, a routine job that involved bathing the red-hot object first in water and then, after it had cooled somewhat, in oil. With absentminded casualness

I tossed the glowing steel directly into the oil bin over by the wall. A fiery splash arose and burning oil spread out over the wall, billowing up clouds of blue smoke. Water is not supposed to be effective against that sort of fire, but I chucked a whole bucketful against the wall and the fire went out, probably smothered as much as anything else. Still I had made a hell of a mess. The worst was that Warder Chao was away that day and his replacement was a zealot who had no sympathy for us. He accused me of attempting to sabotage the factory! That was a terrible charge. Deliberate sabotage can mean a death sentence. He sent me back to the cell to await the government's decision.

Within half an hour I was hearing the dramatized details of my crime over the loudspeaker system. Nothing like a fair trial, I thought. It looked as if they wanted to make an example of me. I was scared as hell and didn't know what to do. It was my friend Dai – old Square-Jaw Dai – who saved me. He had invented some excuse to leave his work for a few moments and came racing back to the cell with some urgent advice.

'Goddammit, Bao,' he said breathlessly, 'get going right now and write them out a confession. The quicker the better. Tell them you weren't careful enough and you overlooked the fact that the oil bath is right under those wooden rafters. Tell them you recognize how serious your actions were, and all the harm they could have caused. Get on it right now.'

Dai was a great man. He had already been in Prison Number One seven years, and there wasn't much he didn't know. I wrote the confession. I pleaded guilty and asked the government to punish me with all the harshness deserved. I signed it and trotted off to the warder's office.

'It's good that you realize your mistakes,' he said gruffly, 'but it doesn't alter the fact that you committed a serious error that could have caused several deaths. We'll take your confession and show it to our superiors. They are the ones who will decide what to do with you.'

For the next two and a half weeks I lived in nervous dread. Not a word came back from that mysterious hierarchy that was judging my confession. Through it all, Dai kept telling me not to worry. What bothered me, though, was that the Meetings of

Rewards and Punishments came only every six months, and the last one had only recently passed. Did this mean I would have to wait more than five more months before my case would be resolved? So I fretted as Dai remained calm. Finally Warder Chao called me to his office one evening. He seemed to be in an expansive mood, almost joking.

'Well, well, well,' he said, 'so it's our foreign prisoner. The moment I turn my back you get into trouble – and you had been making such good progress. I know you're sorry about what happened, Bao, but the best way to show your regret is to avoid mistakes in the first place. It's too late for that now, so this thing has to take its course. Tonight I'll be making an announcement about your case. That's all for now.'

I walked back to the cell hoping that maybe things would work out, after all. Warder Chao's good humour had been a good sign. That evening he appeared in the hallway as soon as Li had distributed the flags for that day's production.

'I know you're all tired,' he said calmly, 'so I'll make this short. Several things have happened in my absence. I'll take the most serious first. Your schoolmate Bao, here, sometimes forgets where he is. He very nearly caused a serious incident, but thanks to the vigilance of the others, it didn't happen. Now I have to decide what to do with him. I have read his confession and passed it on to the government. It's not bad. At least he recognizes he was wrong in his actions. So this time we'll let him go.'

I felt a surge of genuine gratitude.

'In confessing as he did he has made an example of himself that the rest of you can follow. But you all have to remember one thing: The leniency of the government is not without limits.'

'I told you so,' Dai said later, with enjoyment. 'The only way to survive in jail is to write a confession right away and make your sins look as black as possible. Always accuse yourself harshly – exaggerate, even. But don't ever hint that the prison authorities or the government share any of the responsibility.'

A few weeks later I had a chance to put his advice to the test, but I bungled it. Detailed to install a windowpane, I broke the new one I was trying to put in. The property involved was so negligible that I dashed off only a cursory confession for Chao.

'Today,' I wrote, 'I broke a windowpane in a moment of inattention. The pane was very thin and I used too much force. I made a great mistake. The pane belongs to the people. Prisoners are supposed to be producing goods for the people and not destroying their property. I demand that the government punish me as it sees fit.'

Warder Chao called me in. He was disgruntled.

'This confession is not satisfactory. Your emphasis is not correct. You are not to be blamed that the pane was too thin. The people who made the pane should be punished for that, not you. And the prison shouldn't buy thin panes. You say you used force. Well, you have to use some force with your work. But you admitted you weren't paying attention to your work. Why weren't you paying attention, Bao? Because you resent the government? Not paying attention to your work means you resent the government. Resenting the government, you destroyed the pane. I want you to go back and write a new confession. Bring it in to me tomorrow.'

Chastised, I wandered back to the cell and consulted with Dai again. After about ten minutes with him I took up the pen and tried again.

'I hereby confess,' the new confession began, 'that on 14 March 1960, I committed sabotage. While undergoing Reform Through Labour I broke a windowpane. I was thinking of other things. My mind was not on my work.'

I continued in the same vein for two pages and ended with a firm request for punishment. Chao did a double take when he saw that first line.

'Who wrote this?'

'I did.'

'Who told you to write it like this?'

'You did, warder. I thought that if I had the courage to break a window, I might as well have the courage to admit it.'

Chao fixed me with a lengthy gaze, searching for any sign of humour or sarcasm.

'All right,' he said at last. 'The case is closed. But I'm going to hold onto this so that I can show it to you in the future if you slip again. I'm glad to see you're improving.'

'You've saved my skin again, old man,' I told Dai when I got back to the cell.

He was grinning.

'I should have learned something from all these years, no?'

As we drew into the warm spring months I began feeling progressively weaker and my bouts of fever became more and more frequent. Everything caught up with me one afternoon as I was carrying a heavy steel chuck over to a lathe – I lost my grip and the damn thing fell on my toe. Immediately, the pain told me it was broken and that I would have to go to the hospital. Bedroll under one arm, I hobbled across the courtyard, accompanied by a solicitous Warder Chao.

'This is a lousy epilogue to the Great Leap Forward,' I muttered. I was genuinely upset at having made myself unproductive.

'Don't worry,' Chao assured me. 'They won't keep you in there longer than they have to. You might as well get a good rest now that you'll be having the time.'

An orderly showed me to a spacious and neat room with four plank beds covered with straw mats. I dropped my bedroll and sat down. Presently a nurse wearing a white surgical mask – she probably had a cold and wished to avoid spreading microbes – came hurrying in and told me to hand over the bedroll. It was too dirty for her hospital. I was happy to comply, and for the first time since my arrest I had the luxury of lying between real sheets.

Throughout my hospitalization my temperature remained high, despite the normal healing process of my broken toe. Clearly, something else was wrong. Eventually Dr Tan, the head physician, diagnosed tuberculosis. Dr Tan was an interesting case. A prisoner himself, he came to Clear Stream after a futile attempt to escape to Hong Kong.

Before the Liberation he had been an extremely successful and sought-after private practitioner among Peking's foreign colony. Although 100 per cent Chinese, he had been schooled first by French Jesuits and then learned medicine in Aurora University in Shanghai. I enjoyed speaking French with him (technically forbidden, but Prison Number One was a rather relaxed place) and I soon learned his story. The big escape plot, it turned out, had been jointly hatched between him and a Western diplomat. On a seemingly innocent pretext – an infection or something of the sort – the diplomat officially requested permission for Tan to accompany him and watch his health until Canton, the last big city before the Hong Kong frontier. There they figured to find some professionals who could get him across the border for a price. Unhappily for Tan, the police had somehow got word of the stunt; they arrested him in his hotel room in Canton. When the diplomat called for him later in the evening, he encountered one of those marvellous Kafka-Orwell situations.

Dr Tan? There was never any Dr Tan registered here, sir. Surely you must be mistaken. Would you like to see the register?

Doc Tan* got twenty years. He was a funny type, one of the few who seemed totally unaffected by the pressures of the official indoctrination. An unreconstructed reactionary, he could always be counted on to greet the latest loudspeaker announcements and production figures with a snide rejoinder, as if he were dialoguing with those disembodied voices. Of course he was a regular target for denunciations and Struggles, but no one doubted his medical value. It was always pulling him out of rough moments. It was common for the police to come for him when some VIP was especially sick and Tan's colleagues on the outside wanted a confirming opinion. The regime considered him irrecuperable, but useful.

When he told me the X-rays showed unmistakable signs of TB, my first reactions were in French. I had to know how serious it was.

'*Je suis foutu?*' I asked him.

* Dr Tan, upon learning that his request to work in an urban people's commune in Peking (so as to be near to his family) had been turned down and that he will have to continue to stay and work in prison after having served his sentence, committed suicide by hanging.

'On te soignera,' he promised. We'll take care of you. It was my great fortune to be in Prison Number One when the TB was discovered, because here at least they had some of the proper medicaments. I began a regular rimifon treatment and was transferred to the larger TB ward – fourteen of us, all in big, individual beds.

I stayed put in that ward for the next two months. It was during the easy calm of this period that I met and became friends with Koo, a man with whom I would later share some of my worst moments in the camps. In fact he saved my life once, quite literally, by nursing me back to health during the great famine period in 1961. Since he was almost six feet, we called him Longman Koo. Koo was a great man.

The easy life changed on 13 June. We were sitting out in the sunny courtyard when the hospital administrator appeared with two warders and two anonymous officials in faded but immaculate green army jackets. They spoke in low tones and took notes. Sure as hell, something was up.

'We're in for a move,' someone said. 'Every time they look us over that way, it means a transfer.'

How right he was. Four days later a trusty came by to pass out our savings books and told us to check that the amounts inside were correct. Even in the hospital we automatically earned our pocket money of five yuan a month. I briefly thought that maybe we were only going back to our cells; but, even helped along by wishful thinking, that didn't seem realistic. When I saw that the stretcher cases were getting their books, too, I knew it meant we were leaving. The next day we were sent back to our cells to clear out our personal gear.

I was eating my last lunch in Prison Number One when Square-Jaw Dai came over to say good-bye.

'They're transferring you out,' he told me needlessly, but it was a way to break the ice. 'I guess it's so long, Bao.'

I was amazed and touched by what happened next. Dai, the tough old veteran, insisted on giving me a little send-off speech. He was embarrassed, but he went through it, sentiment and all. Apparently he had decided he was my big brother.

'I want to thank you for all the nice things you've done for me, Bao. Just remember that wherever they send you, the thing isn't to be smart or progressive or even have money. What counts is that people like you. There are a lot of engineers hauling buckets of shit in the camps. But if you're pleasant and people like you, they'll help you out. It's the only way to get by in the camps. Remember that.'

He shook my hand and walked quickly away, solid in his blue overalls and wide leather belt. He turned around and waved once. I felt terrible. Later in the camps an ex-Red Army officer, a good Communist cadre who got denounced, told me that the one thing the Communists feared most was human sentiment between individuals. It was the one thing they could never entirely control, and it could make for dangerously conflicting loyalties.

Hsu, the warder in charge of education and discipline, gave us the official announcement. Considering we were all sick, he said, the government had decided to send us to a place more appropriate for recovery. What we needed was lots of fresh air, sun and fresh food. We were being sent to Ching Ho Camp.

It was exciting news. We had all heard about Ching Ho. The work was easy and there was plenty to eat, rumour had it. We were really touched.

Ching Ho: Clear Stream. We would soon be bathing in its pure waters to emerge as better men. Hsu sent us back inside the hospital with instructions to hold a discussion session on the government's consideration to us. The day dragged into night and we weren't called back until 11 p.m. Even this late, the temperature was still hovering near 100°. Guards marched us across the floodlit compound to a courtyard next to the boys' reformatory, where a dozen buses were waiting. All but one of them were full. We invalids piled aboard the empty one. Silence. No smoking. A warder came inside and stood behind the driver to give us our last instructions. Behave normally on the train. Heads should not repeat not be bowed down. If anyone has to go to the latrine, signal to the guard – the fist with the thumb sticking out. Smoking and talking will be permitted. No funny stuff. The guards have orders to shoot.

Our convoy got going at last, and it was around 3 a.m. when we trundled through the lifeless city to the Yong Ding Men railroad station.

There was pandemonium on the station platform. Thousands of prisoners, of all ages and sizes, many on crutches and some blind, scrambled for position around the water tap. The rows of Sepos stood silent and impassive. Gradually, roll calls got us into proper order and we were ready to board when the train drew in. They were beautifully painted green coaches, new and shiny. We were going to the camp in style.

When our train finally left Peking, it was 4.30 a.m. and the sun was already beginning to rise. It was the morning of 18 June 1960. In the dim early light we rolled for two hours non-stop until we came to Tientsin, where there was a fifteen-minute layover to let some other trains pass. On the move again, now in full sunlight, we rushed by great expanses of carefully tended fields.

When we ground to a stop for the last time our car was directly opposite a huge sign whose bold red characters read:

FORBIDDEN ZONE

This was Chadian railroad station. We clambered down to the wooden platform. Facing us was another sign, CHING HO STATE-OPERATED FARM. On both sides of the sign were large, symmetrical piles of dried sweet potato slices. I thought they were meant for feeding pigs. I was wrong.

Chapter Ten

Longman Koo and I stood in the centre of a swarming crowd of nearly two thousand prisoners, waiting for someone to tell us what to do. As soon as we had stepped down from the train, we transferees had been herded down an embankment to a vast, sunken parade ground that might have been an old rice paddy. The sun was already unpleasantly hot – by midday the temperature would be in the nineties – and a fine, greyish dust hung in the air and came grittily into the mouth and nose. So far, the famous Ching Ho farm wasn't measuring up to those pretty illusions we had developed.

At length a warder in shorts and a straw hat clambered onto a table brought out from the station. Since we had arrived in the middle of the wheat harvest, he said, and since it was a difficult year for the crops, there would be no vehicles for us. All but the crippled and amputated would have to walk to the camp – twenty-two and a half kilometres. Perfect, I thought. Everyone wants to do long marches. The warder told us to bow our heads when we passed through civilian villages and to keep our eyes from straying right or left.

We pushed off with the first group, three by three. There must have been a thousand of us. For the first hour we couldn't see much because we were paralleling an embankment that blocked the view, but we finally branched off onto one of the raised roads. It was from there that we got our first good look at the effects of the big drought we had been hearing of. Close up, the fields didn't look as lush and green as they had appeared from the train early that morning. We passed some vineyards with yellow, curling leaves before we came upon the main plantings of corn, in huge fields that stretched away to the horizon. The stalks were still greenish, but the leaves were turning brown,

The crop was stunted and sterile. The famine of 1961 was being prepared.

The sun grew higher and hotter. I balanced my handkerchief on my head to fend off its rays, but the heat was still inhuman. Not a bird, not even an insect, came into view. It was too hot and dry for nature to move. In the distance there was a shady line of trees and some telephone poles. Every now and then a mounted guard would appear silhouetted on one of the roads. Even in times of starvation, their horses were well fed. The guards had to be able to move quickly. Security always comes first.

Shortly before noon we came to the first village. These were people who had volunteered to be resettled and create new agricultural units. Like all communes in China and like the state farms in the Soviet Union, the village announced itself with a garish ceremonial entrance, made of a pair of red brick columns with a plywood billboard between. 'Ching Ho State Farm', it read. On either side of the columns were signs with white characters on a red background. 'Work without laying down conditions', the one at left read. 'Without expecting reward', read the other. Inside the village little supplementary signs urged 'Every effort for agriculture' and 'Everything for a good harvest'.

Kids grouped together and watched us silently. Once I saw an old man stride over and shoo a bunch of them inside. I had a strange feeling of shame. We were an army of outcasts. We refilled our water bottles at the village pump and pushed on. At 3.00 p.m. we passed through another village, but we still had no food. The crops here were fruit and wheat, but it all looked as moribund as the corn we had passed earlier. We plodded on in a stupor of heat and exhaustion. The sun looked down blankly and it shimmered up in reflection from the skimpy yellow wheat. Just to breathe was like fire.

At 4.30 or so, we finally caught sight of our camp in the distance. From our vantage point it appeared only as dull red blotches of colour, dominated by a tall thin construction that looked for all the world like a church steeple. That, I knew, wasn't possible. As we drew nearer I saw that it was the water

177

tower, made of red brick like everything else. The overall effect of our camp was that of a nineteenth-century factory or mill. The rectangular compound was delineated by a high brick wall topped by electrified wire, and the wall itself was surrounded by a moat. At each corner was a watch-tower and in the centre, under the inevitable billboard, the bridge and the main gate.

'Let us make a double harvest,' the billboard proposed. 'One of labour and one of ideological reform.'

We trooped in over the bridge and pulled up beside the high wall of a still-unfinished auditorium whose roof bore a huge red star. Over on the left three more slogans were written down the flanks of the water tower: 'Long live the General Line', 'Long live the People's Communes' and 'Long live the Great Leap Forward'. Surrounding us entirely, and giving the place a stockade effect, were rows of single-storey brick hooches with domed roofs, backed up against the walls. There were our barracks, each one to hold twenty men.

The guards told us we could sit down and take it easy until supper came. Longman Koo and I went around to inspect our new home. It was a mess. The camp was brand new – we were among its first occupants – but nothing had been organized yet, and the buildings were only rough-finished. Obviously, we would have to put it all into shape.

'Hey, look at this.'

It was one of our schoolmates from the hospital, standing over by the kitchen. He had found the agitprop's blackboard. At the bottom he had chalked in a disconcerting message:

'In view of this year's bad crops it has been necessary to reduce the amount of food allocated to the kitchen. Until further notice prisoners' bread will consist of millet meal mixed with corn meal and dried sweet potatoes.'

So those piles out by the railroad station weren't for pigs, after all . . .

At suppertime we received two ladles apiece of a vegetable soup thickened with flour – a sort of vegetable porridge – and five small loaves of millet-corn-sweet-potato bread. It was sticky and glutinous and sweet.

'Do they expect us to work on that?' Koo wondered.

'Maybe they'll give us more tomorrow,' I said, but I didn't believe it very much.

How can I describe the ten days that followed? They were certainly among the most harrowing of my life, and I remember them like some sort of special trial or initiation I had to undergo to prove something. What that something would be I don't know, but it has to do with brute survival.

We didn't realize it then, but our trainload had obviously been rushed down to Ching Ho to help salvage the disastrous harvest. Labour and machines were in short order and it was imperative to get as much as possible from the blighted crops. Our work in the wheat fields lasted only ten days, but they were hellish. Awakened every morning at four by the clanging of a hammer against a section of rail – that universal labour camp alarm clock – we washed and gobbled breakfast as ludicrously incongruous Chinese schmaltz blared out over the loudspeaker system. We were in the fields by five, where a cross-eyed agricultural technician and several warders were awaiting us. They passed out stubby sickles from the equipment cart, and we set to cutting the stalks in regulation style – no sitting or squatting, always bent over at the waist. Three stalks at a time and eighteen stalks to a bundle, to be tied neatly. Of course we had norms, but no one, not even the former peasants, managed to live up to them the first day. At water break time we got the lukewarm, greenish stuff the kitchen had used for cooking vegetables – it might contain some nourishment, was the reasoning, but we all longed for clear, cold water. Lunch was sweet bread and soup and it was followed, from 12 to 3 p.m., by an obligatory nap. We had to keep our eyes closed, even if the sun and the ants made it impossible to sleep. A regulation is a regulation.

The days succeeded each other in dreary repetition of heat, aching muscles and hunger. Koo and I were in relatively good shape, but the weak prisoners only grew weaker. By the fifth day we noticed a pile of rough coffins over on one of the raised roadways, and by the tenth day one of our own cellmates was in one. God knows how many died throughout the camp.

Toward the middle of the harvest, when I was beginning to wonder seriously if I would make it, Koo came up with a

179

surprise that completely changed my morale. I was flailing away at the wheat, unconscious of everything else, when he appeared at my side, profiting from the monetary absence of guards. Longman bent low as if he, too, were sickling and pulled an object from under his shirt. He had a little watermelon in his hand!

'Where in hell did you get that, old Koo?'

He gave a little uncommunicative grunt and wonked the melon in half with his sickle.

'Don't ask questions,' he said, his face already into the cool, red meat. We buried what was left of the rinds.

'Feel better, old Bao?'

'Yeah.'

'You see? We'll always find something.'

Longman was a good scavenger and one of the most loyal friends I ever had. Quite literally, I wouldn't have survived the camps without him.

On the morning of July first – the anniversary of the founding of the Chinese Communist Party – Koo and I and some thirty others were called out of the assembly lineup. The others went off to work and we sat around smoking until the warder appeared. He told us to get our things ready. He had an announcement for us, and it began with that ill-omened phrase:

'The government is concerned with your welfare. Your state of health doesn't permit you to stay on and work in this farm. We are going to send you to a farm where there are better facilities to treat the sick and where the rations are better.'

Longman and I looked at each other, not sure what to believe. When we walked out over the bridge at 7 a.m. our eyes were open and we were ready for anything. Our destination wasn't far. We could walk there in a few hours. The place we were going to was called Northern Precious Village – Bei Yuan Bao Tsun. It had, we learned later, the reputation of being a death camp. But this time, as luck had it, Longman and I would be there only for transit.

We walked in quite good spirits – after all, we were avoiding the usual morning's hard labour – the few miles separating us from the Precious Village. The first thing that struck us when we arrived was that there were no walls or guard towers but simply a cluster of one-storey red brick buildings and a big beaten-earth yard, a rough basketball court and, of course, more slogans: 'Everyone Must Take Part In The Technological Revolution' and 'Trying Means Production'. But these buildings were not for us. We continued past them until we came upon a gate at the northern end of the village. This was more like it, a real prison compound. The open buildings we had passed at the front had been for the free workers and their families.

Our own compound was a distressing sight. Strewn like flotsam on a beach were little groups of old men – scarcely a young person in sight – listlessly going through their various motions of existing. Many of them were slapping flies with paper swatters and carefully placing them in bottles. Flies were useful. There was a nationwide campaign on for the examination of flies, and every prisoner not otherwise engaged had a quota of fifty a day. Extra flies could be saved and used to barter for cigarettes. Some of the men were so weak that they were reduced to crawling; some sat in the shade staring at nothing; some were blind. It looked like something Dante might have imagined.

Eventually a warder came from one of the buildings to take us in charge, and even he was a sorry sight. He had only one arm, his clothes were little better than rags, and he looked dirty and unkempt, like a poor peasant. He regarded us unenthusiastically and led us into a long dirt-floored room, filled with magazines and newspapers and a few books – the library.

'My name is Wang,' he said, 'and I'm one of the brigade leaders. You have been sent here to join the Brigade for the Old, Crippled and Weak, but that doesn't mean you won't work. Those of you who are able will be expected to work.'

He filled us in on our housing, work norms and meals, then led us to a row of temporary sheds made of bamboo matting, where we dropped our bedrolls. The sheds weren't much, but at least they kept the sun away. We went to the kitchen for lunch: one bowl of vegetable soup and a thin piece of bread resembling a chocolate bar, in six sections. The bread was made from black beans and was so soggy that we spooned it up rather than holding it in our fingers. A thin old man in dirty white pants shuffled up curiously to look us over. He was heavily sunburned but skeletal, and when we spoke he showed large, yellow teeth.

'You guys are getting first-class rations!' he exclaimed in surprise.

I was irritated by his intrusion and tried to shoo him away but Koo, who was smarter, smiled and invited him to sit down with us.

'How about a cigarette, classmate?' The old man accepted happily.

'Give him a cigarette, old Bao.' That was one of Longman's tricks. He didn't smoke, so when he wanted to offer one, he asked me.

'How long have you been here?'

'Six months,' the old man answered. 'I'm sick.'

'When you getting out?'

'Never, man. It's one-way traffic here.'

Longman raised an eyebrow, but the old man continued emotionlessly.

'This is where they send expendable people, the ones who are useless in the other camps. Washouts. There's no medical treatment, so not many of us can get better.'

He dragged on the cigarette with pleasure, happy to enjoy the moment.

'But apart from the food, things aren't too bad,' he went on. 'We don't work much. As a matter of fact, a lot of us don't work at all. We can visit each other and take it easy, until . . . Well, you know.'

He smiled and made a vague gesture with his arm.

'You guys are lucky to be eating so well. They must have some special reason for keeping your strength up. I guess they'll put you to work.'

The old man was right. We had been brought to the death camp because most of its inhabitants couldn't work. There were some jobs that had to be done, one way or another.

The old-timer's prediction was borne out later that afternoon, when another brigade chief, a man named Fong, assigned us to carrying earth in the brick-making compound. That night in the hooch we held an informal meeting to choose who would dig and who would carry the baskets of soil. Ten of the weakest were elected as diggers and the rest of us to carry the fifty-pound baskets, two by two. We weren't awakened the next morning until 6 a.m.

'Ah, the late risers!' exclaimed the kitchen worker when we went in for our soup and bread. We set to our job. The two in each team had to carry their basket only a hundred or so yards, and at first it seemed to be easy work. No one was worrying about norms. The baskets grew heavier as the day wore on. At one point I told my partner to take a break and went to the pump to wet the bit of rag I was using as a shoulder pad. A trusty was leaning against the wall indolently.

'May I use the pump to wet my rag?' I asked. I was playing it safe. It's better to ask before you act in prisons.

'You know how it works,' he said with a shrug. 'You want me to pump it for you or something?'

'I just didn't want to break any rules.'

'You ain't breaking any rules. If you were, I'd tell you.'

It was a strange place, this Northern Precious Village. There was scarcely any discipline, no norms and hardly any guards. They weren't needed. Most of the prisoners were either blind or crippled or too weak to run. And we, the strong ones, weren't going to change our easy work for the harvesting we had just gone through. So everything was in order. Four days after we arrived, Warder 'One-arm' called me to his office.

'Tell me, Bao, what did you do before your arrest?'

'I was a translator for embassies, Warder.'

'A stinking intellectual, huh? I thought so. And of course you're a counterrevolutionary, too? And you're in for a long time?'

'Twelve years, Warder.'

'You got off lightly. We have a name for deformed people like you – people whose brains are worse than cesspools. By the time we're through with you, you'll be a new man, Bao. With a new and clean brain. But to remould yourself you have to work with determination. We can only do half the job – the other half is up to you. To carry out the task the government has given me, I have decided to transfer you to Section Six. The transfer takes place immediately. Dismissed.'

When I told Longman I was being transferred from the construction brigade, he said I was lucky. My new work was sure to be easier. That evening I picked up my gear and moved down to Section Six, which was only four hooches down the line. I was happy for that, because it meant I'd always be able to see Longman and the others in the evenings. Friends are the most valuable commodity of all in work camps.

The leader of Section Six was a bald, round-faced prisoner in his fifties, named Yeh, who welcomed me to the hooch with courtly Mandarin politeness. He even made a little presentation.

'Attention, everyone,' he said, 'this is our new classmate, Bao Ruo-wang. I'd like it if we could all welcome him and give him a helping hand with work tomorrow so he'll be able to learn quickly.'

Yeh was a fine human being. Even in Prison Number One, no cell or section leader had spoken so nicely. Incongruously enough, his polite words were immediately followed by an invitation to join my new classmates in a little Struggle. The object of our attentions was seated on an old stool in the centre of the room. He was a skinny little character about twenty-six with enormous black eyes, deeply tanned and dressed in rags. At that moment he was wearing a big patchwork, visored hat he'd made himself, resembling a baseball cap. He was one of the saddest creatures I had ever laid eyes on. He already seemed resigned to the worst.

It was my first meeting with Pan Fu-kang – Small Pan, we called him, to differentiate him from the others who bore the same rather common name. Small Pan was, I think, a quadroon – one quarter white and the rest Chinese – and I forget why he was sent to the camps, but the political police might just as well have given him a death sentence right at the start. He never had been able to make the adjustment to confinement and food rationing. He lived in such terror of dying that he reverted more and more to childhood. By the time I met him, he was already acting like a whimpering baby, and would get even worse. We

184

all liked Small Pan and tried to help him, but it was no good. A few months later I watched him die with a piece of cake in his mouth.

Our Struggle that night broke up in less than half an hour. No one had his heart in it. A few of the cellmates perfunctorily accused Pan of a bad attitude toward work, malingering and slandering the government by his complaints, but it was really only to please the brigade leader. Yeh broke up the session and had the scribe enter in the record that Pan had resisted criticism freely and sincerely offered.

We of Section Six were up the next morning at five for our bowl of vegetable porridge, and it wasn't until then that I learned what our work consisted of: We collected pig shit. We were the fertilizer technicians. I followed Yeh unenthusiastically to the sties. When we were within 100 yards, I could smell them already.

'Don't worry,' he said affably, 'you get used to the stink. Pretty soon you don't even notice it.'

I felt like vomiting. Hundreds of grunting, snorting animals, massive and black, were struggling to get at the potato peels, wild vegetables and miscellaneous garbage that a prisoner was heaving into their troughs. It was hard to figure which smelled the worst, the garbage, the pigs themselves or the excrement. The pig yard was made of brick, like a patio, so that none of the fertilizer would be lost, and their living quarters, rows of slant-roofed pens, were carefully freshened up each day by shovels of fine, dry, sandy earth. Our job was to shovel the sand from the pens after the pigs had fouled it, toss the wet mess into a ditch over on the side and then add straw to the mixture. The pig excrement and urine quickly fermented with the straw to make a horrible, rich, black mess that was high-grade fertilizer. We would then scoop the muck out, pile it in mounds and repeat the process. There are many ways of building socialism.

Yeh called a break at ten, and I remember the moment well because he gave me a tip about making a cigarette camp-style. I was about to light up a normal cigarette when he abruptly stopped me.

'Wait a minute,' he said. 'You're wasting that.'

He broke my cigarette open and dumped the tobacco onto one of the little squares of newspaper prisoners always carry with them. From a little cloth pouch he drew out an equal amount of dried wild mint leaves, mixed it all together, rolled two fat smokes and handed me one.

'Here,' he said with a laugh. 'Have a menthol smoke.'

The rest of the day passed easily enough, and I was surprised at how rapidly I became accustomed to the sour stink of the pigs. Late in the afternoon 'One-arm' wandered by to check on us. He came upon the scene just as I was bending over to remove a piece of shit that had stuck to my sandal. 'One-arm' saw the opportunity for an ideological analogy.

'What are you doing there?' His tone was sharp.

'Cleaning my sandal. It's dirty.'

'Your brain is dirtier than that, and it smells worse, too. Stop that immediately. That is a bourgeois habit. Clean your head instead!'

That evening as we trudged back to the barracks I couldn't help noticing that Small Pan was eating a rotten tomato he had stolen from the pig slops. I was appalled, but the others either didn't notice or didn't care.

'Small Pan,' I said, 'are you really as hungry as that?'

I'll never forget the look he gave me, the sort of look an animal gives when it is trapped.

'Don't talk so nice, new man. Your turn will come.'

He wolfed the tomato down and stared at me defiantly.

'Are you going to report me for that? Go ahead. I don't care.'

Of course Small Pan was right. Even though it took me a lot longer than that, I, too, became a scavenger and ate worse things than rotten tomatoes. A lot worse. And as the ironies would have it, exactly a week after my moralizing remonstrance, our food was made subject to new emergency measures. The farm's autonomously produced food supply had suffered so badly from the drought that the administrators were forced to ask the state for help. It was an embarrassing and difficult position. To cut their demands to the minimum, the farm directors instituted a system of official scavenging. From that week on, our food supply was to be stretched by adding wild vegetables, weeds and plants. Two sections were detailed to collect the various edible stems and leaves from the fields while the rest of us worked. I remember in particular the stems we called *ma erh tsai*, which looked something like green spaghetti when they were boiled, had a sourish taste but, apparently, no nutritional value. Just to keep things fair and square, we also fed wild vegetables to the pigs.

After work that first day everyone but me changed to a carefully segregated set of clean clothes. I didn't have anything else to wear. Yeh took me over to the library to fix me up. The librarian, it turned out, was also the man who gave out clothes – a useful man to know. He was a tall old man named Hsiung, quite distinguished in his horn-rimmed glasses, white jacket and pants and black sandals. Hsiung took me to a storeroom opposite the library where dozens of used shirts and pants were stacked next to a pile of odd shoes. I grabbed one set of everything. It was, I reflected, the first time I had received anything from the Chinese government.

Hsiung was a likeable fellow. Without the least hesitation he told me he had been sent up for thievery.

'I stole lots of stuff,' he said, proudly.

He busied himself with an abacus, then took a slip of paper, entered my name and added some figures.

'What's that for?' I wondered.

'Your pocket money for the next month. Two yuan. You came on the first of July and you get your allowance on the fifteenth. If you work well, that is. If not, we make reductions.'

'Does everyone get allowances?'

'No. Only those who work. And those who don't work get only six ounces of food a day. That's our principle here – if you don't work, you don't eat.'

Hsiung was exaggerating somewhat, but he wasn't far from the truth. I noticed a chart on the wall, with columns and little squares.

'The cemetery,' he said calmly, arranging his paperwork. 'We enter the name in each square so we can keep track of who's buried where.'

His orderliness was fascinating. 'Are the graves dug already?'

'No, Bao.' He smiled indulgently. 'If we did that, they would just fill up with mud during the winter. No, we dig each one fresh.'

'Who does the digging?'

'There's a brigade of volunteers. We have to have that because the death rates are high here.'

'They don't send the bodies back to the families?'

'Oh, yes. They can, yes indeed. But only if the families ask for them – but they have to pay. Once a man's dead, the government's not responsible for him anymore. You're not considered a prisoner when you're dead.'

A few days later I ran into Koo, who broke into peals of laughter when he saw my tattered outfit and smelled my aroma.

'They've got me watching cows now, and I think I'll stay there, old Bao. I'm not a snob, but you smell worse than they do.'

He walked away holding his nose.

The comic relief was fun, but there wasn't much of it. The case of the brigade barber swiftly brought us back to the realities of discipline. I was surprised to learn that we had a barber in Northern Precious Village. It was Yeh who brought me over to his place, a large, square room with a beaten earth floor and three wooden chairs. The barber was a squat little fellow in his forties who stuttered. We chatted pleasantly while he gave me the required military-style trim. He told me he was in on a morals charge, but I didn't ask what kind and he didn't offer to elaborate. We left it at that while I enjoyed the luxury of a shave.

'I wouldn't spend too much time around the barber,' Yeh cautioned me back in the hooch. 'He's a bad example.'

Coming from Yeh that was strange. He was an intelligent, cultured individual who scarcely bothered himself with doctrine. No matter. I wasn't going to argue with him.

I don't remember the date, but it was probably two or three weeks later that it happened. It had been raining all morning and most of us hadn't been required to go out to our jobs. Late in the afternoon the sun blazed through the clouds and started drying up the earth. Suddenly whistles started blowing.

'*Ji ho!*'

It was the call for assembly – and there were to be no exceptions, the warders told us. We straggled out into the courtyard and arranged ourselves in our section order. I was in the front row, next to Yeh. We pulled out bags of tobacco, rolled smokes and waited. The damp earth steamed as the sun beat down on it. Then I heard the sound of chains behind us.

The first one to come before us was Wang, our one-armed warder, and he was quickly joined by the brigade leader in charge of production, a man named Yen, perhaps a dozen guards and finally an official of some sort, dressed in a blue Mao uniform and holding a neat, black briefcase. In the middle of them all was the barber, tied up in chains and fetters. A rope around his neck and cinched at the waist kept his head bowed. His hands were tied behind his back. The guards shoved him directly in front of us. He stood there silently, like a trussed penitent, as the steam wisped up around his feet. Yen had a speech.

'I have something awful to speak about. I'm not happy to do it and it's nothing to be proud of. But it is my duty and it should be a lesson for you. This rotten egg here was jailed on a morals charge – homosexual relations with a boy. He only received seven years for this offence. Later, when working in the paper mill, his behaviour was constantly bad and he stole repeatedly. His sentence was doubled. Now we have established that while here, he seduced a young prisoner nineteen years old – a mentally retarded prisoner. If this happened in society, he would be severely punished. But by doing what he did here, he not only sinned morally but he also dirtied the reputation of the prison and the great policy of Reform Through Labour. Therefore, in consideration of his repeated offences, the representative of the Supreme People's Court will now read you his sentence.'

The man in the blue uniform strode forward and read out the sombre document, a recapitulation of the offences that ended with the decision of the People's Court: death with immediate execution of sentence.

Everything happened so suddenly then that I didn't even have the time to be shocked or frightened. Before the man in the blue uniform had even finished pronouncing the last word the barber was dead. The guard standing behind him pulled out a huge pistol and blew his head open. A shower of blood and brains flew out and splattered those of us in the front rows. I looked away from the hideous, twitching figure on the ground and vomited. Yen came up to speak again.

'Let this serve as a warning to you. I have been authorized to tell you that no more leniency will be shown in this camp. From now on, all moral offences will be punished in the same way. Now go back to your cells and discuss this.'

He glanced down at me and the others who had been hit with brains and blood.

'You people, go have a wash and then go back to your cells for studies.'

Yen may have been deliberately exaggerating when he threatened all further offences with execution, but I am certain no one was tempted to test him. Morals offences are not treated lightly in China. In the socialist countries in general, but even more so in China, deviations from the norm are not appreciated or considered tolerable.

The reasoning is simple: Those who do not behave as normal human beings should be punished, for the purification of society. After the revolution many male opera singers were persecuted because they impersonated women. Sodomy and rape can be punished by death. Females get five years for extra- or premarital fornication. A married man who seduces a married woman gets ten years. A married man seducing an unmarried woman will receive an indeterminate but heavy sentence and his partner a light one. Lesbianism has always been rare in China, but the once-widespread homosexuality is no longer tolerated. I have read of men being raped in Western prisons. In China the guilty party would be shot on the spot.

My work with the pigs became more and more routine, to the point that it hardly bothered me anymore. I reached something of an apogee one day when we were detailed to empty the fertilizer fermenting in the big ditch. We loaded the black, stinking

190

muck into wicker baskets with heavy wooden scoops, but it was awkward for me to bend over on the slippery bank to fill my scoop. I took the example of two other prisoners and simply jumped in feet first – in shit up to my waist. As I was heaving the stuff around, Wong, the man who had compared my intellectual's brain to a cesspool, ambled up to the pig sties.

'Well, Bao,' he said with good cheer, 'you're making progress. I see you're learning a lesson. That's good. Continue that way.'

It might have been because of 'One-arm's' approval that one day not long afterward I was assigned the easy job of guarding the vegetable patch. All I had to do was sit down in the shade, read a book and make sure no one slipped in to steal anything. It was a perfect, restful day's sinecure. Around 11 o'clock in the morning Warder Wong's wife came through the gate with a little basket. I kept my mouth closed and read my book. We were not supposed to talk to any women, let alone free ones and even more so the wives of our leaders. She took some tomatoes and eggplants and went back out without a word. That evening back in the hooch a guard came to fetch me. 'One-arm' wanted to have a word with me.

'Sit down, Bao,' he said, every inch the schoolmaster. 'Now tell me: What mistake did you make today?'

We were at the old game again. 'I don't know, Warder.'

The glare: 'Don't lie. You know the penalties for lying.'

I stared at him blankly.

'What did you do in the garden today?'

'I read a book.'

'That's good.'

'Nothing particular happened. No one stole anything. Your wife came for some eggplants and tomatoes, that's all.'

'So something did happen, didn't it? You even know how much she took, don't you? Did she pay?'

'Warder, I couldn't stop your wife,' I protested, but he drove his point home.

'I told you to stop anyone – that meant even me! Those vegetables are government property, not mine. You know what you're going to do?'

He bent down and came up with his wife's basket in his hand.

'Take this and weigh the vegetables and look on the list to see how much they cost. And then make sure I get charged for that amount.'

He dismissed me and I carried out the little commercial procedure. I've often wondered since how he punished his wife. Communist cadres may be a painful lot at times, but they are the most scrupulous people I have ever known.

On the twenty-fifth of July a heavy consignment of new prisoners arrived, some three hundred in all. They were a terrifying lot.

'They didn't want us anymore in Peking,' one of them told me, and I could see why. There didn't seem to be an able-bodied man among them. Some were even on stretchers, and most of the rest were leaning on sticks or each other. There was no doubt they had been assigned to Northern Precious Village to die.

I was surprised to see among them a man I knew, or what was left of him. He had been an acquaintance of mine since the old days in the diplomatic circle, where he had been a servant in a Western embassy. His problem was he had been too loyal to his employers. When the police asked him to spy on the embassy staff, he refused, because they had always treated him honourably. It is not a good idea to say no to Chinese police. He died in Northern Precious Village while I was there.

At the end of that week Old Yeh interrupted our section's smoke break with an announcement.

'I've just come from the brigade leader's office,' he said. 'The eight of us have been assigned the job of burying the dead. I guess they figure that since we're already doing the dirtiest work, we wouldn't mind taking on the burial detail, too. In return we will all draw maximum rations, get an extra meal when we work at night and be able to keep small things we find on the bodies, like cigarettes and soap bars.'

The very next night we had our first assignment, some poor unknown from among that pathetic batch of arrivals. We heaved him fully clothed into our little handcart with the bicycle wheels and hustled him up to the graveyard on the hill. It was a beautiful evening, with a red sunset and the cicadas singing in the trees. The hole was ready. We dumped him in as he was – there were no more coffins in those days – covered him with his sleeping mat and quickly filled the hole. Small Pan looked on in horror. He didn't touch his shovel. When we came back, we got two extra pieces of bread.

The next morning we were called in from the pigs for another one. This time we had to dig the hole ourselves. While four of them went off to start digging, I and the others fetched the body. This one had been a cripple, but by the looks of him he was an intellectual from a good family. His coat was clean and his coverlet was silk. We gathered his fountain pen and books to send to his family and heaved him into the cart. My toe ached with each step up to the graveyard. I had hurt it several days earlier and now it was infected. That was going to cause me more trouble later, but for now my only concern was to bury our unfortunate classmate.

As I approached the graveyard I saw a strange scene. Everyone was standing around the freshly dug hole and suddenly one of them – it turned out to be Small Pan – detached himself from the others and threw himself at the feet of the guard witnessing the burial. Two of the men in the section, Shau and Chang, pulled him away.

On the way back Yeh told me Small Pan had gone a little bit crazy when he saw the body coming. He begged the guard to send him back to Peking, even to the Transit Centre if they wanted. He was sure he would die if he stayed on in Northern Precious Village. The poor little bastard was right. Of course we had to Struggle him back in the hooch. No one wanted particularly to do it, but the guard had given us orders. We compromised by giving him a group-criticism session, avoiding the rancour and insult of a Struggle. We advised him to go to the warder and make a clean breast of his doubts and explain his attitude.

Small Pan agreed and left the room at about 8 p.m. to give it a try. When he came back, he was in tears. Pan cried more and more toward the end of his life. Yeh yelled at him to cut it out – weeping in prison was a sign of resentment, as if the government were oppressing him in some way. Small Pan stood there in that little peaked cap he had made out of extra pieces cut from his jacket, his shoulders heaving in grief.

'How would you feel if the warder threatened to put your ration down to eighteen catties a month?' he sobbed.

Eighteen catties. That made about twenty pounds. Yeh didn't press the point. 'Sit down and do your lesson,' he said.

The infection in my toe soon spread up my leg through the lymph glands and formed a gruesome boil on my groin. When it started bubbling, I had to go see the doctor. At least he was honest with me. The combination of my TB and the bad rations made the boil extremely dangerous, but it still wasn't the time to operate. We could do nothing but wait. Panicked at the thought of a generalized infection finishing me off, I went to see 'One-arm' and made an exceptional request to be transferred back to Peking. If I was going to die, I told him, I wanted to be near my family. He gave me a scolding for my improper attitude and ordered me to write out an admission of ideological fault. I should have known better.

In the burial detail we had a brief experience with the magic black box, an invention of some zealous cadre. Coffins had long since disappeared, since the wood was urgently needed for other purposes, but the authorities of Northern Precious Village evidently felt that form should be served nonetheless. The result of their concern was the black box – a special, reusable coffin with a sliding bottom. We would place the box directly over the hole and then, so to speak, pull the rug out from under the corpse, which would pile headlong into its final resting place. Warder Wang finally did away with this grisly pretence, and I admired him for it.

One night late in August we got a call that there was a fresh corpse for us. Half our section was away doing something else, it turned out, so there were only four of us left. Two of them went to dig the grave, but the one who was supposed to help me had cramps and couldn't leave the hooch. I went to the Black Shed alone, pulling the rickshaw cart behind me. The Black Shed was a special place reserved only for prisoners who were dying. When a prisoner was in his last hours, he was carried there to expire alone, out of sight of the others. It was better for morale. Often there were two or even three of them in there at a time.

The guard who had called me out helped me load the corpse, still in its bedclothes, into the cart, but then he took off. I was left to carry out the burial alone. More than a mile, I had to walk with it behind me. The moon was nearly full but I didn't look back. His head thumped against the side boards as we climbed the path; it was as if he were still alive and protesting. When I buried him, his eyes were still open. The next morning I asked 'One-arm' to make sure I would never have to do a night burial alone anymore. In September we averaged two deaths a day and by October most of those three hundred who had come from Peking on 25 July were dead.

Summer was finished in the middle of September. The sun was still warm when it showed itself, but the skies were almost constantly cloudy and the rains came more regularly. When the cold became acute, Yeh gave me a tip – snuggle up to the pigs for warmth. Far from running away, the animals actually seemed to enjoy our company in such close quarters. I huddled next to their opulent black flanks, watched the rain and pondered the vagaries of fate that had brought me there.

Throughout the whole time with the pigs, my pal Koo kept hustling and helping me out as he had done in the days of the wheat harvest in Branch Farm Three. A master scavenger, he set something of a record one week by catching a chicken and then a hedgehog, which he shared with me and a few other friends. That was, of course, counterrevolutionary behaviour, but little matter. Longman cooked the animals in the classic peasant style, first gutting them and then applying big gobs of sticky mud around them to make a ball of clay. The ball hung for a few hours over a fire and when Longman broke it open, it fell away from the cooked chicken, pulling the feathers with it. A little wild garlic and some salt from the horse trough made it a memorable feast.

I finally had my operation in the first week of October. Naturally there was no anaesthetic, and since the doctor was not a practitioner of acupuncture, I had only a rag to bite on as he opened up and lanced my boil. The operation was a success, though, and I could feel myself getting stronger with each of the five days of rest that 'One-arm' gave me. I passed the time loafing around the cell and reading periodicals in the library. Now I could watch the progress of the burials on Hsiung's cemetery chart with a professional eye.

On 13 October, I was out in the fields with the pigs when Yeh told me the warder wanted to see me. When I got back to the compound, I saw a wooden horse cart in front of his office. And Longman was standing there! Something was up. Because of our good efforts and our positive attitude, 'One-arm' told us, we were being transferred back to Number Three Farm. We were a rare oddity, Koo and I. The traffic to Northern Precious Village was almost entirely one way; we were some of the few to go back to the living.

'Zheng chü,' said Old Yeh, who had come to see us off – Keep striving.

'Sure, Yeh,' I said. 'And good luck to you.'

I never saw Yeh again. I suppose the burial detail eventually got him.

Chapter Eleven

This time we spent only a week in Ching Ho. Koo and I were assigned to digging irrigation ditches, but it was only to mark time. We learned the real reason for our precipitate transfer on the cloudy afternoon of 20 October, when the education and discipline warder called all prisoners into the auditorium for a special meeting. The building had been more or less completed in the three and a half months I had been gone; the banners and slogans around the stage made a properly impressive setting. As Longman and I were taking our places we noticed some new faces in the crowd – fresh arrivals from Northern Precious Village. They had just come in that morning, they told us. They were about a hundred and, no, they didn't have any idea why they had been transferred. The warder introduced a tall man in olive-drab tunic and blue pants – Ching Ho's deputy director.

'Today I have good news for you,' he cried out. 'You are going to set up a new farm. You are going to the Northeast [Manchuria]. You people have been especially chosen for this honour. You will have the glorious task of producing more food for the country and raising the people's standard of living.'

'Come on, applaud!' demanded an agitprop somewhere in our midst. We brought our palms together in the open-handed Chinese manner.

'In the next few days the government will issue you warm clothes,' the deputy director continued. 'You may write your families or even invite them for a visit if you wish. You will be leaving in four days.'

There was no way any of us could bring our families down here on that short a notice, but form had been served by telling us that visits were not forbidden.

'This is a period of great joy,' he went on. I felt like an enlisted man on the Crusades. 'You must volunteer, but we can't take all of you. We will examine you to see who is fit.'

I followed the flow of traffic and found myself in front of a warder with a pen. I was volunteering for the famous Hsing Kai-Hu – the Lake of Emergent Enthusiasm.

In the days that followed we naturally enough repeated the delicious hearsay about the abounding food up north, the lakes full of fish, the woods of wild boars and berries and the fields of soybeans, rice and fruit. But there were a few old hands who had already been there. They gave us some of the other sides of the picture.

Prisoners wore handmade straw shoes in the winter, they said, because in anything else, in any manufactured boot known in China, one's feet were bound to freeze. There was a special kind of grass up there called woo la ts'ao. The trick was to take this soft, pliable stuff and line the straw shoes with it to absorb the moisture that brings on frostbite. The winter temperatures went down as far as forty below, but prisoners weren't obliged to work outside beyond thirty below. Work norms were calculated on a seven-day week – no time off at Hsing Kai-Hu. In summer, huge, powerful mosquitoes filled the air. The only way to coexist with them – the Chinese have succeeded in virtually eliminating flies but mosquitoes had still defied them – was to take to the fields wearing a net over the head and gloves on the hands. And woe to the prisoner who felt an irrepressible call of nature! Incontinent field hands quickly learned to light a bunch of smoky weeds when they dropped their drawers, but the more courageous mosquitoes attacked anyway. At night, of course, no one dared sleep naked.

On the positive side, the land was so fertile that it needed hardly any care – so rich, in fact, it was loaded aboard trains and shipped to the poorer regions of central China to be used without further treatment as fertilizer. The thaw arrived late in April and the winter freeze in October. In the months between, rice and soy were planted by simply being strewn over the fields. The crops germinated on the black, oily loam without needing help from man's hand.

On the twenty-fourth 1,700 of us piled into trucks to be driven back over the twenty-two and a half kilometres we had walked under the sun from Chadian railroad station. As our train

198

pulled away to the north the last sign we saw of Ching Ho was a billboard identifying Number Three Limestone Quarry. The long journey was under way.

Each one of us was toting a bundle containing a six-pound black padded jacket that closed with buttons up the front and a belt at the waist, black padded pants, a pair of padded green rubber and canvas boots and a fur hat with ear flaps. Since the train was barely heated, Longman and I opened the bundles and put on our jackets straight away. Our only long stop that day was a twenty-minute layover at Mukden (Shenyang). The next morning at dawn we hit Harbin, China's northernmost major city, built by the Russians during the time of the great tsarist imperialism. We sat there two hours. In the distance, through the smoke from the chimneys, we could make out the onion domes of the Orthodox cathedral in the grey early light.

Our terminus was Miyun, a small city in Hei Lung Kiang Province. Forty or fifty canvas-roofed army trucks – Russian Molotovs – were awaiting us and we piled in for the ten-hour ride north to our staging point. Two soldiers guarded the back of each truck. Between every fifth vehicle was a jeep with more soldiers. The rest of us made ourselves as comfortable as we could on the cold steel floors and watched the countryside roll past. It was nearly 8 p.m. and getting dark when we came to Mi-Hsien, our transit point. The air was sharp and bracing and clear. We could see the stars clearly. Everything about the place gave an impression of robust, business-like efficiency. Barely visible in the penumbra were symmetrical rows of sixty-man tents, each one lit inside by a single oil lamp. The brightly lit kitchen tent was manned by smiling civilians who generously scooped out our first hot meal in two days, an unforgettable noodle dish, thick and brimming with soybeans. Though we were fairly shaking from the cold, we were alive with excitement and enthusiasm. Everything seemed abundant up here in Manchuria, and strangely unprisonlike. We found that the civilians were happy to barter us the strong but high-quality local tobacco for whatever we cared to put up. I reluctantly parted with my fountain pen against half a pound and Longman, even though he didn't smoke, got the same amount. Tobacco leaves

199

are better than money in the camps. We hustled back to the dormitory tents, burrowed contentedly into the straw covering the beaten earth floor and fell into deep slumber.

It was still dark when the hammer hit the rail the next morning and the cornmeal mush the civilians ladled out to us was laced with onions – a delicious departure from tradition. Longman and I ate in a hurry and were still standing near the wooden tubs after everyone had been served. To our joyful surprise the kitchen worker scooped us up an extra portion from the bottom of the tub. Seconds in jail!

The rest of that morning and part of the afternoon we followed new, well-maintained dirt roads farther north. We were already within the vast confines of the camp area and all around us we saw not only cultivated fields but also barracks, watchtowers, villages and other prisoners going about their work. In the vegetable fields, not yet entirely harvested, were some of the biggest Chinese cabbages I had ever seen. Everything seemed orderly and well tended. Our guards made no attempt to block our view or to stop us from talking or smoking. Hsing Kai-Hu, it was becoming evident, was not a place where ideology counted more than work.

We reached our farm unit at 4 p.m. The brick dwellings, one of the latest triumphs of the Construction Battalion, looked solid and comfortable enough. As our trucks drew to a halt we were astonished to see that the resident prisoners had arranged a reception ceremony for us. A big paper banner bore the message 'Welcome to Our New Schoolmates'. All around it were beaming faces and waving hands; they chanted slogans of brotherly greetings, beat on little drums and rattled cymbals. It may sound amusing to the Westerner, but I can assure you that we were deeply touched. We who were accustomed to being treated like vile, crawling things were actually being welcomed as heroes! There were buckets of warm water and pots of tea brewing. When we jumped down from the trucks they gave us cigarettes and offered to carry our bundles. Do prisoners anywhere else in the world behave so marvellously? I doubt it.

After a cup of tea and assignment to barracks we were called together again to listen to a husky officer in a blue padded uniform, sheepskin coat and a brown fur hat with a prominent red star.

'You are in Number Nine Farm,' he said. 'It is a special place because it is located on some of the worst land in Hsing Kai-Hu. It was set up for people who wanted to make an extra effort and show their gratitude to the government. Since then we have built up vegetable fields, a fruit orchard and a soybean processing plant. We also produce some meat from pigs and other small animals. My name is Hsu. I don't expect any trouble from you but you must know that the door to my office is always open if you have ideological problems or bad thoughts to discuss. You may voice your problems to me whenever you like. The only thing I ask is that you observe the rules. Since you need a rest, you won't have to work tomorrow, but you should spend this free time making an ideological preparation for the day after tomorrow, when your work will start.'

After Warder Hsu's speech we had a first-rate meal of soybeans with pork and a sort of gruel containing cornmeal, onions and cabbage leaves. One of the residents offered me a smoke from the local leaf. I almost turned green when I inhaled. It was the strongest stuff I had ever tasted.

'You'd better mix it with some vine leaves,' he said with amusement. 'It's a little hard to take at first.'

Our next day was devoted to studies and learning more from the veterans about how unbelievably cold the winters could get. Inevitably, there were more stories about men freezing to death. One nice touch bequeathed by the Construction Battalion was that our cell units were radiantly heated. The brick huts were in lines wall to wall and between each one was a hollow space for fires. Even the beds, made of planks laid over hollow brickwork, could be radiantly heated in the same fashion. In a place of honour in the library were photographs of the ten prisoners who died in 1955 putting out a brush fire and who had been pardoned posthumously. We were told to emulate their spirit.

The work we began the following morning was almost enjoyable – tying up the spreading leaves of the giant cabbages which were about to be harvested. There were no norms; we were directed to work as hard and as conscientiously as we could. Improper attitude, rather than low production, was the criterion for cutting a man's rations. We responded to this indulgence by giving ourselves totally to the job at hand. I can understand now how intelligent it was to treat the prisoners of Hsing Kai-Hu so fairly – it wasn't the sort of place that could have been built on short rations. That was obviously why the Japanese had failed with their driven, intimidated slave labour. After a few days in the fields I was truly happy to be in the barren lands.

Fifteen days later my world fell apart. I was called in to see Warder Hsu on urgent business. He looked grim.

'It is my duty to inform you that you are in deep trouble,' he growled. 'Two other men, too. I won't tell you now what it is that is wrong, but I want you to go back to your cell and think about it. Think what it could be. Tomorrow there will be someone from Peking to speak with you.'

I was horrified. 'Is it something from my past?'

'No. It is something that happened since your arrest. Tomorrow answer all the questions truthfully, even if you are afraid.'

When I returned to the cell, I saw that Longman had been called in, too, and another classmate, a man named Chi. What the hell could it be? I spent a restless night trying to figure it out. At nine in the morning a couple of jeeps came for us. I was scared. We drove for thirty minutes to the headquarters of Number Nine Farm, a rather new grey brick building with an overhanging wooden eave. The guards hustled us into a wooden-floored waiting room with a cast-iron stove in the middle, a portrait of Mao and a map of China on the wall and a soldier drinking tea in the corner. We waited.

After ten minutes a guard led me into a room where an officer in a blue uniform of thick flannel sat behind a plain table, inspecting me from behind bushy eyebrows. Warder Hsu was with him. They told me to sit. I didn't have to bow my head, though.

'You are a foreigner,' said the man in the flannel uniform. 'A Frenchman. Why didn't you tell them that at Ching Ho when they transferred you?'

So that was it. I felt relieved.

'I didn't know I had to. I volunteered with all the rest.'

'We're not blaming you for volunteering, but you should have gone to see the warder or the director of the prison.'

'But that wouldn't have gotten me anywhere,' I protested. 'Five months ago, when I was being transferred out of Prison Number One, I told a warder I was French. He said nationality didn't matter. All prisoners had to listen to the orders of the government, he told me.'

'Well, nationality does matter,' he said gruffly. 'It was a mistake to send you here. Go to your cell and get your stuff ready. You're going back.'

Longman and Chi got the same treatment. Neither one of them held a foreign passport as I did, but they both came from what is known as 'overseas Chinese' – families who had emigrated to work elsewhere and established residence abroad. Apparently the Sino-Soviet border even then was such a delicate trouble spot that there was a standing rule to allow no foreigners or persons with families abroad into Hsing Kai-Hu. We were a dejected trio to board the train back south that 29 October.

Illustration of Chinese police caution: Koo, Chi and I and the two soldiers guarding us had an entire car to ourselves all the way back to Ching Ho. We made the journey in utter silence, too intimidated to talk among ourselves and too lowly to talk with the guards.

A jeep was waiting for us at the Chadian railroad station. Everything was the same as we had left it except that it was colder now. The three of us were driven to Branch Farm Three and incorporated into a temporary brigade run by two warders named Yang. To differentiate them, we called them Young Yang and Old Yang. For three days we did miscellaneous clean-up work until a reorganization of the camp put us into Team One of the Fifth Brigade. There were sixteen of us in the team, and it was quite a cast of characters. Besides me, there was one other half-breed, Lo, who was a quarter American. Classmate Soong had been an acquaintance of mine in Prison Number One and he was – I hesitate to use the word – beautiful. He was one of those rather common cases of effeminacy that occur among Chinese males. Graceful and slender, he resembled Mia Farrow, but he was also deadly serious and one of the best workers in the camp. In society he had been an apprentice at the Peking Opera.

The most extraordinary-looking member of our team was named Lin, a powerfully built old man of sixty-five or so who had been a war lord general in the twenties and then later with the Nationalist Army. With his barrel chest, Fu Manchu moustache and completely bald head, he could have stepped from the pages of a popular Chinese adventure saga. His story is sad. We'll come to that presently.

Leong was the son of a rich Shanghai family that had fled to Hong Kong when the revolution came. I don't know what his reasons were for staying behind, but he eventually got denounced, arrested and sent up. The family sent him occasional food parcels, but such was their ignorance of camp life that they invariably filled the packages with luxury items – smoked delicacies, perfumed soap, candies and the like. Once he even received a big tin of *pâté de foie gras*. The only time I saw him happy with the parcels was when he found a two-pound tin of refined lard. That was useful – he could mix it in with his soup to make it richer.

There were also two English-speaking intellectuals, Ku, a young student from Peking, and Jimmy Chin, a man who became a great pal of mine, the Cambridge graduate who was arrested because he thought English texts should be used for teaching the English language. Small Pan was back among us, too, the poor little fellow. He had been released from Northern Precious Village but the change scarcely made him any happier. By now he had become a chronic malcontent and complainer.

Longman was named cell leader, which was fine with all of us. He was one of those rare persons whom everybody automatically trusts, a man of good faith. His deputy was named Lo. Longman found himself appointed to one of the easiest but most tortuous jobs of all – kitchen worker, in charge of divvying up and distributing the rations. He did what he could for us when food became dramatically scarce later that fall, but his goodwill couldn't help our hunger much.

And then there was Sun – Lao Sun. Sun had been a cop and

a good Communist, a graduate of the Police Academy and a member of the new Democratic Youth League, but the pleasures of the flesh did him in. He was strikingly handsome, stocky and fair skinned and there must have been some Turkestani blood in him because his eyes were wide rather than slit in the Chinese manner. He spoke with a heavy Shansi accent. He told me his story one drizzly afternoon when we were scrounging through the cabbage fields for odd leaves and stems to augment our rations.

'Something went wrong with my ideology,' he said with a light laugh. 'I don't know if you could call it counterrevolutionary, but the fact is I got sent up for illicit sex relations. The girl was my boss's wife. The police chief's wife, can you figure that? It wasn't very smart of me, but she insisted and I finally just couldn't turn it down anymore. They sent me to the brick factory first, but then I got transferred here.'

We rolled a cigarette – the standard fat camp cigarette of newsprint twisted closed at either end – with my fresh Manchurian leaf. As we were smoking, a new guard trotted over to give me a dressing-down. It was illegal for me to pass anything of mine to Sun, he reminded us, and illegal for him to accept.

'This tobacco belongs to the government,' I lied. 'It was issued to me in Hsing Kai-Hu Camp. What the government gives me I have the right to give to others, don't I?'

The guard didn't know where he stood on that one. He didn't pursue the matter. He was one of those bastards who was quick to spot any infringements of regulations but who couldn't be bothered to bring water to the workers in the fields.

'I used to be like that,' Sun said ruefully. 'Always trying to gain merits. I used to report to my boss how many times the villagers farted. We cops would be eating stewed pork and eggs and rice and the ordinary people would be eating wo'tous. We had meat two or three times a week and they had it twice a year. When I see people like that guard, I'm happier to be here. At least we're honest. Our standard of living was fifty times better than theirs. We had our own special kitchen with all the sesame oil and bean oil we wanted. And the state called us Communists. Communists, my ass.'

Sun's comments about oil were especially pertinent. Oil is absolutely basic to Chinese nourishment. The rations of a prison or camp or commune are invariably described in terms of how much oil is used. Oil gives strength. Without it a man can't work. In the bad times the peasants had only boiled and steamed foods, usually grains and vegetables, and almost never meat. A peasant caught killing a pig would go straight from the farm to the camps. The government used all its ingenious powers of persuasion to tout substitute foods. In 1958 and 1959, for example, there had been bumper crops of sweet potatoes. For one Chinese cent – less than half an American cent – you could buy a catty (1.1 lbs.) of them. The farms even sold them on credit to get rid of them in a hurry, and delivered them. The newspapers were filled with articles extolling the nutritive value of sweet potatoes – superior in calories to rice and in protein to wheat – and suggestions for recipes. There were sweet potato breads, chips, cakes and desserts of all kinds. Once back in the Interrogation Centre, we had been allowed to buy individual batches of sweet potatoes for ridiculously low prices. There was a big shipment that had to be eaten before it rotted. For two days we starving prisoners glutted ourselves on those damn things, and then were floored by diarrhoea for two more. The experiment ended in a hurry. It wasn't conducive to confessions.

In 1960 and 1961, while I was in Ching Ho, the sweet potato crop was mediocre. Suddenly newspapers started calling them positive menaces to the health, purveyors of stomach problems and even diabetes. The people were well served to be rid of them. That was economic planning for you.

Sweet potatoes bring back a vivid memory of a little vignette I witnessed later in the fall, when the ration situation was becoming catastrophic. Two prisoners were arguing over in a corner of the compound, and one of them exclaimed:

'You've got no face.'

That is a very strong insult for a Chinese. It means he is shameless, abject, despicable. The other man – I recognized him as a classmate named Lei Ying-fang – simply said, 'I'm hungry.'

I saw what it was about as I got nearer. Lei had grabbed some half-rotten sweet potato peels from the garbage heap and was rinsing them under a tap. With perfect calm he picked them apart and ate them as we watched. Lei wasn't a pretty man – in fact with his round face and thick, fat nose he resembled nothing so much as a pig – but he knew how to keep himself alive and didn't worry about niceties. Like Sun he, too, had been a good Communist, but he had erred and was sent away for three years of Education Through Labour. His stubborn nature led him to continue making critical remarks, though, and one day he was transferred over to Lao Gai as a recurrent offender. Lei taught me a lot about foraging later on. I eventually became so adept at foraging that before I left Ching Ho I had learned how to get nourishment from horse shit. Really. You'll see. Read on.

For a week or so I carried bricks until the weather turned seriously cold. Since I had nothing but light summer things to put on my back (the warm Manchurian gear had of course been confiscated back at Hsing Kai-Hu), Young Yang ordered me to stay inside until suitable clothing had been found. He cut my rations during this period of enforced rest, but only by fifteen per cent. Young Yang was fair. I spent the time lounging, reading and studying my written Chinese.

Bored one afternoon, I decided to visit the cell where the old and sick were segregated. For one thing, it was the only properly heated room in the place, aside from the warders' quarters. It was really a cell for prisoners beyond hope. They lay in the straw and waited. I remember a senile old priest who was sucking candy like a baby. He had a little hoard of the stuff, and he counted it all day long. He took the clear wrapper paper from one of them, held it up to his eye and peered through it to inspect me. Another was knitting socks and one man with a supply of tobacco rolled cigarettes, undid them and rolled them again – anything to pass the time until they ate, fell asleep or died.

Finally Deputy Cell Leader Lo came up with some clothes for me. I could go out and work the very next day. He thrust at me a pair of blue pants with a large olive-green patch on the right knee. With that and an old padded jacket, I was all set.

'Where'd they come from?' I asked.

'He doesn't need them anymore,' Lo said.

I went back to the fields picking up cabbage leaves in company with Lin, our own war lord. It was a pleasure to be around such an energetic and resolutely cheerful man. I retain a mental image of this strong old soldier working in the fields or heaving away with a spade digging ditches, his pants tied up at the waist with a string, his padded jacket often unbuttoned to cool him from his efforts. He had been arrested right after the revolution and given ten years. Lin knew more about the camps than any of us and enjoyed regaling us with endless stories of how things used to be in the old days before ideology had come in to freeze attitudes. The camps weren't too bad at first, he said. They were almost like men's clubs, where everyone pitched in to do his share.

'At first I thought it was beneath my dignity to work,' he said, 'and no one pushed me to do anything. In those days they were still respecting my former rank. The guards told me I'd get bored doing nothing. Well, they were right, but not at first. I didn't care about labour. I used to spend my days hanging around creeks and irrigation ditches looking for crabs and fish. When the boys came back from the fields I'd have a bucket of boiled crabs waiting for them. It finally got to be a routine – I'd scrounge around to see what I could come up with and they would make up the share of work I was supposed to do in the fields. That went on for a couple of months, but finally I realized they were doing a hell of a lot more work than I was. So I went to the guards and asked them to let me go to work in the fields.

' "We ain't got no horses for you, General," ' they told me.

'That was all right. I went to work. It took me quite a while, but I caught on. The camps taught me the value of labour. I'm thankful to them for that.'

We all liked and admired Lin, and we looked forward to his release from Reform almost as much as he did. As the old-timer of our bunch, his sentence was coming up to its finish on Christmas day of that year – ten years to the day. He would be able to become a free worker and fulfil his dream of dying not in a camp but at home with his children and grandchildren. It was one of his favourite subjects of conversation.

A week before his release our cell was directed to make up

its collective appraisal. It was the first time I had taken part in the process of ideologically ushering a fellow prisoner out. Each of us had to give his opinion of Lin's merits at the end of his term, determine to our satisfaction if he had indeed reformed himself and judge whether he was worthy of the government's leniency. Within three hours our little document was completed and Lin had a clean bill of health. We passed the paper around, signed, and sent it off to the warder.

Two days later, a Saturday, a guard called Lin to the warder's office. He was back only fifteen minutes later, thunderstruck. He opened the door to the cell and leaned mutely against the jamb, oblivious to the cold air rushing in. His face told us that something terrible had happened, but no one dared ask. At length Lin walked in, took his place on the bed and sat staring into space. We read and smoked in silence. That evening he finally told us what had happened.

'I have something very painful to say, schoolmates. I know how much you have been looking forward to my graduation, but I'm afraid it won't be for some time yet. When I went to see the warder, he had a man from the People's Court with him. He told me that I had never confessed sincerely and that I had been bamboozling the government for all the years of my sentence. When I asked him what crimes he held against me, he accused me of being a mass murderer.

'I couldn't believe my ears. Then he told the story of how some men from my regiment had massacred a Communist village during the war against Japan. There were many terrible things like that, I knew. The Communists had not been any more innocent than the Japs or the Nationalists. But I hadn't even been there at the time of the massacre he spoke of. I was away and left the command of my regiment to another man. How could they accuse me? They told me I still bore the responsibility because I was in charge. They're going to look into the matter and let me know what steps the government has decided to take.'

The answer came back on 5 January 1961 – twenty more years of imprisonment. Old man Lin collapsed and was carried off to the infirmary. He came back a month or so later, but he was never the same again. He hardly spoke anymore, and didn't even bother to try working. He used to wander around the farm mumbling to himself. They finally came and took him away.

Meantime, Small Pan had died. The winter started off badly. After a couple of weeks in Team 1, Pan started spitting blood and became too weak to work anymore. Even he knew it was terminal TB when they transferred him to the little hut out in back for the dying cases. Longman and I and some of the others visited him, but that did nothing for his condition, especially since he was on the reduced rations of the hopeless. Late one afternoon a fellow prisoner told us he wouldn't last through the night. Longman and a few of us went to see him. He was huddled in his bedclothes against the back wall of the shed in a sort of nest he had made from the straw on the floor. His face was grey and there were big dark rings around his eyes. He could barely talk.

'I'm finished,' he whispered. Longman tried to reassure him but he convinced no one. Embarrassed and at a loss for words, Longman asked the ritual question if there was anything he'd like us to do for him. To our surprise, he had a very specific request. Small Pan was always hungry.

'I wish I could have a piece of cake.'

It hit us like a hammer. All the poor little guy wanted on his last night was a lousy piece of cake, but he might as well have been asking for the moon. Where in hell could we get cake? Koo worked in the kitchen and he couldn't even get an extra wo'tou. I was amazed to hear him promise we'd be right back with the cake – he had had an inspiration. Out in the yard he explained it to me: We would steal the cake from young Warder Yang's office.

Jesus Christ! His audacity was stupefying. My four years of reform had effectively leached any such larcenous and illegal thoughts from my head, but of course he was right. Prisoners had the right to receive food packages from time to time and for safekeeping they were always locked up in the warders' offices. There was bound to be some cake in there. All we had to do was get to it. Longman went straight to our team and asked a man named Wong to come out and have a little talk with us. Wong was a common law prisoner who was in jail for safecracking. He agreed unhesitatingly.

'Just give me one guy for a lookout by the big gate and another outside the warder's door,' he asked.

We arranged it. That evening when Young Yang had gone to the canteen for his dinner, Wong attacked his padlock with a piece of bent wire. Within ten minutes he was back with a piece of almond cake. Longman and I took it to the death shed. Small Pan was barely alive. Longman bent down and placed the cake in Pan's mouth. He died without finishing it.

We went back to the cell and ate our supper in silence. Before lights out Wong showed up and offered us a smoke. He had real fresh tobacco! We asked him where it came from, but we already had a pretty good idea.

'Well,' Wong said, 'when I was feeling around there in the dark trying to find the cake I smelled this good stuff. It was right next to me and I couldn't resist grabbing a handful.' We had a smoke in Small Pan's honour.

As the autumn drew on into winter our food situation steadily worsened. With the bad harvests there simply wasn't enough to eat in China, and as outcasts of society, we prisoners naturally got the short end of the stick. Lei Ying-fang's half-rotten sweet potato peels didn't seem so disgusting anymore. As in Northern Precious Village, official foraging teams had long since been appointed, and the wild plants and vegetables they had gathered, now dried like shocks of hay, became a staple part of our rations. Mixed in with our soup and wo'tous they added no nutritive value, but at least gave a certain bulk. Cornmeal mush, that old standby, became a luxury for feast days only. Now the daily fare was the black, soggy sweet potato bread, laced sometimes with pea flour or the coarse millet flour ground up with the husks, which the prison administration euphemistically labelled 'unconventional cereal'. On some good days there were bits of raw carrots in the soup, or cabbage or turnips – categorized as Class A vegetables. There was never any meat or fat anymore.

In November two brigades of Lao Jiao people arrived to join

us Lao Gai types. There were 600 of them, and none of them looked too good. Though they were technically considered citizens, they did the same work as we did and ate the same rations. That didn't sit too well with some of them. They complained. A warder named Liu called us all together in the auditorium to give them the word.

'We have received complaints from some of you. You have a right to complain because you are still citizens, but you seem to forget that Lao Jiao people have committed serious mistakes, otherwise you wouldn't be here. Lao Jiao people are here to expiate their mistakes by hard work. As far as the farm administration is concerned there can be only two kinds of treatment meted out here – one for people who have never made any mistakes and another for those who have. Well, all of you here have made mistakes, so far as we are concerned Lao Jiao and Lao Gai are the same. Now get back to work.'

So much for the complaints. For a short period that month I was on the stable-cleanup detail. Compared to the pigs, the horses smelled like perfume, and they never complained when we swiped little chunks of their salt. A bag of salt is always handy in the camps. In a storeroom behind the stables we discovered a sizeable cache of sugar beets. We hid them under our jackets and brought them back to the cell. They tasted sweet and spicy.

The toughest work of all was hauling brick in the bicycle-wheeled rickshaw-style carts for the various construction projects. Two prisoners manned each cart, roped into teams like horses. Since the ropes easily rubbed through the thin cotton jackets, we improvised cloth yokes by sewing together sections of rags to make a garment like a rudimentary football shoulder pad, with a hole in the middle for the head to pass through. From the remains of an old tent we fashioned canvas spats to keep the mud and pebbles out of our shoes, and the same canvas worked all right as rough work mittens. Like the Russian prisoners in Siberia, we sealed our loose clothing by tying bits of string tightly at the ankles, wrists and at the waist – everything to keep our body heat from escaping.

The fall of 1960 was exceptionally cold. By the end of November it was already well below freezing. Half-starved as we were, our energy didn't last long in the cold. We were a sorry, inefficient bunch of labourers. On the last day of November the farm director called us together to announce some new measures. But first, of course, there had to be some rhetoric.

'The situation at home and abroad is very good,' he began with the superb gall of a veteran ideologue. 'At home the production has never been so high and all efforts are being bent to overcome any economic hardships that still linger on. Improvement is assured for 1961. Abroad, the days of the imperialists are numbered and they are facing defeat on all fronts. What I have come to tell you is that you have more reason than ever to be grateful to the government. The government realizes that we have been living through a temporary period of difficulty caused by abnormal factors beyond our control.'

'Listen to him,' Sun whispered. 'I bet he's going to lower the rations again.'

'You must realize that this period of economic difficulty will soon pass. Meanwhile, the party and the government know you are not physically up to what you were before. Therefore, considering the level of rations, it has been decided to combine work and rest. Without more rest you won't be strong enough to do the big job that has to be done in the spring. Starting tomorrow, December first, your working hours will be from 10 a.m. to 4 p.m. In the cold season it is difficult to begin before 10 a.m. anyway, and it gets dark by 4.30, but in society the workers don't have it as easy as that. From now on you will be working only six hours, but since the government is concerned for your welfare, it is leaving your rations at the same level – exactly what you have been getting for nine hours of work. We expect you to show your gratitude by doing in six hours what you have been doing in nine.'

The result of the new discipline was a slower pace of life, with more free time and more sleep – also more studies – but it didn't make us any stronger or less hungry. The food supplies remained at subsistence. In the last days of the cabbage harvest we were all mobilized into the cold, muddy fields to get all the vegetables in before the snows rotted them. Inside the brick silos

213

where we carried them, the scene was comical. Every time a guard turned his back whole teams of harvesters plunged their heads into the fat cabbages and ate out the hearts like bunnies.

One afternoon, as I was standing in the mud picking cabbages and talking to myself, someone slogged up and slapped me heavily on the back. I almost lost my balance, and turned around in anger, but I had to smile when I saw it was Jimmy Ch'in. He was dressed in a ragged, ill-fitting black outfit, rubber shoes and a padded cap with a visor he had fashioned himself. He looked like hell, but he was smiling as he peered through his steel-rimmed glasses.

'Cheer up, old man!' he said in English. I wasn't particularly in the mood.

'What the hell's there to be cheerful about, Jimmy?'

'Well, John, just think how lucky we are – fresh salad all around us every day. All we need is a little mayonnaise.'

Ch'in had a twenty-year sentence then, and had no hope of getting out. He was too old and his health wasn't good. Still he always remained cheerful. He didn't even seem to regret having come back to China from England to serve the revolution that had sent him to prison.

'What they do to you or me is really immaterial,' he told me once. 'We've seen the good life, John – we can daydream on what we've already lived. But most of these poor guys have suffered all their lives and never known anything but that. They're still good, kind people, though. They've been told to hate intellectuals but they've always treated me like a gentleman. Once when I was in the Transit Centre folding book leaves – and I was one of the slowest – a guy behind me, a poor, ordinary worker, saw a louse on my shoulder and took the time from his folding to crush it for me. He didn't have to do that. He knew my background, but he didn't hold it against me. I was so grateful to him I could have cried.'

At one very bad point that winter I allowed myself to give way to depression. I told Ch'in I had given up hope of ever getting out. Things couldn't be worse, I said. But Jimmy, the good university dialectician, set me straight.

'Things couldn't be better,' he announced.

'Jimmy, don't play games,' I remonstrated. 'You're a smart guy but something's wrong in your head.'

He smiled. 'John, I'll prove it. We're eating, right? Not well, but we're eating. Now, we might want an extra wo'tou or maybe some meat, but we know we'll never get it. It's impossible. There isn't any, so we won't get it. That's why I say things can't get better. That's all. What we have now is the best. But things could get worse – if we got sick tomorrow, they could cut our rations in half. Then things would be worse, wouldn't they?'

Ch'in gave me his crooked little smile and tapped me on the shoulder.

'It's a cockeyed world we have here, John. The pessimists look ahead and the optimists look back.'

Chapter Twelve

By the end of November I had picked up the rhythm of existence at Ching Ho. I was a professional prisoner by then, and felt that I knew how to survive any of the physical or spiritual trials the place could throw at me. In the end I did survive, but it was a much closer thing than I thought it would be. If I was able to adapt to the harshness of the climate, the rough working conditions, the intellectual humiliation and even the semi-starvation of drastically reduced rations, there was little I or any of the others could do about the recurrent waves of disease and debilitation which chose to visit us. As Solzhenitsyn wrote of the Soviet camps, many better men than I broke and many stronger ones died. The strange laws of chance always play.

In the thirteen months that remained before me at that prison farm I was plunged into such a series of personal experiences and human encounters that the outside world I rejoined afterward often seems pale and less significant by comparison. My head so swims with images of what I went through myself, or that others told me about, or that I learned of by accident, that if they come out here in a somewhat kaleidoscopic jumble, forgive me: They are the essence of what it is like to be down and out in a Chinese labour camp.

The signal that truly desperate times were upon us came in early December, when a horse-drawn cart entered the compound and a prisoner detail began unloading the cargo: dark brown sheets of an unknown material, rigid and light, each one measuring about three by five feet. No one had any idea of what they were. Two weeks later we were called into the auditorium to hear the answer. The stuff was paper pulp, and we were going to eat it. Food Substitute, the prison officials called it – *dai sh'pin*. I'll never forget the words. Since there wasn't enough food to go around in China, the search was on for something to replace it and we prisoners had the honour of being the guinea pigs for the various ersatzes the scientific community came up with. The warder describing the new nutritional policy told us that paper pulp was guaranteed harmless and though it contained no nutritive value, it would make our wo'tous fatter and give us the satisfying impression of bulk. The new flour mix would be no more than thirty per cent powdered paper pulp. It will go through your digestive tracts easily, he said with assurance. We know exactly how you will feel.

Sure enough, our wo'tous the next day were considerably bigger and we had the pleasant sensation of putting more into our stomachs. They tasted like the normal loaves, but were a bit limper in texture. We ate them without complaint. That evening I saw Ma Erh-kang, the prison doctor. A prisoner like the rest of us, he had no particular respect for most of the warders and certainly none for their medical capabilities. He told me he was worried about the ersatz.

'If I were you, Bao, I'd try to eat some fatty things,' he advised, but it was an empty thought under the circumstances.

'You're joking, Ma,' I said. 'Where in hell am I going to get fat?'

He shrugged and looked preoccupied.

'I don't know, but I don't like that stuff. It may not contain anything poisonous, but I wonder what it will do to the digestive tract. Paper absorbs moisture.'

For a while it appeared that his fears were groundless. The bigger wo'tous were popular with the prisoners and they seemed digestible. At the start, anyway. There was hardly any jealousy or complaint; in fact, when the Health Preservation Diet was announced a few days later. We should have been alarmed by the ominous title, though. P'ao Ca'ien Fan, as it was called in Chinese, was established especially for those prisoners who would be holding key jobs during the winter months and who in the past had earned merits by displaying a proper attitude toward labour – and whose strength would be needed for the crucial spring planting. About 30 of the 285 in our brigade won places on the list, and among them were Sun and Soong, the one we used to call 'the Stakhanovite' for his tireless enthusiasm for doing right and serving the government. The Health Preservation Diet consisted of millet flour without ersatz and a soup made from whatever vegetables could be found, often laced with horsemeat or some kind of oil. Even that diet disintegrated as the winter went on, though. After a month or so the only difference was that they had a larger portion of vegetables.

On the second day of the diet old Sun was already too embarrassed to eat his food with us in the cell, as he had done the first day. He ended his personal crisis with one dramatic and illegal gesture. When he walked back from the kitchen his painted tin mug was brimming with a soup of horsemeat, vegetables and fat. He paused long enough to make certain that everybody was watching – and then emptied his mug into our communal soup tub.

'Your health needs preserving, too,' he growled. 'You can report me if you like.'

The Stakhanovite was confused. He wasn't used to breaking the rules. No one thought he would report Sun, but he obviously didn't know what to do now.

'Don't think you're so well off, Soong,' Sun said sharply. 'Next spring they won't expect these people to work so hard, because they've had a bad winter, but guys like you and me are going to be slaving because we've had all that good food. We'll need all the help we can get.'

Soong slopped his mug into the tub. I suppose it must have been those two extra portions of fat over the next two weeks that saved our cell from having any paper-pulp deaths. By Christmas day the whole farm was in agony from what was probably one of the most serious cases of mass constipation in medical history. Sounds comical, doesn't it? It wasn't. Just as Doc Ma had predicted, the paper powder absorbed the moisture from our digestive tracts, making it progressively harder to defecate as each day passed. And painful. Men were bent double with cramps. Even soapy water enemas did hardly any good, for those few who had the honour of using the single apparatus in the farm's medical inventory. I had to stick my finger up my anus and dig it out, in dry lumps, like sawdust. The prison authorities finally backed off in alarm, gave us straight mush and instructed us to drink lots of water. I never saw it personally, but we heard that many of the older and weaker ones died trying to shit their guts out. I do recall a little scene in the fields, though, when Sun and I walked by one character squatting down by the edge of the road, shaking and sweating with the effort in spite of the cold.

'Look at that,' Sun spat out with surprising rancour. 'Another one of Mao's benefits for you.'

After paper pulp flopped, someone in central planning came up with the bright idea of trying marsh water plankton. Since plankton was said to be almost 100 per cent protein, the idea seemed brilliant – in theory. They skimmed the slimy, green stuff off the swampy ponds around the camp and mixed it in with the mush either straight or dried and powdered, since it tasted too horrible to eat unaccompanied. Again, we all fell sick and some of the weaker ones died. That particular plankton, they discovered after a few autopsies, was practically unassimilable for the human body. End of plankton experiment. At length our daily ersatz became ground corn cobs, mixed in with the wo'tou flour. Afterward it was adopted as the standard food supplement for the country at large. We had been pioneers.

Two little images stay with me today from that period around Christmastime 1960. They have no connection or even, I suppose, any particular significance except to illustrate what life was like then and how men could react to it. Fertilizing the fields was the most important job at that time of year, and the selection of our labour teams changed from day to day, depending on who was available and strong enough to go out. Sun and I were watering down one of the big manure dumps one afternoon, tossing buckets of water over the straw and shit to help it ferment. We worked in silence, trudging back and forth from the water trough with the Chinese yokes on our shoulders, balancing two buckets apiece. It was muddy and cold and stinking and we were hungry and weak. Sun put down his buckets and stopped moving altogether. The look of resignation and bitterness that crossed his face was all the more surprising in that he had always been one of the strongest and most stoic of us all.

'Tell me, Bao,' he asked numbly. 'Do you think I'll ever have a full meal again?'

'Sure, Sun,' I said automatically. 'Sure you will.'

But he wasn't in a mood for facile optimism. He gave me a dirty look.

'When, Bao?'

Poor Sun. Poor all of us. We went back to work and never brought up the subject again.

For four or five days around the same time I was detailed to team up with Shau, a man from another cell, carting manure out to the fields. I remember him now for the Christmas present he made me.

Shau was probably the strongest prisoner at Ching Ho. In society he had been a pedicab driver, and he had broken into the trade as a boy in the old days of the rickshaws, pushing his uncle's rig from behind to help him in Peking. He was a dramatic-looking man, tall for a Chinese, with broad shoulders, a head he always kept shaven smooth and the musculature of a weight-lifter. As happens so often with large, strong men, he was the gentlest of us all and shrank from conflict as if fearing his great strength. He was famous around the camp for his capacity to absorb work, but instead of gaining merits by over-fulfilling his norms, he used to let the weaker prisoners claim part of his production so they could hold onto their rations. That was ideologically incorrect, of course, but no one – least of all the warders – thought of questioning him about it.

Over the days we worked together on the bicycle wheel cart, we talked easily and reminisced about places we both had known in Peking. Like most illiterates, he had an excellent memory and grasp of colourful detail. Some of his preferred pedicab customers, it turned out, had been my friends and colleagues the American Marines. He remembered them as good tippers who used to give out presents on their big holidays.

Shau also had the best vision of anyone I had ever known, and he used it to become Ching Ho's champion cigarette butt scrounger. 'Radar Eyeballs', they called him, and he had an uncanny knack for discovering stray butts left behind by guards or free workers, even if others had already searched the area. As with food, real tobacco had grown increasingly scarcer as winter came on. A cigarette butt windfall meant not only a valuable piece of barter currency, but for the man who finally smoked it a few luxurious moments of surcease from the despairing tedium of camp life. (The Chinese have always been heavy smokers. Mao himself smokes about fifty cigarettes a day.)

On Christmas the wind was blowing heavily but the day was otherwise dry and sunny. Shau and I had been spreading manure over the wheat fields all morning long and well into the afternoon. It must have been around 3 p.m. when we trudged over to the embankment in the lee of the wind to take a break in the sun. We lay down on our backs and stared up at the sky.

'The foreigners' big holiday was a week before New Year, wasn't it, Bao?'

Shau's question was so unexpected right then that I hesitated for an instant, getting my thoughts straight. He didn't know the name for Christmas, but he remembered the ceremony of the presents. When I told him he was absolutely right in his reckoning, Shau reached inside his black jacket and drew out a little square packet of neatly folded newsprint. He held it out to me.

'Here's something for your holiday, then.'

I was surprised and a little embarrassed by this gesture, but I took it nonetheless. Inside the newsprint packet was a lovely cigarette butt about an inch long. I automatically asked him if he would share it with me, but Shau would have none of it – it was to be my present alone. I smoked it after supper that night, for my Christmas celebration .

For the New Year we had a modest feast, in spite of the famine conditions. Longman Koo came from the kitchen to give us the good news on the night of 30 December.

'All right, there's some good news for the team,' he said. 'The government has done the impossible to give us a good New Year.'

'You turning agitprop now, Longman?' someone asked. It was true that that sort of speechifying was unlike him, but he probably felt the occasion called for a certain solemnity.

'Skip the formalities, Longman,' I said, 'Are we going to get something extra or not?'

'Yeah,' he said. 'One cake of dried rice apiece. That'll make about half a kilo when it's steamed.'

We all agreed that was pretty good, considering the circumstances.

'And there'll be two ounces of meat apiece and some vegetables,' he added. 'And two ounces of sugar and two pieces of cake. That's it.'

We didn't complain. With the shape the country was in, that was even generous. We worked happily on New Year's Eve day, looking forward to supper that night and the New Year's day lunch. That night like most of the others I went to wish a happy New Year to Warder Yang.

'Don't thank me,' he intoned, all baby-faced and pink-cheeked. 'Thank the government. As long as you behave and accept the reform programme, you'll be all right. I wish you a Happy New Year, too, and hope you will receive the greatest possible leniency from the government.'

There were bones with the meat in the New Year soup this time, and we ground them down with our teeth and swallowed everything, then cleaned our basins with a splash of water and drank the water. There were no study sessions that night. We went to sleep feeling blissfully close to satiety and certain that the next day there would be one more good meal.

I entered 1961 with what my warders would have called a high ideological level. My reeducation was successful to the degree that I believed what the warders told me, respected the guards (most of them, at any rate) and was convinced that if the government didn't exactly love me, it was at least doing everything reasonably within its power to keep me and my comrades healthy, considering the bad times. I also knew well that it was very much to my interest to keep my behaviour as close as possible to the letter of the law. As a foreigner, I was the only one who stood any chance whatsoever of leaving the prison and getting out of China for good, although to tell the truth, I never believed I would. Still, I didn't want to jeopardize any chances.

My intransigent purism began to take its toll, though. Since I refused to forage in the fields or to steal food systematically as many of the others did, I grew weak and easily fatigued. My legs felt like cotton and my head was always spinning. I went to see Dr Ma.

Ma was a man everyone liked. Around forty-five when I met him, he had been a successful practitioner before the revolution, with his own clinic in the west side of Peking. His downfall came as the result of an abortion he performed for the wife of a party cadre. Abortion is a legal operation in China but the cadre suspected his wife of infidelity and denounced Ma for having acted without securing proper authorization. He had already been in Ching Ho for two years by the time I arrived and had managed to turn an empty cell into the semblance of an infirmary.

I told Ma I felt terrible but didn't want to be taken off work. Leaving work sounded like a nice idea in principle, but it entailed a forced rest of at least three days at half rations. Ma was familiar with the dilemma. He reached into his drawer and took out three small packets of pink paper and one larger one, green this time.

'Take one of the pink ones before every meal,' he instructed me. 'The green one you can take when you like but I recommend it later, after supper.'

Back in the cell I opened one of the pink parcels and mixed the white powder into a glass of water. Aspirin, as usual. Curious, I unfolded the green paper as well. To my delight I saw it contained pure tobacco, enough for ten cigarettes. Doc Ma knew how to take care of prisoners. Over the next few days Sun and I shared the smokes.

With the increasing scarcity of food, we prisoners developed quasi-religious gestures around its presentation and consumption. It is axiomatic that persons on the verge of starvation and yet regularly supplied with a small quantity of nourishment eat slowly in order to prolong the pleasure, but I wonder how many others ever went to the extremes that we devised at Ching Ho. It was even, in its own manner, a philosophical proposition.

'I go through a battle every time I eat,' a cellmate named Wo explained to me once. 'If I eat the food right away, it will be gone soon; but if I try to keep some for later, then I'm even hungrier. I never know what to do,'

Eating, and occasionally smoking, was the only creature pleasure we had left, and devouring a furtive cabbage leaf behind a guard's back wasn't the same as the ritual of the meal, where we had our leisure. Bits of food that I now eat in two or three minutes I would draw out for twenty minutes then, in ceremonial, slow-motion mastication. Small, bite-size morsels we divided even smaller. About the only things we didn't subdivide were individual grains of rice. Many of my friends solved Wo's dilemma through self-discipline by eating only half of their wo'tous in the morning and holding onto the rest all day long, as a supplement for supper. They carried the food treasures in bags hung around their necks, beautifully made little things that closed at the mouth with a drawstring and were decorated with their names sewn in with coloured thread.

The objects of eating, of course, had their own cult. Everyone fashioned his own chopsticks and the cleverer ones sharpened the ends to spear rice grains, or pieces of wo'tou or, if it was a special day, meat. Naturally enough, the honoured chopsticks had to have their custom-made cloth covers, also decorated with name or monogram. In the early months of 1961 spoons became the rage – everyone scavenged around for scraps of metal to tap out into the desired form. I personally missed this fad because I still had an olive drab aluminium spoon my wife had brought me back in Prison Number One. The champion stylist of all, though, turned out to be Lo, our assistant cell leader. Early in January he began scraping away at a ten-inch piece of cast-off bamboo with that traditional prison tool, a piece of broken glass. He whittled and polished until it was flat, and I assumed at first he was just passing the time. Lo kept at it over the days, and what emerged in February was a hybrid instrument with a delicately fashioned knife at one end and a spoon at the other. Lo took his meals with his creation from then on, cutting his wo'tou with the knife end and then flipping it over to spoon it into his mouth. I was mad with desire to own one of them but Lo's price was too high – six cigarettes. I had long since resigned myself to living without it when we discovered by chance one day that I had gone to school with his uncle. To honour our discovery he especially whittled me a knife-spoon. I carried it with me throughout the rest of my time in jail as my second most treasured possession, after my Chinese-English dictionary. When I was released and expelled from China, the police took it from me and threw it away in spite of my protests. It could be of no use to me, they explained. It was such a beautiful object that I had never even eaten with it. Lo had spent probably twenty hours making it.

On 20 January the cadres sprang a surprise on us in a special meeting called by Brigade Chief Yang in the frigid, unheated auditorium. There had been perfidious rumours, Yang said, that the guards and warders were eating well while the prisoners starved. To put an immediate end to this subversive talk he ordered us to make a tour of the cadres' kitchen. The guards lined us up by fives and herded us across the compound and into the kitchen. The place smelled good, all right, but we could see that they, too, were eating the sweet-potato flour mixed with corncob ersatz. There was cabbage and vermicelli, too, but no wheat flour or meat. The only difference we could perceive between their rations and our own was the larger portion of oil in their soup. Yang warned us against any more antigovernment chatter, but assured us that prisoner delegations could continue the kitchen visits whenever they asked. There were no more complaints after that. Chinese Communists are often painful fanatics, but they are straight and honest.

Honesty wasn't helping me get any stronger, though. I was continually short of breath as I stumbled around the fields and suffered dizzy spells more and more frequently. I started losing my hair again and my fingernails took on the same brittleness as in Grass Mist Lane. One morning after I fainted in the fields, Sun sent me to see Dr Ma again. He clucked his tongue and sighed with displeasure when he took my blood pressure.

'You're not in good shape, Bao,' he said at length. 'I've got to prescribe a long rest for you.'

I was alarmed – that would certainly entail a major cut in rations. I begged him not to do it.

'Your blood pressure is unbelievably low,' he told me. 'Have you been sticking to regulations? Excuse me for asking, but do you forage?'

'Not much,' I said. I had always tried to maintain ideological purity on that question. Ma gazed at me through his heavy glasses, pursing his lips.

'Well, you're a man of honour, Bao, but as a doctor I have to tell you that it doesn't pay to go on acting that way. You're in a bad way. Even if I put you on the highest medical rations I can get, it won't do you much good. Sometimes it's better to be a little less strict about interpreting the regulations.'

This was surprising heresy from a man whose position made him something close to a prison official. In effect, he was recommending insurrection, however limited and personal.

'I've got people here who are too far gone to help,' he added. 'I wouldn't like you to get that way.'

He pointed to an œdema case I had already seen before. He was a man of about forty who appeared to be in no pain at all as he sat propped up in a corner reading a paper. His legs and feet, though, were swollen to grotesque proportions, the result of months of compulsive water-drinking as an antidote to hunger. He might never walk again, Ma confided to me. I decided I would go foraging.

My first professor in the art was Leong, the scion of the wealthy bourgeois family who used to receive the elegant parcels from Hong Kong. He seemed an unlikely one to be a forager, but the situation had its own internal logic, since his parcels were relatively rare and never very nourishing. Further, he was frail and almost perpetually sick. Rather than attempting to force a full day's work from him, the warders chose to ignore him, cut his rations to the absolute starvation minimum of 300 grammes per day and let him stay behind in the cell doing what he pleased. Leong spent the day looking for things to eat, stalking through the compound with a cotton bag around his neck and a pointed stick for spearing things. For two days I observed him in his routine around the various refuse heaps, picking through the meagre mess for bits of edible leaves or stalks. The half-rotten outside leaves of cabbages were his principal fare. He boiled them several times over and dried them in the sun.

When they were ready they had the salty, crunchy consistency of HiHo crackers. I made myself a foraging bag.

On my first day back in the fields I managed to come up with nothing better than two shrivelled turnips and a few pieces of old cabbage leaf. Soong the Stakhanovite laughed when he saw it.

'That ain't much, Bao,' he said. 'I think you need some help to get started. Come on.'

Soong grabbed the fork of his pull-cart and made straight for the hothouses. Full of apprehension, I followed. He parked the cart near the door, took a quick, expert look around, then pulled me inside the warm, humid interior.

'We're not supposed to be inside here,' I whispered absurdly.

'Don't worry, Bao. We've just been dumping a load of shit, right? Grab yourself a turnip.'

There were long rows of fresh young vegetables. I found one that looked promising and pulled. I hit the jackpot – it was big and fat and beautiful. I stuffed it quickly into the bag under my jacket and we beat it outside again. That night while Sun and Soong kidded me about losing my ideological virginity, I ate and ate that turnip. It was delicious.

'Good, ain't it?' said Soong with satisfaction. 'Only from now on, remember to keep a few extra for a rainy day.'

As a special demonstration he opened his bag and laid out his selection for me to see. He had turnips, cabbage leaves, some soybeans and even some garlic cloves marinating in a bottle of brine. This was scientific foraging – he could even leave part of his hoard behind when he was in the fields. Our cell, at least, was close enough so that no one would think of stealing from another. I was learning, but a few days later Warder Yang caught me red-handed. He appeared in the cell when I had the foraging bag open before me. He ordered me to follow him to his office with the vegetables. I knew I was in for at least a lecture.

'I thought you were a man of honour,' he began, 'but now I see you're no different from the others. What you have done here' – he enumerated the items one by one on his fingers – 'is, first, proof that you are discontented with what the government is giving you; second, stealing government property; third, inducing others to criminal activities; and fourth, unhygienic. You can ruin your health with dirty food. If you do it knowingly, you are making a serious mistake. I want you to take all this stuff and throw it out.'

He stood there sternly in his uniform, a father figure no older than myself, ordering me to actually destroy food. I felt a surge of desperate rage.

'Warder Yang,' I protested miserably, 'please don't say that. It took me days to find this stuff. Put me in solitary if you like, but don't make me throw away food.'

There was a long silence. He watched me with resignation – I almost would have thought fatigue.

'Bao, in the future will you be able to tell your children what you did without a feeling of shame? You'll outlive these temporary economic difficulties, but will you be able to face yourself after stooping so low?'

'Warder, it's one thing to talk about honour here, but you're on the other side.'

'Yes,' he agreed quietly, 'but my stomach's made out of flesh and blood, too, Bao. Just like yours. Go on back to your cell.' He made a little waving gesture with his hand. 'And take these with you.'

I scooped up my treasures and trotted back, filled with admiration for my jailer, but shame-faced too.

Of all the ones I witnessed, the most terrible collision between hunger and the petty world of regulation involved another prisoner, a man named Hsu from the Fourth Brigade. It happened on the day before Chinese New Year, when I had orderly duty in the visitors' room. It was an easy job, and generally uneventful, consisting mostly of stoking the little coal pot stove, keeping hot water ready for drinking and running errands for the guard. The guard screened visitors, witnessed the meetings and went through the formality of weighing the food parcels visitors brought. In principle the limit was five kilos, but the more understanding warders like Young Yang rarely put them to the test. The guard I had that day, though, was a literal-minded bastard without any humanity in him, the sort who looks for trouble.

He got everything he could hope for in the day's first visitor, a soldier in officer's uniform who was carrying two heavy parcels under his arms. The guard received him next to the long table under the portrait of Mao. At the far end of the table, there was a clock and a set of scales.

'I've come to visit my brother,' the soldier said, producing the invitational postcard from the camp director that authorized him to be there. The guard sent for Hsu. He was handsome, this Hsu, obviously the soldier's older brother. His pants were tucked into boots Russian style and his black padded jacket and scarf gave him a piratical air, accentuated by a heavy, three-day beard. The guard stepped up and intervened just as the lieutenant was pushing the parcels across the table to his brother.

'I have to examine this,' he said. 'Please open them.'

Deliberately, he went through the contents piece by piece until he had everything lined up in military order. One bag contained canned foods – fish, meat, chicken, a bottle of oil, preserved fruits and finally some apples and persimmons. In the other there were fifty small loaves of wheat flour bread. The guard counted them.

'He is permitted only five kilos,' he said with the satisfied finality of the born bureaucrat. As he was about to put the bundles on the scales the soldier protested.

'It's Chinese New Year,' he said. 'Can't you let him have just a little bit more this time?'

'No. Five kilos and no more.'

'I came all the way from Tsing Tao,' the soldier tried, still hoping to win him over. 'What can I do with the extra stuff?'

The guard shrugged, unmoved by the dilemma. 'Take it back.'

'I'm a member of the armed forces. I suppose you were, too. Can't we talk comrade to comrade?'

'I am.'

The poor soldier was getting nowhere, and his brother didn't dare join the debate. He kept his mouth shut, but darted his glance back and forth between the two.

'Would it be possible for me to see the prison director, then?'

'What for? Right now I'm in command here.'

The soldier finally became angry and unthinkingly tried a dangerous flank attack. He should have known better.

'In that case, comrade,' he said firmly, 'I would like to see your superior.'

The guard left without a word, perfectly confident of the outcome of this set-to. It was another ten minutes before he returned with Liu, the education and discipline warder. It was quite clear that the guard had filled him in on the situation and that he had prepared his act.

'Well, well,' he said with a phony smile. 'What seems to be the problem here?'

The poor visitor was taken in by the comedy. He thought he glimpsed a ray of hope.

'I was just telling the other comrade that I get to see my brother here only once a year. I've come very far for this visit and I've brought him some New Year presents. I admit it's more than the regulations allow, but I thought maybe you could make an exception in this case.'

Liu picked his way through the pile of food, making little grunts of displeasure. When he lifted his gaze back to the visitor he was ready with his speech.

'You brought all this?'

The soldier nodded. Liu let fly.

'And you call yourself a member of the armed forces? What sort of ideological standards do you have, anyway? What are all these delicacies here? They don't come from the local markets. The peasants and workers can't enjoy this sort of thing, can they? But because you are in the armed forces and have been given the glorious honour of protecting the fatherland, the working classes have made sacrifices to provide you with these things. They have given these things to *you* – not to a counter-revolutionary! You are committing not only a mistake, but an error of principle. This counterrevolutionary isn't your brother. He is your enemy! By bringing him all this food do you mean to insinuate that we are treating him badly here? I won't even ask you where you got the food tickets to procure fifty loaves of bread.'

The soldier had been ideologically trapped and knew it. All he could do now was to wait for the end of the tirade and hope for the best.

'Comrade,' Liu snapped, 'you will now please give me your unit number and the name of your commanding officer.'

He had no choice but to comply. The request was perfectly reasonable and congruous with the Communist ethic. And besides, Liu was a member of the national security police.

'Now take all this back,' Liu said absently as he returned his notebook to his pocket. 'This prisoner isn't entitled to any gifts. And, by the way, he would tell you himself that he doesn't need any parcels from you. He lacks nothing here. Isn't that right?'

'Yes, of course,' answered Hsu obediently. 'That's quite right.'

As we moved into the fifth period of winter, our old obsession about food was joined by an abiding concern about the weather. For the Chinese, winter lasts exactly eighty-one days, which they divide into nine periods of nine days, beginning 21 December. By the third and fourth periods the temperature was regularly dropping to the vicinity of twenty below zero centigrade, a situation that inspired us with a permanent anxiety. According to regulations, we were not required to go out to work if the temperature was twenty below in still air, or fifteen below with a wind blowing. Every morning we waited for the gong to tell us whether or not we would be heading for the fields. How many times have I lain with the others, fully clothed under the covers of our bed, hoping against hope that one or two degrees would save us from work – while at that very moment a trusty was climbing the ladder up the big wooden gallows where the section of rail hung. When he hit it with the hammer – always nine strokes – it could be heard for miles around. There would be a pause, and then nine more strokes.

'Tchoo gung!' a warder would cry, and we would reluctantly pile out for assembly.

Our study sessions naturally increased with the cold and the hunger. The aim was to keep our minds occupied during the long days indoors, develop our reliance on the government and forget as much as possible about eating. These almost never-ending studies constitute the great Chinese invention in penal theory and the main difference between their prison camps and those built by the Soviets. A Chinese prisoner is practically never left alone to think his independent thoughts. Studies of one type or another occur every single day of his jail life. If I refer to them only occasionally, it is to avoid repetition, but the Western reader should know that not a day passes without studies.

Occasionally, miraculously, the sessions in the camps would turn out to be comical. I recall in particular one session that ended in total debacle. The theme we were given that day was 'loving labour', and our study period happened after an unusually tough day in the fields. Longman Koo was directing things.

'Each one of us will tell what he thinks it is to love labour,' he said. 'Someone will preside with me this time. Bao, you start.'

'Loving labour is forgetting what you were in the past,' I said, 'rolling up your sleeves, disregarding everything else around you and concentrating on your job. It is overfulfilling the government's norms and doing your level best at all times. It is not complaining or asking for favours or special treatment.'

'No, Bao,' Soong objected, 'you're not explaining what it means to work well. You are speaking like a theoretician and a stinking intellectual.'

It is one of the constants of Chinese Communist vocabulary that an intellectual is always 'stinking'. Like the Soviets, the Chinese ideologues cordially despise and mistrust the intelligentsia because of its irritating tendency to form its own ideas.

'Loving labour is doing more than the government asks,' another cellmate said, but Soong wasn't at all satisfied with the way the talk was going.

'No,' he insisted, 'you're all wrong. In the first place, all of us are here because we're enemies of the government. Of course you speak about doing more than the government asks, but that's just empty talk. What if tomorrow there's a force seven wind blowing and the temperature is fourteen below. Not fifteen, but just fourteen. And we're here in the cell after breakfast, waiting. Well, every one of us will be hoping they don't hit that rail, won't we? But we're here to redeem ourselves, not to relax in the cell. It's at times like that that we have a chance to show how much we love labour. The two prisoners who spoke just now weren't loving labour – they were only showing enthusiasm. But I'll bet neither one of them would go out fifteen minutes early in the morning and wait under the rail hoping they'll come out and hit it. Now *that* would be loving labour. I'm sorry to say that none of us here loves labour like that.'

Warder Yang heard Soong's talk and didn't like it. Like many of the other cadres, he would go from cell to cell checking on studies and noting enthusiasm. He concluded that the attitude of our team was far from serious and that, further, we were flailing around with totally unorthodox theories instead of remaining safely within the framework of the General Line. He ordered us to drop labour for now and take up another theme: 'Socialism is good.' We would get our thoughts straight by meditating for fifteen minutes beforehand.

That was a mistake. Yang should have known better. We were bone-tired from our day of preparing the fields for spring planting. Nothing was more welcome than a nice little meditation. Within minutes most of us were fast asleep. When Yang came back to check on us, his presence was announced by a gust of cold air as he opened the door. It woke us up, but not before he had understood perfectly well what had happened.

'What's this? What's this?' He was the very picture of outraged virtue.

'We, ahh . . . were meditating socialism,' Soong stammered, but he was thoroughly unconvincing. Yang stood there glaring at us, hands on his hips.

'If I questioned you one by one,' he said, 'you'd swear on your grandmothers' heads that you were meditating and that you know socialism is good. I know that. But I also know that deep down inside you're also saying that socialism doesn't feed you enough.'

'Look, Warder,' Sun said without a hint of sarcasm, 'you said it, not us.'

Yang looked down at Sun, sighed and went back out into the night.

A couple of days later we got a chance to find out if we really did love labour. It was time to get the fields fertilized, and absolute priority was to go to spreading manure from the big heaps we had been watering down and ripening throughout the fall and early winter. Every available cart was to be pressed into action and they would be manned by twos – one to shovel in the load and the other to pull the cart. There would be other teams to spread the manure where we dumped it. It didn't appear objectively to be such a bad job, but the hitch was that it had to be done in ten days – every single field, and many of them lay more than two miles from the manure dumps. Each cart was to be fully loaded with at least 240 catties of manure, and guards would check to make sure there was no cheating. The individual norm was to be six round trips a day. A single slogan appeared on every agitprop blackboard after that, written out in beautiful Chinese calligraphy with coloured chalk:

'Load as much as possible, run as quickly as possible, unload as quickly as possible.'

The fatalities of topography had it that the course was in almost all cases uphill from the manure dumps to the fields, but there was nothing we could do except to choose the strongest as pullers, the weakest as loaders and hope for the best. That night we had only a short study, devoted to the techniques of spreading manure, and turned in early.

On the first day of the campaign our cell failed to make its norm. There was simply too much work and not enough time. Warder Yang told us we would have to start getting up earlier. For the next nine days we were out in the fields before sunrise, making our first trips in the dark and galloping back with the empty carts in the first rays of the dawn. We finished at noon on the last day of the Chinese lunar New Year – not a speck of manure was left, and the fields were ready for planting. Our reward – it coincided with the New Year festivities rather than the Fertilization Campaign – was a cattie of rice apiece, meat stew in place of vegetable soup and a movie in the auditorium. All around me in the dark I could hear the crunchcrunchcrunch of my fellow jailbirds eating cabbage leaves from a pile of heads which felicitously had been stored in another corner of the building.

Some weeks later our Fifth Brigade was disbanded and incorporated into the Fourth Brigade. Our entire team went over to the new brigade intact except for Soong, who was rewarded for his enthusiasm by being made leader of Team Seven. His place in our cell's sleeping order was taken by the Reverend Father Hsia. What a man he was! If all Catholic priests were like him, there would never be any crisis in the Church.

Father Peter Hsia was a Trappist monk from Yangkiaping, a small, frail, sunburned man in his late sixties with prominent, bushy eyebrows and only a few wisps of white hair on his head. Very soon after he arrived in the cell he approached me and began asking dangerous questions. I was extremely wary. He could have been a provocateur, for all I knew.

'John is a Catholic name,' he said softly. 'Are you a Christian, then?'

He had seen my name written above my sleeping spot on the bed and had made the same translation any educated Chinese would have done. The second part of my Chinese name, Ruo-wang, is the Catholic transliteration for Saint John. I preferred to stay away from the subject entirely.

'That's none of your business,' I told him.

'My name is Peter,' he said, and then clammed up. He wasn't going to push it.

In the fields the rest of that winter Father Hsia gave himself to his work with incredible conscientiousness, in spite of his frailty. He was forever apologizing to us, every time he slipped or made a mistake or carried less than the strongest ones.

'Sorry to be holding you up, schoolmates,' he said whenever something went wrong.

We all liked Hsia and as the weeks passed I even drew out of my shell and guardedly discussed religion with him when I was sure no one could hear. Koo was so impressed by his attitude that he took it upon himself to order the rest of the team to help the old man with his norms whenever he was in trouble, to ensure that he held on to his Class A rations. Even that bothered Hsia.

'You shouldn't do that,' he protested. 'It's against regulations. If I can't finish my work, I have no right to the higher rations.'

Koo told him to shut up and leave the decisions to him. But late in April it became apparent that there was at least one cellmate who didn't approve of the little priest, when I and some of the others were called in one by one to see Warder Yang. He used the hallowed cat and mouse style.

'Bao, are you withholding something from the government?'

I didn't know what he was talking about, and said it.

'You know Christian activities are not permitted in the cell.'

I waited for him to go on.

'What's this I've been hearing about Hsia? I hear he's been praying in bed.'

Yang was quite right, but I was certain he had no proof. 'If he has been,' I said, 'I'd be the first to know. I don't practise Christianity anymore, but I can still recognize prayers.'

'Do you mean to say these accusations are unfounded?'

'No, I didn't say exactly that.'

'Well, then, what's this mumbling people have been telling me about?'

'Brigade leader,' I explained as reasonably as I could, 'you have to realize that Hsia is an old man. Old people talk to themselves – it even happens to other people, too. Sometimes when I can't get to sleep, I tell myself stories.'

'Shen jing bing,' he said disgustedly. 'You're all lunatics.'

After Koo went through the same interview he returned to the cell in a controlled fury. There was a subtle hint of threat in his voice when he spoke.

'I have something to say to classmates who make reports to the government. I want you to know that I am all for it. It is the duty of every one of us. Confiding in the government means you are on the road to redemption. But let me say one thing more: If anyone makes false reports to the government, he is committing a crime. Lying to try to gain merits is one of the worst criminal activities there is.'

236

'What are you getting at, Koo?' someone asked.

'I'm just telling you what the warder said. If any one of you thinks I have spoken wrong, you can go see him yourself.'

The incident was closed with that, and we never did discover who had told on Hsia. Of course he did pray in bed, but it was barely audible. He also used to give confession in the fields to some of the prisoners who had remained Christian. During breaks when we would lie down to rest in the sun, the prisoner wishing to confess would simply take his place next to Hsia and tell him his sins while looking up at the sky. We could see their lips moving, but they were always careful never to look at each other or make any kinds of gestures. Hsia probably would have loved to be able to make the sign of the cross, but it was just too risky. 'Your sins are forgiven,' he would say up to the sky, and the prisoner would wander away.

Hsia trusted me to the point that he knew I would never report him, so he often lowered his caution when he was around me. Once I overheard an amazing exchange when a very devout Christian came to him for advice about stealing. Like all the rest he had been keeping himself alive by grabbing extra food, but the morality of theft still bothered him.

'Do the guards know you people are stealing food?' Hsia asked him.

'Well, sure. They know that foraging goes on.'

'Well, then,' the old man went on easily, 'if the government knows you are stealing and lets you get away with it, then the government is pretty kind, isn't it?'

'Yes,' the prisoner agreed worriedly, but that was hardly the conclusion he had been looking for. Hsia had been holding it back as a surprise.

'Do you think God will be no better than the Communists?' he asked. 'Don't worry about that anymore.'

Father Hsia was certainly the finest Christian I have ever met. The great Catholic martyrs may have endured more pain than he, but their faith could hardly have been any greater than that of this stubborn little old man who kept the faith of the Western missionaries alive in the camps after all his foreign superiors had left China when the going got rough. He deserves to be sainted.

Chapter Thirteen

As winter gave way to spring we prisoners were frankly employed as draught animals with no pretence that we were to be considered anything else. In those days tractors were still not produced on a large scale, and horses and oxen were scarce – everything was scarce in 1960 and 1961. All the work of preparing the ground, levelling and terracing, moving rock and loam, digging and maintaining irrigation ditches, fell directly upon us. As of 1 March, our slower, more restful winter schedule was replaced with a ten-hour work day. We were back to the old routine, weak from malnutrition and disease but still expected to perform as fresh, strong labour. Some lasted, but a lot didn't. I was among those who couldn't keep the pace.

The production warder, a wiry, bowlegged peasant named Chao, never tired of reminding us that our future rations were directly at stake. The work we did now would determine how much wheat and rice would be harvested and hence how much of it we would get. As an added inducement to enthusiastic labour he divided his workers into relatively small groups and decreed a policy of Socialist Emulation – challenges between teams with food bonuses as the rewards. On every agitprop blackboard the teams were numbered and the categories schematized as in the Transit Centre – rocket, airplane, automobile, bicycle, oxcart and the final ignominy of turtle.

I began the season in that typical Oriental labour of dragging a weighted levelling board through the rice paddies. A rice paddy, of course, must be absolutely level, since it is built to contain a constant depth of water for the young shoots. Every paddy must be reworked at springtime and the classical system is to flood them and to drag the leveller along behind a beast of burden. In Ching Ho two prisoners took the place of the beast and the leveller was a wooden plank a foot wide and four inches thick, weighted with sixty pounds of bricks. My partner and I were hitched to ropes at either extremity of the plank. We were only a mediocre team, though, never rising above automobile.

Three incidents, all of them directly related to the hunger and the harsh working conditions, remain with me now from that bad springtime. The first was when Lei Ying-fang, the master forager, cracked up. Hunger was behind it, but it was finally his nerves that gave way. I heard about it later from Sun, who was there in the fields with him when it happened. Lei had been complaining more and more bitterly with each hungry day of work. When the lunch cart came out to their station, he grabbed his portion of wo'tou and broke it in half under a warder's eye. To the general surprise, he began to curse loudly and hurl imprecations against the government for first starving him and then forcing him to eat a wo'tou that was half ersatz.

'Be quiet and eat your lunch,' the warder said, trying very reasonably to avoid trouble, but there was no stopping Lei. He spat and hurled the offending loaf to the ground – a purely criminal gesture no warder could ignore. He had Lei bound head to foot and detailed two prisoners to dump him in a bicycle cart and bring him back to the compound for a stretch of solitary. We had to Struggle him later.

Then there was Lam, a Chinese who chose the wrong way to forage. Lam was about fifty and had been in Ching Ho since 1951 – one of the real old-timers. I never knew him personally, but he had a good reputation as a student and as a hard worker, and several times had been named Activist of Reform Through Labour. His big trouble came when a warder found a bag of corn hidden among his personal belongings in the cell. That was against the rules, of course, but what made it a grievously serious offence was that it was seed corn. He had stolen it from the supply shack. We heard talk about his folly but didn't learn what the consequences would be until Rest Sunday, the single day off our schedule gave us, after thirteen days of steady work. At 4 p.m. the entire Fourth Brigade was called to assembly in the auditorium, where Warder Chao did the talking. He got to the point in a hurry.

239

'One of you has stolen from the government,' he barked out. 'Stand up!'

Down in front, Lam arose slowly. His head was already bowed.

'I called you in here while it was still light so you could see this individual. Look at him! Lam's past behaviour has been good. He has often been an Activist. He is enthusiastic in his work. He studies well. He has made lots of progress. He has withstood the trials of bad times. During these days of temporary economic difficulty anybody can be weak, but that's when you should try your hardest to be strong. He didn't. He stole a bag of corn.'

Chao paused to let the importance of the moment sink in. Chinese Communist cadres are born histrionics.

'A bag of corn. What is a bag of corn? Nothing. Maybe twenty cents. But that bag of corn seed contained enough grain to grow an acre – enough to feed a whole team for a year! Stealing from the kitchen or the fields is one thing, but this prisoner tampered with production. He committed sabotage, and that is unforgivable.'

The prison director, who was up on the stage between Warders Chao and Yang, stepped forward to read out Sung's punishment, which they had decided earlier: five more years to his sentence.

With Gold Mountain's corn it was something different. Very much different. Liu Chin-shan was a short, square-faced peasant whose name meant Gold Mountain and whom I got to know when we were paired together for awhile, in the horse stalls and out in the fields with a harrow. He never spoke much, but I soon saw that he was as accomplished a scavenger as Lei Ying-fang and nearly as good a cigarette scrounger as Shaw, the pedicab jockey. He was one of the rare ones who disciplined himself to rise an hour before reveille to scour the compound for butts in the cadres' and free workers' areas. Illiterate farmer that he was, he had a straightforward thinking process that went to the point with unerring accuracy. I once saw him win an exchange with Warder Yang, a far subtler and more educated person. A puritan, like most of the cadres I have ever met,

Yang couldn't restrain himself one afternoon from criticizing Liu for picking up and smoking old butts.

'You know, you might get a lung disease from them,' he remonstrated.

'That's all right,' Liu answered with superb indifference. 'I've got one already.'

Yang was amazed and shocked. 'Well then,' he said, 'do you want your life to be cut short?'

Liu cocked up an eye and gave him one of those wonderful sardonic smiles of which the Chinese are masters.

'Why ask me, Warder? Ask yourself.'

It was Liu who taught me that when a man is hungry enough, he can find nourishment anywhere. It happened during one of the long lunch-and-siesta periods, when we were with our harrow. This time he didn't lie down and rest but instead built himself a little fire. Presently I noticed he seemed to be cooking something in his enamel mug.

'What did you find?' I wondered. I hadn't seen him doing any foraging.

'None of your business,' he grunted. I got up and walked over. 'Can I look?'

Liu shrugged. I lifted off the lid and saw to my surprise that the basin was half full of kernels of corn. I wondered if he could have been as stupid as Lam. That seemed unlikely, though. Liu tossed in some rock salt stolen from the horses.

'You got your food basin?' he asked.

'Sure.'

'Get it.'

When I returned with my basin he ladled out three spoonsful. Liu said nothing. He nodded his head and I ate the corn. It had a strange, powerful taste, like ammonia. That didn't bother me in the least. It was hot and salty. It was food.

'More?'

'Sure.'

'Where'd you get it?'

As before, he just grunted. Later, when we were working the harrow, he let me in on the secret.

'Old Bao, you didn't notice anything because you're a lousy

intellectual who doesn't pay attention. But when we were in the stables the other day I saw a lot of undigested corn in the shit of the guards' horses. So I picked it out and washed it off. That's what we just ate. I learned the trick when the Japs raided our village and took away all our food. We had to eat the corn from their horses' shit. That and bark from the trees.'

I didn't tell my cellmates about my meal that afternoon, not even Sun or Longman, but I needn't have been so finicky. There were others who had done worse. That fall I met a prisoner who told me how he and a friend had found they could eat the worms they found in the shit of cows and oxen. The worms were fat because they had been in the intestines of the animals, ingesting their food along with them. Medically speaking I suppose they were clean, and almost pure protein, but the thought of the worms still put me off. The prisoners washed them off, roasted them and snipped off the two black ends before consuming them. Compared to that, the occasional cockroach was a luxury.

Later Liu showed me how to find the artfully camouflaged eggs of praying mantises. They always laid them in the crotches where a tree limb joined the trunk and they were invariably the same colour as the bark. The eggs were about the size of Brazil nuts, and each one had its own little yolk and white. They were delicious.

The comical side of our existence was rarer, but it was there nonetheless – like the morning when one of my cellmates awoke with an exultant cry.

'Pao ma!' he exclaimed. 'I've been horse racing.' Horse racing is the Chinese slang for having a wet dream. That was a remarkable feat, considering the state of debilitation we all were in.

'Shut up,' Sun told him. 'You let the warders hear that, and they'll cut your rations down. You've got too much energy.'

The question of sexuality in the camps fascinates everyone, especially Westerners. Since my release scores of people have asked me how we were able to endure the lack of women. Weren't we prisoners, the younger ones at any rate, tormented by unfulfillable erotic fancies? The simple, surprising answer is no – not at all. In the first place, Chinese as a general rule are more reserved (or should I say less frenzied) about sexual matters than Westerners. But far more than that, the combination of perpetual hunger, lack of vitamins and the exhaustion brought on by hard physical labour had brought us to such a state of decrepitude that we were, for all intents and purposes, impotent. Survival was our only preoccupation. And one last point not to be forgotten – sexuality was and still is ideologically incorrect in China, especially in the camps. Need I repeat how dominated we all were by ideology? Westerners may be amused by it, but Mao is literally capable of preventing his people from copulating. If that isn't ideology in action, nothing is.

Not long after the May First feast (a bowl of rice, some meat in our soup and a movie) our cell received its first genuine celebrity, a funny-looking character of about forty with a hook nose, soft brown eyes and pocked skin, who stuttered and walked with the shambling gait of a duck. His name was Li Wan-ming, and he had been the original model for one of the most popular stage plays ever produced in post-Liberation China, *Looking Westward at Chang An*, by Lau Saw, the same man who wrote the famous *Rickshaw Boy*. Lau Saw was a sort of Chinese Gorky, who wrote devastating novels about social conditions in the old days and then gave himself to satire after the revolution, which was something less than wise. He was jailed during the Cultural Revolution and not heard from since.

Before, during and immediately after the Hundred Flowers, *Looking Westward* was *the* stage hit of China. It was an engaging bit of entertainment, based on the adventures of a particularly cheeky socialist con man and political swindler – Li Wan-ming, the very man who had just arrived in our cell – who had managed to persuade hundreds of bureaucrats, party officials and innocent bystanders that he was a courageous veteran of the Korean War. He had landed the easiest of jobs by widely displaying photographs of himself in the uniform of the People's Volunteers, complete with the requisite medals. To top

243

off his act he fabricated a certificate stating that he had been wounded in combat. This bogus hero was accepted into the elite ranks of the party and selected for a trip to the Soviet Union, during which he was supposed to get both treatment for his wound and deepened studies of Marxism–Leninism. When the Soviets discovered that he was virgin of wounds and knew nothing of Marxism–Leninism, he was sent back to Peking, where his story quickly fell to pieces. He had made his military photographs, it turned out, by cutting and pasting pages of magazines and then rephotographing the pictures with his head stuck on someone else's shoulders. The paper for his medical certificates he had stolen from a local health office and the official stamps he had carved himself out of smoked bean curd. He disposed of the stamps by eating them after the documents were in good order. I saw the play three times in Peking and loved it. But I never dreamed I'd be sleeping next to the original.

'You know, I never got any royalties from the play,' he complained to me once. 'And Lau Saw exaggerated my story. He exploited me.'

What amazed me was how party officials could have accepted this poor, stuttering, mythomaniac as a war hero.

'What would they think if they could see you now?' I asked him.

'Well,' he answered with an utterly straight face, 't-t-t-they just *might* see me. They're in the c-c-c-camps, too.'

That same month I ran into an old acquaintance, Tsui Yan, a man I first met in Grass Mist Lane. He had nothing much to recount that I didn't already know, except for one interesting, poignant little detail – they were folding no more book leaves in the Transit Centre. With the heavy demand for plastic goods, they had teamed up with Prison Number One to produce wallets. Now the prisoners were sewing plastic instead of folding paper. But they were still launching rockets and satellites.

Tsui's arrival coincided with that of about 100 juvenile delinquents sent to us for a term of Education Through Labour. They were the meanest, most terrifying little bastards I have ever had the misfortune to meet. The oldest was only seventeen

– because at age eighteen they are considered majors and pass over to the adult side – and the youngest around nine or ten. They had been dispatched from Peking to form their own Youth Brigade. After watching them perform awhile I could understand why the capital wanted to get rid of them. They were full of dirty tricks and generally got away with them – after all, since they were only undergoing Lao Jiao, they were still considered citizens. Several times bands of them waylaid poor, hungry prisoners carrying rations back from the kitchen, beat them up and made off with their food. And since they were younger, they even ate more generous rations than we did! It was a terrible situation. When we marched past them in formation on our way to work they taunted us by shouting 'Huai dan!' (rotten eggs) or 'Hun dan!' (S.O.B.). We couldn't answer back.

It all came to a head the day they stole our team's clothes. It was on a Rest Sunday, and we had piled into the bathhouse for a wash – but when we came out, our clothes had disappeared. The little brutes had simply walked off with everything, so they could rifle our pockets at their leisure and take their pick of the best clothes. We had to wait there for almost two hours while the guards went off to recover whatever they could. That escapade finished our co-existence. From then on the boys were strictly segregated from us men. Luckily for us.

Early in May Dr Ma put me on health rations. I was obviously growing weaker every day, and the advent of the warm weather could do nothing to change my condition. Nor, it turned out, could the health ration. By wheat-harvesting time I could no longer fulfil my work norm, and Longman Koo had to make the unpleasant choice of lowering my rations to Class B. The team had carried me for several weeks, but not all the goodwill in the world was enough to prevent some of them from grumbling about a man not doing his share. And besides, it was impossible to hide my low performance from the warders indefinitely, especially old Chao the peasant. I lost Class A.

Within two weeks I was so far gone that Longman and Sun had to carry me to the infirmary. Amoebic dysentery was the main problem, but I was anaemic as well and had drastically reduced blood pressure. All the signs of malnutrition and debilitation were there. I was a wreck. Old Hsia, who never gave up even tried to convert me to Catholicism. He advised me to pray and reminded me that man doesn't live by bread alone.

'No, Hsia,' I agreed, 'but it helps.'

'Don't worry, old Bao,' Longman said confidently. 'We won't let you down. Just do what the doctor says and you'll be right back with us.'

'Sure, old Koo,' I said, but I didn't believe it. I was too exhausted to care.

The infirmary had a floor of beaten earth over which straw had been strewn, held in place by a double row of bricks in the shape of a large L. Koo dropped my sleeping cloth down between two other prisoners and helped me lie down. There were two paneless windows, which had been covered over with paper in the winter but now were wide open to the outside air. One of them gave out next to a ditch latrine and the other to the main kitchen, where they started working at two in the morning. The noise from the kitchen kept us awake, the stink from the latrine made us even sicker, and the flies – the rare, canny ones who had escaped the various extermination campaigns – walked on us with proprietary arrogance. Dr Ma did what he could, but it was a lousy place to be sick.

The hospital rations were a definite improvement over the normal fare – wheat-flour noodles, bread, dried meat and sometimes some red-bean paste – but I was feeling too terrible to eat any of it. At around 7 p.m. that first day Sun appeared for a visit, sunburned and still dusty from the fields. He was wearing blue shorts, camp-made sandals and a straw hat.

'Well, old Bao, how are you?'

'No good, old Sun. Bad.'

I wasn't looking for pity. At that moment I felt utterly hopeless. I was dying of starvation, but I couldn't put anything inside me and I wasn't even hungry.

Sun leaned down and whispered to me urgently. In his voice there was the same bitter intensity I had glimpsed in him on occasion before, so different from the natural nobility of his character.

'You're going to die, then, just like that? You're going to let them kill you?'

'Sun, no one's killing me,' I protested, but I knew how his mind was working. No one is more rancorous than a fallen Communist.

'Fight it, Bao,' he said, 'fight it. We want to get you out alive. Can't you understand that?'

I was too tired to argue. 'Okay, Sun,' I promised, 'I'll try.'

'Good. We'll come back and see you again tomorrow. Now take these.'

Sun had three eggs in his hand! It was unbelievable. Scrounging a turnip or a cabbage heart was one thing, but eggs were almost unheard of.

'Where in hell did you get these, Sun?'

'They've been boiled,' he said blandly, avoiding my question. 'If I were you, I'd eat the shells afterward, too. Calcium. And there'll be no traces.'

I tried to protest again, but by now it was only for the sake of form. Sun strode out even before I could finish. I knew that the only place where he could have found eggs was in the warders' chicken coop. He had been taking big risks there. The next evening Longman came in with a big enamel mug, decorated with a bright, optimistic floral design. Inside, there was a stew of wild vegetables, frog meat and a few grains of rice from the bottom of somebody's provision sack. It was thick and hot. He spooned it out for me. As a little gourmet gesture he had flavoured it with a pinch of salt swiped from the horses.

My team's intensive-care programme continued for about three weeks in all. By the second week of July, I was sitting up on my pallet. As soon as I was able to totter to my feet, I asked Warder Yang to put me back to work in the fields. It was healthier out there, I figured, and I was fed up with the infirmary.

'If you could see yourself in the mirror,' Yang said, 'you wouldn't be asking me for that. The wind would blow you away out there, Bao. I must say you have the proper attitude, but stay in the hospital and fatten up first.'

I spent the next month or so tidying up in the infirmary and helping out with odd jobs in the kitchen. It wasn't real work, but it passed the time and made me feel useful, while the rest of my schoolmates were out in the fields fighting for a good harvest. I would lie in the straw before sunrise and hear them forming up their work details as Chinese schmaltz boomed out over the loudspeakers. 'The Asters Are in Bloom' was one of the most favoured tunes, and there were Indonesian waltzes, too. It was an incredible atmosphere.

One drizzly day in August a new warder I had never seen before came to the infirmary to look us over. He was dressed in a white shirt, khaki shorts and sandals, and seemed totally efficient. He took down our names and asked us about our health histories. When he had left, I asked Dr Ma what his visit was all about.

'Nothing good or bad,' he replied obliquely. He often spoke in riddles – it's an old Chinese habit. The next morning the new warder was back again. This time he had that bastard Liu with him.

'The government is always concerned with your welfare,' Liu said, and I thought to myself: Here it comes. It *had* to be some sort of bad news. 'Number Three Farm is a production unit and as such has neither the means nor the time to care for the sick. For this reason the government has decided to transfer you to a place where there is proper medical care. It is called Camp 585, and it is especially designed for the needs of the sick. Now get your things ready. You are leaving immediately.'

Those of us who could walk climbed onto a truck and the rest were carried aboard. We rolled over dirt roads through the fields for several hours before drawing up in front of a roughshod hamlet of red brick and whitewashed buildings surrounded by a flat mud embankment into which was stuck a large wooden panel with the numbers 5-8-5. We clambered down and when I caught sight of the old one-armed warder I had known before, Wang, I realized that this must just be a larger version of Northern Precious Village, the dying farm. Wang remembered me perfectly well, and on the strength of our past acquaintance made me group leader of our bunch.

We spent the rest of the afternoon and evening settling in one of the whitewashed cell units, finding out about rations and generally getting acquainted. Very quickly I saw some familiar faces from Northern Precious Village and got filled in on the situation. The old place had been requisitioned, they told me, when the agronomists had found some crops that would grow well in the surrounding soil. Camp 585 was to be the new consolidation point for all the weak, crippled and aged, and not many of them felt there was any chance of getting back out alive. We were 400 in all, and we ate twice a day, mostly the extras from the other production units. That wasn't much in those days. I shuffled around in the mud of the courtyard, watching some desultory foragers over by the kitchen waste heap, depressed and feeling hopeless and abandoned. It really looked like the end of the road.

The same tiresome, pointless routine continued the next morning, still under a fine, grey drizzle. Since we had no jobs and no work norms, the only activity appeared to be waiting to eat. Some time after noon Warder Wang called me to his office.

'You're leaving,' he announced without ceremony. 'You're going back to Number Three Farm. Get your things.'

I was astonished and exhilarated. Suddenly my future seemed more possible. I didn't know it then, but I learned later that it was Wang himself who declared me undesirable for 585. It was a very conscious and pointed gesture: He meant to save my life. He knew all too well that 585 was nothing but a death farm.

My exceptional bounce back to Number Three Farm didn't work without complication, though. This time I was accepted into the infirmary with only Class C rations – exactly half what the normal workers were getting. Evidently someone in the hierarchy, probably Warder Liu, had decided that I had shown myself to be a malcontent by having refused the government's benevolent offer of medical treatment in Camp 585. It wasn't until I had written a formal letter of protest to the camp director, explaining that I had been retransferred without my consent or prior knowledge, and had always acted in good faith, that Liu relented and allowed me back in the cell on Class B rations.

'Letter of protest' may sound wildly improbable for those

who do not understand the Chinese prison system or the mentality of the cadres. As I learned in Prison Number One, everybody, even a prisoner, is encouraged to speak his mind honestly and fully, for the government wants to know what goes on in a man's head. In this manner if the thoughts are erroneous or not in synch with the party line, they can be corrected. No one would have thought of preventing me from sending my letter up the chain of command. The strange, Alice-in-Wonderland world of forms must always be served. My jailers had absolute authority over my body and soul, but they were obliged to hear me out. On my side, though, it imported that I be careful with my ideology. Free speech is encouraged especially if it remains within the acepted channels.

My recovery after I returned from 585 was surprisingly rapid. I don't know whether to ascribe it to the ministrations of Dr Ma, the diet supplements of Sun and Longman, or simply fear of the death farm, but I was soon out in the fields with the others. One of the first big jobs that fell to us was to weed out the rice paddies and loosen the earth around the young shoots – the classical Chinese bent-back, straw-hatted labour that illustrates millions of prints, cigar boxes and coffee tables in the West. It was the timeless image of Asia, and I was happy to be back inside it. The greatest pleasure of working in the paddies (besides serving socialism) was catching the frogs that proliferated there. I never could understand how they could be so numerous when the past few years had been so disastrously lean, but there they were, and none of us questioned our good fortune. They weren't even particularly difficult to stalk – often they would literally jump into our laps. We would skin them on the spot and eat them raw. The system is to start with the mouth, and the head comes off with the spine. Those with greater discipline would save the meat in their mugs with a little water (at that time of year we always carried our mugs with us, stuck down in the folds of our clothes) and then dry it in the sun to make a type of jerky. Salted, they had a delicious, delicate flavour. Sun roasted them on a stick and they tasted like bacon. Later in the summer when there were more wild vegetables, we would make all kinds of stews with them,

Around wheat-threshing time I witnessed a terrible suicide. Just as we were sitting in the shade for our midday meal of soup and wo'tous, a prisoner in a tattered white shirt and blue pants appeared in the field next to us, running with desperate energy toward one of the big wheat-chopping machines set into the ground. Before anyone had a chance to react, or cut off the machine, he had dived down into the blades. I never knew why he did it, but it wasn't rare for prisoners to get out of the camps that way. This one ended up in pieces.

In early September, Sun let me in on something of a secret, or at least an explanation of why the cellmates had taken such good care of me when I was in the infirmary. We were working the paddies then, and it was around 3 p.m. when he ambled over to me.

'Come on, Bao,' he said, 'don't knock yourself out. It won't get you anywhere. Let's have a smoke.'

Why not? There was no warder in sight, and discipline was somewhat more relaxed now that the wheat was safely harvested and the rice seemed to be all right. We settled back against the bank of one of the raised roadways that intersected the paddies, took off our straw hats, drew out our little squares of newspaper and rolled ourselves a couple of vine-leaf smokes. Sun gestured broadly out at the fields.

'Look at that, Bao, isn't that a magnificent sight?'

It was difficult to tell whether or not he was being sarcastic, for in point of fact it *was* a magnificent sight. It was a cinemascope day with an intensely blue sky pocked with rich, billowy cloud formations. The vast series of paddies before us stretched limitlessly to the horizon with nothing breaking the geometric pattern except the one long row of acacias and poplars over by the main highway. The dikes and pathways that separated them marched along in disciplined order. Everywhere we looked there were men, bareback or in black shirts, bent to their work, impervious to the world about them, each one lost in his personal universe. There were thousands of them.

'Isn't that wonderful?' Sun asked again. 'All those people, and none of them will ever make it out, me included. Lifetime contract. You're the only one who's different, Bao. You might get out the Big Door some day. It could happen to a foreigner, but not us. You'll be the only one who can tell about it afterward if you do. That's why we wanted to keep you alive, Bao.'

I was touched, but didn't quite feel his optimism. 'I don't know if I'll live that long, Sun.'

That wasn't theatrical pessimism on my part. Since August 1960, more than three-quarters of our brigade had died or been dispatched to Camp 585. There weren't many of us left.

'Don't you worry,' Sun said firmly, 'as long as you're here, you'll live. I can promise you that. And if you get transferred to other camps, there'll be other people who think like us. You're precious cargo, old man.'

Sun laughed and sloshed back out into the paddy.

One of the transfers into our team that summer was an overseas Chinese from Indonesia named Lu Ke-hsi, who surprised me with his knowledge of the degenerate outside world. I used to call him Luke. He was young and handsome, around twenty-five and, though scrawny, a good worker. One afternoon in the fields I happened to be humming 'Cherry Pink and Apple Blossom White' to myself when Luke appeared next to me and joined in without missing a note.

'Where'd you learn that?' I couldn't help wondering.

'Indonesia,' he said proudly. 'And I know plenty more.'

We were like kids discussing bubble-gum cards. I was transfixed when he gave me a rendition of 'Tennessee Waltz'. It took me right back to the old days before my arrest. Luke had forgotten the words, though, and asked me to help him. It was absolutely forbidden to write anything in a foreign language, but he slipped me a piece of Kraft processed American cheese, part of the booty from a parcel from his family, to refresh my memory. The cheese inspired me to let him have not only 'Tennessee Waltz' but 'Vaya Con Dios' as well – a little bonus. I wondered what the warders would have made of those secret, illicit messages if they had ever captured them. Later on Luke gave me a chocolate bar for the words to 'I Went to Your Wedding'.

With the corn harvest, we naturally tried to steal as much as possible for our own use, but the guards were vigilant and we were rarely able to make off with more than one ear apiece. They were clever, these guards. Every day upon returning from the fields they formed us up and had us search *each other*, in pairs. It saved them the time and tedium of going through all of us themselves, and was more effective than would appear at first thought – they knew very well how much we feared that they might double-check our searches. As a result, the teams quickly learned to 'uncover' some contraband in every search. The guilty man for the day was agreed upon in advance. This way each one of us took a few demerits every month for the good of the group. And as far as the warders were concerned, form had been served.

On 1 October, National Day, we had a nice feast of stuffed Chinese bread, a big bowl of vegetable soup and rice and cabbage cooked with diced pork. After the meal we were sitting around outside relaxing and telling stories when old Warder Chao strolled over to join us. He was wearing a faded blue jacket and shorts, and politely asked our permission before sitting down with us. He drew out his tobacco and filled his pipe. We shut up and respectfully waited for him to speak. When a warder joins a group, however informal it is, he's in charge.

'Today I'm going to tell you about the Ten Manifestations of Negativism and Laziness,' he said without the least hint of self-consciousness. 'They are known as Hsiao gee Hun Pao.'

He spoke slowly and instructively, popping out his fingers one by one as he enumerated them.

'One: To work only when the warders are looking. When he turns his back, you slough off.

'Two: Pretending you're working hard. Just going through make-believe gestures with your tool when you're really doing nothing. But never forget: The warders have a third eye. We know more than you think.

'Three: Going to the latrine all the time, or pretending you have the shits. Six times in the morning and six in the afternoon, ten minutes each time, and that's two hours you've stolen from the government.

253

'Four: Wandering around all the time pretending to be looking for tools.

'Five: Unnecessary talking together about work procedures. Too much talk and not enough action. You should come straight to the warder if you want to know what procedures to use.

'Six: Keeping your work to the minimum by doing the same thing over and over again, under the pretext that you want to do it perfectly.

'Seven: Setting norms below your capacity; deciding in the morning how little you'll do so that you can take it easy all day long.

'Eight: Talking with other teams under the pretext of exchanging labour experiences.

'Nine: Patting yourselves on the back at the end of the day when really you have done very little.

'Ten: Taking a long time to walk out to work and then leaving your work early under the pretext that it takes a long time to get back.'

Later in the evening we learned that the long-rumoured boost in rations would not come with the harvests after all. Just before the film (it was 'The Five Golden Flowers' that day, a Maoist fairy tale) Liu climbed up to the stage to give us the news.

'There has been some discontent running through the brigades,' he observed. 'Some people have dared to say that the People's Government hasn't kept its word because you haven't gotten a big boost in your rations. Well, you are already eating a couple of ounces more now than in the winter, so you have no complaints. We cannot allow a few professional provocateurs to incite you to laziness in these important times, so just to make that point clear we are going to give two of the worst offenders what they deserve.'

He ordered the guards front and centre and they dragged two prisoners off for a week of solitary apiece. It looked like we would stay hungry for a long time.

One of the best ways to forget our food troubles was by smoking. Real tobacco was just about nonexistent by then, and we replaced it with all sorts of baroque imitations, mostly con-cocted from dried leaves. The men with real tobacco in their pouches were the closest thing in Ching Ho to millionaires. Plenty of prisoners, for instance, would happily trade half their lunch for enough tobacco to roll one smoke. Smoking, or just the thought of it, used to cause weird frenzies of voluptuousness. It finally got to me, too, the day I heard that Gu Wen-xuan, a smart-aleck in one of the other teams, had received a parcel with sixty leaves of high-quality tobacco. Those sixty leaves became an obsessive image inside my head. The more I tried to repress my craving, the worse it became. I finally had to go and at least ask him his terms.

'Well, let's make a fair exchange,' he said with cordial equa-nimity. 'We both have things the other wants. So how about your Roget's *Thesaurus*.'

The bastard – of course that's what he would go after. Gu spoke some English and this would obviously be a treasure for him. He was a hard bargainer. I tried other propositions but he was adamant. It was the *Thesaurus* or nothing.

'Fuck you,' I told him in English. He didn't need a *Thesaurus* to understand that.

'That's all right,' he said blandly. 'Any time you want, the offer still stands.'

For the next days, whenever I saw someone smoking, my mouth watered. It was torture, like there was something tickling my lungs. A week later I went to see him again.

'I don't have much left,' Gu warned me. 'Look at this blanket – I got it for only four leaves.'

I felt terrible. I wanted to punch him in the nose for his profit-eering, but at the same time I felt like begging him for a smoke.

'Tell you what,' he said. 'I'll make it fifteen leaves. You can choose the ones you want yourself – big or small, as you like.'

I caved in. I handed over the *Thesaurus*. I kicked myself afterward, but those smokes tasted wonderful.

A few weeks later my wife came down for a visit with little Yung. It was the first time I had seen them in about a year and a half, and by then we had become virtual strangers. I wasn't even certain that Yung recognized me; he answered my questions with all the shy diffidence usually reserved for schoolmasters. Cowed by the guard, Yang and I exchanged platitudes about how well the government was taking care of us. They had brought some cakes, and we ate them together in silence. The poor kid, I couldn't help noticing, was almost as hungry as I. I asked him what he had had for lunch that day. Sweet potatoes and cabbage and rice, he said, in the free workers' canteen before the visit. The government had been excessively kind, my wife added. No one had asked them for food coupons or money.

God knows she was short on money. Despite the governmental rhetoric about families of prisoners being provided for, she and the boys were only one step up from hunger and destitution. She had never been able to land a job because she was 'not qualified'. She was then earning fifteen yuan ($6) a month by doing housework and watching over sick people in the neighbourhood.

They missed the last train for Peking that night and Warder Yang had them put up in a visitors' dormitory. The next morning I was permitted to accompany them to the main gate and say good-bye. During the lunch break I went to Warder Yang's office and thanked him for the unusual consideration he had shown me and my family.

'Your behaviour has not always been perfect,' he said, 'but we don't feel that that should deprive you of the pleasure of seeing your loved ones. Sometimes visits like that can inspire prisoners to greater efforts. So if you are really grateful to the government, don't just say it, do something about it. Show your thanks by deeds.'

I worked as hard as my strength permitted me, especially one day in mid-November when Warder Chao set us all loose in the late afternoon to forage freely for unpicked carrots and sugar beets in a field that was to be ploughed over. We made a beeline out there and happily grubbed through the cold, moist earth like dogs digging for bones.

'Hell, we're better off than Mao,' Sun wisecracked. 'Our food's fresher than what he gets.'

I was too busy crunching through a dirty beet to answer. We came back with bulging forage sacks that night.

I had two ideological problems around the end of that month. One concerned the Soviet Union and the other pissing. Surprisingly enough, it was the second that got me into the deepest trouble. It happened on a cold, blowy night at study time, when I left the cell to go out and take a leak. When the cold north-western wind caught me, I felt less inclined to do the 200 yards over to the latrine. I walked over to a storage building and pissed against the wall. After all, I reasoned, no one would see me in the dark.

I was wrong. I had barely finished when I received a very sharp and swift kick in the ass. When I turned I could make out only a silhouette, but the voice belonged to a warder.

'Don't you know the sanitation rules?' he demanded. 'Who are you?'

I gave my name, and what happened next was a lesson I'd never forget.

'Oh, it's Bao Ruo-wang then, is it? You have no excuse for this, Bao. Your legs are perfectly good.'

He was quite right, of course, but the mood of despair that I was in made me throw caution to the winds. I became very arrogant.

'I admit that I am wrong, Warder, but what I am doing is only a violation of prison regulations, whereas you have broken the law. Government members are not supposed to lay hands on prisoners. Physical violence is forbidden.'

There was a pause while Silhouette considered, and I expected the worst. 'What you say is right, Bao,' he said with measured calm. 'If I admit that I have made a mistake – and I will bring up this subject at our [the warders'] next self-criticism session – would you be ready to go back and write me a thorough confession?'

I was surprised by his reaction. I was touched, too: for here was a warder admitting his mistake before a prisoner. An unheard-of thing! What else could I do but blurt out: 'Yes, Warder, I certainly will.'

I didn't want to push my luck any further. I had gained a quibbling point, and I decided that my own confession would have to be an impeccable one. Square-Jaw Dai's lessons were just as valid here as in Prison Number One. When I burst back into the cell, I announced in a loud voice: 'I have just committed a grave mistake. I pissed against the wall.'

They regarded me with bemusement. 'Who in hell cares where you pissed?' one of them said. 'You're interrupting the studies.'

When I told them how the warder caught me and the little 'conversation' we had, they understood. The cell leader could not help saying to what lengths the government was prepared to go in order to reform us. I sat in my place and began preparing my confession. At the Weekly Examination of Conscience a few days later I read it out aloud for the entire cell to hear.

'What I did may appear on the surface to be not too serious,' I added after I had finished reading, 'but on further examination it demonstrates a disregard for the teachings of the government and a resistance to reform. By pissing I was displaying my anger in an underhanded manner. It was a cowardly act. It was like spitting in the face of the government when I thought no one was looking. I can only ask that the government punish me as severely as possible.'

The confession went up to Warder Yang and I waited. I was bracing myself for another bout of solitary. Two nights later Yang came to the cell with his verdict.

'A few days ago,' he said, 'one of you thought he was above the law and committed a big mistake. You all know who he is and what he did. I have read Bao's confession and I find it just barely acceptable. We'll let him go this time, but don't think this means you can always weasel out of trouble by just writing an apology.'

I heaved an inward sigh and made a silent vote of thanks to Square-Jaw Dai.

If my second ideological problem had a less immediate effect on my dossier, it was far more frightening, not only for me but for my fellow prisoners and for the Chinese population in general. It concerned Sino-Soviet relations. Things had been deteriorating for quite a while, but the moment finally arrived when the public masses had to be told what the party already knew, that the great socialist ally to the north, the one everyone had known until then as 'Elder Brother', was in reality an evil fraud. All of China – we, the scum of society included – had to readjust its thinking: It was time for white to become black.

Our ideological retooling in Ching Ho began with the three newspapers regularly circulated for our studies, the *People's Daily*, the *Peking Daily* and the *Kwang Ming Daily*. Khrushchev, we read, had attacked Stalin at the Twenty-second Party Congress even more virulently than before, and had even ordered his body removed from the Lenin crypt. Chou En-lai had returned precipitously without waiting for the congress to end. The Russian press obliquely attacked China through Albania, calling it dishonest and ungrateful for the past Soviet aid against fascism. The *People's Daily* responded with a similarly indirect formulation, accusing the Soviet Union of letting Albania down by withdrawing technical help. In short, the world was falling apart.

What was most terrible for us was the fear of guessing wrong. We had learned our ideological recitations by heart long ago and felt comfortably able to respond to any new situation with the proper series of catechismic catchphrases. But now we were suddenly, cruelly, thrust into dangerously uncharted waters. We treaded with desperate care, afraid that one slip of the tongue could mean another five or ten years. 'It is better to say little', says a Chinese proverb, and we stuck to it like limpets. Warder Yang constantly encouraged us to speak our minds but he had little luck at the start. I vividly recalled my stretch of solitary after having opened my mouth about Tibet and all the others had had similar experiences. We edged into the new ideological positions with all the maidenly attention of bishops in an opium den. More than two weeks passed before anyone could bring himself actually to cast concrete accusations against the Soviets. It was a painful time.

Since then I often wondered whether the ideological flip-flop had something to do with the strike, and now I believe it must have. Our living conditions had not improved one bit, our rations continued to hover just above subsistence, and the ersatz was still an integral part of our diet. When winter returned to torment us and at the same time the government suddenly directed us to make a mental ninety-degree turn, it was simply too much for some of the men. On the morning of 8 December, I was astounded to see a strike form before my very eyes. It was the only strike in the forced-labour camps I had ever encountered, or even heard of.

The work lineup that morning didn't seem any different from others, except that this time when the warder asked about sick call, fifteen men stepped forward. What was unusual was that they were some of the best men of the brigade, many of them cell leaders or activists of Reform Through Labour. And Longman Koo was among them! I don't know if they expected the rest of us to follow them, but we were too astonished to do anything but stand there and watch.

'You have five minutes to get examined by the doctor,' the warder said roughly.

'We won't go to work,' one of them replied. 'We're not sick.'

Amazing. Obviously, this was an unprecedented problem, one that had to be handled with special care. The warder put me in charge of our team and marched us off to the fields. In the evening when we came back, Longman's place was empty, so I also became *pro tem* cell leader. The strikers had been grouped together in one cell, we learned, but the guards wouldn't allow any of us near them. Several more days passed before it was decided to put them in a special punitive cell with rations of corn mush and water. Warder Chao promised that all resisters would be *compelled* to work for socialism. I saw Longman once after that, and then for only a few minutes, in the presence of guards. I never learned how and when he had decided to take such drastic action. He had gone through all the worst times without a hint of weakness, but then just threw up his hands and stopped trying.

I didn't know it, but I would be leaving Longman, Sun and the others behind in a few weeks. The last extraordinary experience I had at Ching Ho was the Christmas mass of Father Hsia. Our teams had spent most of the month of December in miscellaneous agricultural housekeeping, such as marking boundaries for rice paddies, cleaning out irrigation ditches and cutting brush. The morning was bright and clear that Christmas day, but the temperature was close to zero, and a force five wind was roaring down from the northwest. The eighteen men under me were laying out paddy markers on Field Strip 23, a plot of clean ploughed earth about two miles long and 120 yards wide, in which we were to mark out sixty paddies, set down the stakes and then turn it over to other teams who would set up the system of irrigation ditches. I divided the section into five teams of three each and sent the remaining three to gather scrap wood for a bonfire.

It was around 9.30 when I noticed a solitary figure approaching me across the strip. Even quite far away, I could tell from his gait that it was Hsia. The earflaps of his ragged old cotton hat danced in the wind as he hurried over to me, and his faded khaki army overcoat and black padded pants were splattered with mud. With the exaggerated politeness characteristic of him, Hsia asked me if he could have a break for a few minutes. I had nothing against that, but he knew we had a deadline for the paddy job – couldn't he wait until lunch? Embarrassed and pained, he looked down at his boots, toying absently with the red-and-white markers he still held in his mittens.

'Don't you remember what day it is today, John?' he asked me in English.

Of course. I had been thickheaded.

'Go on, old man,' I said, 'but be careful.'

He smiled gratefully and scurried away across the road and down the embankment to a dry gully where a bonfire was burning, and where he was shielded from the wind and the view of the warders. A quarter of an hour later, I saw a bicycle against the sky in the distance – a warder was on his way. I hustled over to the gully to warn Hsia.

As I looked down the embankment I saw that he was just finishing up the mass, in front of a mound of frozen earth which he had chosen as an altar. He was making the traditional gestures of priests all over the world. But his vestments here were ragged work clothes; the chalice, a chipped enamel mug; the wine, some improvised grapejuice; and the host, a bit of wo'tou he had saved from breakfast. I watched him for a moment and

261

knew quite well it was the truest mass I would ever see. I loped down the embankment, and when the warder passed on his bike he saw only two prisoners warming their hands.

Two days later I was transferred – Warder Yang pulled me out of the morning formation and ordered me back to the cell. The main thing that concerned me was the possibility of being sent back to 585. I had fainted in the fields a week or so before Christmas and had been hauled back to the cell in one of the bicycle carts. I poked gloomily at the fire in the stove and waited. Very shortly I was joined by five or six Koreans from another brigade. They were just as much in the dark about our special treatment as I was. At mid-morning Warder Yang told us what was happening.

'The government has decided to send you back to Peking,' he announced. 'Don't forget that wherever you are sent, you are still undergoing Reform Through Labour. Continue to work hard and obey the government.'

When I asked him if I could say good-bye to Koo, I was pleasantly surprised when he nodded his head. He walked with me to the punishment cell and ordered the guard to let me in. Longman looked drawn and tired and depressed. We had been through a lot together since Prison Number One. I felt like hell to be leaving him.

'I'm glad you're leaving,' he said as we shook hands. 'I'll say good-bye to Sun for you.'

'Okay, Koo,' I said, and I found that I was in tears.

'No displays of emotion!' the guard ordered severely.

'Suan la ba [Stow it],' I said, and brushed past him out into the courtyard. Warder Yang didn't say a word.

Chapter Fourteen

At three in the afternoon a truck came to pick us up. Besides myself all the others were Koreans, and it wasn't until then that I realized that our transfer from Ching Ho involved foreigners exclusively. As we bumped along past the frozen fields a muted sensation of dread came upon me when I saw we were taking the road to Camp 585, and it turned to active horror when we turned into that familiar gate. I couldn't believe it – had Warder Yang only been setting a trap for me? False alarm. The stop was only to pick up a few more passengers. The truck turned back toward the Chadian railroad station.

The sun had set by the time we arrived, around 7 p.m., and the platforms and the little barracks-style waiting room were teeming with the dark, muffled figures of hundreds of prisoners. Most of them, I learned, were Lao Jiao people from Manchuria – something like 700 in all. Presently a warder called us out to the platform and shouted out that we would have to wait several more hours for our train. He confirmed that our destination was indeed Peking.

'*Hao ji la!*' someone cried out from the middle of the group – 'hooray'. But the warder was not amused.

'You will not comment on the government's decisions,' he said angrily. 'Show gratitude.'

We lined up for an evening meal of tea and three wo'tous apiece. As I was edging my way back from the line underneath one of the floodlights I found myself face-to-face with Old Man Wong Ai-Kuo, the one who had worn the elegant pyjamas in Grass Mist Lane. His hair was thinner and whiter now and he had become so emaciated that his skin was waxen and strangely transparent, as if I could see through it to his skull. He looked like an incongruously gracious beggar, in the same old Western-

263

style overcoat I had seen in the Interrogation Centre, red woollen sweater, baggy grey pants much too big for him and, inexplicably, bedroom slippers. His rheumy old eyes looked me over inquisitively.

'I've seen you somewhere, haven't I?' he asked.

'You're damn right,' I answered in English. 'I'm Bao Ruowang, from the Interrogation Centre.'

'Ah, yes,' he said, 'ah yes. You look terrible.'

'You should have seen me last year.'

I politely avoided commenting on his appearance, but I imagine he had few illusions on that score. We exchanged news for a few minutes before returning to our respective units. I took my place on the platform with the Koreans.

Their leader was quite a character, a celebrity in his own right, a good-looking, lithe young man named Rhee. The first part of his name, Yung Jün, most appropriately, meant 'Ever-Handsome'. I was to live quite a few adventures with my friend Ever-Handsome. He was one of the cleverest prisoners I had ever met, and certainly the most daring. For some reason, perhaps only because he was Korean and not Chinese, the ideological indoctrination never quite took hold on him. He had achieved a high personal notoriety as one of the rare prisoners to stage a successful escape from the camps. I had heard a good deal of talk about him in Ching Ho. He filled me in on the rest of the details himself.

Rhee had chosen the adventurous life early, when he crossed over from North Korea to China in 1954. Life in the North was grim, he said, but even more so it was repressive and boring. He struck out for his own brand of freedom by becoming a 'big wheel', a man who lived by stealing from trains and riding around China with false papers. Neither theft nor forgery posed a problem for him. Rhee managed to baffle the police for two years, but was finally caught and arrested in 1956.

He first started serving time in Hsing Kai-Hu, but was sent back to Ching Ho in the summer of 1960 after falling seriously ill. During the long period of convalescence that followed, he became a sort of unofficial orderly for the bedridden prisoners and some of the warders. He made himself useful by running miscellaneous errands, shopping at the cooperative whenever anyone had a bit of money, taking messages and the like. The guards became accustomed to his passe-partout functions and allowed him free movement throughout the camp. Bit by bit over the months he socked away small change.

His big chance came in August 1960, when a batch of fresh fruit was put up for sale in the cooperative. Rhee took everyone's orders and money to pay for their purchases. In all, it came to around forty Chinese yuans (about sixteen dollars). He changed into the cleanest, best repaired clothes (among his many talents, he was a very able tailor) and set off on foot for the co-op. But kept on going, straight to the Chadian railroad station, right to where we were sitting now as he told me about it. Everyone along his route assumed he was a visitor, because he looked too well dressed to be a prisoner. Completely familiar with both railroads and police psychology, he bought a ticket south, the opposite direction the cops would expect from a Korean. He lost himself in Shanghai, where his affable manner and good looks quickly found him a woman to take care of him. After a couple of months he borrowed fifty dollars from her and moved on to Tsingtao, where he repeated the same routine. He was discovered when his papers were checked the first time he tried to get a hotel room with his new lady friend. Rhee came back to Ching Ho in chains and the entire population of Branch Farm Number Three was called to a special assembly to witness his humiliation. To make him a good example for the rest of us, they gave him a full month of solitary. It was already November then and the fact that he survived that terrible month made even the guards admire him. Rhee was tough.

Our transfer train finally pulled in under the moonlight at half an hour before midnight. Our team was assigned to the coach nearest the locomotive and I sat with Rhee and six other Koreans up front. The guard told us we could talk if we wished, but only in whispers, so the others could sleep. We could go to the latrine, but had to request permission each time.

I knew of only one other escapee during all my years in the camps, a Chinese who was caught a couple of days after he left

Ching Ho. Less enterprising than Rhee, he had quickly fallen afoul of the numerous checks and constraints that govern normal civilian life. Every citizen must carry identification papers; to eat he needs coupons; to travel or lodge himself he needs authorization. It is not altogether impossible to escape from Chinese jails, but – to what? Every one of us had heard dozens of stories about families bringing escapees back to their prisons by main force. We didn't have any illusions about flying the coop.

I dozed and nodded through the next several hours until our first stop at around 5 a.m.; but even in my stupor of half-sleep, I couldn't help noticing that my Korean mates went to the latrine over and over again. I assumed they had been drinking too much water.

Our first halt was at a town called Fengtai, not far from Peking, where we came upon a horribly tantalizing sign of civilization – a food kiosk, where they were selling roast chicken. We peered dolefully through the locked windows and daydreamed. The train bumped off again, and it was at 7.30, under a bright sun, that we pulled into Peking's Yong Ding Men station. We piled out to an eerily empty platform, from which stray civilians had long since been cleared. A line of guards met us, absolutely rigid and impassive in their padded olive-green overcoats, each one clutching a submachine gun and staring out at us from behind gauze surgical masks. Orientals favour these white masks as a means of preventing the spread of colds, but seeing them on every one of those guards was a chilling experience. They were like faceless automatons, except for the white steam of their breath.

From behind the masks muffled voices ordered us to form up in groups and make ready to move off. We climbed into beautiful, red Czech buses and drove through Peking's busy streets in comfort. A brief surge of hope dwindled and then went out entirely when we passed through the area of Prison Number One, but went on beyond it. We watched the shops opening and the housewives firing up little coal-ball stoves on their front steps, waiting for the coal-balls to burn off their smoke before bringing the stoves back inside to cook their meals. There were vendors

266

selling fruits and vegetables and steamed bread. Everywhere people pedalled bicycles, serious and intent on their destinations. As we passed out of town the rice fields appeared again and then an industrial village where furnaces were melting iron ore – real, proper furnaces this time, not the whimsical toys that enthusiastic peasants had created during the Great Leap Forward – and finally at around nine we arrived at a red brick complex of buildings surrounded by a wall, topped by the inevitable watchtowers and electrified wire. We rolled through the main gate, but there was no banner or sign to identify the place. Before us were two four-storey buildings and another of the same height but immensely greater proportions, clearly a factory. We sat down on the cold ground and awaited orders.

There was no prepared speech for us this time, only a rather officious young warder to lead us inside one of the buildings, up to the fourth floor and into a long grey corridor, where the Koreans and I were assigned to the first room on the left as we entered from the staircase. It was distressingly barren. The concrete floor was naked, the walls were unpainted and not even half the windows had panes in them. One light bulb hung from a wire in the high ceiling. The only source of heat was a stove out in the hall. The warder didn't bother to explain, but he was just temporarily moving us in to camp in this unfinished building. To make the place suitable for sleeping, he told us, we could find straw and bricks downstairs. We piled straw on the floor and held it into place with a double row of bricks, like in the Ching Ho infirmary. We plugged the open windows as best we could with paper and sat in the straw together, backs to the wall, cold and bored, awaiting further orders, or at least the next meal. Very soon there was bad news: The warder had been informed too late of our arrival and he had no food vouchers for us. We would have to wait until evening to eat. We were cold and tired and hungry and uncomfortable; the transfer was beginning to look like a bad deal. I stared into space and tried to make my mind a blank.

'You hungry?'

Rhee's voice came crashing into my reverie.

'I don't appreciate the joke, Rhee,' I answered testily. He

reached inside his shirt and handed me two small round loaves of bread. This Korean was amazing!

'What about the others?' I wondered, but even as I said it I could see that they were chewing. The bread was made of wheat flour and it was delicious: feast day material.

'Have a smoke,' Rhee said after I had finished, and this time I didn't say anything. He reached into his pants and pulled forth a leaf of real tobacco. It was like watching a magician at work.

'Don't worry,' he said casually. 'There's plenty more.'

'Rhee, I don't mean to pry,' I said, 'but how in hell ...?'

I caught myself. A basic camp rule is not to question good fortune, but it didn't bother him in the least. On the contrary, he rather enjoyed my bafflement.

'Remember when we went to the latrine all the time on the train? You didn't really think we had to piss that much, did you, Bao? Well, the fact is that one of the guys found a bag of bread and a pile of tobacco leaves in a cupboard in the back of the car near the latrine. Must have been the warders' rations, I guess.' A look of solicitous concern flashed over his intelligent features. 'Well . . . we stuck it all down our pants. There were so many of us on the train they'll never know who took the stuff.'

We had a nice little snooze after the snack and cigarettes, but it was broken up by the same young warder, who told us we should be studying instead of sleeping. He took down our names and appointed one of the Koreans cell leader. There would be no more sleeping until bedtime, he added. When we could hear the warder's footsteps going down the stairs, we scrambled out into the hallway and crowded around the stove. One of the Koreans couldn't resist the gourmet's temptation to toast a little hunk of bread on the stove. When the delicious smell went wafting through the building, the warder came galloping back.

'Where'd you get that?' he demanded angrily.

'At Camp 585,' the Korean answered, not a bit discomfited. These people were as clever as they were cheeky. 'I saved it from my rations.'

'What's your name?'

'Kim,' he said with the same regal calm. 'I'm toasting it because the doctor said it was better for my digestion.'

The warder glowered, but had no real response. He said he would check that story out. Kim nodded and ate his bread.

At 5.30 p.m. we received our official ration of bright-yellow wo'tous and lukewarm cabbage soup. We warmed it on the stove.

The next morning a fat little man named Chia, the prison director, gave us some details about our new home. It was called Liangxiang Prison, he said, and to the outside world it was known as the New Capitol Electrical Machinery Factory. The complex had been built originally to produce elevators, but the production was switched first to steel tubing and now to aluminium goods. We were never to mention either of the two names in letters to our family, but tell them simply to write to P.O. Box 265. After a final send-off about labour enthusiasm he dismissed us for lunch. We heated our soup on the stove again. When the young warder came by, he accused us of hedonism.

For several days the prison seemed to be at a loss over what to do with us. There were no work assignments for us at all. We passed the time lounging and talking with veterans about what sort of a life we could expect. For one thing, any illusions we harboured about food were rapidly dispelled – the famine made conditions no easier here on the outskirts of Peking than in Ching Ho. Rations would be roughly the same. They told us that the only place where prisoners still got decent food was in good old Prison Number One. It wasn't the model prison for nothing.

Lingxiang, whose name meant 'Virtuous Village', was quite new, the factory having been thrown up by the Construction Battalion only about a year before and the barracks even more recently. Our building wasn't yet completed. The compound was located about twenty miles southwest from Peking, on the Peking–Hankow railroad line. The aluminium goods that Director Chia had mentioned were mostly cheap cast pots and pans. The irony of that was evident: The reason we had to turn out pots and pans was that millions upon millions of Chinese families had tossed theirs down the steel hoppers during the Great Leap Forward. The two main living quarters were simply

269

called the West and East buildings; the West being for free workers and the East for Lao Jiao people plus a couple of hundred sick prisoners from all over Peking and, for some reason, us foreign jailbirds.

Naturally, there was a set of solitary cells – just in case – and the story I heard about them warmed my heart. Either through misplaced zeal or a perverse wish to please prison disciplinarians, the men of the Construction Battalion had at first built a particularly inhuman solitary block. No more than four feet high at the ceiling, three feet wide and long enough only for a man to sit with his legs folded, the cells were more like dog kennels than human housing. When Director Chia saw them, he immediately ordered the Construction Battalion's chief architect and five of his foremen to spend five days inside their creations. After they were released they rebuilt pleasant new cells that differed from the standard cells only in that they had no windows. They were the nicest solitary units I had ever seen. I was happy not to try them, though.

The walls around us in Liangxiang were about thirty feet high and 600 yards long at each side of the square, with a guard tower at each of the four corners. There was a big, double-doored main gate, and only one other breach in the wall, a little wooden door at the back, which the prisoners called Tai Ping Men, the gate of peace. The only prisoners who passed through that door were in coffins. Completing the buildings were a makeshift hospital, mostly filled with hopeless overflow cases from 585, a central kitchen, a delousing station and various storage sheds and agricultural outbuildings for servicing the large vegetable garden we prisoners were responsible for tending.

The free workers we began running across were a sorry lot. They looked as if they *belonged* in prison. They were lazy, unskilled and dirty. Evidently they had concluded that nothing was worth the effort anymore, and in a way they were right. They were constantly hungry, under the order of guard and warder, and locked up at night just like the rest of us. The only difference between our condition and theirs was the home visit privilege. Nothing else counted. True, they now received salaries, but they had to spend them on food and clothing, which were no longer gifts of the government. These free workers just didn't give a damn.

Behind the West Building were the guards' barracks and canteen, their basketball court and the big vegetable garden with the greenhouse in front of it. The biggest building of all, the factory, was a cavernous, hangarlike structure as tall on the outside as our living quarters but with no floors on the interior, an immense shell covering about an acre of ground, filled with the equipment for turning out our Liangxiang brand kitchen gear. Ten yards from the wall and running parallel to it all around the compound was a broad strip of gleaming whitewash – the forbidden line. Anyone venturing beyond it in the direction of the wall was to be shot without question or warning.

At night the corridors of our building were patrolled by honour squads taken from the ranks of the prisoners and – rare luxury – we were allowed to sleep with the lights off. Besides myself, our cell contained seven Koreans and two Japanese. Wai Chiao Zu, it was called, the Foreigners' Team. Life was easy enough at the start since we had nothing to do, but the drawback was that until we were assigned regular work shifts, we ate the low-category rations – 33 catties a month.

The first change in our routine came on 3 January, when a tall man in an old military tunic, peaked cap and surgical mask came to our cell. He introduced himself as Li Tien-you, one of the prison doctors. In Chinese his name meant 'Heavenly Friend'. He went through the men one by one, checking their medical histories. When he came to me, he asked if I were a foreigner.

'I'm a Frenchman,' I said perhaps a bit grandly.

'You don't look it,' he threw back. 'And I've been to France. You look like a beggar. Have you seen yourself in a mirror lately?'

I thought he was insulting me. For a man trained as I was to ideological and behavioural conformity, he seemed to be unconscionably rude.

'I am here to be reformed,' I reminded him tartly. 'In the past I have been told that the government doesn't humiliate or take liberties with prisoners.'

Heavenly Friend wasn't in the least put out.

'I'm not a member of the government,' he said. 'I'm a free worker. I was just being funny, man. Take it as a joke. And you needn't call me doctor. I'm in here for studies, just the same as you.'

Heavenly Friend turned out to be a good man, once I had grown used to his style. His road to prison had been much like Sun's. A functionary in the Ministry of Health, he had accompanied several Chinese delegations abroad, but it all ended during a conference in Karlovy Vary, where he let himself be tempted by a female comrade from the Czech side. When he returned to Peking, he was accused of illicit sexual relations. Somewhat naïvely, Heavenly Friend had assumed that making love with a sister party member was ideologically satisfactory; but for his superiors the only consideration that counted was that she could have been a secret agent. He got three years and had already worked them off and had become a free worker by the time our paths crossed.

Heavenly Friend finished his examination and accorded a few days' extra rest to me and another Korean who had serious TB. After my rest period was up, I made a small effort at gold-bricking – it was cold as hell outside, and I was a lot more comfortable in the cell – by telling the cell leader I still didn't feel up to par. But he ordered me out to join the crews anyway. I had no choice but to obey, and the next morning I grumpily marched downstairs and across the compound with the others, following them to a toolshed where we picked up stout poles, lengths of string and a bunch of dusty burlap bags. Bringing up the rear, I ducked after them into a low-roofed shed.

'Come on down here,' the cell leader said, and jumped into a pit dug into the earthern floor. I followed gingerly and found myself standing on a huge pile of sweet potatoes. So *that* was our job – toting them to the kitchen. Meanwhile, they were all there for free, as many as we could eat. I apologized for my earlier recalcitrance.

'Don't overdo it,' one of the Koreans warned. 'Eat them slow or you'll have trouble digesting.'

We sat in the cold and humid darkness of the shed for half an hour, crunching away like rats, before we got our delivery service.

Over the next few weeks I frequently caught sight of two large, pale-skinned prisoners who were the only non-Orientals I had seen in jail since Bartek. They were descended from White Russian settlers, and now had no place to go home to, even if they were released. They looked strikingly out of place as they stood in the yard surrounded by Asians, especially the one called Butolin, who had a great, Rasputin-style beard and a Russian peasant blouse gathered at the waist. Both of them, I heard, were doing time in Lao Jiao for incorrigible rowdiness.

Chinese New Year fell on 5 February, and as a special treat we were allowed to buy five packs of cigarettes each, at fifteen Chinese cents apiece. I remember them well because of the name involved, a low-quality brand called 'Courageous Man'. The very same cigarette had existed in Kuomintang days, but then they were known as 'Red Man' and identified by the colour portrait of an American Indian chief. With the advent of the Communists, though, the pack caused ideological problems. Such cigarettes should not be sold any longer, theoreticians concluded, because they were an insult to a minority oppressed by imperialism. The cigarette was popular with the masses, however, so revolutionary logic found a way to keep them in circulation. Hong Shih, meaning Red Man, became Yong Shih, Courageous Man, and everything was in good ideological order again. The Indian chief was replaced with a picture of the legendary Chinese hero Wu Sung, killing a tiger with his bare hands. When the Hundred Flowers rolled around, the party people decided to update the images with an accent on modern times. Wu Sung was lifted for the one and only true Courageous Man of our times, a soldier of the People's Liberation Army, posing with a big red flag and the sun behind him. By 1962 the quality of the tobacco had become execrable. No one in camp drew any parallels, though.

Our New Year meal was meagre again this time, but Rhee predictably found a way to get himself a little bit more. Taking advantage of our jailers' anomalous respect for religious form – doubly curious in that religious practices in themselves were forbidden – Rhee declared himself a Moslem, which entitled him to a pork-free diet on the big feast days.

'Hell, I'm no Moslem,' he cheerfully admitted to me, 'but I don't like pork so much, and you're usually better off if you're exceptional for things like this.'

Sure enough, when supper came around that night, his portion of beef was appreciably more copious than the pork and vermicelli the rest of us ate. This time we had man'tous with the stew instead of wo'tous – slightly bigger loaves, and made from finely ground, leavened wheat flour instead of corn.

After supper the Koreans gathered in the hallway and sang their country's moody, wailing folk songs. As the strangely evocative voices rose around me I grew fretful and depressed, thinking of my family. Their New Year, I knew, would be even hungrier than ours this time, since my wife had written me to tell how she had lost her ration book. For a whole week, it turned out, she and the kids had to get by with what they could scrape up, around the house – precious little – and 'bean soup', the green-grey sour residue that remains in the bottom of a pot when soybeans are prepared, so cheap it could be had in any food store for next to nothing. I had already written to invite Yang to the first visiting day after New Year, but had no idea if she could make it. The next day my spirits rose when I ran into Fourcampre in the yard. He told me he had seen them. They would be coming for sure.

Fourcampre was a Franco-Chinese *métis* like me. I had known him vaguely in my childhood, but it was in Liangxiang that he became my good friend. He shared with me the little he had – cigarettes and food he received from his family. He had just recently turned free worker, and so had the occasional chance for a visit to town. I began relying on him more and more to be my eyes and ears for the outside world. He was always willing to help. That soon got us both into trouble.

On the night of New Year's Day my larcenous Korean mates decided to take unilateral action to augment our cell's food supply. They had been making ready over several days of preparation and observation, and when their plan went into effect, we all took part. After the warders had gone home to their families and the prisoners' honour patrol had passed our door, we scuttled treacherously down to the kitchen, set up lookouts and went to work. One of the Koreans rapidly assembled five lengths of bamboo pole, which the others had concealed under their clothes, one apiece, and fixed a stiff wire hook to the end. As usual, the kitchen window had been left slightly open to let out steam. On a table before us was a big pile of freshly-made bean curd. We had buckets ready. The new curd was so firm that when the hook bit in it held fast and lifted up from the table like magic. For his second act the Korean hooked some cabbage leaves and a whole bundle of vermicelli. We were all set to call it a day until one of our cell's two Japanese, a fellow named Yoshida, put in a bid for the gourmet style. What, after all, is an Oriental meal without soy sauce? Yoshida had his drinking mug with him, and he attached it to the wire. With impressive calm and precision he reached his scooper into a big earthern pot of soy sauce on the same table. He ladled three mugsful into our bucket. Back in our quarters we made a stew in a communal basin and heated it on the stove out in the hall. It was a damn sight better than what we had eaten earlier in the evening.

As Fourcampre had predicted, my wife showed up on visitors' day, 11 February. We talked at a table by the whitewash warning line next to the main wall, and by the time the visit was over I was more depressed than ever. It was obvious, even from the platitudes we exchanged in front of the guards, that she and the children were in a bad way. Yung, the little one, was with her and he solemnly handed over a little package of biscuits for me. Selfishly I took it, without bothering to think that he probably needed it as much as I. When I was eating them that night, I swore I would repay him 100 times over some day. As they were leaving I asked the warder, a straight guy named Wang, if they could have three dollars from the pocket money I had earned, but my wife refused. She needed nothing, she said. The government was taking good care of them. In her first letter after her visit she told me that Warder Wang had slipped her the three dollars from his own pocket. I immediately went to thank him for the gesture.

'There's only one way to thank the government,' he said stiffly. 'Work diligently.'

I was willing, but not very able. The recurrent TB I was afflicted with had weakened me considerably, and the dizzy spells still hadn't left me. I decided to try the infirmary on the ground floor, since all Heavenly Friend Li ever had for me was aspirin. I was pleasantly surprised to see that the head doctor was a man I knew – Yen, the bearded Northeasterner who had been my second cell leader in the Transit Centre.

'Well, so it's Fa Kuo Bao [French Bao],' he said affably. 'How did you get here?'

'With the other foreigners,' I said, and told him about my symptoms. They could hardly have amazed him – in 1961 and 1962 almost half the prisoners I knew had TB. Doc Yen found an important cavity in my right lung, but admitted there was little he could do about it except to assign me to the light-labour brigade. Two days later I left my Koreans and moved downstairs with the sick men. I and one old Mongolian who almost never opened his mouth were the only foreigners. Heavenly Friend came by and told me I was lucky to be there. He knew of plenty of prisoners sicker than I who were still working out their norms in the yard or the factory.

There were, in fact, far too many sick prisoners in those days for the government to cope with. The last couple of years of famine conditions had taken a frightful toll not only in death but even more so in disease and debilitation. Camp 585 was overflowing and so was every hospital and light-labour ward in every prison and camp in the country. All these useless bodies were unproductive; the government, in its concern for the welfare of its convicts, came up with an ingenious solution – Bao Wai Chiu Yi, the Medical Parole Programme. This allowed the sickest and most thoroughly disabled men to be sent back to their families, to die there or regain their health. Everything considered, it was cheaper and much better public relations for the men to do their dying at home. Bao Wai Chiu Yi was an admirably cynical gesture. Being a foreigner, I was not eligible; but even beyond this the warders knew quite well that my wife could do nothing for me. The first batch, 100 of them, left on a Saturday afternoon in March. We were called out to bid them farewell and hear a speech from one of the ideological warders on this enlightened new policy.

We of the light-labour brigade lived in tents down in the yard not far from the latrines, and we passed our days in such chores as scraping bark from tree branches with pieces of broken glass, to be used by other prisoners for making wicker baskets. There were twenty of us in our tent, and the leader, a middle-aged Manchurian named Kuan, had had his own little bit of exposure to Western culture – he hummed a tune called 'Moonlight on the Colorado' all day long, until it nearly drove me mad. Naturally, our decreased work loads were mirrored by lowered rations. I was down to $28\frac{1}{2}$ catties now, or $142\frac{1}{2}$ wo'tous a month – above starvation level, but not much. The consolation was that as a foreigner I benefited from a new rule proclaimed that very year that accorded me a double portion of vegetables. The reason apparently was that since foreigners stood less of a chance of receiving food from their families, they should be compensated. I was still permanently hungry, though. After a month in the tent I asked to be put back on the regular work details.

'Your duty is to do as the government tells you,' Warder Wang said. 'The government will look after you. Leave the question of your rations up to the government. When the time comes for you to leave the light-labour unit, you will go, no matter what your wishes are.'

Of course.

I was shocked to find that we had an informer in our tent. My memories of prisoner solidarity in Ching Ho had perhaps made me careless; there were still plenty of prisoners who believed in mutual surveillance. The incident with the informer occurred while I was finishing up my lunch and the gong rang to call us back to work. As was my habit, I was eating slowly to make it last, and the gong caught me by surprise.

'I wouldn't like to go to work before I finish eating,' I grumbled, and gobbled down what I had left. The Chinese phrase was 'Mei yo ch'i hao.' A day later a warder came to the cell and directed me to make a public confession for having said the food was bad – 'Mei ch'i hao de' in Chinese. Taken off guard, scared and confused, I tried to defend myself, but didn't make much of an impression. Luckily for me, good old Kuan remembered the incident and spoke for me.

'Warder,' he said, standing respectfully, 'Bao has been misquoted. I heard him the other day, and he only said he didn't want to go to work without having finished.'

Another classmate backed him up and I was saved. We never did find who the informer was, but the warder let him know then and there that he was not pleased.

'It is good to report to the government what goes on in the cell, but you have to be frank and honest. If you take the government for a fool and begin informing in order to settle grudges, you will have to suffer the consequences.'

Late in May the East Building was finally completed and we moved into one of the new cells, the best I had ever known in Chinese jails. They had the same form as the room where I had camped with the Koreans, but now that they were properly installed, they were paragons of luxury – whitewashed walls, high ceilings, plenty of light from the twin windows, central heating, fluorescent lighting and twenty straw mats on the floor, twelve on one side and eight on the other. The cadres were overweeningly proud of this building, and they made us maintain the cells with the same meticulous attention to petty detail as the boot camps my Marine friends used to describe. For instance, I was in charge of the windows, and had to clean out the corners with a sharp little stick after polishing up the pane with damp newspaper. Every morning there was an inspection for dust. Our books, water mugs, toothbrushes and other miscellaneous small gear had to be placed precisely in their assigned spots. The warder demanded that we polish the wooden floor so that he could see his own reflection in it. All this was a far cry from the filth Chinese prisons were notorious for in the old days.

One of their more understandable innovations around that time was the weekly lice inspection. The idea was an intelligent one, I knew, but all the same it was a ludicrous sort of routine we went through – every one of us stark naked in the cell, teamed off two by two, picking over each other's bodies like so many curious monkeys. And we had to inspect with utmost care – a man harbouring lice could theoretically be accused of spreading germs.

In mid-June a security hysteria seized Liangxiang. The Nationalist, hoping to capitalize on popular discontent bred by the famine, had attempted landings at several different spots along the coast. As usual, though, they miscalculated – the Nationalists were born bunglers – and the uprising they hoped for turned out to be against them as invaders. They never got anywhere, but their potential threat was taken very seriously. Our mail privileges were cut off, visiting privileges cancelled, and we were ordered to devote every study session and reading period to the threat from the Taiwan clique. The worst part of the new measures, though, was the night security – every single window in the prison had to be firmly shut and curtained from dusk to sunrise. I never quite understood the rationale behind this, but I suppose it had to do with the possibility of sending or receiving signals. In the heat of June in Peking, this was a terrible trial and a prisoner in another cell got himself into trouble over it. Many of us had trouble sleeping at all in the bolted, stuffy rooms, and it was common to see the silhouettes of men creeping over to the window in the middle of the night to stalk the first rays of sun, when the windows could be opened. This man in the other cell had been standing at the window since 3 a.m., peering out through a tiny opening he had made by pulling the curtain back. At four or so, when he perceived a faint glowing in the east, he threw open the window and heaved a sigh of relief.

'Thank goodness,' he said, mostly to himself, but loud enough so others could hear, 'the day's here at last.'

The following Saturday, when the Weekly Examination of Conscience came around, an ideological warder appeared in the cell. To the general surprise, he told the prisoner to stand and make a clear account of himself before his classmates and the government. The government would be lenient if he spoke fully and frankly. The poor man gaped and stammered as the warder turned on his heel and strode back to his office.

'Come on,' the cell leader said pitilessly. 'You heard what he said.'

What else could he do as head of the team? An order was an order, even if he had no idea what it was all about.

'But I don't know what he's talking about,' the poor man protested.

'Make an effort,' the cell leader said, helpful this time. 'Try to think what it could be.'

After a great deal of sighing and anguish one of the cellmates, obviously the one who had informed, accused him of wishing for the return of the Nationalists – hadn't he exulted the other day that a new day was dawning? So *that* was it . . . He furiously denied any such intent, but the authorities were hunting witches in those days and they refused to accept his denials. We Struggled him for three days until he finally threw up his hands and said, okay, he had been hoping for the Nationalists.

I was transferred again, this time to a special sick cell, after a Health Ministry X-ray unit confirmed the TB I already knew I had. I moved up to the fourth floor again and my jaw dropped (but I should have known) when I saw that my new cell leader was none other than Ever-Handsome Rhee. I don't know how he had managed it, but God knows he was full of tricks. He must have thought of something better than the toothpaste ploy. A couple of wise guys tried that one with bad results. The point was to get transferred off work and into a medical ward by persuading the X-ray machine that they had bad cases of TB, and their method was simple – they ripped little pieces of lead from a toothpaste tube, and stuck them to their chests under their undershirts. The lead, they figured, would show up as spots on their lungs, but they overdid the stunt. The doctor took one look at the fluoroscope screen when the first plotter went through, called a warder over and pronounced the men dead. That ended that funny business.

Anyway, I was reunited with Rhee and happy to be there. He immediately slipped me a pack of cigarettes. He got them from other prisoners, he explained, by the old Ching Ho general services technique, the most profitable of which was his tailoring business – pants, jackets and even caps from any old cloth a

280

prisoner managed to scrounge up. Rhee could do anything with his hands.

Everything considered, life was pretty good in the sick cell.

As a foreigner under the new rules I was allotted not only extra vegetables, but a ration of 300 grammes of tobacco a month as well. That didn't mean I had enough to eat, but the tobacco helped me forget the penury of food. One of the cellmates became so obsessed with food that his anxieties turned into a minor form of madness. He was perpetually convinced he was being cheated in the distribution of the wo'tous and that others were eating microscopically larger amounts. At first Rhee tried calming him by offering to exchange his portion of wo'tous any time he wished. That worked for a few days, until his paranoia saw a sinister, doubly clever back-twisted plot behind the deal. All right, Rhee tried, from now on you can choose your own wo'tous from the tray as it comes in from the kitchen. It was quite incredible to see the man eyeballing the wo'tous one by one, measuring and comparing (there was a no-touch rule) before making his choice from the big pile. But even that ended one day when he looked up from his calculations, turned and threw out an accusation that proved to be the last straw:

'How come you guys always put the smallest ones on top?'

After that Rhee gave up and ordered him to take what he got, and shut up about it. Another memorable character in the cell was an old fellow named Wong, who had worked as an army medic for the Nationalists and the war lords before them. He sometimes made himself useful by helping out Heavenly Friend Li and Doc Yen; but they didn't like to use him very much because he was a doctor of traditional Chinese medicine – herbs and acupuncture. That particular folk science was not then held in the esteem it now enjoys, and most of the prisoners used to refer patronizingly to Wong as 'the Mongolian doctor', Chinese slang for a quack. He took the kidding with aplomb, and offered to stick needles into anyone who cared to receive them. There were precious few takers. His great day came when one of the warders was stricken with a terrible toothache. For some reason it was impossible for him to get into Peking that day, and the APCs that Yen gave him had no effect whatever. Desperate and racked with pain, he called for Wong and his needles. It was child's play for him to relieve the pain – toothache is one of the easiest things for acupuncture to cure.

Wong became a hero. From that moment on, he treated prisoners side by side with Heavenly Friend and Doc Yen. I, too, had a toothache fixed by Wong in a matter of seconds, but the most extraordinary sight was the way he took care of the one epileptic we had among us – he stuck a whole selection of needles in his upper lip and toes, and it calmed him every time. Quite astonishing.

In September, Rhee was discovered to be too healthy to remain among us, in spite of all his guile. His place was taken by a serious young man named Chou Fu-rui, who had been a teacher in a mining district not far from Peking. He had made the mistake of speaking his mind on the subject of education. As a bright young teacher, someone in the local party apparatus had asked for constructive suggestions, and he gave a little twenty-minute talk recommending that control over the curriculum be left with the professionals rather than to party cadres whose concern was more with ideological purity than scholarship. Naturally, he was accused of attacking the government.

'They gave me one year for every minute I spoke,' he told me.

Chou's fall from grace recalls a little vignette, a bit of fun I had around that time with a particularly odious zealot in the cell, one who enjoyed informing. We were speaking of sentences, and I told him that I deserved to be in for one day.

'One year, you mean?' he corrected me, but he knew that wasn't right. He was perplexed.

'No,' I insisted. 'One day.'

He reported me for mocking the system of reform. When the warder inevitably came for an explanation, I had my catechism prepared.

'He must have misunderstood,' I told the warder in all innocence. 'I only meant that I was thinking in the spirit of the Great Leap Forward.'

The warder shrugged and went back to his office. There was nothing more to be added. The slogan of the Great Leap Forward was 'One Day Equals Twenty Years'.

I learned quite a lot about life as a free worker through my friend Fourcampre, whom I saw more and more often around the compound those days. A free worker was better off than a mere prisoner, perhaps, but not all that much.

'You know what going back to society means?' Fourcampre once asked me in that didactic, question-and-answer style so much favoured by the Chinese. 'For me it meant moving from one building to another. And paying for my food.'

Free workers were formed into brigades organized exactly like ours, were locked into their cells at night, arose at the same hours and performed the same work, held the same daily study sessions, weekly examinations of conscience and quarterly ideological summaries, not to mention the automatic adherence to the principles of mutual surveillance, accusation and denunciation expected of them. True, they were permitted home visits twice a month if they had the money, but they were also eligible for solitary if their ideologies slipped. Of their average salary of twenty yuan a month, about fifteen went for food and tobacco and the rest on such items as uniforms, electricity fees and the general odds and ends of camp life. It didn't leave much for spending in Peking. But at movies the first ten rows were reserved for them. That was something.

I often discussed the free-worker situation with the chief warder, a man named Tien, whom I came to admire as a friend and father confessor. We used to have talks at least once a month, and he actively encouraged them, since they fostered dependence on the government. Like all the good warders I had known, Tien strictly adhered to the Maoist principle that if a prisoner had something on his mind, he should say it through, holding absolutely nothing back. The man who speaks his mind, Mao said, commits no fault.

'What's the use of us making big efforts to reform ourselves,' I once asked him, 'if we end up with just about the same thing when we're through?'

Tien didn't even wince.

'You've got your political notions all mixed up,' he said patiently. 'I'm afraid you're straying farther and farther from the government. What you must remember, Bao, is that if this place is a prison for you, it is a factory for the free workers. And the government watches over them very carefully. Most of you come to these places with no training or skills, and it takes the government lots of time and money to bring you up to the proper technical levels for the jobs you do here. Do you seriously think all that time and money should go to waste?'

That was a hard one to answer. Tien had something there. He went on easily.

'The records of the free workers are such that we have to be wary of them. It's true that they have expiated their sins, but it is one thing for a man who has never been condemned to show dissatisfaction and another for a man who has already committed crimes.. If you drop a plate on the floor, Bao, there will always be cracks no matter how carefully you glue it back together again. So why not just keep them on in the jobs they know? The government is served, and in the long run they're happier. It's logical, Bao.'

Old man Wong became a free worker while I was in Liangxiang, but by then he was too old to work or contribute anything to the community. And in fact he didn't even want to. I ran into him on a staircase one afternoon as I was going down to the laundry. He had been moved to a corner of the building where they kept the unproductive old folk. He and nine others shared one fairly large room with a common bed – Liangxiang's own Senior Citizens' Lodge. Physically he looked better than at our last meeting in the Chadian railroad station, and I told him so.

'Young fella,' he said in English, 'things couldn't be better. Or worse. Things are just what they are. I offered my knowledge to the state and the state didn't want it. I offered to teach or translate and they didn't want that, either. So now I'm living on fifteen yuan a month and they give me thirty catties for a ration. That's okay. When I save a little money, I go into town and have a meal or see a movie, or I buy a book. You can come and visit me when you like, and borrow books. And we can talk some English together, no matter what they say.'

Wong didn't give a damn any more. He had lived through so much that there was hardly anything more the jailers could do to intimidate him. Several months later while I was cleaning windows, I saw him being pushed over toward the solitary block, with a guard twisting his arm behind him. I don't know what offence he had committed, but I'm certain it was ideological.

'Wong's problem,' Heavenly Friend Li told me once, 'is that he's too American. He just can't get over it.'

As my internment in Liangxiang drew into 1963, my ideological progress had become so striking that Warder Tien appointed me deputy cell leader to Chou, quite an honour for a foreigner. Although I was still ill-nourished and not at all healthy, I had taken to the rhythm of the place by then and was, in my own strange fashion, happy. The news from home was bad, and my wife was coming up with the first oblique references to a possible divorce (her only real chance for regaining a decent style of life), but what could I do about all that? She was on one set of rails and I on another, and all I could hope for was that she find a way out of her poverty and humiliation.

Through the spring and into the summer of 1963, living conditions improved slightly for us prisoners: We now had a meal of rice or wheat flour at least once a week. As a sick person my jobs were only nominal – picking metal scraps from slag heaps and cleaning sand from aluminium castings – and I devoted myself more and more, as Warder Tien suggested, to studies and self-criticism. When my zeal was rewarded with definite signs of approval, I responded favourably. I gave myself more and more easily into long, rambling discourse about imperialism, Soviet revisionism, serving the people or whatever other subject was in vogue for the moment. Being deputy cell leader, I was expected to talk more, but I scarcely needed prompting. I paid less and less attention to what had been my previous style of objectively assessing life, until I became a virtual stranger to the cool rationality the Catholic mission schools had taught me as a boy. I had become, if you like, brainwashed. Or was it that I had simply accepted the bargain that my life in Liangxiang tendered to me: Follow the path marked out for you, don't make trouble, and you will be comfortable. I fell into it. It was easier.

The single notable exception to my good behaviour was the letter I tried to send to the French consular agent in Peking. The one thing that stuck like a nettle in the back of my mind was the way France had abandoned me. Of course I wasn't important enough for Quai d'Orsay to make a diplomatic issue over, but it rankled me that the country of my passport had apparently written me from the face of the earth. I was coming dangerously close to giving up on France entirely. In the six years I had now been imprisoned I had received nothing more than two cartons of cigarettes, a little cash, and my family only laughable little handouts of money – and the consular agent knew me quite well from the old days. France and China were without diplomatic relations at the time, but he was the one person recognized by the diplomatic community as representing France's interests, and furthermore was well paid for it. I decided to act, but to do so I would have to go beyond regulations. I asked Fourcampre to carry a note to the agent the next time he had a leave for Peking. I slipped him the note in the latrine. It was written in French:

I am writing you in haste. Mr Fourcampre at great personal risk has agreed to deliver this. As you know from my wife I have been sentenced to twelve years of labour. I assure you that the Chinese authorities are treating me correctly but my personal situation is such that my family is in a bad way. My own needs are modest. I need only some clothes and two dollars a month to help me through this bad period. Thank you in advance.

Fourcampre, who was illiterate, took the note unquestioningly, which I appreciated as a rare gesture of friendship. It could have been a plot to kill Mao, for all he knew, but he carried it gladly because it was from me.

And then he was caught with the note.

I had made the mistake of assuming that free workers were not subject to searches like the rest of us, but the guards grabbed him by the front gate and shook him down. I was called in to see Warder Tien without knowing what had happened.

'Tell me, Bao,' he began, 'are you satisfied with your ideological status? Do you feel that you have been supporting the government as you should?'

It was the old game of cat and mouse. Warders never come straight to the point, preferring to lead up to their conclusion by a well-orchestrated series of questions. It is almost an established ritual. And for my part, I had to play the innocent, even though I was now 90 per cent certain of what it was all about. A prisoner loses face if he breaks down too quickly, and surprisingly enough the warder does, too. He should be allowed to play out the logic of his little game.

'The government never speaks needlessly,' he continued. 'It always knows what offences you have committed.'

'I can't recall anything.'

And so it went, for five or six more minutes until we arrived ineluctably at the point when Tien decided to end it.

'You know, Bao, that convicts are not allowed to have relations with individuals undergoing Lao Jaio, let alone free workers. But do you know the penalty for passing notes to the outside? Especially in a foreign tongue?'

I admitted everything. That night the deputy director of the camp got on the loudspeaker system. It sounded pretty bad.

'Two persons in this factory have committed a most serious offence. They have attempted to send a message to an imperialist agent. One of them is Free Worker Fourcampre and the other is Prisoner Bao Ruo-wang. Their plot was uncovered thanks to the vigilance of the guards. Both of them must give a thorough accounting of their crime – if not, the consequences are too horrifying to contemplate. These two are ordered forthwith to solitary confinement.'

Poor Fourcampre,* the innocent messenger, got four days, but I was luckier – Doctor Yen examined me and told Warder Tien I was not fit to undergo solitary. He could not vouch for my survival. I might have imagined it, but I could have sworn I saw him wink at me when the guard's back was turned. They sent me back to the cell.

'You must know that no government in the world treats its enemies with such generosity and leniency as we,' Warder Tien

---

*Louis Fourcampre was allowed to leave China in February 1964 upon the establishment of diplomatic relations between France and People's China. He is now living and working in Paris.

told me, and I was ready to believe him. 'That's why our Chairman Mao and the party are so great. Be thankful for that, Bao.'

He told me to give him a written report on my crime. I described the entire incident in five pages and added my translation into Chinese of the note I had slipped Fourcampre. Then I waited. A few days afterward I was called to the office of one of the new ideological warders, a tall, strong, bearded man in an officer's uniform of the People's Liberation Army.

'Your confession,' he said, 'while not profound, is acceptable. Your translation of the letter is good. Luckily for you, you didn't slander the People's Government when you asked the Frenchman for help. You should know that if he wanted to help you, he would have done it without your asking. He knows where you are. In this case, considering that your motives were not reprehensible, we have decided to be lenient with you. From now on if you have hardships, come to us. You don't have to ask elsewhere. If we can help you solve them, we will; if we cannot, we will at least give you an explanation.'

'The government is doing enough for me already,' I insisted. 'I can't expect anything more. Besides, the consular agent gets money from the French government to help French citizens. It's his duty to help me.'

'There are channels for that.'

'But they don't do me any good.'

'All right, then. What is it you want now?'

'Permission to write him again.'

'You know the regulations, Bao. Prisoners are allowed to correspond only with their direct families. But I suppose you could ask for an exception to be made in your case. Write a request to the factory director.'

I pondered the situation a few days before I started the letter. The important thing was to aim for what I wanted, but to remain within the logic of correct ideology to get there. Once again, the catechism would have to serve me. This was the letter I wrote:

REPORT
To: The Factory Director

Convict Bao Ruo-wang of Team Four, Seventh Brigade, respectfully submits the following to the Factory Director –

Of late, as a result of certain study sessions, I have been assailed by serious ideological problems which, if left unsolved, could have an adverse influence upon the reformation I am undergoing. It is because I place my full reliance upon the Government that I am now exposing my innermost thoughts. I hope that after having given this report due consideration the Government will help me solve my problems and give me the necessary education to set me right once again.

From newspaper articles concerning the treatment meted out to Chinese subjects illegally detained in camps by the Indian expansionists (*People's Daily*, 12 & 28 Aug. 1963), I have learned that Chinese consular officials have been denied the right to correspond with their compatriots, to visit them and to provide them with articles they need. Moreover, these Chinese detainees are permitted to write only two letters per month to the Chinese consulate, and in the English language only. As a result of the unreasonable restrictions imposed by the Indian expansionists, the Chinese detainees are now living under precarious and straitened circumstances.

My first reaction to these shameful details was indignation and shock. However, I must admit that very soon these reactions gave way to a different manner of thinking, a very dangerous manner of thinking. In other words, I began to have bad thoughts. I asked myself: 'Why does the Chinese Government accuse others of doing things that she does herself? Why does the Chinese Government demand of others what she is not willing to do herself?'

Speaking more concretely: The Chinese Government accuses the Indian expansionists of not permitting her consular officials to visit Chinese subjects illegally detained in concentration camps, or to provide them with necessities. The Chinese Government accuses the Indian expansionists of placing inhuman restrictions upon the detainees regarding correspondence. This attitude of the Chinese Government is correct and praiseworthy; it demonstrates the concern that China has for her own people. But what about China herself?

Months ago, I requested permission to write the Frenchman X. for some material assistance. This man, X., looks after the interests of France and French residents in China, although he is not officially recognized by the Chinese Government as a diplomat. In the past I have received some small assistance from him and the Government permitted it. If you care to look through my dossier, you will note that X. sent me a carton of Chien Men cigarettes in March 1959, and again in December of that year, plus the sum of 15 yuan (U.S. $6) in October 1962. My request to write him has not been answered to this day. The Chinese detainees are allowed to write two letters a month but I, apparently, am not allowed to write even one. The fact that the Chinese detainees have to write in English has provoked protests from the Chinese Government. In a like manner, I am obliged to write all my correspondence in Chinese, which is not my native tongue. Is it surprising, then, that I am beset by serious ideological problems?

There is a Chinese maxim: 'Set yourself up as an example.' But how can I pursue my reformation as the Government wishes when the Government demands of others what she is not willing to do herself?

I know perfectly well that the thoughts I express here are erroneous, and that they cast slander upon the Chinese Government. However, these thoughts exist in my mind and I would not be sincere if I kept them hidden from the Government. That I have such bad thoughts is not surprising – after all, that is why I am in prison. My purpose in exposing them here is to obtain the education needed to correct them. I hereby request that the authorities give some consideration to my state of mind and accord me the help for which I have so much need.

It was more than two weeks before there was any reaction. Obviously my special case had bounced back and forth in the Public Security offices in Peking. I was finally received in the office of a discipline and education warder named Hseuh. Right away, I could tell from his manner that things hadn't gone too badly. He was brusque, a bit officious, but on the whole accommodating.

'You have a nerve,' he began, 'to make disparaging remarks about the government while undergoing Reform Through Labour. Do you realize what the consequences for actions like that could be?'

'Yes, Warder,' I said humbly, 'but I was trying to be frank and sincere by exposing my innermost thoughts to the government – even if they are wrong and bad. I have been taught that prisoners who reveal their thoughts to the government commit no sin and will go unpunished.'

'Who said anything about sanctions?' Hseuh asked stiffly.

'I would like to report to the member of the government that you did mention the word "consequences".'

'Hum,' he said. 'Yes, I did, indeed.'

One small point for me.

'However,' he went on, picking himself back out of trouble, 'I meant that the consequences would be frightful if you persisted in harbouring evil thoughts. You know that the government is always ready to listen to you and to help you solve your problems. Now tell me – what exactly is it you want from this man X.?'

'I would like some material assistance.'

'The government is looking after your needs.'

'I know, but I would like to be able to help my family, too.'

'Have no worries about them,' he said with the same fatherly assurance that all government officials always employed when they spoke about Yang and the kids, while doing next to nothing to help them. 'We are living in a new society now. The government is conscious of the hardships of people.'

'I was only trying to lighten the burden of the government.'

That was a lie and we both knew it, but it was the correct ideological response. Hseuh accepted it favourably.

'Your attitude is correct and good, but let the government make its own decisions. Now, then, regarding what you wrote in your report, we never turned down your request to write this Frenchman. We were merely studying the matter. The fact that you show yourself to be impatient indicates that you do not trust the government entirely. The government will solve all your problems in due course. You may write this man X., if you like, but you know that there is no guarantee he will help you.'

'Permit me to report to the member of the government that I have a new bad thought.'

He accepted that less favourably.

'What kind of bad thought?' he asked suspiciously.

'I am worried because you tell me I may write X., but at the same time you are predicting that nothing will come of it. I am wondering if this means my letters will not be mailed.'

'You are speaking honestly, Bao, but you are also insolent. You may be assured that your letters will be mailed. Knowing the characteristics of the bourgeoisie, though, I doubt that he will come to your help. But go ahead and try.'

I thanked him and made a move to take my leave. But Hseuh wasn't quite through yet. He wanted to send me off with the right attitude.

'Do you realize now,' he asked, 'how wrong you were in making all those baseless accusations against the government?'

'Yes,' I agreed humbly. 'I beg the government to forgive me.'

'All right then,' he said with satisfaction. 'You may return to your team now.'

As I was passing through the door he had one last thought.

'The letter must be in Chinese. And it must bear no return address. Just the P.O. Box number.'

Chapter Fifteen

I never did hear from the French consular agent. I sent out eight letters in all, and he never took the trouble to answer one of them. I hid my bitterness behind a mask of imperturbability and sank myself even more deeply into the stream of life in Liangxiang. I was already skilled in the presentation of study-session material, but from then on I became one of the absolute stars, ready to hold forth on any subject the warders might demand of me. But they always came back to the same one – Soviet revisionism. China had become obsessed with the infidel Russians.

My gift of eloquence even earned me a nickname – 'the story teller', they used to call me, and the only one of my mates who could lead studies as impressively as I was Ai Min, the one they used to call 'the theoretician'. Ai Min was a phenomenal character, a one-armed, one-eared bear of a man, who had been not only a party member but a colonel and political commissar in the army as well, a veteran of the Long March. When the two of us were speaking well during the extra-long studies then in fashion, we were unbeatable; I would set the stage with drama and colour and he would take it from there with Marxist-Leninist-Maoist chapter and verse. I had always had the good luck in the camps to be befriended by men more experienced and knowledgeable than I – Square Jaw Dai, Longman, Sun and the others – and Ai Min was the latest. The most valuable, too, when I consider the monstrous mistake he saved me from not long after I had met him.

Like most of the ex-Communists I met, Ai was utterly honest, straight and hard-working, but his intimate experiences with the sources of power had given him a certain disabused attitude toward sacred institutions. I recall particularly well the time he defined dialectics for me. Earnest student that I had become, I had asked him for a striking illustration of the use of dialectics, one I might use myself in study sessions. Instead, he brought out his own brand of Marxist-Leninist humour.

Imagine, he told me, that a group of journalists from the West is invited to Peking and receives first-class, top-priority treatment from the government, with all the trips and interviews they requested, the best food and lodging and a sumptuous banquet for their departure. When the first articles appear in the Western press a few days later, they are unanimously pejorative and heap odium upon the regime. The Peking ruling circles erupt into a frenzy of indignation, but the Great Man himself remains calm and unmoved.

'Be happy they wrote such things,' he advises. 'We should start worrying when the bourgeois press writes nice things about us.'

When, several days later, some more newspaper and magazine articles arrive and they are filled with flattering accounts of the new life in China, consternation runs through the ranks of the party. All but the Great Man.

'Why are you worrying?' he wonders. 'This proves that even the rotten bourgeois press has to admit the progress we have made.'

The point about dialectics, Ai said, is that they can answer anything satisfactorily.

My ideological progressiveness had made me such a prize that I was appointed to take over the education of a special cell of fifty unusually backward illiterates, who until then had proven to be virtually impermeable by the new line which the rest of us had assimilated long since. 'Persons of low cultural level', they were designated, with euphemistic understatement. Mostly ex-peasants, labourers or mental deficients, they were the ones who had spent their past study sessions either asleep or in witless stupors. Nothing, apparently, had registered in them. I was given three months to set them right. Warder Tien made it a point to tell me that the results would be viewed as a test of my reformation. I approached the job as a supreme challenge.

When I first entered the classroom-cell where our course was to be given my students greeted me with all the intellectual animation of lumps of coal. I foolishly began my presentation in the rarified political terms that would have been appropriate to someone like Ai. Disaster: I could see their eyes glazing over as if by Pavlovian reflex. Obviously I would have to be more direct.

'What do you know about Khrushchev?' I threw out.

'What's that?' one of them asked. I swear it. He didn't even know whether Khrushchev was animal, vegetable or mineral! I was obliged to explain that he was not only a man, but first secretary of the All-Union Communist Party of the USSR.

'Ah,' came the pleased exclamations of recognition – 'Elder Brother.'

It was my moment for revelation.

'No, he is not Elder Brother,' I said slowly and firmly. 'Khrushchev is a huai-tan – a rotten egg.'

This time there was reaction from the crowd. Their complacent pudding faces began to register doubt, perplexity or outrage, depending on how much they could remember from studies of the past years. A few of the bolder ones told me to be careful when I spoke of our great ally. I redoubled my insults. The group began chattering and grumbling agitatedly.

'We're warning you, Bao,' one of them said, 'any more talk like that and we're reporting you.'

They were already sharpening their blades. When I continued once again in the same vein, the room exploded into a clamour of shouts and protests. Half of them were calling for a warder by then, and it didn't take long for one to arrive.

'What's going on here?' he asked at the doorway. 'Is this the way you people study?'

'Warder,' a spokesman for the group said, 'we're sorry, but Bao here has been insulting Elder Brother Khrushchev.'

He had trouble with the name, but the warder knew what it was all about. He held up his hand and the room fell silent.

'Listen,' he said carefully, 'Khrushchev is not only a huai-tan. He is the biggest bad egg on earth!'

He turned on his heel and went on back to his office. My fifty students looked up at me with mouths agape, dumbfounded. Now, finally, it was their turn to learn that black was white. With painful, step-by-step care, summoning up all the colourful detail I could muster, I began explaining to them how the unthinkable had happened. My only problem in those three months was that I never succeeded in persuading them to take Albania seriously. When I told them that the population of our doughty little ally was only around a million, they sniffed with exquisite Chinese scorn. Only one million! Not worth considering. One of my students even permitted himself the speculation that if we 600 million Chinese got together we could sink Albania by merely pissing on it.

But Russia was big and contiguous and very much a threat. It had been so, right from the start, Ai Min told me.

'We never did like them,' he said, recalling the early, enthusiastic days after the Communists had triumphed. 'They have always lived in a world apart from ours. When the Americans came to China, they took over the best hotels and houses and apartments, but we could see that that was natural behaviour for them – what else would you expect from capitalists? But when the Russians came in, they made us build new hotels for them!'

By the end of 1963 we had made certain that there wasn't a soul among the prisoners who didn't hate the Soviets with energetic passion. We were clean and on the track again. Among my students, though, there was one particularly ironic case. The man had remained perplexed and tormented throughout my crash course and at the end he told me why: He had been arrested and sent to jail in 1956 for having spoken of the Soviets just as we were speaking now. No matter how hard he turned it over in his mind, something seemed out of place. Didn't that mean that he now deserved a pardon? I promised to bring the matter up with the authorities. It was no trouble at all for Warder Tien to straighten me out.

'First of all, Bao,' he told me, 'this man got into trouble in 1956 because he attacked the party for being subservient to the Russians. If he had only attacked the Russians it would have been different – he wouldn't have had such a big sentence. And

296

then what he said wasn't as important as why he said it. What he said might be progressive now, but in 1956 it was antigovernment propaganda. Do you see?'

I did. I took it without protest or quibble. I was such a model prisoner by then that once when Warder Tien upbraided me for having spoken in the cell about a minute after lights out (I had wanted to finish my sentence), I felt sincere pangs of remorse. One minute of self-indulgence like that, he warned, might have prevented another prisoner or two from sleeping properly, which in turn could have affected the factory's production. With the zeal of a true convert I began searching for new ways to serve the government and help my fellow man. All the greater was my enthusiasm in that it seemed evident that France had abandoned me. The model we were all urged to follow in those days was the good soldier Lei Feng, whose posthumous diary had been turned into something of a national monument. The message of the diary was that neither he nor any other Chinese person could rest easy as long as there were still persons on the face of the earth oppressed by capitalism and imperialism. Besides Lei Feng there were also the good soldiers of Nanking Road in Shanghai, contemporary saints who used to go to extraordinary lengths of self-denial, such as walking the twenty kilometres to and from the fields where they worked, instead of spending a few pennies by taking the bus. For my part, I took to going barefoot in the warm months, in order to save the government the expense of shoe leather.

My reformation was all the easier since it was in the hands of Warder Tien, whom I admired for his humanity and personal honesty. Like Warder Chao in Prison Number One, he had the uncanny ability to see into a prisoner's mind and anticipate his thoughts before he dared articulate them. As our living conditions continued their slow rise in 1963 he took to assigning ration increases according to each man's need rather than to his production figures. Unlike most other warders, he never resorted to using rations as a form of blackmail. The pain he took to judge each prisoner's case individually was rewarded by our entire loyalty. He had by far the lowest rate of men under his responsibility being sent to solitary. Everyone behaved.

Even when things were at their worst Tien had been able to control his charges with his own brand of applied psychology that never needed to be complemented by force. The best example I can recall was the escape incident. It happened in October of 1962, when things were at a high tide of hunger and confusion. He called the brigade together shortly before nightfall, lined us up in fives, and marched us out toward the main gate. We stopped twenty yards from the gate and he climbed onto a stool for a little talk. The cadres had been hearing persistent rumours, he said, that certain bad elements among the prisoners had been talking about escaping. This could be a dangerously corrupting influence on the rest of us. Something had to be done. With a dramatic flourish he ordered the guards to open the gates!

'I don't want you to have ideological burdens,' he said with a perfectly straight face. 'We're making it easy for you. Since some of you have been talking behind the government's back, here's your chance to carry out your thoughts in the open. You can go on out the gate now. No one will stop you.'

He clambered down from his perch and began striding back to the main building. Then he stopped, turned, and threw out one final line:

'Before you leave you'd better think about where you're going to be eating from now on.'

Of course no one left. We filed obediently back to the cells and were happy to have our wo'tous. Tien had us, as the saying goes, eating out of his hands. Tien could certainly be firm when the occasion called for it, but he nearly always avoided coercion. There was the time, for instance, when he shamed a prisoner into correcting himself. The man in question was rather old, over sixty, grumpy and probably a little bit senile. But whatever the reasons, his offence was to have turned on his family and insulted them on visiting day, screaming imprecations and actually throwing their gift parcel to the ground. It was shocking behaviour, but Tien was careful not to apply the obvious solution of solitary. Instead, he called us together with the offending prisoner in the front of the group and made an hour-long speech to the old man about his unworthiness. He ended it by ordering him to write two apologies – one to the government and one to his family.

On another occasion involving visitors, Tien turned a deaf ear, deliberately tolerating improper and scandalous talk from a prisoner who had suffered deep humiliation. It happened when he was visited by his wife and their son, a mean little brat of around ten or eleven. The kid was wearing the red scarf of the Communist Young Pioneers, and he had learned his lessons well.

'I didn't want to come here,' he brayed proudly, 'but my mother made me. You are a counterrevolutionary and a disgrace to the family. You have caused grave losses to the government. It serves you right that you are in prison. All I can say is that you'd better reform yourself well, or you'll get what you deserve.'

Even the guards were shocked by his tirade. The prisoner returned to the cell in tears – itself forbidden – muttering, 'If I had known that this would happen, I would have strangled him the day he was born.' Tien let the incident pass without even a reproach.

The only time I saw him reduced to using force was when he came up against Chung the hunger striker. Chung Kao-hung was his name, and he was a tall, handsome man in his thirties who had done university studies and whose brother was a divisional commander in the People's Liberation Army. Arrested as a rightist element for irrational antigovernment talk in 1958, he had since become utterly obsessed by the immense amounts of money the superpowers were spending on missiles. His head was full of facts and figures on the subject. Over and over again he told us how much the Soviet Union, America and China were spending on sophisticated military hardware, and how much better it could be spent on food. As his personal, and marvellously fitting, weapon of protest, Chung chose the hunger strike. The first time he struck, he fasted for ten days before he was thrown into solitary for recalcitrance. He was perversely delighted – that only meant the hunger strike could be more effective. He won his masochistic battle that time and made his point. When it pleased him, he took up eating again. But the next time it happened Tien was prepared. He allowed Chung to stay in his dirty corner of the cell until he was too weak to get to his feet, then had him fed glucose intravenously.

'As long as that thing drips,' Tien told him, 'you won't die. You'll just stay like that in your corner. It's up to you to decide how you want things.'

Chung couldn't bear the thought of a perpetual half-life. He gave up and never went on hunger strike again.

In the beginning of December I was assigned for a few months to a small cell with only five others. Now that I was officially off the sick list this was, apparently, one further step along the way as the Peking Bureau of Public Security tried to figure what to do with me. The most memorable aspect of life in that cell was the gin rummy. We had only nominal work – light gardening – and not even the extended study sessions could totally fill the day, so I taught my cellmates American card games. They especially took to gin rummy, and within a few weeks beat me at it regularly. That year, too, there was an unexpected Christmas present. Heavenly Friend Li called me to his dispensary, ostensibly for an examination of my lungs, gave me a shot of glucose, and slipped me a whole bottle of vitamin pills. By then it was clear to me that my situation was going to change, and probably for the better. There had been too many indications, too much kindness from the government of late. And above all there had been The Lure some weeks before Christmas. The Lure was an important turning point for me.

It happened on an afternoon late in November, when I was summoned to the office of Prison Director Chia. There were four warders in the office with him. That was very strange. Apprehensively, I took my place on the stool in the corner. Chia told me I did not have to keep my head bowed. After the usual formalities about my name and age and criminal activities, he opened the proceedings.

'Today the government has something very important to discuss with you. It concerns the progress of your reform.'

He let that hang in the air. There was a long, portentous

silence. I kept my mouth shut. Chia flipped through some papers.

'It says here that you are a French citizen. Have you ever been to France?'

What was he getting at? He knew very well I had never left Chinese territory.

'Are you married?'

Again, questions to which he knew the answers. Jailer rhetoric.

'I beg to report to the director that I am married to a Chinese wife and have two children.'

Chia looked pleased. He had reached the point for his speech.

'So, Bao. Theoretically you may be French, but you are really Chinese, aren't you? There is Chinese blood in your veins from your mother. You were born and raised here, and you have been nourished on Chinese food. Your wife and children are Chinese. You even look Chinese. Where is the French in you, Bao?'

He had a point there and he knew I knew it. He probed a little further.

'I don't have the feeling the French have ever done much for you, either. It seems to me they even look down on you. You know the French are racist. You may consider yourself to be French, but do you think they do? For the French you're just a half-breed. The consular agent still hasn't answered your letters, has he? Do you think he would treat a hundred per cent Frenchman that way?'

Chia had come to my weak points in a hurry. The consular agent's cowardly and heartless attitude toward me and my family was the one thing I could not forgive. As a manner of defence, I obliquely suggested that maybe he had not received the letters, but I only got a dressing-down for that from one of the other warders. Was I trying to suggest that the government was going back on its word and had not mailed my letters? No. Of course not.

'The People's Government is taking care of you,' Chia went on. 'The Government gives you food and drink and clothes and even pocket money. You have committed crimes against the government, but still you are getting all sorts of considerations. And at the same time your own people are neglecting you. Have you ever thought about this?'

Had I ever! But I didn't carry it to the same conclusion as he.

'Do you ever wonder if there's any reason for holding onto your French nationality? What does it get you? We know you want to be with your wife and children. Your crimes have caused them a good deal of hardship. You are a heavy burden to them now, but there might be a way out for you. There may be a chance.'

I felt the thrill of excitement and fear that comes when big decisions are at hand. I listened very carefully.

'The only way the government can tell if you have reformed yourself is by actions. If you really regret your past mistakes, you have to prove it to the government. Do you really want a new life? If you do, you have to break with the past. You have to decide whether you still want to be associated with the imperialists or whether you want to come over to where there is light. If you made that decision, it would be the best proof for the government that you have learned your lessons well. Then there would be no more reason to keep you here – you would be thoroughly reformed!'

Chia's syllogism was perfect. That was quite an offer he was hinting at. Still, I had lingering doubts.

'People who know foreign languages like you can get good jobs, Bao,' he suggested. Luckily for me I retained a clear image of Old Man Wong. Chia went on.

'There are quite a few foreigners working for the government. Their living conditions are excellent. All we can do is point the way for you, though. You have to make the decision.'

'I don't know if it would be right for me to give up my nationality,' I said.

'We're not asking you to do that,' Chia insisted. 'We have only lain some facts on the table. Think about them, that's all. Don't say no or yes now. Just go back to your cell and think about it.'

That was the end. I rose from the stool to go. Then one of the education and discipline warders had an inspiration – he called me over to have a look at myself in a full-length mirror next to the director's desk. I looked like a cadaverous tramp.

'What's your sentence?' he asked.

'Twelve years.'

'And you've served how many now?'

'Six.'

'Halfway,' he said. 'Do you ever wonder if you'll make it through the next six?'

They sent me back to the cell. I was depressed and troubled. If what they told me was true, it seemed that I had a pretty good chance of bettering my lot if I renounced my French nationality. Somehow, I had to balance all the factors and make a decision. It was Ai Min who made up my mind for me. He told me that the answer to my dilemma was the simplest thing in the world. There was nothing to consider. Walking around the vegetable patch, he filled me in on his reasoning. It was time for question and answer period again.

'What are we, Bao, you and I and the rest of us?'

'We are convicted felons undergoing Reform Through Labour for the sins we have committed against the party, the people and the government.'

'Yes, that's true, but put it more concretely.'

'We are enemies of the people.'

'Good! Do you remember what I told you once about this? The Communists don't feel obliged to keep promises to their enemies. As a means to an end, they feel free to use any scheme or ruse that happens to serve them – and that includes threats and promises. Even if they do let you out, which isn't sure, your dossier will follow you wherever you go, and there will always be that black mark of Lao Gai. The very first mistake you make, you'll be back here again – and then you'll *never* get out. But with your French nationality you'll always be different from the rest of us. You'll always have some hope, even if it's slight. Give up that piece of paper, and you'll just be another jailbird. You understand?'

'Yes, old Ai,' I said. 'Thanks.'

'Don't thank me. Just use your head. And remember another

thing – Communists don't have any respect for turncoats, either.'

So I didn't bite on The Lure. I owe more than gratitude to Ai for his advice. Without it, I wouldn't be here now. On 13 January, I was called in to see Chia again. This time there were eight warders with him! And in the middle of them all, seated behind the desk with Chia, was my interrogator from Grass Mist Lane.

'Sit down,' he said. His voice was positively friendly. I took my place on the stool.

'I was here on some other business,' he said with studied indifference. 'And I happened to hear that you were here. I thought I'd check on your progress.'

That sounded like an obvious invention, but I certainly wasn't going to dispute it.

'I haven't seen you since 58. Would you like to smoke?' He threw over a nearly full pack of Chung Huas, the same brand Mao smokes. 'Tell me about what's happened to you since then.'

Coming from an interrogator, that was no light request. In careful detail, watching my ideological step, I produced the entire history of my life as a convict. I went through five cigarettes as I talked and I didn't finish until nearly 5 p.m.

'It looks like you were the wrong person in the wrong place at the wrong time,' he said, stubbing out his cigarette with a wry grimace. 'What I'd like you to do now is write me a full ideological report. I want to know all about your thoughts and impressions. Tell me about how you viewed your crimes then and how you do now, and what you think of the government's sentence.'

'That will take a lot of time.'

'That's all right.' He turned to Chia. 'Give him all the time and material he needs. Take him off work if he needs it.'

And he had one final word for me before dismissal: 'Continue your good behaviour. You won't regret it.'

Even without Ai's advice I could see that the report was of highest importance – like a final exam. Still, I didn't allow myself any illusions about graduation. That would be only destructive folly.

I went back to the cell and started writing. The government provided me with a pack of cigarettes every second day. Unlike my work in Grass Mist Lane, my report was in Chinese this time, the fruit of my studies at Ching Ho and Liangxiang. I spent two months composing the report.

I wasn't even halfway into it when, one day at the end of January, a radio bulletin came over the loudspeakers at suppertime: France and China had established diplomatic relations. To emphasize its importance, the announcement was read twice. The warder told us to make that the subject of our study sessions that evening.

Being French, I was the obvious choice to lead the talk. I spoke for an hour and a half, starting with thumbnail histories of the Fourth and Fifth Republics, the Algerian War and on to a comparison of Chinese and French cooking and cultures. Both countries, I didn't fail to point out, were trying to free themselves from domination by a superpower. When I had finished, Warder Tien called me in. He asked me to tell him what I thought personally about the establishment of relations.

'It is of greatest international importance,' I said. 'And it is clear that the relations were extended on China's terms.'

'You have no more views? Nothing personal, as a Frenchman?'

'No.'

'Were you thinking that you might be released from prison?'

That was the first time any of my jailers had actually come out and said it. I suppose I did have those thoughts in the back of my mind, but I did my best to erase them. And above all I wasn't going to admit them to a warder. That would be ideologically stupid.

'I don't think my efforts have been strong enough for that,' I said. 'I've hardly been doing enough work lately to repay the government for the food I'm eating. And then, why should the French government start doing anything for me now?'

'You've come a long way, Bao,' he said.

The next day my ration was increased to forty-four catties, even though my other cellmates were eating only thirty-five. It meant an extra wo'tou at lunch and one and a half more at suppertime. This sudden concern over my well-being was troubling. I had to work even harder to drive thoughts of release from my head. That same week I was given a copy of *Lettres de mon moulin*, by Alphonse Daudet, and was asked to translate it into Chinese. It would be a useful service to the government, the warders told me, but I knew very well that Chinese translations of it already existed. So now they were trying to help me brush up on my French . . .

Physically, the winter was no trial for us that year. Living conditions were on the rise all over China and the improvement was reflected in our style of life – the edge of desperation had disappeared. Our rations, though not exactly copious, were sufficient now, especially for us in the light-labour cells who had nothing but little pickup chores to perform around the compound and even more so for me, the privileged foreigner. Curiously, studies were emphasized more than ever. I could not have known it at the time, but the increased importance of indoctrination, the endless preachings about self-effacement in the manner of Lei Feng and the soldiers of Nanking Road's good 8th Company, were preludes to the Cultural Revolution. As food and consumer goods became more and more abundant – 1964 was a very good year – certain segments of the party, with Mao at their head, grew wary of the effects of the relatively easy times that had come upon us. Everywhere the 'candy-coated bullets' of embourgeoisement threatened the purity of the revolution. Vigilance was called for for the moment; it was only admonition, but it was building inexorably toward the mass hysteria the country was to know after I had left.

In February I discovered I was a bachelor again. Yang had divorced me. I received the news in a curt, almost cursory meeting with one of the warders.

'Your wife is more progressive than you,' he drawled. 'She has severed her ties with you. You should be proud your sons have a mother like that.'

So that was that. I could hardly blame her, but I did feel a twinge of resentment at not being kept abreast of matters. The warder told me that the actual legal proceedings had been carried out in November. I returned to the cell in a daze, wondering what new roads life had in store for me now. All I could perceive was a blank. Anything could happen.

In April I was named a cell leader. As a foreigner I had never expected such an honour, but my ideological progress had been so striking and my work in studies so effective that when an opening occurred I was the one chosen to fill it. There were plenty of openings that April, for the simple reason that three-quarters of the prison's population had been sent off to open a new camp. Our drastically reduced effectives, mostly old and sick, moved down to pleasant cells on the ground floor. Ai Min stayed in the same cell with me, so I found myself in the astonishing and somewhat embarrassing position of being the ideological guide to a man who had been a political commissar.

Within a few weeks Liangxiang began filling up again. The first to arrive were some 250 court-martialled ex-soldiers, part of the unfortunate group that had remained faithful to Peng Teh-huai, the disgraced former minister of defence. Peng had unwisely chosen to remain favourable to Elder Brother when the Sino-Soviet dispute began gaining momentum. Inevitably, he was branded a revisionist and disappeared. The soldiers arrived in a convoy of buses, still wearing their uniforms but stripped of badges and insignia. It was quite impressive to see them jump out and fall into precise formations before marching swiftly over to their cells. They always remained aloof from the rest of us, even though they were theoretically undergoing the same programme of Lao Gai. Perhaps this restraint was a result of orders; I never did find out.

Three days after the soldiers had been installed, another convoy – flatbed trucks this time – arrived with overflow from Prison Number One. They looked pale and sickly compared to the soldiers, and their faces betrayed apprehension. Anyone who leaves Prison Number One knows that the next step has to be down.

In May came the second Medical Parole Movement. I remember it particularly well because of Huang Kuo-chiang, one of the men in my cell. By the time I met him Huang was seriously afflicted with T B. He was among the first to be named to the 200-man parole group. He was looking forward to returning to the little village where he grew up, he told me, but at the same time he felt dreadful premonitions: Since his arrest, he had not received a single letter from his family.

The poor man was back after only ten days. We were sitting on the bed preparing for studies when he suddenly appeared at the door, sunburned, dusty, breathing heavily and looking absolutely stricken.

'I couldn't take it,' he said. 'I had to come back. The warder let me in. He says I can have my old rations back.'

Over the next few days I pulled the painful story from him bit by bit. He had been released with seven yuan and a one-way ticket in his pocket. When he arrived in the village, his own father cursed him as a criminal element and ordered him to remain seated on a stool under the sun until he checked with the police to see if the letter of medical release he bore was really valid. After a week of being coldly tolerated by his family, taunted by children and scorned by the rest of the village, he decided that the only home he had was Liangxiang. He took what money he had left, bought a return ticket and literally begged Warder Tien to allow him back inside the gates. It was only because Tien was exceptionally lenient that he relented.

In August I was given another book to translate – *Le livre du savoir-vivre,* published by Editions Montsouris. A sort of French book of etiquette, it was filled with advice on how to behave in polite company, what to say at marriages and baptisms and how to eat, dress and correspond correctly. I was told I could take my time. The others could handle my portion of the work in the vegetable patch. Perplexed, still not willing to allow myself any glimmers of optimism, I went through it until I knew by heart how to handle myself in society – French society.

On 30 August, my interrogator was back in Chia's office. This time he didn't pretend it was an accident.

'I've read your ideological report,' he said. 'Your best progress has been with the Chinese language. You've got it almost perfect now. But what concerns me most is the result of your Reform Through Labour. What you have written here is positive, though it could be better. I've decided to accept the report, but I want you to keep on thinking about how you can improve your ideological status.'

I promised to do my best. His off-hand comments were, in fact, complimentary in the extreme, and I was thrilled and flattered. What was more, he had quite a piece of news for me.

'The French embassy has asked several times to visit you. Until now we have not allowed it. This isn't the place for a visit. It's not suitable and it's too far. What we are going to do now is transfer you to another place nearer their embassy. You should be ideologically prepared for a visit from the French. I don't think I need to explain what I mean. Get ready to leave as soon as possible.'

Early the next morning one of the ideological warders, a man named Sung, called me to his office for a rambling speech about what I should have learned in my two years at Liangxiang. I heartily assured him that I felt nothing but gratitude for the government's teachings. When we were finished, Sung called in a trusty with a new outfit for me – a new blue suit, underwear, black Chinese sandals, a towel and some soap. He also handed me eleven yuan.

At four in the afternoon Director Chia officially turned me over to two plainclothes men from the Peking Bureau of Public Security. They led me to a black Pobeda hardly newer than the one in which I had ridden the night of my arrest in 1957. This time there were no curtains, though, and I was permitted to hold my head up. We rolled through the outskirts of Peking and then into the city itself, finally turning into the gate of Prison Number Two, the new Interrogation Centre. Kung Deh-Lin, it was called, the Grove of Virtuous Deeds. The old Interrogation Centre,* where I had made my confession, had been torn down to make way for some buildings of the Chinese Academy of Sciences.

A guard led me through a maze of cells and showed me into a small private one, deadly silent. There was a bucket in one corner, a small raised bed and a stool. I put my bundle down on the bed and began arranging my little collection of personal

---

*The old Interrogation Centre was Tsao Lan Tse Hutung No. 13 (Grass Mist Lane) mentioned at the beginning of this book.

gear and books. The guard came back with a pallet mattress. He asked if I had enough clothes and whether or not I was hungry. I thought I was – it was habit never to refuse food – but when he returned with a plate of sautéed potato shreds, wheat flour man'tous and soup, I could hardly eat it. I was far too unsettled and nervous. And when I thought of Sun and Longman and the others in Ching Ho, it made me feel even less hungry.

'The government is being too good to me,' I said, but the guard wasn't impressed. He ordered me to eat every scrap. After I had, he told me it was bedtime.

The next day I had three meals! The place was like a hotel. In the afternoon they took me out for a walk in the exercise yard. Over at the far end I caught sight of a Westerner who looked strikingly American. I never did discover who it was, but I now presume it must have been one of the unfortunate CIA operatives from the Korean War, Fecteau or Downey who were not to be released until the 1972–73 improvement in Sino-American relations. That evening a doctor came to examine me.

'You'll be getting good treatment,' he said like a man who knew. 'You need to put some weight on.'

That was true enough.

Chapter Sixteen

For two more weeks I stayed on in my private cell eating myself goggle-eyed, reading old newspapers and trying to fight off boredom as I waited for the French to come and visit me. After all the years of living in close quarters with dozens of school-mates at a time I found the solitude oppressive, even if the living conditions were better than I had ever dreamed. After ten days of it I wrote the warder a note asking to be sent back to Liang-xiang if the embassy people weren't going to show up soon. That was probably why he let me in on the Struggle session – occupational therapy.

It turned out to be a nice little triumph for me, one that was constructed directly from my practical knowledge of ideology and the realities of jail life. From time to time during this period of fattening up I had been able to hear prisoners being Struggled – Prison Number Two was, after all, the new Interrogation Centre – and I could only sympathize with those poor victims who were at the threshold of their incarcerations. Then one morning after breakfast, as I was sitting on the bed glancing over a paper, a guard told me the ideological warder wanted to see me in his office. He had an interesting proposition for me.

'I understand you're rather an expert at studies and Struggles,' he said. 'You've attended a dozen or more, haven't you?'

'Yes,' I said with a certain pride. 'I've Struggled and been Struggled.'

'Well, we might be able to use your experience. We've got a prisoner here we've been Struggling for a week without any luck. Why don't you have a try?'

He filled me in on some of the background of the case. I promised to give it my attention right away. First, though, I had to go back to my cell for a little preparation. I opened my bundle and put on the dirty old patched clothes I had brought with me from Liangxiang. The guard watched me, his VIP prisoner, with scarcely concealed bewilderment, but I told him not to worry. I knew what I was doing. When he led me to the Struggle cell, I told him to shove me in as if I were a new prisoner just arriving to be interrogated. I kept my head bowed low and hurtled awkwardly into the noisy, crowded little room.

'We're having our meeting now,' the cell leader said. 'Sit over there and I'll speak to you later.'

He seemed quite sure of himself for a man who had been directing a fruitless Struggle for seven days. Even if the warder had not filled me in, I could have judged from the type of insult being thrown out that the man they were Struggling was an intellectual. He was gifted with the stubbornness of a peasant, though, and sulkily held fast against the onslaught of insult and threat. He simply refused to talk, despite all the jeering, screeching faces. After a few hours the cell leader called a break and told me to give a short report on myself. I went through the normal procedure – name, age, background and crimes I was accused of.

'Start working on your confession,' he said. 'Don't be like him and hold out against the government.'

I repaired back to my little corner of the bed and contemplated the familiar old scene, the agitation, the shakings of the fists, the harsh, repetitive words spat out with apparently sincere hatred. Stinking intellectual. Scum of society. Ass licker. (That one was theoretically forbidden, but the cell leader let it pass.) Shameless. Sly and cunning. Bad element. Rotten egg. No skin, no face. They threw everything they could think of at him. Once, in a moment of boredom, I craned my head back to see out the window through the edge of the curtain.

'What are you looking outside for?' one of my cellmates angrily corrected me.

The Struggle continued. I kept my mouth shut. At around 4 p.m. the cell leader – irate and frustrated by now – pointedly gazed over to my edge of the bed. I was a handy one for him to pick on.

'Why aren't you talking?' he demanded. 'Do you sympathize with him or what? Just because you're new here doesn't mean you have the right to do nothing. Everybody has to talk. Give us your views.'

Good. I knew there would be a chance like that sooner or later.

'My, my, my,' I said politely, 'the way you people work this session. How disorganized!'

Some faces turned in surprise. It was easy to take charge with these beginners.

'There shouldn't be all this confusion and disorder,' I went on. 'Now, I'll tell you my views and afterward you can discuss whether they're right or wrong. Is that all right with you?'

The cell leader waited, curious to see what sort of phenomenon I was.

'From the way you've all been talking since this morning,' I said, 'it seems that the only counterrevolutionary in this cell is that guy over there. I guess that means the rest of us are a bunch of heroes. Party members or something. I think we're forgetting that we're counterrevolutionaries, too – just as dirty as him. We all stink as bad as he does.'

Brief uproar. Grumbling of angry voices. One of them shouted indignantly that I was insulting my fellow schoolmates. I was ready for that one.

'You'd better put his remarks on the record,' I suggested to the cell leader. 'I have insulted him. That means he's not a counterrevolutionary. He hasn't committed any sins. Or he doesn't recognize any. He thinks he shouldn't be here.'

That shut him up in a hurry. And even if it hadn't, the session was ideological child's play. They had forgotten that the object of a Struggle was not just to correct a recalcitrant enemy of the people, but to learn about one's own sins at the same time.

'All of us here,' I said importantly, 'are stinking bad elements, including the cell leader. You'd better think about reforming yourselves before you feel so sure about jumping on other prisoners. And let me tell you another thing: You're going to need each other in the camps, because the only way to survive there is to count on each other. So I think you'd better change your attitudes. I have been appointed by the warder to take over this session. Now let's see what we can do.'

The cell was magically pervaded with quiet respect. The cell leader moved back up against the wall without complaint. It was obvious he felt nothing but relief. Later, after our meal, I called the Struggle victim aside for a little talk.

'You're being dumb,' I told him, 'and also masochistic. You let these people swear at you and insult you and all you can possibly get from your attitude is a longer sentence. The only way to get them off your back is to go to the warder and make a clean confession. It's just like Chinese medicine: If you take it in little sips, all you'll have is the bitterness; the only way to do it is close your eyes and throw it all down.'

He smiled for the first time since that morning. He had finally understood. I walked back to my cell with another mark of merit on my dossier.

On the afternoon of 18 September, the guard opened my door and told me it was time for a shower. All right. Anything you say. When I returned to the cell a barber was standing there with a stool, clippers and a pair of scissors. On the bed were a blue Mao suit, socks and Chinese slippers. The barber trimmed my hair and shaved me. I climbed into the Mao suit, which was a good fit. The guard led me to the director's office. From the sofa where he was sitting he motioned me over to an easy chair next to him. Now it was adult-to-adult style. Things had changed quite a bit from the days of the stool in the corner and the bowed head.

The director told me that in a few minutes I would be receiving a visit from the French. How I spoke to them would be considered as a direct reflection of the progress of my reform. I would be allowed to speak only in Chinese or French. A hidden tape recorder would be registering every word I said. I should be careful.

Two guards led me to a large, bare-walled room with a table in the centre, a couple of decks for the interpreters on the side, and a set of sofas against the wall. We entered by the back door, and I could see the tape recorder already turning, hidden from the front of the room by a screen. I sat down on a chair beside one of the sofas. In less than a minute the door at the far wall opened and two Europeans were ushered into the room. Both were members of the French embassy in Peking: Marc Menguy and Jean Colombel. What happened next dispelled to a great extent the bitterness that I harboured all along within myself at being let down all these years by the French.

Marc Menguy came toward me, right hand outstretched, and as we shook hands, he said warmly, 'We have come to let you know that we haven't forgotten you.' It was a very touching moment for me. What was said may have sounded rather melodramatic under the circumstances that I found myself in, but it wasn't a simple sentence of greeting and encouragement that was being pronounced for my sole benefit. As a matter of fact, with that brief sentence Menguy was actually asserting France's position vis-à-vis a prisoner of the Chinese who happened to be a French citizen. He was making an official affirmation. In other words, France cared.

Menguy and Colombel came to see me at the behest of the French ambassador to China, Lucien Paye, but, from the way they talked to me, they made me feel that they came rather as friends than as bureaucrats carrying out instructions. This was so unexpected and so vastly different from the attitude of the so-called consular agent that at first I felt rather uneasy. The questions that Menguy asked me throughout the visit showed that he had a genuine feeling of concern for me.

'We have been trying for quite some time to see you, but the Chinese authorities have not permitted the visit until now,' Menguy began.

I thanked him.

'We have heard that you were ailing. Are you feeling better now? Do you need anything special by way of medicines?'

'The Chinese government is taking good care of me.'

'How about food? Are you eating all right? Do you need anything extra?'

'My rations are sufficient: the government is seeing to that. My food is better than what the guards get. I have three meals per day: at eight a.m., at noon, and at six p.m.'

Menguy followed my exposition carefully, nodding his head.

He went back to his questions, trying to find out more about the position that I was really in within the time limited to the visit.

'How about meat? Does your diet contain enough meat?'

'I can't tell you how much meat I get,' I said, 'because I don't have the scales to weigh it, but it is more than enough by Chinese standards. I am perfectly satisfied.'

'How about your cell? Do you have enough light? Are there any windows?'

'There are two windows in my cell: one big one and one small one. I get exercise for an hour every day except Sundays and holidays.'

'And cigarettes – can you smoke if you want?'

'I am allowed to smoke as much as I want during exercise period outside.'

'Well, then,' Menguy said with satisfaction, 'everything seems to be all right. Is there anything else you would like from us?'

'I would be grateful if you could let me have either a French-Chinese or an English-Chinese dictionary and maybe some newspapers.'

'I think we can arrange to send you copies of *Le Monde* and *Le Figaro.*'

'No, thank you, Monsieur Menguy! Those are bourgeois papers. I would prefer to have the latest copies of the *Peking Review*. And some novels by Maupassant or Balzac, if you could manage that. And some warm underwear.'

Menguy kept nodding his head, while Colombel took it all down. Before they left, Menguy informed me that he had a message for me from the French ambassador: 'Monsieur Pasqualini, you must not lose courage but must continue to behave well as you have done up till now. We have heard that you are studying Chinese and that the results are rather excellent. Continue your studies so that someday, when you will be in France, you shall be able to make your modest contribution. I have been authorized to inform you that our ambassador has already begun to take up your case with the Chinese authorities in the hope of obtaining for you a pardon and the remission of the remainder of your sentence. Therefore, it is very important for you to give us your co-operation by not giving the Chinese authorities any cause for complaint as regards your behaviour and by refraining from doing anything which might compromise the efforts of his excellency. I am sure that we shall not be disappointed with you.'

Thus, just before leaving, Menguy not only reiterated France's position, but also let it be known to the prison authorities that the French government had the intention of doing everything within its power to get me released. It was a very comforting thought.

Back in my cell I could feel elation and excitement surging through me, but I wondered about my performance. Would the warders approve of the way I had handled it? And would Menguy think I had been brainwashed? I got a hint of an answer that evening when the guard brought my supper. With it were two packs of Gauloises, a carton of Chung Huas, a tin of 555 State Express and ten yuan. This pampering was a good sign. The guard informed me that the government was looking over some books the French had brought for me. If they were approved, I could have them soon.

After supper I was feeling good. 'Bao gao!' I cried out. The guard came to the slot in the door.

'I request the member of the government to tell me if I might be allowed to have a smoke in the cell.'

I knew that as a general rule it was forbidden but since I was enjoying such de luxe treatment I thought it would be worth a try. To my pleasure and surprise, he passed a single match through the slot.

'Try not to burn the place down,' he said. He watched carefully as I lit up a Gauloise and put the match out. The cigarette was so strong that I choked on the first few puffs. It reminded me of the good old Hsing Kai-Hu native leaf. After I had finished, the guard told me I was wanted in the director's office.

'The government is satisfied with the visit,' he told me. 'I have to admit that you have made a little bit of progress. We especially liked the way you dealt with the tricky questions where they tried to trap you. That was very good, what you said about the meat and the scales. But do you really think they will keep on helping you? Do you think they have your best interests at heart? Do you have any illusions about them being able to get you out of prison some day?'

That was easy to answer. I didn't even blink.

'Of course not,' I said with emphasis. 'I know I can't rely on the French embassy for that. If I started having those sorts of ideas, it would mean I was relying on the imperialists. It would prove that I wasn't reformed. I am in prison because of sins I have committed against the Chinese People's Government. No one has the right to interfere with the internal affairs of the Chinese People's Government.'

The words rolled off my tongue with all the ease of pre-digested slogans. I wonder how much of it I truly believed and how much was pure habit. But there was one thing of which I was utterly certain – it was what they wanted to hear.

The director sat and looked probingly at me for a long moment.

'Do you really mean that, Bao? Are you really being sincere?'

'Look through my dossier,' I suggested. 'I think you will find that my attitude has always been the same.'

Another prolonged silence.

'Yes,' the director said absently. He called for a guard to bring me back to my cell.

On October first, they gave me a kilo of apples, half a pound of candy and an assortment of cakes in addition to the regular meals – full helpings of beef, pork, raviolis, noodles, bean curd and vegetables. I was feeling like a maharajah with a guilt complex. I knew Yang and the kids were not eating nearly as well as I, but all my requests to see them had gone unanswered so far. On the fifth, the guard informed me that they were in the prison visiting room to see me.

'Jieh jian,' he said. Come along.

I followed him to the room with the big table in the centre. Yang, now my ex-wife, was there with Yung. Mow, the eldest, was already old enough to have been sent away for 'volunteer' work on a state farm. It was the first time I had seen Yung in about a year. He was getting to be a big boy – he was ten now – but I was distressed to see how shabby and worn his clothing was. In spite of the cold he had only sandals on his feet, without socks. He told me his socks were hanging up on the line to dry, but I wasn't so sure he even had any. I asked the witnessing warder if I could give him the ten yuan (about U.S. $4) that the French had left me. Of course, he said, but it was time to call the visit to a halt.

'Bao has made some progress,' he told Yang, 'and you should rejoice for that, but you should tell him how well the government is taking care of you and your sons. Apparently he doubts.'

'Warder, I didn't say that,' I protested. 'I was just trying to find out why he had no socks.'

Yang declared that the government was taking good care of them all. The meeting was over. It was the last time I saw Yung. I returned to the cell feeling miserable. There was precious little I could do for them, but I wanted to make at least a gesture. I spent the next few days taking apart the little padded mattress I had brought with me from Liangxiang and re-sewing it into a jacket for Yung. My increasingly liberal guards not only didn't object to the activity, but even provided me with scissors, needle and thread. My tailoring was hardly up to the standards of the magic-fingered Rhee, but at least I knew it would keep the boy warm. I finished it in a week and gave it to the guard to pass on to my family.

Meanwhile, I had had a second visit from the embassy. This time it was only Mr Colombel. He said things were going well for me. I could have reasonable hopes for the future. On the thirty-first the guard opened my door and tossed two books onto my bed, a Chinese–English dictionary and a dictionary of idioms. They both had come from little Yung, I learned. He had waited for several hours out in the cold street in front of the prison, hoping to be let in to see me. Rules were rules, though, and there was never a chance for him to come inside without all the formalities having been worked out beforehand. At least the guards had been good enough to take the books from him and bring them to me. He had bought them with part of the ten yuan I had given him.

On the morning of 5 November a warder came in with yet another set of clothes for me to try on. There was a Western-style grey woollen suit this time, with Chinese-made leather shoes and a white shirt. Both the shoes and the shirt were too big, so he took them away and reappeared later that afternoon with another set, which fitted this time, except for the collar of the shirt. The next morning my guard opened the door directly after reveille and told me to put on my new clothes. He led me out to a courtyard where a jeep with two pistol-bearing Sepos was waiting for me. There were no handcuffs this time.

We drove through the familiar streets of \ Peking, dodging bicycles, and when we passed the People's Congress Hall in midtown, I suddenly realized where we must be heading – the Supreme People's Court. It was an imposing edifice, baroque and pillared, topped by the inevitable red star. We hustled through the high-ceilinged hallways, our feet ringing on the polished wooden floor, our progress marked by the regularly spaced brass spittoons that are *de rigueur* in any Chinese public building.

The courtroom we entered was a big, theatrelike place panelled with dark wood with a raised platform in front for the judges, the usual witnesses' chairs and an oversized portrait of Mao on the back wall. Up on the dais were an assistant judge, a secretary and a prosecutor. The proceedings began as always.

'What is your name?'

'Bao Ruo-wang.'

'What were you originally called?'

'Pasqualini.'

'Spell it.'

We continued down the checklist of my past, my nationality, crimes, sentence and reform. The judge read a statement that was surprisingly short.

'In view of the fact that Pasqualini has shown sincere signs of regret for his sins, the Chinese People's Government has decided, as a measure of special leniency, to remit the remainder of his criminal sentence and to order him deported from the country. He will be taken to the border under police guard and there will be handed over to the competent authorities.'

That was all there was to it. Relief had come as swiftly as the ceremony that had condemned me to the camps. It wasn't even

10 a.m. yet. Back in the jeep one of the Sepos ordered me to hold my head up higher.

'You're not a prisoner anymore,' he said irritably. 'Why are you bowing your head like that?'

'Habit,' I said. 'Sorry.'

As soon as we were back at Prison Number Two I was called to the director's office. He was nothing but smiles as he shook my hand.

'How does it feel to be free?' he asked cheerfully.

'I won't know until I'm out of prison.'

'True,' he said. 'Quite true. Well, you'll be out soon. In the meantime, your ex-wife is here to see you.'

Our last meeting was nervous and strained, and would have been even without the presence of the guard. What more could we say to each other that we didn't already know? She wished me luck wherever I happened to land. I promised her I would provide for the kids, even if I never saw them again. This time they had a jeep to drive her back home.

The director called me back to his office and told me to prepare myself for the trip to the border. I made the mistake of asking him if it would ever be possible to bring my children out of China after me. For the first time in weeks his voice became harsh.

'Bao,' he said, 'if you had asked that question yesterday, I don't think you'd be leaving now. They may be children to you, but to the government they are citizens of the People's Republic of China. Their future is assured here. Even if they wished to, which they do not, the government would not permit them to give their lives over to a corrupt, bourgeois society.'*

In my cell there was a huge pile of raviolis waiting for me, but I had little appetite. I ate five or six and told the guard I was finished. When the kitchen worker came for my tray, he contemptuously dumped what I had left into the bucket on the floor. I was shocked.

'That's wasting food,' I said angrily, but the guard stood there

---

*I have started formalities to get my children out of China one by one. The French Government has given them the necessary entry permits; they're still waiting, however, for an exit visa.

impassively and the cook only shrugged. It was an anguishing experience to see the uneaten raviolis lying in the bottom of the dirty bucket.

On the afternoon of the tenth, I left Prison Number Two. My departure began with the most thorough search I had ever undergone. After I had been stripped naked and minutely inspected the guards went through my clothes and belongings. It was here that I lost the wooden knife-spoon that Lo had whittled for me in Ching Ho. The only objects they left me were my three books – the two dictionaries Yung had bought me and the old one I had brought through the camps. The guards drove me to the Peking Central Station and put me aboard a 'soft' compartment that had been reserved in advance. Chinese trains are divided into soft (padded seats) and hard (benches) sections, in order to avoid the unpleasant, anti-Marxist connotations of first class and second class. My welcoming committee was awaiting me inside the compartment – a moustachioed plainclothes man from the Peking Bureau of Public Security.

'Sit down, Bao,' he said. 'Have a smoke.'

He even lit it for me. Before he turned me over to my official escorts he wanted to make a few last ideological points.

'We are a young country, Bao, and the young often make mistakes. The best proof that the government is good is that you are alive and well today, even though you may have gone through some hardships. What you say about us when you are outside China is your business, but we all hope you will stress the positive sides.'

We took leave of each other with a cordial handshake and my journey out of China began. Fittingly enough, one of the two men escorting me was the very same Sepo who had handcuffed me in my house seven years earlier. They took their places opposite me and we rolled along in silence, listening to the music from the loudspeaker overhead. I had nothing to say to them and they didn't care to chat together in front of me.

For the first twenty minutes of the ride I gazed intently out the window, looking for a glimpse of Liangxiang, which I knew lay close by these very same tracks. It was with a curious mixture of emotions that I finally caught sight of the red brick

322

buildings in the distance – joy to be leaving it for good, but also a kind of melancholy nostalgia for all the good friends I would never see again.

Not long afterward a fresh-faced girl with a long pigtail, one of the train attendants, poked her head into the compartment and asked whether we would be taking our supper here or in the dining car. Here, the Sepo said, and she handed him a menu, which he passed on to me. It was then that I had an inspiration. The fact that I had just seen Liangxiang helped it along.

I put the menu down.

'I'd like a bowl of soup and two bowls of rice, please.'

My escorts glanced at each other and smiled.

'Ah, come on,' the Sepo said. 'Take something better than that. We've got to take good care of you.'

He still hadn't caught on to my game.

'No thank you. Just soup and rice.'

'Don't worry,' the other one said. 'Everything's paid for. You can order anything you want.'

I kept my face severely expressionless. 'I haven't even finished expiating my sins,' I said. 'How can I presume to order luxurious food?'

'That's all right,' the smiling Sepo said. 'What's past is past. The government has forgiven your sins. It's finished. Over!'

'I should try to lighten the burden of the government as much as possible,' I intoned. 'Surely you see what I mean.'

One of them started to protest, but gave up in mid-sentence. They had been cornered and they knew it. They looked at me glumly. They couldn't tell whether they had an ideological robot before them or whether they had simply been had. But in either case, they had no choice when it came to ordering their own suppers. That was how that evening I had my last small victory over the police – all three of us ate a bowl of soup and two bowls of rice apiece. Could a guardian of the New Order show himself to be more bourgeois and luxury-oriented than a scum of society?

The rest of the two-day trip to Canton was uneventful, except for the fact that from then on my escorts took their meals in the dining car, relaying each other so that one of them always stayed behind with me while the other ate. As for me, I kept to my soup and rice. We went through Hankow, across the river to Wuhan and then directly on to Canton.

I spent the night of 12 November in the Canton Provincial Jail. The director apologized for this indignity, but explained that no other facilities were available. And, more specifically, would I mind sharing the cell with another man? I shrugged. That was the last thing that could bother me right then.

My cellmate for that final night turned out to be another Franco-Chinese *métis* like me, an older man named Rousset, from Shanghai. He had been released from a normal civilian jail rather than from Lao Gai, and he was not at all happy with the idea of having a room mate. It was the first time that such an outrage had been inflicted on him. He complained to the guard when he saw my Chinese face, but relented and welcomed me as a comrade when he discovered I was as French as he. We smoked two of my Gauloises as a token of our new found friendship.

My last day in China was Friday the thirteenth of November.

Rousset and I boarded a morning train for Shumchun, the Chinese terminus town at the Hong Kong border. This time it was open seats instead of compartments, and we sat in the middle of a mixed crowd of Asian and Western businessmen returning from the Canton Trade Fair. China has truly come a long way, several Englishmen agreed among themselves. Everyone seems well fed and happy. Plenty to buy in the stores. It might just be the model for the future. Rousset and I sat in our government-issue suits and held our tongues. Airs from Chinese opera came from the loudspeakers. Our two guards sat discreetly in a far corner of the car.

At Shumchun the guards led us through our own border formalities apart from the other voyagers. Naturally, we were searched again, and the man in the foreign exchange booth allowed us to change our Chinese money for no more than six Hong Kong dollars apiece (U.S. $1). The rest (my savings of pocket money from jail came to ten yuan) would be sent to our families, he promised. The border police told us we could write a last letter, which the government would post free. We scribbled them out hastily and handed over the unsealed envelopes.

324

The customs inspector wrapped a sturdy band of paper around my three books, affixed a red wax seal to it and let us through into the transit restaurant.

It was some time after noon that we sat down for our final meal, since a meal was on our programme. I told the waiter I would prefer not to have any fish because of my allergy to sea-food. He nodded and returned in ten minutes with a large omelet. To my surprise he also unloaded from his tray an assort-ment of chicken, pork, vermicelli and vegetables – eight dishes in all. He was indignant when we told him there must have been some mistake. We were only two, and we weren't even par-ticularly hungry.

'Who ordered all this?' he asked irritably. 'Now that we are just emerging from the period of temporary difficulties [I was interested to see that waiters and warders used the same euphe-misms] no one should be wasting food like this. There's enough here for six people!'

Rousset* indicated the plainclothes guard at the table next to us. The waiter turned to remonstrate with him but shut up when he saw the card from the Peking Bureau of Public Security.

'Ah, all right, comrade,' he said. 'If that's the case, then it's all right with me.'

At 1.30 they brought us out to the Chinese side of the Lo Wu Bridge. At the far end I could make out the English policeman in his colonial uniform. Over to the right steam locomotives chuffed back and forth in the Shumchun freight yards. Their spokes were painted brilliant crimson and rimmed with white; the tenders they pulled bore painted red flag emblems signifying how many times their teams had overfulfilled their work norms. The boxcars parked on the sidings were covered with billboard-size Chinese characters forming the slogans 'Long Live the General Line' and 'Long Live the People's Communes'. It was a bright, warm, optimistic, sunny day.

*Louis Rousset succeeded in getting his wife and four of his children out of China a year or so after his release. Being French citizens only minor difficulties were involved in getting exit visas, which is not the case for my children. Louis Rousset is now living in the Paris area and working for the Paris Airport Authority.

The guard held us up a few more minutes for an identification photograph. Just as he was about to click the shutter, another guard shouted and ran toward us. Seizing Rousset's hat, he threw it roughly on the ground. It might obstruct the picture, he said. Was he joking when he explained that the picture would be circulated to all the Chinese border posts, in order to prevent us from sneaking back in some day?

When they had finished, the guard told us we could be on our way. I picked up Rousset's hat. We walked across the bridge without looking back.

More about Penguins and Pelicans

Penguinews, which appears every month, contains details of all the new books issued by Penguins as they are published. From time to time it is supplemented by *Penguins in Print*, which is our complete list of almost 5,000 titles.

A specimen copy of *Penguinews* will be sent to you free on request. Please write to Dept EP, Penguin Books Ltd, Harmondsworth, Middlesex, for your copy.

In the U.S.A.: For a complete list of books available from Penguins in the United States write to Dept CS, Penguin Books, 625 Madison Avenue, New York, New York 10022.

In Canada: For a complete list of books available from Penguins in Canada write to Penguin Books Canada Ltd, 41 Steelcase Road West, Markham, Ontario.

Some Books on World Affairs and Current Events
published by Penguin Books

Some Books on World Affairs and Current Events
published by Penguin Books

Some Books on World Affairs and Current Events
published by Penguin Books

Some Books on China published by Penguins

Russia, China and the West

Isaac Deutscher

His great biographies of Trotsky and Stalin were evidence of the knowledge and insight with which Isaac Deutscher approached the affairs of Russia and the Communist world. These attributes inspire the posthumous collection of articles he wrote between 1953 and 1966, the period from the death of Stalin to the start of the Vietnam war and the Great Cultural Revolution in China.

Here, with the immediacy of contemporary journalism sobered by years of close study, he discusses such critical events as the Hungarian rising, the abortive Summit Conference, and the Sino-Soviet dispute. Deutscher once declared that it was his aim 'to concentrate attention on the essential motives and long-term aspirations of Soviet policy'. He fulfils this aim superbly in these essays: linked by the editor's commentary, they provide both a continuous account of Russia in her relations with China and the West and a fascinating guide to some of the less-known internal political and economic tides inside Russia, China, and the Soviet bloc.

China: The Quality of Life

Wilfred Burchett with Rewi Alley

Since 1927, when Rewi Alley first arrived in Shanghai, China has been in turmoil. How have the Chinese people reacted to the enormous changes that have taken place and where do they find themselves today?

In search of the answers to these questions, Rewi Alley and Wilfred Burchett travelled the length and breadth of China, talking to the people in the villages and communes, in their factories and farms. They visited Tachai, the famous agricultural Brigade where, with sheer communal effort (and very little else), the peasants have turned a wilderness into fertile farmland; the oilfield of Taching; the enormous irrigation complex on the Huai river; and, taking the enquiry outside central China, they investigated the position of the minorities who form a large part of the population in Yunnan, Szechuan and Tibet.

'Our central interest,' says Wilfred Burchett, 'has been to measure the changes that have occurred in recent years in China and to set them in perspective against what we knew of old China. We tried to understand also how ordinary Chinese citizens conceive that much-bandied-about term: "quality of life".'